SPACE BETWEEN US

SPACE BETWEEN US

JAMAAL AFLATOONI

This book is a work of fiction. Names, characters, places, and
incidents are either product of the author's imagination or are
used fictitiously. Any resemblance to actual events or locals,
persons, living or dead, is entirely coincidental.

Printed in the United States of America

First Printing, 2019

ISBN 978-1086874815

Cover designed by Lance Buckley.
Interior text layout by Leo Baquero, leo_baquero@hotmail.com

For Eliana

"The earth is but one country and mankind its citizens."

-Baha'u'llah

PROLOGUE

The timer on the lab table struck thirty minutes, beeping loudly in the otherwise silent room. Everyone was waiting intently, especially John Greer. This was Dr. Greer's ninth attempt in the past eight months at completing an experiment that could conceivably be the greatest discovery in the history of humankind. It wasn't an easy task—this was his ninth attempt for a reason. Constructing something so complex and meticulous required hours of preparation, not to mention the long, arduous nights of little-to-no sleep. And on some evenings, many more than he liked to admit, Dr. Greer made it a habit of staying up late and staring into the darkness, running the details of the experiment over and over in his mind on an endless loop, looking for answers as to why it had failed yet again, why he was always coming up empty.

Dr. Greer removed his round glasses and rubbed his chocolate-colored eyes, which looked weary, ringed with circles so dark they appeared to be almost bruised. His normally olive-skinned complexion was ghostly pale, the result of too many days and nights locked in this cavernous space, bent over test tubes, watching, waiting, hoping one day he'd succeed. That one day, he'd finally get it right. The room was quiet, hushed, as the other scientists wondered if maybe this time he'd finally done it.

The test had failed the first eight times due to improper calculations. On the first three attempts, the pH balance in the petri dishes was off, which had resulted in a small pool of green sludge. Tests four through six were burned up in test tubes, due to inaccurate temperature control. Tests seven and eight were also disappointing, as they did not receive the amount of oxygen needed to bring life to the specimen, to animate it the way Greer had envisioned it for all of these years of hard work. Years when he often felt defeated at the end of a sixteen-hour day, when he'd arrive home and slump into a chair in the living room, staring into space, still consumed by what continually eluded him. But now it seemed as if a ray of hope had somehow entered the room and hovered there just above the beaker.

They needed to wait twenty-five more minutes in order to know if the specimen had survived its way through the heat of the test tube, and been given enough oxygen to sustain life. This process alone, from start to finish, took nearly four days, with a handful of people all playing a part in its completion. All of their hard work and hours of preparation would be realized in a matter of minutes. There was an electric charge in the air and Dr. Greer felt almost as though his dark, close-cropped curls were standing on end.

Twenty minutes now. The room was silent. Dr. Greer sat in his chair with his head down and his eyes closed. There was nothing he could do at this point but wait. The bright lights overhead felt blinding and Dr. Greer's clothes felt as if they were sticking to him—the room was hot and airless, despite drafts of cold air wafting in through the vents. The other eleven men and women in the room stood there and waited, waiting to see if their time and labor had finally paid off. Some couldn't bear to watch the timer tick down, while others looked on and observed every second, their faces expressionless as the clock counted down to zero.

Fifteen minutes, then ten, then five. The timer had reached two minutes and thirty seconds when an enormous blast sounded from the test beaker, which contained the ingredients of the specimen. Everyone's gaze shot over to the beaker at once, as this magnitude of a blast had never occurred during previous attempts. A thick, gaseous substance had erupted out of the top of the beaker, and the liquid beneath it had begun to turn a peachy color, one that almost glowed with an otherworldly intensity. The team looked at one another quizzically, unsure whether this was a good sign or not. They had never witnessed anything like this in the previous eight attempts, but then again, there was no mention in the instructions that such a blast would occur.

Dr. Greer looked over at the time.

"One minute!" he shouted, his voice wavering with excitement. The last sixty seconds seemed to be ticking down so slowly that it felt to Dr. Greer like an hour had passed. Everyone in the room stood there gazing at the beaker as clouds of white smoke slowly poured out of it, drifting up into the air. But by the time it had reached ten seconds, most of the gas in the beaker had cleared.

The timer struck zero, and the alarm beeped loudly. Dr. Greer slowly walked over to the beaker while the rest of the group looked on anxiously. He looked over the top of the glass tube to see what was inside. Then, he slowly turned around to his team, his face breaking into a smile, and said in a low voice, his expression both elated and tinged with relief, "I think we finally did it."

CHAPTER 1

"Darwin . . . Darwin. Darwin, do I have your full attention?" the doctor said.

Darwin Sanders looked up from having stared at the floor for a good thirty seconds; he blinked slowly as the room came back into focus, the proliferation of green plants tucked into corners; the plush, cobalt blue couch he was sitting on; the fireplace and its dark marble mantle, with a series of tiny white streaks running through it.

"There we go. Eye contact."

The psychiatrist smiled, and to Darwin the man's pale gray suit jacket seemed very bright, like the sunlight streaming in through the windows. The room was too bright, even with the sheer white curtains that covered the long glass panes, the thin material swaying in the breeze. Darwin closed his eyes, still feeling fuzzy, almost half-asleep, then willed himself to open them again. To act normal. Whatever that was.

"Sorry, what was it that you asked?" Darwin said, blinking rapidly, and trying to focus on what the doctor was saying. His arms and legs felt languid and heavy, like he'd been buried for ages in a vat of wet sand.

"Well, I asked how your sleep has been recently," the doctor said, looking closely at Darwin. The man's eyes were rimmed with darkness, as though the doctor himself hadn't experienced a restful night's sleep in some time. "Were you having another vision?"

Darwin was quiet. He knew people thought he was just crazy, but these visions he was having seemed to be real, almost as if they were memories. Darwin shrugged and looked up at the doctor. He had a dark complexion with a silvery gray beard, and short, silver hair to match.

"Yeah . . . Yeah, I guess I was," Darwin said quietly, looking down at the floor for a moment.

"And what happened in this vision? It seemed to be a relatively short one, compared to some that you've had in the past."

"I could see it again, the mountain range. This time I was walking alongside it. I was alone, as always. But I could hear people off in the distance." Darwin frowned, his forehead creasing as he remembered. The jagged peaks of the mountain in the distance, rising out of the bright blue sky. The noises, like Morse code, strong and insistent, emanating from the depths of her long throat.

"And what could you hear? What were they saying?" the doctor asked, leaning forward a little and watching Darwin intently. So intently that the hair on Darwin's arms stood up, his skin flooded with the unsettling sensation of a million tiny insects walking back and forth across his limbs.

"I couldn't quite make it out, but it wasn't English, that's for sure. It was almost like they were speaking in some kind of weird clicking noise, but it might have been because I was so far away." Darwin's cheeks flushed; he was aware that this all sounded ridiculous, if not borderline insane. He wondered how long he had before a bunch of men in white coats busted in and carried him off to the nearest mental institution.

"Did you ever reach the people?" the doctor continued.

"No, no. I could only hear them off in the distance."

"How do you know for sure that they were people, what if they were animals, since you couldn't make out a distinct language?"

"I don't know, it . . . it just didn't sound like animals," Darwin said with a confused look on his face as he stared at the opposite wall, which was decorated with a series of brightly colored, abstract prints in gold frames, scattered here and there. "They sounded happy, like they were enjoying themselves. I didn't feel any negative feelings at all."

"Hmm, I see," the doctor said, crossing one leg over the other. "So, Darwin, when you're having these *visions*, as you like to call them, do you ever feel a sense of low energy or a different sensation after you snap out of them?"

"I feel . . . tired. Confused. But also . . . I don't know. I feel a little empty when I come back," Darwin replied, trying to read between the lines. Was he sick, he wondered, squirming uncomfortably on the soft couch. The cushion beneath him felt soft as velvet as his hands grazed the surface, trying to reposition himself.

"But why do you feel these are even visions or premonitions? What if they are simply thoughts that have entered your mind? A lot of people daydream, but they know that it's not real," the doctor said practically, then started writing notes in his notepad, the pen scratching hard against the paper. Darwin wondered what the guy was writing. Probably something like, *Delusional teenager. Arrange transport to nearest psychiatric facility immediately.*

"I just . . . I just have a feeling that there is something more to this. It's not just daydreaming," Darwin said slowly, carefully, aware that what he was about to say would no doubt sound completely insane to anyone outside his own head. "It's as if it really happened. And the only thing I can think of is that these are events that have taken place that I don't remember happening, but then I'll have a flashback to it later on in life."

The doctor looked Darwin straight in the eye, without saying anything, his face impassive. He jotted down more notes. Darwin knew what the man was thinking—that Darwin had been imagining it all, every vision, every dream. He'd heard it so many times, his entire life, from his parents, other doctors, and his grandma. No one ever had an explanation that made sense to him. Why was he having these visions on a consistent basis, he'd wondered every time one happened, and then would drift off to that strange yet somehow familiar mountain range and those odd clicking noises that filled his brain. What did it all mean?

"So, Darwin, you're sixteen years old now, right?" the doctor asked, looking briefly down at his chart to corroborate, then looking up again. Darwin nodded. "And you started having these visions when you were, how old?"

"Around seven. They started out as very brief moments, but over time they turned into long instances. The first people to notice were kids at school in my second-grade class. I wouldn't respond to them when I had these episodes." Darwin clenched his hands together. He never liked talking about the visions, as they always made him nervous. What if they had life-threatening implications as he got older? What if it was cancer? Or brain damage? Darwin swallowed hard and then looked away, his pulse suddenly racing.

He caught sight of himself in the gilt-edged mirror on the wall directly across from the couch. He immediately looked away. Usually he tried to avoid mirrors at all costs, but sometimes they were inevitable. He forced himself to look at his reflection again, taking in the sandy hair that fell over his forehead and the profusion of white spots that mottled his skin.

Darwin had been born with vitiligo, a rare disorder that caused a loss of pigmentation in various places across his whole body, but most prominently on his face. As a result, his skin somewhat resembled the fur pattern of a dalmatian—even the hair on his scalp and body was white in the areas where his skin lacked pigmentation. Darwin remembered shaving his head on his first day of seventh grade, desperately trying to remove any evidence of his mismatched hair, but it just exposed the mottled skin on his scalp. That's when Darwin's mother began dyeing his hair once a month. But this didn't stop people from gawking unabashedly at Darwin's spotted face and skin. Weren't the visions, or whatever they really were, bad enough? Did he have to look as weird on the outside as he was on the inside? "Everyone has their crosses to bear, Darwin," his grandmother Ethel always said. But Darwin felt like he'd been burdened with more than his fair share of crosses—and then some.

"Well, let's do this," the doctor said firmly. Darwin looked away from the mirror, trying to concentrate on what the doctor had been saying only moments before. "What are some things you like to do for fun?"

"Um, well, I like to read a lot, and I like going on walks with my mom," Darwin said.

"Okay, good. When these things are happening, are they real?" he asked.

Darwin paused for a moment.

"Well, yes, of course," he said, slightly confused by the doctor's obvious question.

"Right. Now with these so-called visions that you have, are they real?" Darwin knew what the doctor was getting at, now, but he still felt like he wasn't being understood. Not at all.

"Well . . . they seem very real to *me*. They may not be real in the present time or present location, but they feel like they are real when they are happening."

"The thing is, though, Darwin, your visions or premonitions aren't actually real. When you go into those states, you are removed from the present reality," the doctor said, while looking intently at Darwin to see if he understood. Darwin didn't say anything, though. "See, what I'm trying to get at here, Darwin, is that these visions are simply thoughts or daydreams, if you will. Everyone has them. Yours might be more visual or even physical when you're thinking about them, but in reality, they aren't real," the doctor finished, putting the notepad he held in his hands onto his lap.

Darwin looked at the ground again, feeling like yet another doctor had misunderstood him. They were all the same. Every doctor. Darwin had always called the incidents "visions," but the doctors always referred to them as "psychotic episodes," which was kind of inaccurate, since Darwin wasn't psychotic in the least. What the doctors meant by this was that the episodes he was having weren't "real," and were what some might consider out-of-body experiences.

The doctor began to elaborate, but as he did so, Darwin simply stared at the floor, tuning the doctor out, a familiar feeling of disappointment washing over him. He had met with so many doctors over the years. Every appointment was filled with the same feeling, that there was a thick, transparent wall between him and whatever doctor was treating him, and he couldn't get through it. He was banging his fists on the glass, but his voice was muffled by the thick pane between them. The feeling was very depressing, in that he was experiencing and seeing something that nobody could understand, and that he himself could not explain.

But the good news was that Darwin hadn't been experiencing the visions as often as he used to. Currently, he was having them on a monthly or so basis. It was to the point where Darwin no longer told people when they happened, unless it was obvious. He knew that these episodes worried his parents, particularly his mother, so he felt it was best to keep them from his family to avoid causing them any more stress.

"Darwin," said the doctor again, interrupting Darwin's reverie. "You mentioned that you like taking walks with your mom. Does your dad come on these walks as well?"

"Not really," Darwin said, shifting again in his seat and bouncing one foot against the Persian carpet beneath him, wondering how many minutes were left in the session.

"And why is that?"

"I don't know, he just never wants to go with us, I guess." Darwin shrugged. "He's always busy with work and stuff."

"Does that bother you?"

"I mean, no. Not really. I get along better with my mom, anyway. I'm not that close to my dad."

"And that's because he's not around due to work, or is it something else?" the doctor asked, his pen poised in midair.

"Some of it is because of work, but my dad is just . . . strict. I feel like me being around him annoys him," Darwin said with a sigh.

"Well, I'm sure it might come off that way, but I'm sure your dad loves you, too. Maybe it's worth having a conversation with him about it? Or maybe set up some time for some father-son bonding? You have to make time for that, if you want to be able to feel more comfortable around him."

Darwin nodded like he understood, but he knew that was never going to happen. His father rarely made plans to spend time alone with Darwin, and on those rare occasions when he did, they usually involved Darwin helping his dad take out the trash or the recycling.

"All right, well, let's wrap up for the day. I'm going to go talk to your parents for a bit, okay?" The doctor stood, placing his notepad on top of the imposing mahogany desk in the corner of the room, a top that was completely obscured by papers and books. "Why don't you check out some of the new magazines in the lobby? I've got some comic books there as well," the doctor said with a smile.

Darwin nodded and made his way out of the room, a sinking

feeling taking up residence in his gut. Why did he have these dreams? Why did he look the way he did? Why couldn't he just be like everyone else?

"Darwin . . . Darwin?" his mother said loudly. Darwin, startled, realized his mom had been saying his name for a while now. "You okay, honey?" she asked, looking at him with her pale blue eyes, her wavy blond hair blowing in the wind.

She always loved to drive with the windows down, even during the hot, airless Texas summer. Darwin realized he had dozed off as they were driving back home from the doctor's office. The flat plains of subdivisions flashed before his eyes as he looked out the window, the sun baking the pavement of Crimson, the town where he'd lived his entire life.

"Uh, yeah. Yeah, I'm fine, Mom. What's up?" Darwin asked, rubbing his eyes with his fists roughly until bursts of color, electric blues and greens, exploded behind his closed lids.

"I was asking what you wanted for dinner tonight. Your dad was thinking maybe we could barbeque, since we're getting toward the end of summer and it might be one of the last times we're able to."

Darwin's mom was, by nature, a planner. She wasn't happy until she had everything in the considerable future mapped out. It didn't really bother Darwin, though. He found it kind of comforting.

"Yeah, that sounds great to me, Mom," Darwin replied.

His mom nodded briskly and hummed with the radio, reaching over to turn up the volume. Nothing seemed to make his mom happier than driving the winding, manicured streets of their small town, the subdivisions rising out of the hot sun like a mirage in the distance, the pastels of the houses reminding Darwin of the candy he'd received in his Easter basket each spring for as long as he could remember.

They arrived home around 5:30, and Darwin's mother immediately went to the grocery store to buy ingredients for the barbeque. His dad went straight to the den to watch sports on TV, and Darwin reluctantly decided to join him. When Darwin entered the room, his father looked up at him but didn't say a word. Instead, they both sat there staring at the TV. From time to time, Darwin looked over at his dad, who steadfastly refused to make eye contact. After a half-hour of this, Darwin gave up, figuring there was no point—if his father didn't want to talk or spend time with him, there was no use in him making any effort either. With that, Darwin got up from his chair in the den and went straight up to his bedroom.

Darwin sat in his desk chair and began to finish his book on social inequality. It began with countries like Sweden and Finland that had economic systems in place designed to reduce the extremes of wealth and poverty among their populations. These countries had managed to thrive. He breezed through a few pages when suddenly he noticed a figure out of the corner of his eye, outside the window.

A man was walking in the distance, heading toward the house, a dark figure moving ominously forward. Darwin got up from his desk chair and slowly made his way to the edge of the window, standing to the side so the man couldn't see him. He watched the man walk up to the front yard and pace back and forth on the sidewalk, by the gate of their house. Darwin drew back the curtain as he peered out into the night.

Darwin watched the man intently, and just then the man looked up at the house and around the area of the front yard, almost as if he were inspecting something. Every so often, the man looked around, as if to make sure no one was watching what he was doing, his face slightly obscured by his gray hat. He paced back and forth for a good three minutes and then left, making his way down the block.

Darwin wasn't sure what to make of it, but the appearance of the man made him feel uneasy, though he wasn't sure exactly why. Darwin sat back at his desk. He was trembling slightly, his body vibrating like leaves in the fall wind. Why was this man casing his parents' house? And if he wasn't casing it, then what was he doing out there? Darwin leaned back in his chair, wondering if he should tell his parents, but dismissed that thought as rapidly as it had come. He knew better. After all, what if it was one of his visions—or even a daydream, as the doctor had said? There was no way he was going to wind up back in the psychiatrist's office for yet *another* evaluation.

All of the doctors eventually came to the same conclusion: that Darwin suffered from schizophrenia, which was most likely caused by a combination of low self-esteem and the persistent loneliness he'd felt throughout much of his childhood. But something about that diagnosis rubbed Darwin the wrong way. And it wasn't just that he'd been labeled mentally ill, along with everything else that was wrong with him. It was that even though the diagnosis made sense, it just didn't *feel* right. Darwin knew somehow in his very bones that his visions weren't schizophrenia, that nothing was wrong with his brain. But if it wasn't that, then what was it?

The sound of the garage door opening broke into Darwin's thoughts, startling him. He jumped from his chair. His mom was back from getting groceries for the barbeque. If he was going to tell anybody, it would be her and not his dad. The only other person he would feel comfortable confiding in was his grandmother, as she was usually open-minded and not quick to judge. She also wouldn't obsess about it and worry like his mom definitely would. She would probably get even more overprotective than she already was, and for the first time, Darwin wasn't sure he could bear it.

When Darwin came down for dinner an hour later, he was even quieter than usual. He didn't say a word to either of his parents. His father didn't say much either, since Jane always did the majority of the talking, chattering on about her day at the hospital and her patients. Darwin pushed his food around on his plate, suddenly not hungry.

"Darwin, is everything all right? You haven't said a single word since sitting down." His mom's blue eyes crinkled in worry.

"Oh . . . um, I'm fine. I'm fine. Just kind of tired," Darwin replied, using the tine of his fork to stab at the mound of green, leafy salad his mother had foisted on him.

"Aren't you hungry? You've barely touched your food," his mom asked again, motioning to Darwin's plate.

"I'm not that hungry. I feel like we ate lunch not that long ago."

"Well, lunch was almost seven hours ago, dear," his mother replied with a smile and a shake of her head, as though Darwin's absentmindedness was somehow endearing. "Just don't forget to take your potassium."

Darwin picked up the two beige, oblong pills next to his plate and popped them in his mouth, washing them down with a glass of milk. His stomach churned every time he thought about the man in the gray hat standing outside their house, looking up at Darwin's window as though waiting for him to appear.

"Why aren't you eating?" his father asked loudly, breaking into Darwin's thoughts. Darwin looked up at his dad, not really sure what else to say other than what he had already told his mom. "Don't you feel well?"

"I feel fine, I just . . . I'm not that hungry for some reason," Darwin replied slowly, knowing that doing so was sure to anger his father further. His dad looked at him suspiciously, his eyes narrowed, as if he suspected Darwin wasn't being entirely truthful or had something to hide.

"Your mother worked hard on making that tonight, so unless you're sick, you eat it!" His dad pointed to Darwin's plate with his fork. Darwin didn't respond. He started eating quickly, even though the thought of consuming anything didn't sound appetizing. His father went back to eating.

"I hope you like it, Darwin," his mom said in a soft voice that made Darwin's heart contract in his chest. Chewing and swallowing seemed almost impossible, but he forced his jaws to move.

"Yeah, it's great, Mom, thanks," Darwin said. At that point, Darwin decided against telling her about the man waiting outside the house. If he said anything about it, she would eventually give in and tell his father, which was the last thing Darwin wanted.

Darwin knew his mom was afraid of keeping things from his father. If his dad found out, especially if a secret pertained to Darwin, it would only anger him more, and things would most likely end in a huge argument, his dad storming out of the house, slamming the door behind him so the whole house shook. One time, his dad hadn't come back home until the following morning, creeping back in just as the sun began to streak across the sky. Where he stayed that night, Darwin had no idea. His father had told him he did it to clear his head. But it always upset his mom when his dad walked out like that, without saying another word. Darwin couldn't even count the number of times he'd come downstairs in the eerie quiet after a blowout to find his mom sitting on the sofa, her head buried in her hands as tears dripped over her fingers. No. Darwin knew it wasn't safe to confide in his mother, to tell her about the man. It would only cause more problems, and Darwin had always felt like his very existence was trouble enough.

Darwin finished his meal and asked to be excused. His father nodded without making eye contact. Darwin put his plate in the sink, careful not to let the silverware clatter and annoy his father even more, and then made his way up to his room. As he closed his bedroom door behind him, Darwin crept over to the window to see if the man had returned. Outside, the sky had begun to darken to a midnight blue, but he didn't see anything other than the leafy profusion of bushes and plants in his front yard.

Darwin sat for a few minutes, looking out, waiting, almost holding his breath, but no one appeared. He sat on his bed, pulling a wool blanket at the end of the mattress around his shoulders because he was suddenly shaking again. Though the early fall weather in Texas was warm and close, the room slightly humid, he felt a chill. *Don't let me dream tonight*, Darwin begged the four walls of his bedroom, the sky, the universe, even though he didn't know whether his words fell on deaf ears. *Please . . .* he thought again as his eyes slowly fluttered shut. His body felt heavy and limp, and he lay back on the bed, his head on his pillow, the blanket wrapped around his shoulders until a black wave overtook him and he fell into a half, disturbed sleep.

CHAPTER 2

The alarm went off at 6:30 a.m., and Darwin slowly opened his eyes then blinked a few times as the sound of Bach's "Minuet in G" filled his ears. Darwin loved classical music and refused to wake up to anything other than the compositions of his favorite composers: Bach, Stravinsky, or the tinkling melodies of Chopin, music that reminded him of water running over smooth gray river rocks. He stretched his arms overhead for a moment before reluctantly removing the warm covers to drag himself out of bed.

Darwin trudged into the bathroom to wash his face and comb his hair. His glacial blue eyes stared back as he took in his reflection; a lock of sandy hair fell over his forehead that, for an instant, camouflaged the constellation of white patches scattered across his skin. He sighed, taking in his image, dismay overcoming him. At that moment, he couldn't help wishing he looked, well, normal.

"Darwin! Breakfast is ready!" his mother called from downstairs in a cheery voice.

"Be right there!" Darwin shouted back.

He looked back at himself in the mirror, taking in his angular jaw and wide-set eyes. It wasn't just the spots that drew stares and cruel comments from kids at school. Darwin was also short for his age, extremely thin, and the size of his head was in the bottom fourth percentile for males his age. The doctors attributed this to his premature birth six weeks before his mother's expected delivery date. Darwin had come screaming into the world weeks before he was ready, and it seemed like his body had never had the chance to

17

fully catch up. He let out a sigh, running his hands through his hair, hoping that this year might somehow be different, that he would finally, magically, fit in.

Darwin had always had trouble making friends, not because he wasn't pleasant to be around, but because nobody seemed to want to get close to someone who looked so "different." There were rumors at school, harsh whispers in the halls and in the lunch line in the cafeteria, that Darwin was diseased, contagious, that if anyone got within five feet of him, they'd start breaking out in white spots too. But the funny thing was that vitiligo wasn't contagious at all. When he was younger, he used to hope and pray fervently every night before bed that somehow his pigmentation would return, and he'd wake in the morning with his skin a smooth, even hue. But despite his prayers, his spots continued to look much the same as they always had.

Darwin finished getting ready and made his way downstairs to have breakfast. As he entered the dining room, he could smell sausage cooking on the stove, and saw his mom scooping a mound of scrambled eggs onto a plate. The smell made Darwin's stomach turn violently, and he took a deep breath in an attempt to steady his nerves. His father was reading the newspaper at the kitchen table, sipping his morning coffee.

"Morning, kiddo!" his mom cried cheerfully as she saw Darwin enter the room, flashing him a smile, her blond hair styled in a soft, wavy bob that stopped at her chin. She wore a pair of pale green scrubs, sensible white shoes with cushiony soles that she wore to work every day peeking out from the hems. "What can I get you— eggs, sausage, fresh fruit, toast, waffles, pancakes? I've got it all ready to go, whatever you'd like." As usual, his mom was completely over the top. Why make one breakfast when she could make six? Darwin shook his head, unable to stop the smile that played at the corners of his lips.

"Just some waffles would be great, Mom. Thanks," Darwin responded, a little overwhelmed by the effort his mother had clearly gone to on his behalf.

"That's it? You don't want anything else for your first day?" Jane replied. Her pale eyebrows furrowed slightly in concern. Darwin usually ate a big breakfast, but today his stomach felt like it was tied in knots.

"Um, maybe some fruit, too, I guess. I'm just not that hungry," Darwin said, trying to keep his voice casual. He didn't want to admit it to his parents, but he was nervous to be starting school again. He knew his mother would worry, and his father would be disappointed if he told them that he was experiencing all his usual first-day jitters, wondering what his classmates would say to him or if he would make any friends that year. But he was trying to stay positive, trying to convince himself that the first day of school was a new beginning, an opportunity to study interesting subjects, and maybe, *maybe* make some friends.

"Okay, my boy, just let me know if you change your mind and want something else," Jane said as she bent down to kiss Darwin on the cheek.

"Morning, son," his father said without looking up from his newspaper. As usual, his dad looked like he'd been up for hours—and he probably had been. A perpetually early riser, his dark hair was already combed back from his round face, and he was dressed in a crisp white dress shirt and a pair of dark pants with creases so sharp they looked as though they might draw blood if Darwin got too close. Methodical, exacting, and uncompromising. That was his father. "Sleep well last night?" his dad asked in a tone that sounded more like an interrogation than a question.

"Yep," Darwin replied, though he hadn't at all. He caught his mother staring at him with her eyes narrowed, as though she somehow knew he'd spent the night tossing and turning in a half-dream state, his covers twisting around his torso like a straitjacket. Even when he did finally slip into a kind of half-sleep, he'd woken up at what seemed like just a few minutes later, gasping for air, the room uncomfortably close.

"Glad to hear it," Dave said as he turned to the financial section of the newspaper. "You going to make any friends this year?"

"Dave! Don't be like that, he has friends!" his mother interjected defensively, before Darwin could respond.

"Oh . . . that's okay, Mom. Yeah." He shrugged. "I'm going to try to make some friends this year," Darwin said in what he hoped was an optimistic voice.

"Son," his dad said rather impatiently as he finally looked up from his newspaper, the light glinting off the pair of black reading glasses he wore, "you may look different to some people, but you're still a person just like anybody else. Don't let anybody tell you that you're different."

"Uh, right. I won't, Dad," Darwin said.

Even though Darwin was one of the smartest students in his class, even though he always tried to be helpful around the house, he seemed to always fall short of his father's expectations. Darwin never knew if perhaps his dad was ashamed of him for his appearance and lack of a social life, or if he blamed Darwin for the fact that his mother had no longer been able to conceive any more children after Darwin was born. Maybe his dad had adopted his own distant father's style of parenting. Or maybe his father really *was* ashamed of him. Darwin knew that his dad had always wanted a large family, as he himself was one of six children and enjoyed being surrounded by family, but because of Darwin and his difficult birth, his father's dream of having a house filled with children would never become a reality.

"He's right, sweetheart. Just remember to be yourself, and focus on the important things, like your education and your health," Jane said warmly, reaching out to pat Darwin gently on the shoulder, before glancing at her husband, who had already disappeared once again behind his newspaper. She sighed then reached for a medicine bottle at the center of the table.

"Don't forget to take your pills, Darwin," Jane said as she set down two potassium tablets on the table in front of Darwin, next to an empty glass that she was now filling with orange juice.

"Thanks, Mom."

"And don't forget to take two more at lunch," she warned, the bottle rattling as she handed it to him.

On top of the vitiligo, Darwin was born with an extreme and seemingly permanent potassium deficiency—the doctors said his body seemed incapable of retaining the sufficient levels of potassium that it needed to function. When he was ten years old, Darwin had avoided taking his potassium tablets for three consecutive days,

convinced that the potassium was causing his skin to lose pigmentation and that if he just stopped taking the pills, he'd wake up one
day soon, his skin as even-toned as everyone else's. Then, in the
middle of a fifth-grade math exam, he collapsed. Darwin was in the
hospital for two days as he recovered, receiving potassium through
an IV. The doctor informed his parents that if he had gone another
day without taking his potassium, he might have died.

After that incident, his mother, who was a nurse by profession,
began taking Darwin's health even more seriously than before. She
began monitoring his potassium intake, and later insisted that he
wear a wristband that allowed her to continuously monitor his blood
pressure, his insulin level, and his heart rate. Soon after, she began
monitoring everything Darwin watched on TV, which had always
seemed a little excessive to him, but if it made her feel better, then
he was happy to comply. At least, he used to be. When he was old
enough to leave the house unaccompanied, she wanted to know
where he was at all times. It was all extremely overbearing, to say
the least, but until recently Darwin didn't really mind, as his mother
was also so warm and loving, the polar opposite of his dad, who
rarely cracked so much as a smile, and hugged Darwin maybe once
a year, if he was lucky.

Darwin finished his breakfast slowly and took his potassium
tablets, washing them down with the orange juice, and went back
upstairs to grab his backpack.

"Well, are we ready?" his mother exclaimed from downstairs.

"Almost!" Darwin shouted back. Darwin gathered his things
and sat down in his desk chair, taking a moment to think about what
he wanted to accomplish this upcoming year: make friends, join a
sports team, get straight A's . . . but if he was honest with himself,
he knew that none of these goals were really *that* important to him
in the grand scheme of things. As he sat there thinking, he realized
that what he wanted most of all was to find himself—cliché as it
sounded—and to be true to who he was. Whatever that was . . . He
resolved not to spend the year trying to conform to other people's
expectations, though he knew it was easier said than done.

Darwin marched down the stairs to find his mom waiting by the
door. "Let's get going!" she said merrily. She was always annoying-

ly positive, no matter what obstacles lay in his path, and sometimes it drove him a little nuts. "I still can't believe you only have two years left of high school, Darwin," she mused, shaking her head in disbelief. "Seems like just yesterday we were starting your first day of school in kindergarten. Pretty soon you'll be heading off to college." Before Darwin could respond, her eyes turned glassy with unshed tears, and she smiled brightly through them as they headed to the car.

Darwin slipped into the passenger seat, and his mom began humming to herself tunelessly as she started the ignition, surreptitiously wiping her eyes with the back of her hand. He could never quite understand how his mom generally seemed so happy and content, able to brush off almost every mishap or slight and move on like nothing had happened, while his father was the very definition of stern and unapproachable. She never seemed to let her husband's negativity affect her. She was almost pathologically pleasant and upbeat.

As the car pulled out of the driveway, Darwin noticed his neighbor, Jake, from across the street walking to school. Jake, who was Darwin's age, was short and a little pudgy, with extremely round cheeks, his dark hair shorn to his scalp in the buzz cut he'd worn even since Darwin could remember. Despite the fact that he lived so close, Darwin never spent time with Jake. He wondered what would happen if he started walking to school every day. He would probably cross paths with Jake most mornings. They might even become friends. His heart leapt a little in his chest at the very thought of it.

But Darwin's parents never let him walk to school, not since the day he was almost kidnapped. Darwin was in third grade, three blocks from home, when two men pulled up next to him in a van and tried to grab him. It was strange to say the least, given that crime was practically nonexistent in their neighborhood, and rarely occurred in their small town of Crimson.

Darwin sat back in the passenger seat while his mom continued to hum to the radio. He thought about that day when he was walking home from third grade; it was by far the most traumatic thing that had happened to him in his life, and psychologically it still had an impact on him. Sometimes in the night he'd wake in a panic, certain that hands were about to grab him, the sheets soaked in sweat, his heart hammering in his chest.

It had started out as an ordinary day; his teacher, Mrs. Scott, had finished up that day's lessons with a review of times tables. Darwin always finished his times tables worksheets before the other students, as math was, by far, his favorite subject. Mrs. Scott had instructed the children to place their chairs on their desks and line up at the door, her bright red hair shining in the sunlight that streamed through the windows, her aged but capable hands herding them toward the doorway. As the other children frantically packed their bags, anticipating the bell that would release them at any moment, Darwin made his way to the door, his backpack already on his back.

"Hey, Darwin, can you, uh, help me out with this last one?" one of the boys sitting next to him at the line by the door asked. Darwin, taken aback, turned around to see Fletcher McCrouger pointing at the last problem in the times table. Fletcher, unlike Darwin, was big for his age, with long brown hair that habitually fell over his soft, doughy face, hiding his eyes from sight.

"Sure!" Darwin answered, eager to help. Students did not often initiate conversation with him. Darwin looked at the worksheet and saw Fletcher was stuck on 8 X 11. "I don't know why, but the eleven tables always get me stuck," Fletcher said.

"Yeah, I have a little trick for elevens," Darwin said, more confidently than he felt. "When multiplying numbers by eleven, you can start with the first and last digits, which will remain the same, unless there is a carryover, and then you would insert the sums of the adjacent pairs of digits sequentially in between," Darwin finished.

Fletcher looked up at Darwin, his face awash in utter confusion, a look of almost panic in his eyes.

"Here, let me show you an example," Darwin started again. "With single digits, it's easy—when you multiply a single digit by eleven, you just duplicate the single digit. So, for example, 5x11=55, 7x11=77, and so on," Darwin stated, writing the equations on the side of Fletcher's worksheet as he spoke. He could tell from the way Fletcher exhaled heavily in relief that this strategy made more sense to him. "Now, for multiple digit numbers, here's what you have to do: say you want to multiply 354x11. Then, 354 begins with a three," Darwin said, and wrote the number three in the corner of the page. "Then the next digit is a five, so you add those two numbers, and get eight. The next digit in 354 is a five. So, you add 5+4 to get nine." Darwin tacked a nine to the end of the number eight at the corner of the page. "Then you take the very last digit, a four. So, the answer is 3,894," Darwin said in a satisfied tone as he handed the pencil back to Fletcher.

"Whoa, how did you do that?" Fletcher asked, his eyes wide with astonishment.

"I didn't do anything—it's just a little trick I learned when multiplying by eleven," Darwin replied. "Does it make sense?" he asked Fletcher.

"Yeah . . . Only, I can't believe it's this easy! I wish it was like this for all of the other times tables," Fletcher said with a little nervous laugh. He looked thoughtful for a moment, then took a deep breath and said, "Do you think we could study together sometime? My parents said they'll buy me an Xbox if I get A's in math for the rest of the year," he said, shrugging his shoulders as if it was no big deal.

"Sure, no problem!" Darwin responded excitedly. Fletcher seemed really nice. He didn't seem to notice or care about Darwin's spotted skin.

"And if I get that Xbox, you can come over and play!" Fletcher said.

"That would be great!" Darwin's parents didn't allow him to play video games, but he wasn't going to pass up an opportunity to hang out with a new friend, even if he was terrible at it or his parents considered it a waste of time. They didn't have to know about it anyway, Darwin reasoned with himself.

The rest of the students had lined up behind the door and were anxiously staring at the bell. When it rang, Ms. Scott made her way to the door, opening it, and the students began pushing and shoving, eager to get home for the day. "All right, class, straight line, straight line, no pushing, no shoving," Ms. Scott shouted over the commotion. "And don't forget to finish your model of the solar system!"

Darwin had already finished his—in fact, he'd completed it the same day it was assigned. He had used Styrofoam balls for the planets and wire, pipe cleaners, and felt to create rings for Saturn and Uranus. Darwin loved space—it was so open, vast, and seemingly empty, yet full of beautiful things, if one knew where to look—the stars overhead sparkling in the inky blackness of the sky, strung together like a series of diamond necklaces. The idea that there was this massive universe out there, which was mostly unexplored, and how Earth was just a tiny fraction of the overall makeup of space, fascinated him endlessly. Maybe it was the fact that space allowed him to think about things that took him away from this world, a world where he would never quite fit in.

As the students left the classroom, many of them made their way to the pickup line, where they found their parents waiting for them. Others waited to board the school bus. Darwin said goodbye to Fletcher just outside their classroom, then made his way through the playground, where a number of students played on the swing set and monkey bars while they waited for their parents to pick them up. Darwin felt his heart sink in his chest, just watching them and listening to their happy, joyful chatter. Whenever Darwin approached, they would often run away, when he came close. This had happened a few times in second grade, and Darwin didn't want to face that experience again. The chorus of, "Don't go near him! He'll give you a disease," kept running through his head as he navigated the playground, his eyes downcast.

Darwin walked through the playground at a steady pace, without stopping to look around or make eye contact, heading toward the gate. As Darwin approached, he saw one of the staff attendants monitoring traffic while packs of children crossed the street. This particular attendant was always nice to Darwin and knew him by name. He was large and round with a big white beard, with more than a passing resemblance to Santa Claus. "Hey there, Darwin, how's it going?" the man asked in a jolly tone.

"Good! A boy in my class asked me to help him with his math today, and he said that if he gets A's in math for the rest of the year he'll get an Xbox and I can come play it with him if he does!" Darwin said enthusiastically. He had been excited to tell someone about this new information; anyone, really.

"That's great! Putting those brains to good use, I see," the man said kindly.

"I guess so," Darwin said nervously as he looked down at the ground with a smile.

"All right. buddy, your turn to cross the street now. I'll hold up the traffic." The man stepped out into the street, holding up his sign directing cars to stop while Darwin crossed.

"Thanks!" Darwin said as he crossed the street and started to make his way home.

He walked on his normal route, passing the house with a huge trampoline in front of it that he always wished he could have a go on. After walking the first block home, he would pass the couple that had a Saint Bernard in the front yard. The enormous dog would always bark at the top of his lungs when people passed by their front gate. Darwin had walked to and from school so many times now that the dog no longer barked at him, but instead just watched him intently as he passed.

But that day, as Darwin turned the corner, the dog began to growl menacingly. Darwin, finding this very unusual, turned to look at the dog. It barked viciously twice then continued growling. Darwin noticed the dog wasn't looking at him, but rather looking somewhere behind Darwin and to his right.

Darwin turned around to see what the dog could possibly be looking at, but he didn't see anything out of the ordinary. The whole street was clear, with not a single person walking by. There were no other animals, not even another car. Suddenly, Darwin saw what appeared to be a man's leg sticking out of the side of a bush in front of a neighbor's house across the street, in a position that suggested that the man was lying down on his back. Darwin slowly walked toward the bush, not sure what to expect. Was it a homeless man? Unlikely, given the fact that Crimson's homeless population was few and far between and it looked as though this man was wearing a slightly soiled pair of beige cargo pants. Perhaps it was the neighbors' gardener taking a rest after trimming the bushes.

As Darwin approached the bush, the leg moved quickly out of sight. Darwin jumped back, startled, and paused for a moment.

"Well, whoever it is, he's awake," Darwin muttered to himself.

As he took a step closer, the dog suddenly began barking wildly. Darwin heard some rustling, then saw a man emerge from behind the bush, looking straight at him. The man was wearing ripped beige cargos, a white T-shirt, and sunglasses. His hair was oily and disheveled, and his face scruffy. Darwin guessed he had to be around his late thirties. He looked as if he hadn't taken a shower in days. Darwin suddenly felt very uncomfortable at the way the man was staring at him, unflinching, with his hands in fists by his side.

Darwin immediately turned around and began walking away from the man, without saying anything, with the dog still barking madly in the background. Then he heard the man's footsteps following in his direction. Darwin began walking more quickly, his pulse racing and his heart pounding in his chest, afraid of what this man might be capable of. *What does he want*, Darwin thought over and over as he heard the sound of the man's footsteps begin to pick up as well, as did the howls of the dog who was still barking like crazy. Then Darwin began to run. He was a fast runner for his age, but he knew there was no way he would be able to keep ahead of a fully-grown man. The man started running as well, and Darwin could sense him on his heels. He saw a garbage can to his right and knocked it down behind him as he passed, in an attempt to throw the man off. But the man jumped over the garbage can and continued to chase Darwin down the street.

As soon as Darwin was about to round the corner to the next block, the man grabbed his backpack and wheeled him around. "Get off me!" Darwin screamed. "What do you want?" The man didn't answer, and placed his hand over Darwin's mouth to silence him. Darwin began to flail, screaming as hard as he could, but his screams were muffled by the man's meaty hand. He could still hear the dog barking in the distance, and hoped that the neighbors would come out and see what all the commotion was. Darwin then heard a car speeding in their direction; someone was coming to his rescue, he thought, relief coursing through him. Darwin looked up and could see a windowless van, fast approaching. The man then lifted Darwin and started moving quickly in the direction of the van, Darwin still screaming as loudly as he could through the hand covering his mouth. The side door of the van swung open.

"Quick! Get him in here," a bearded man inside the van said. Darwin was filled with a sudden dread, the sour taste of bile in his mouth as he realized that the person in the van was not coming to his aid, but rather to the aid of his kidnapper. Darwin began to flail as much as he could, knowing that if he didn't attempt to make noise, these men would capture him. The bearded man grabbed hold of Darwin's flailing arms as the other lifted him into the vehicle.

Just as Darwin began to wonder what they could possibly want from him, he caught sight of the neighbor's dog. He had somehow gotten out of the gate of the front yard and was charging as fast as he could toward Darwin and the two men. The dog lunged at the man who had just lifted Darwin into the van, locking his jaw onto the man's arm in a savage grip. "Ahh!" the man shouted in pain as blood began to run down his arm. The man started punching the dog in an attempt to free himself from the dog's grip, but the dog held on relentlessly, his head moving this way and that as the man struggled to pull his arm free. His accomplice then exited the vehicle and attempted to push the dog away. Darwin seized what he realized would be his only opportunity to escape and opened the opposite door of the van. He jumped out of the car and began running down the street, his heart thudding in his ears. *Run*, he thought. *Don't look back.*

Darwin heard one of the men shout, "He's getting away!" followed by a shuffle of footsteps behind him. Moments later, he heard something hit the ground, then one of the men shouted "*AWAY, AWAY!*" Darwin turned around momentarily and saw the dog circling the second man, the one from inside the van. The dog's teeth were bared and there was blood on his muzzle. Darwin continued sprinting down the street as fast as he could. Running out of breath, he ducked quickly behind a tree in someone's front yard and looked back toward the van. The two men had managed to free themselves from the dog. The second man was helping the first, who was clutching his bleeding forearm, into the van. The man then shut the passenger doors, hopped into the driver's seat, and began quickly driving in Darwin's direction. Darwin inched around the tree trunk as the van zoomed by. He peered out from behind the tree to watch it speed off into the distance.

Darwin then sank into a sitting position against the tree trunk, not fully believing what had just happened. His heart was pounding so hard it felt like it was going to jump out of his chest, and his shirt was practically soaked through with sweat. As he sat there, Darwin's heavy breathing started to slow, and he wondered what he should do. Maybe he should hide a while longer, in case the men came back. He sat there for another minute or two, looking around nervously to see if the coast was clear. There was no van in sight. Finally, he emerged from behind the tree and looked down the street to where the attack had occurred. He saw a lot of blood on the asphalt where the van had been parked minutes earlier. A few feet away on the sidewalk was the dog, sitting on its hind legs and surveying the road ahead, almost as if it was waiting for the men to return. Darwin couldn't have been more grateful to the large beast for rescuing him. He didn't even want to think what might have happened had the dog not been there.

Darwin began to make his way back up the street toward the dog, cautiously, making direct eye contact. He then reached out his hand slowly and gave him a couple of pats on the head. The dog began to wag his tail—something Darwin had never seen him do before. Darwin sat there for a little while, petting the dog, feeling his heart rate slow, returning to its normal, steady pace. "Thank you, you saved my life," Darwin whispered, looking into the dog's soulful brown eyes. The dog gave him a little lick on the hand and started walking back toward its owner's home. Darwin then began walking quickly in the direction of his own house, wondering how he was going to explain this to his parents.

Darwin never saw the men again, or the van, but the memory of the incident would stay with him forever. When he told his parents what had happened, Jane was absolutely frantic, demanding that his father install an expensive security system, complete with cameras. Dave was angry. The neighbors were shocked. And Darwin was scared. He often woke up in a sweat after dreaming that the men had found him at home and were trying to kidnap him from his room.

Two weeks after the incident, the dog that had saved Darwin went missing and was never seen again. Darwin's parents sent out a police squad to find the two perpetrators, in addition to hanging up flyers featuring a sketch artist's drawing of the two men, based on descriptions Darwin had provided. From that day forward, Darwin was not allowed to walk to and from school ever again. The two men were never found or identified.

"Here we are, dear," Jane said, bringing Darwin out of his reverie. He looked up and saw that they had arrived at school. "I know you're already a junior in high school, but you still need to give your mom a kiss," Jane said, grinning. Darwin sighed heavily in exasperation, but still leaned over and kissed his mom on the cheek, if grudgingly. "I'll pick you up at three," his mom called out as Darwin exited the car.

"Thanks, Mom, I'll be waiting at the front entrance," Darwin said quickly, giving his mother a smile as he shut the passenger door. As Jane drove away, Darwin turned around to see all of the students making their way into the building. *Maybe this year will be different*, he thought optimistically, trying to fight the old familiar feeling welling up inside him, that tightening in his chest that dropped down to his stomach, tying it in knots—that feeling that told him he'd never fit in, that he'd never be good enough. He shook his head once, as if trying to loosen the thought from his brain, took a deep breath, and made his up the steps to the front door.

CHAPTER 3

Darwin walked through the double doors of Crimson High, hearing the excited babble of students speaking to one another animatedly after a long summer apart, their chatter filling his ears like tuneless music. There were packs of kids exchanging hugs, and he heard snippets of conversation as they recounted stories of their summer vacations. He saw several familiar faces as he maneuvered through the crowd, but there were some new ones too. He locked eyes with a pretty girl he'd never seen before. She had long, chestnut-colored hair that fell to her shoulders like a silken waterfall and bright blue eyes, her deeply tanned limbs extending from the white V-necked T-shirt and pair of faded denim shorts that she wore. A thin gold bracelet shone on one downy arm, glittering in the sunlight. But before he could say anything, or even smile, she gave him a quizzical stare before quickly turning the other way, grabbing the shoulder of the dark-haired girl next to her and whispering in her ear.

Darwin's cheeks flushed scarlet as he looked down at the schedule he held tightly in one hand, to see what his first class was—Social Studies with Ms. Edmond. He began making his way up the stairs to the third floor of the building alongside several other students who were now shuffling to their various classrooms. He passed Fletcher along the way, the same boy he'd helped with the math problem on the day of his attempted kidnapping. Darwin's short-lived fantasy of a friendship with Fletcher had evaporated when, in the days following the attempted kidnapping, he informed Darwin, red-faced and stammering, that his mother didn't want them hanging around each other. He couldn't even look Darwin in the eye, but instead stared at the linoleum floor and mumbled almost incoherently. Fletcher was now the captain of the baseball team, his pudgy, undefined features having morphed into an angular handsomeness over the years, and he was now friends with everyone. Everyone, that was, except Darwin.

Darwin walked through the door of Room 304 of Ms. Edmond's classroom and scanned the room for an open seat. He made his way toward a seat near the front of the room and started unpacking his notebook and pens. He then heard a few quick footsteps and saw an unfamiliar student take the seat next to him.

"Hey, I'm Tyler," the student said as he stuck out his hand to introduce himself. Darwin, perplexed, looked around to make sure the boy was actually talking to him, and not to the student on Darwin's left. High school kids didn't usually shake hands.

"Hi . . . I'm Darwin," Darwin said as he extended his hand to shake Tyler's, still hesitant that he'd misunderstood him. Tyler was sitting, but Darwin could see that he was very tall and bulky, with dark hair and blue eyes the color of a stormy sky. Darwin couldn't help but notice that Tyler looked slightly older than a typical high school student—he even had some gray hairs here and there on his head, like someone had sprinkled a handful of salt throughout his dark locks. He certainly dressed like a kid though, baggy jeans, a graphic T-shirt, and a chain necklace. Darwin watched as Tyler unpacked a notebook from his backpack and looked back at Darwin, his expression open and friendly. Friendlier than Darwin was used to, that was for sure.

"I'm new here, just moved to the neighborhood a couple weeks ago," Tyler said as he began to open his notebook to a blank page. Darwin nodded sagely. He'd known immediately that Tyler was new. After all, why else would he introduce himself so openly when everyone else treated Darwin like a leper just because of his skin?

"Oh cool, where from?"

"Washington, DC. My parents were getting kind of tired of it, they needed a change. My dad just got a new job here," Tyler said. "So, we moved. What's it like here, anyway? I haven't really had a chance to check it out."

"What, the school?" asked Darwin quizzically.

"The school, the town, everything," Tyler asked with a slightly crooked smile, as if Darwin's reticence to spill the dirt amused him in some way. "You like it here?"

Darwin sat there for a second, thinking about how to respond to the question. *Is there anything worth noting about the school or the area? Is there anything to like, even?*

"Um, it's not bad, I guess. It's sort of your standard upper-middle-class town. Nothing too special about it, but I'm probably the wrong person to ask," Darwin replied with an apologetic half-smile.

"And why's that?"

"Well," Darwin said, figuring he might as well be honest, "I don't get out a lot. I'm what you would probably call more of an introvert."

"Hm, I see," Tyler said, narrowing his eyes slightly.

Darwin expected that would be the end of their conversation, and Tyler would turn around and talk to the girl next to him.

"Well, there's nothing wrong with that. I mean, everyone has their thing. Like some people are outgoing and like to party and others keep to themselves, you know? You've just got to be you and do what makes you happy," Tyler said with a shrug of his shoulders, as if it were the most natural thing in the world.

Darwin, who was opening his backpack, stopped and quickly looked up at Tyler.

"But there's nothing wrong with experiencing new things and getting out more, just to see if you like it, if it's not for you, then okay, whatever. But you gotta try, you know?"

"Yeah, I guess that's true," Darwin said pensively.

He wasn't sure what it was, but there was something about Tyler that he liked immediately. Perhaps it was the way that Tyler seemed so calm and collected despite the fact that it was his first day at a school where he didn't know anyone. He exuded the kind of ineffable confidence that Darwin wished he had more than anything, a kind of calm collectedness that made him seem like he could handle just about anything that came his way. But more importantly—and this was the strange part—was that Tyler didn't seem to notice Darwin's appearance, or even give it a second glance. For some reason, he treated Darwin like he would anyone else.

Just then, the bell rang.

"Okay, class, take your seats. Take your seats," Ms. Edmond said. She was tall and thin with short brown hair, and habitually wore a large black pair of round glasses that were Coke-bottle thick and almost seemed to cover her whole face.

At the sound of her voice, students began shuffling around to get to their desks. Three girls charged through the door, late, while giggling.

"Settle down, ladies," said Ms. Edmond sternly, glaring at them as they took the remaining empty seats.

"Now, class, before we begin, we have a new student who I'd like to introduce," Ms. Edmond said, as some of the students began looking around curiously. "This is Tyler Barros. He recently moved here from Washington, DC. Tyler, would you like to tell us a bit about yourself?"

Tyler got up from his chair and strode to the front of the class-room, shoving his hands into the pockets of the faded, ripped jeans he wore.

"Hey everybody, um, my name is Tyler and I'm from DC. Back home, I played a lot of basketball and baseball, those are my two favorite sports. So anyway, I'm looking forward to getting to know you all." Tyler finished with a grin and made his way back to his seat as the class started clapping. Tyler sat down and gave Darwin a little nod.

Even though it seemed like Tyler really liked him, Darwin wondered how long it would really last. After all, once Tyler found out that Darwin was basically a social pariah, he'd probably start ignoring him entirely in favor of the more popular kids.

"Okay, class, let's get started, shall we?" Ms. Edmond said.

The bell rang at 8:45 a.m., signaling the end of first period. Darwin began to gather his things and looked at his schedule once again.

"Hey, what class do you have next?" Tyler asked as he packed up his bag.

"Oh, English with Randall," Darwin replied.

"No way, me too," Tyler said with a slow, lazy grin. "What other classes are you in?" Darwin and Tyler compared schedules and noticed that they were in every class together, with the exception of sixth period, at which time Darwin had Spanish while Tyler had Band. Tyler seemed delighted by the fact that they shared the same classes, which took Darwin aback, but also made him even more hopeful. Maybe he was being overly cautious. Could this be the start of an actual friendship?

Darwin and Tyler made their way to all of their morning classes, sitting next to each other in every class except for AP Math, which had assigned seating. AP Math was a senior-level course, and Darwin, who for years had achieved the highest math scores of all the students in his class, was surprised to see that Tyler, another junior, had qualified for the same advanced level. But Darwin reminded himself that he shouldn't judge a book by its cover; clearly, Tyler wasn't doing that to him.

AP Math was their last class before lunch, which Darwin was looking forward to. His refusal to eat much at breakfast was catching up to him, and by the time the bell rang for lunch, he was ravenous, his stomach growling noisily. As he packed his books and shoved them into his backpack, he realized that the tantalizing scent of burgers and fries wafting in through the open door from the cafeteria only heightened his hunger.

Darwin normally ate his lunch alone, outside on the front steps near the school parking lot. He thought about asking Tyler if he wanted to join him outside, but decided that maybe he would give him some space. After all, they had virtually every class together. Besides, Tyler probably wanted to meet some other people, who were no doubt avoiding Tyler while he kept Darwin company.

"What do you usually do for lunch?" Tyler asked Darwin.

"Oh, um, I usually just eat on the steps near the parking lot," Darwin replied, his face crimson again with embarrassment. Admitting as much was basically like holding up a sign that read: *LOSER*. *Oh well*, Darwin thought, shuffling his feet and shifting his weight from side to side. *He's going to find out sooner or later. It may as well be now.*

"You mean you guys don't eat in the cafeteria here?" Tyler

35

asked, with a slightly confused expression.

"No, people do . . . I just don't. And I usually bring my lunch from home, so I don't need to go to the café anyway to get food," Darwin said, looking at the ground, unable to meet Tyler's gaze.

"Well, do people ever go out for lunch? If they have their own car, I mean," Tyler said.

"Yeah, some people do, usually seniors, but I don't have one," Darwin responded as they began to make their way out of the classroom and down the hall.

"Do you have a license?" Tyler asked.

"No. My parents won't let me get one, not yet, anyway. Besides, I don't think I'm ready for it, I can barely touch the pedals," Darwin joked with a small laugh. Darwin wasn't tiny, but somehow, he still hadn't grown taller than 5'5".

Tyler looked down at Darwin with a smirk. "Well, why don't you just start practicing? You'll get better at it."

"I don't even have a learner's permit," Darwin protested. "Plus, that's easier said than done, especially when you don't have a car to practice with and your parents freak out the second you're behind the wheel and pulling out of the driveway."

"Well, you could use my car to practice and I'll even go with you, show you how it works," Tyler said, slinging his backpack over his shoulders and adjusting the straps before sliding his thumbs underneath them.

"You have a car?" Darwin asked.

"Yeah, it's not much but it gets me where I need to go," Tyler said with a grin. The two began to walk down the hall toward the cafeteria. "So, what do you want to do, you gonna eat outside?"

"Yeah, I guess—"

"Actually," Tyler interrupted, "how about I grab something from the cafeteria and meet you on the steps. Sound good?"

"Yeah, that works," Darwin responded, trying to sound casual, though inside he was surprised that Tyler wanted to eat lunch together. *But why?* A nagging little voice inside of him piped up. *I mean, he's been with you all morning. Why would he want to eat lunch with you?* "I'll see you in a bit," he said, forcing himself to act naturally, to smile, even though on the inside he was anything but confident about what was happening. He wasn't even really sure he understood it. Tyler was good-looking and had the kind of confidence that would've made him instantly popular with Crimson's elite. If he'd spent any time with the jocks and the popular kids, they would've seen right away that Tyler was one of them. What possible reason could he have for wanting to hang out with Darwin?

"Cool. I'll meet you out there," Tyler said with a nod and a smile as he walked off toward the cafeteria.

Darwin made his way outside and found his usual lunch spot on the second step of the stairs at the front entrance. While he waited, Darwin looked up at the clear blue sky and took a moment to appreciate the day, the white puffy clouds steaking across the sky, the sun shining down, warming his skin that was still prickled with goose bumps from the relentless air conditioning that made the classrooms feel positively arctic on hot days. Darwin knew that sometimes the world was harsh, and he had experienced more than his fair share of bad days. But he tried to remind himself that life always had its up and downs, and that bad times were always followed by good ones, that what mattered was how people conducted themselves in the face of hardship. That's what his mom always told him, and Darwin tried to keep that perspective as best as he could.

Just then, Darwin saw Tyler making his way down the steps, a basket of chicken strips and fries in his hands. "Wow! You didn't tell me they have a stocked cafeteria in this school, man," Tyler said jubilantly as he drew near Darwin. "I mean, seriously, how do you bring your lunch every day instead of eating in there? They've got sandwiches, pizza sticks, fries, chicken burgers, and, like, a ton of candy! And it's super cheap," Tyler said incredulously, as he sat down next to Darwin, stuffing a chicken strip in his mouth. "And pretty good, too!" Tyler added, his mouth full of chicken. Darwin had never seen anybody this excited over cafeteria food before. Maybe the schools in DC were filled with processed burgers and slimy deli meats served by old lunch ladies wearing hair nets. "So, what did you get today?" Tyler asked, peering over at Darwin's lunch bag.

"Um, it looks like the standard PB&J, some chips, some carrot sticks, and juice," Darwin said as he pulled each item from his lunch bag.

"Ah man. I'm telling you, give the cafeteria a shot sometime, way better than a smashed PB&J," Tyler said sympathetically, while shoving a handful of fries in his mouth and chewing loudly, smacking his lips.

The two sat there, eating side by side, A few students entered the soccer field and began playing a pickup game.

Tyler noticed Darwin gazing at the field. "Do you play any sports?" Tyler asked, taking a swig of the Coke he'd bought and wiping his mouth with the back of his hand.

"Not really, I'm not very athletic, and too small for most sports that require physical contact. What about you? You like basketball and baseball, right?" Darwin said, remembering what Tyler had said when he introduced himself to the class earlier that morning.

"I could watch them all day," Tyler said, setting the can of Coke on the ground. "And since I'm not good enough to play them professionally, my goal is to become a sportscaster someday. Just talk sports all day, have fun, and get paid to do it. Man, that would be the best." Tyler said somewhat dreamily before picking up the can again and taking another swig of his soda.

"If you couldn't do that, though, what else would you do?" Darwin asked curiously, biting into his sandwich.

"Hmm, that's a good question, haven't really given it a ton of thought—I always thought I would go into sports broadcasting. But I guess if I chose a backup plan, it would probably be something in law enforcement, like a detective or undercover agent, that would be pretty cool," Tyler said as he continued to chew on his chicken strips. "But I'll tell you one thing, I would never want to be a doctor, that's for sure," Tyler said with a small chuckle.

"Why not?" Darwin asked.

"I don't know, I just don't think I could handle all of that memorization they have to do, I'm also a little squeamish when it comes to blood and stuff like that," Tyler replied with a shudder, as though the very idea pained him, and Darwin could tell that Tyler wasn't joking now—it really did gross him out.

"What do your parents do?" Darwin asked.

"My parents?" Tyler said, his blue eyes full of confusion, as if the question was not only completely unexpected, but almost bizarre.

"Yeah, you said you moved here because of your dad's new job . . ."

"Oh right, of course," Tyler said quickly, pausing for a moment before answering. "My dad works in construction and my mom's a teacher?" he replied, as if he wasn't quite sure. Darwin watched as Tyler smiled once wanly, then looked away.

"Oh, that's cool, what kind of construction does your dad do?" Darwin asked, wondering why Tyler clearly didn't want to talk about his parents. *Maybe they don't get along*, Darwin thought as he waited for Tyler to answer. *I mean, look at you and your dad.*

"He builds houses mostly and . . . other types of properties," Tyler responded vaguely, while looking down at what little remained of his food. There were a few fries left in the little paper boat, ketchup smeared across the bottom in a viscous puddle that reminded Darwin of a bloody wound. Tyler looked off to the side, where a group of guys were playing basketball. The sound of the ball against the pavement reverberated in Darwin's ears. "So, what are the girls like here?" Tyler said quickly, changing the subject.

"Girls? I don't really know too many girls. Well, I mean, I sort of know Mindy Simmons, she's nice—and really smart," Darwin said as he continued to eat his sandwich.

Mindy. Just her name in his mouth made Darwin feel like the world was tilting on its axis; sweat broke out along his temples, underneath his arms.

"Mindy Simmons, huh? Is she in any of our classes?" Tyler asked with that lazy grin, the one that probably got him every girl he went after, Darwin thought.

"No, she's in the grade below us, she's a sophomore." Darwin tried to make his voice nonchalant, but despite his efforts to sound like it was no big deal, the words came out shaky and uncertain.

"Ahh, I see. So, are you gonna go after this girl?" Tyler said with that same cocky smile.

"Go after? What do you mean?"

"Like, are you trying to hit her up? Ask her out? You know, that kind of thing," Tyler said.

"Oh! No, it's not like that at all, she's just a cool person and she's nice to me. But there is no way she sees me like that," Darwin said, looking around instinctively to make sure that no one else was within earshot.

"Well, how do you know?"

"I just know. Besides, she has a boyfriend. She doesn't see me as anything other than a friend," Darwin said, wondering if Mindy actually even considered him a friend at all. Maybe she just talked to him out of pity. It wasn't exactly inconceivable.

"Well, boyfriend or not, that shouldn't stop you from pursuing her, if you like her," Tyler said enthusiastically, as if this information was no deterrent at all.

"But I never said I liked her, I just said she was nice," Darwin said defensively, crumpling his now-empty brown paper bag in his fist and balling it up.

Darwin did in fact like Mindy Simmons, but never told anybody that, and certainly never planned on telling Mindy. She was very popular and had a boyfriend who was athletic and good-looking, and Darwin was, well, just Darwin—a kid with a weird skin condition who didn't have any friends.

"All right, all right. No need to convince me," Tyler responded lightly. "Anyway, point her out next time we pass her in the hall, so I can check her out, okay?"

Darwin nodded, his face reddening again at the thought of checking anyone out, including Mindy. It wasn't like he didn't notice how pretty she was. But why spend your time looking at things you can't have? Even thinking about her as anything more than a friend was pointless. Darwin didn't need anyone to tell him that.

But even so, late at night in his room, Darwin couldn't help thinking how shiny her hair was as it swung past her shoulders like a dark curtain, how bottomless her eyes, as if she could see right through him, as if she somehow knew what he was really thinking every time he looked at her.

The bell rang, signaling the end of lunch. Darwin and Tyler drained the last dregs of their drinks quickly and made their way back to the front entrance. Their next class was Biology with Ms. Anderson. Darwin had taken one of Ms. Anderson's science classes the previous year, and had enjoyed having her as a teacher. She was kind, and always recognized the hard work Darwin put in. She was a bit more eccentric than most teachers, and as a result, she always found a way to make even the dullest scientific topics fun.

"Ugh, Biology. I've never been too great at it," Tyler said to Darwin. For the first time, Darwin noticed that Tyler looked almost nervous; his friend's brow was wrinkled with worry.

"No problem, this is actually my first time taking Biology, too. We'll see if I'm even good at it, myself," Darwin responded with a chuckle. Darwin and Tyler entered the classroom, which was filled with long, black lab tables. The walls were decorated with various diagrams of the human body. Darwin and Tyler sat together as students continued pouring through the classroom door.

"All right, class, take your seats," Ms. Anderson said as she walked to the front of the class. As usual, she was dressed in a long, batik-print skirt in orange and pink, with a matching pink blouse that billowed around her willowy frame. Her fingers were loaded with shiny silver rings, one on each finger. Piles of silver and turquoise bracelets weighed down her wrists, so much so that Darwin was perpetually afraid that one day her bones might snap in two. It was as if she'd never quite grown out of the hippie era of the 1960s, and continued to dress as if she were about to attend Woodstock.

"Darwin! Good to see you again," she said as she passed by his table.

Once at the front of the room, Ms. Anderson addressed the whole class again.

"Welcome back to school, everyone. I hope you all enjoyed your summer holiday. Now, I'll go through the syllabus with you in a moment, but first I want to warn you that Biology will be one of the most challenging courses you will take this semester," she continued, her eyes serious as they swept the room. "How the physical body works in humans, as well as in the animal kingdom, is an incredibly complex topic, but at the same time, very fascinating. We'll learn about different organs that animals and humans possess, and how those organs are critical to their survival. We will also dissect some of these animals, so you can learn to identify organs and other body parts."

Many students exchanged excited whispers and gleeful looks, and the classroom was suddenly full of noisy, heated chattering. Some had heard from upperclassmen that they would be able to dissect worms, fetal pigs, and minks. It was almost like being a surgeon. Darwin was particularly excited about this. He had always been interested in anatomy and biology, mainly due to the fact that his own body seemed slightly different from others, and he always struggled to understand why.

Tyler, on the other hand, didn't look too pleased. His face was ashen, and he was literally cringing as he listened to Ms. Anderson's announcement. Darwin saw Tyler swallow hard, and remembered from their conversation at lunch that his new friend was squeamish about blood.

"Don't worry. I'll help you out with the dissecting," Darwin whispered to Tyler, who gave him a grateful nod, a little of the color returning to his cheeks after a few minutes passed.

The rest of fifth period went by rather quickly, as did the rest of the day. When the bell rang after the final period, and the students began gathering together their belongings and heading quickly out the door, Tyler looked over at Darwin and said, "All right, man, guess I'll see you tomorrow. Thanks for showing me the ropes today."

"No problem, and yeah, we'll probably be sick of each other by the end of the semester, with as many classes as we have together," Darwin responded with a little laugh, still unsure of exactly why Tyler wanted to spend any time with him at all.

"Ha-ha, I'm definitely going to need your brain to get through this year," Tyler joked as he picked up his backpack and threw it over his broad shoulders. With a nod at Darwin, he left the room.

Darwin finished packing up his binder and pens, and made his way into the crowded hallway. He then went to his locker, removed some books he knew he would need for homework that day, and began maneuvering his way through the crowd when he heard, "Well, if it isn't the freak show himself!"

Darwin looked around, and realized he was in the northwest corner of the second floor. This was where the popular students usually hung out. A few of the students laughed cruelly. Darwin didn't look up, but kept walking, trying to ignore them. He knew without looking who had made the comment—it was Billy James.

Billy was the star wide receiver on the football team and already had been offered a football scholarship at Michigan State. He was big and tall, broad, strong, and handsome. And worse yet, Billy knew it. How could he not, what with all of the attention he got from girls? Which unfortunately fed his already overblown ego even more.

As Darwin walked away, he heard Billy shout after him, "I thought maybe he wasn't going to show up this year—figured his parents finally came to their senses and locked him up in his room to avoid scaring the rest of us with his *disease*," Billy continued, his voice dripping with sarcasm.

Darwin thought about stopping and firing back in defense, but he knew it wasn't worth it. His attempts to defend himself in the past had never gotten him very far. In fact, Billy and his cronies seemed to enjoy Darwin's agitated reactions, and would only pester him further if Darwin retaliated. Darwin had learned long ago that the less he reacted, the more he would be left alone. And that was all he really wanted—especially when it came to Billy James.

Darwin started moving quickly to get out of there as fast as he could, while he heard roars of laughter from the group of jocks behind him. When Darwin got to the bottom of the stairs, he stopped and stood there for a moment to collect himself before meeting his mom outside. He didn't want Jane to see that he was upset, because he knew it would only make her upset. Instead, he wanted to tell her what a great first day he'd had, meeting Tyler and starting his new classes. Darwin took a deep breath and proceeded to walk outside.

He spotted his mom pulling up into the pickup line. He made his way over to the car, passing other students waiting to be picked up. Jane, with a big smile on her face, began to wave rapidly once she spotted him. Darwin opened the door to get into the passenger seat. "Hi honey!" she chirped, pushing the wire-rimmed glasses she often wore for driving back up on her nose. "How was your first day?"

"It was actually pretty good! I'm really looking forward to Biology," Darwin said as he placed his backpack on the floor of the car and buckled his seatbelt.

"That's great! What else?" his mom continued as she maneuvered out of the parking lot.

"And I—well, I made a new friend," Darwin said quickly, the

words coming out in a rush, tumbling over one another in a heap.

Jane looked over interestedly. "Really? Who?"

Darwin could tell that she was trying to sound casual, as though Darwin often told her that he made new friends, when it was almost never the case.

"His name is Tyler, he's from DC. His parents moved here for work. We have almost every class together," Darwin said, while looking out the window nonchalantly.

"Well, that's great, honey, maybe you two will become good friends, since you'll be spending so much time together. I'm sure he's a bit nervous, being the new kid, so it's great that he has you to show him around," his mom said while patting Darwin on the knee, clearly proud of him for stepping outside of his comfort zone.

After they arrived home, Darwin went up to his bedroom, sat on his bed, and pulled out the new book he had ordered online a few days prior. Being an only child, Darwin had a rather large room with a big bed and his own computer, which he used often for school and researching topics. His room was always clean, and he hated having clutter around where he worked, as dirty spaces didn't allow him to concentrate. He had a few posters on his walls, one of Albert Einstein quotes and some others that were space optical illusions. His room faced toward the front lawn and was above the garage. It was also up to Darwin to entertain himself, and since his parents rarely allowed him to watch TV, books were really the only thing he had.

Darwin could hear his mom downstairs humming while she made dinner. He opened his book, titled *Social Inequality: The Story of Capitalism*. These were generally books designed for people much older than Darwin—they were essentially college textbooks—but he found these types of topics interesting, and would often end up learning a great deal from them, despite some of the material inevitably going over his head. Darwin spent a good two or so hours reading, highlighting passages and making notes in the margins. Before he knew it, he was already halfway through the book.

"Dinnertime!" his mother shouted. Darwin marked his place in the book and made his way downstairs.

Darwin's father had just arrived home, and was still in his work clothes. He wore a dress shirt, slacks, and a blazer every day without fail. "How was your day?" his mom asked while bending over the stove to peer into the oven.

"Just another day, nothing too exciting," Dave replied.

"Well, I hope you're hungry, because I made your favorite— lasagna," she said, beaming while opening the oven door and pulling out a deep casserole dish, the steam rising to obscure her face. Darwin thought that his mother was an amazing cook, even though he realized that he was a bit biased. Still, the delicious scents wafting through the air were undeniable. The smell of mozzarella and tomato sauce, with just a hint of garlic and basil, permeated the kitchen, and as his mother set down the dish on the kitchen table, Darwin could see the cheese still bubbling and steaming from the heat.

"Oh! What did I do to deserve this?" his dad said enthusiastically.

"Well, it's really for Darwin, celebrating his first day of junior year," his mom said, smiling over at Darwin as he sat down at the table.

"What were you doing up there, honey?" she asked as she cut into the lasagna, pulling out a large piece and placing it on a plate for his dad.

"Oh, I was just doing some reading," Darwin replied.

"What were you reading?" his father asked aggressively, reaching down and picking up his fork, one hand hovering above his steaming plate.

"Oh, um . . . it was just a book on social inequality," Darwin said as he looked down nervously.

"Social inequality, huh?" Dave said with a little scoff. "And let me guess—it says that this country of ours is unjust because we support the right to earn a living freely, without regulating the amount of money people make? Or that in order to make this economy run properly, you need wealth to be distributed equally, even for those who are lazy and do nothing with their lives. Is that it?"

"Well, not really," Darwin said slowly, realizing too late that he was on dangerous ground. "They talk about some of the great things other countries have done to maintain a free, laissez-faire system, but also to ensure that wealth is more evenly distributed, so you still have to work hard in order to be successful." Darwin nervously played with the lettuce leaves with his fork, his hand sweating against the cool metal. The tension in the air was as thick as molasses—and building steadily. Darwin had the uncanny sensation that the room was getting smaller and smaller, the plaster walls threatening to smash him completely, like the trash-compactor scene in *Star Wars*, one of his favorite movies.

"Ha! Good one, and I assume these are countries that failed in the past, like Communist Russia," his dad said, laughing under his breath.

"No, because that was a Communist system. More along the lines of countries like Sweden," Darwin said, now looking up at his dad and swallowing hard. Darwin knew what was coming, but he couldn't seem to stop himself, even though he knew that he should.

"Pshh, Sweden. Like their country ever meant anything in this world," his father said, mumbling under his breath while aggressively rolling his eyes, stabbing at his lasagna, and bringing a forkful to his lips.

"Now Dave, that's enough, can we just enjoy our dinner together?" Jane interrupted, pleading with her eyes, not just with her voice.

"Just because there are some countries that aren't as powerful doesn't mean they don't have good systems and laws in place that help their people," Darwin said forcefully, realizing that he probably shouldn't push anymore, but he just couldn't seem to help himself.

"Oh! So, you think that just because a nation can distribute their money more evenly, that makes them better?" his dad said before he could even take a bite, putting the fork down on his plate and raising his voice even more.

"I . . . I didn't say that, I just meant that—"

"You tell me how it would be fair for us to be lazy and do nothing but still receive handouts from our government, or work in a factory and get paid as much as the manager running the place?" his father started, shouting. His eyes bored into Darwin's, the look of anger piercing Darwin like a laser beam.

"But . . . that's not how it works, Dad," Darwin said quietly, hesitating now so as not to anger his father even further. "The system isn't about being lazy, it's about working together collectively for the common good."

"If I hear one more word about this, you'll go to your room without dinner," his dad said, pounding his fist on the table, which caused Darwin's mother to jump a little in her chair, her blue eyes wide and startled. "Do I make myself clear?"

"I just don't see anything wrong with social organization that's regulated by the community as a whole," Darwin said quietly. He knew he had said too much at this point. His father had said his piece, and wasn't going to back down—he never did.

"That's it! Up to your room, now!" his father said as he pointed upstairs.

"Why are you ruining this perfect evening after his first day of school like this?" his mother moaned in disapproval, glaring at his father.

"You can blame your son for that," his father said, his pointer finger still outstretched.

"Well, at least let him have his din—"

"Upstairs, I said!" his father shouted as he stood up, his face red with exertion.

"It's okay, Mom, don't worry about it," Darwin said, making his way out of the kitchen.

As he walked up the stairs, he could hear his mom crying quietly. Darwin always felt bad for her, as she had absolutely no say in the majority of decisions made in the family. She always worked hard, but was never recognized for it. His mother could spend all day on her feet at the hospital, but still somehow managed to take care of the house and prepare dinner for them all every night without a single complaint. He didn't like the fact that his dad was so hard on him, but it bothered Darwin even more that his father routinely made his mother upset. As far as Darwin was concerned, she was the last person who deserved that kind of treatment.

Darwin closed his bedroom door behind him and took a deep breath. He knew he shouldn't argue with his father, as it would only turn into trouble, but Darwin was tired of his dad dictating what he should feel and believe. He flopped down on his bed, looking aimlessly at the book he'd been reading before dinner. He thought about reading further, but figured that maybe it wasn't the best time, given what had just happened. Instead, he lay in his bed looking up at the ceiling, thinking about school. All Darwin wanted to do was to make his parents proud, but he wasn't going to sacrifice what he firmly believed in order to make them proud. He knew his mom would be proud of him regardless, but pleasing his dad was a different story.

There was a knock on the door, and before Darwin could react, his mother walked into the room. Darwin propped himself up and moved the book away quickly, thinking it might be his dad. "Hey there, how are you doing?" Jane asked, carrying a tray loaded with a large piece of the lasagna and a glass of water, her lips drawn into a tight smile. "I know he said you couldn't have dinner, but obviously he didn't mean it, and besides, how could I let my boy go without dinner on his first day of school?" Jane said, setting the tray down on Darwin's desk.

"Thanks, Mom, you didn't have to do that," Darwin said as he scooted toward the corner of his bed.

"Look, Darwin," she said, taking a deep breath and turning to face him. "I know your dad is hard on you, and sometimes he can be very . . . aggressive in arguments, but I want you to know that he loves you very much," Jane finished as she let out a deep sigh and then took a seat next to Darwin on the bed.

"Sure doesn't seem like it," Darwin said quietly, while looking at the ground.

"It's just . . . you know your dad, he didn't have the best childhood, and he grew up in a difficult time. I think he just wants what's best for you," Jane said quietly, reaching over and rubbing Darwin's head with the flat of her hand.

"How is that what's best for me though, Mom?" Darwin said, moving away from his mother's touch as his anger flared up inside him once again. "Not letting me be myself or figure out life on my own? I'm not a little kid anymore," Darwin said, turning away from his mother.

"I know, sweetie, I know. But I think we'll always view you as our little boy, no matter what, even when you're fifty," Jane said with a little chuckle. Darwin shook his head and rolled his eyes, clearly not finding it funny. "Anyway, I'll let you be. Just don't let this kind of thing get to you so much. No matter what your father might say when he's angry, he knows you're a good kid," Jane said as she made her way out of the room and closed the door.

Darwin fell back on his bed with a heavy sigh. He continued to look up at the ceiling, thinking of how great it would be when he moved away for college and was on his own. Just two more years, but it seemed so far away, shimmering there in the distance, just out of reach.

Darwin could hear his parents arguing downstairs. He couldn't hear exactly what they were saying, as their voices sounded muffled, but he assumed it was about the argument that had just taken place at the dinner table. Most likely, his dad was upset at his mom for bringing him his dinner. His mom was probably defending him, which would, in turn, make his dad even angrier that his mother was on Darwin's side and not on his.

His parents had been arguing for quite a few years now, and it had gotten to the point where it happened on an almost-daily basis. It often appeared as if sometimes they couldn't stand each other. Darwin couldn't figure out how his parents had ended up together, as they were so different from each other. He rarely ever saw them happy, or at least not faking it the way they routinely did in front of guests, or even in front of Darwin himself. He remembered them being happier when he was a child, but those were faint memories, and it hadn't lasted. *What has changed about their relationship*, he wondered. *Did they ever love each other?* They must have, as it was hard to understand why two people who couldn't stand each other would even get married. Was this—the fighting, the disconnection—just something that happened to all married couples over time? Or was it the years spent together raising Darwin that had taken their toll?

Darwin ran his hands through his hair and then lay back on the bed, yawning, his eyes closing as he drifted off into a troubled sleep.

CHAPTER 4

The weather was cold, the sky gray and impenetrable. Darwin could feel the brisk wind on his body, but for some reason he didn't feel the need to warm himself. It was almost as if his body was being kept warm internally, a feeling he'd never experienced before. Darwin looked up at the rainforest he'd been walking through, déjà vu coming over him in a wave. This place seemed awfully familiar.

Patterns of multicolored, circular leaves with small points at the ends covered the trees above, something Darwin had never seen before. He couldn't quite figure out where he was, so he continued to walk through the cold, breezy rainforest. Every step made a loud crunching sound as he walked over what looked like a pile of fallen branches that were different colors as well: maroon, green, yellow, even blue, and purple. It was unusual, he supposed, but pretty nonetheless.

He heard what sounded like the wails of sirens in the distance. He made his way in the direction of the noise. As he walked, the trees slowly started to blossom, flowers unfurling on the colored branches that bent and twisted slowly, almost as if the branches were stretching. The trees froze. The flowers were lined up with the biggest ones closer to the trunks of the trees, becoming smaller the farther they extended from the branches. Darwin's mouth hung open at the spectacle, but he wanted to continue moving, to find out what was making that blaring noise ahead.

The sound became louder as he drew closer. He could see an opening through the thick trees, and he walked toward it cautiously.

Darwin made his way through, covering his ears at the same time, and then suddenly the sirens stopped. He looked around and noticed a mountain range off in the distance. He recognized it immediately. It was the same mountains that had often appeared in his visions— the same visions that his doctor had told him weren't real.

The sirens went off again, but this time not as loudly, almost as if they'd moved farther away. Darwin started making his way toward them, leaving the rainforest and heading toward the mountains. He looked up into the sky. Now that it was no longer blocked by the thick trees, he could see a multitude of stars. Although it was daylight on the ground, everything in the sky was pitch black and covered by the shimmering, twinkling stars.

He looked to his right and saw a small, circular, violet cloud hovering in the distance, covered in shining pinpricks of light. As his breath caught in his chest, Darwin realized excitedly that it wasn't in fact a cloud at all; it was another galaxy. A galaxy that was so close he could see it with his naked eye. It was very similar to the galaxies Darwin had seen in images from the Hubble telescope, or images his teachers had shown him in science class.

As Darwin looked up, he was distracted by other noises coming from his left. Unlike the sirens he'd heard earlier, these were strange clicking sounds. When he approached the clicking, the sounds slowly morphed into long streams of low-pitched tones that echoed across the nearby plains and mountains, inexplicably resembling the kinds of sounds that whales make in the sea.

Darwin began walking quickly toward the clicking and whaleesque sounds. They weren't being made in any particular pattern, but it began to sound like two separate tones harmonizing together. Darwin reached a tiny canyon. He would have to climb down in order to proceed further. He looked back to see how far he had gone, and realized he was quite far from the rainforest. He made his way down the canyon slowly. When he arrived at the canyon floor, the terrain felt like he was walking on sponges; his feet sank half an inch with every step, causing him to wobble. Suddenly, his foot sank down farther, and all at once he lost his footing. Darwin could feel himself starting to fall, which then turned into a tumble.

"Ahh, ooh, ouch!" Darwin yelled as he tried to regain control

and stop himself from sliding farther. He finally grabbed a hold of the ground by sinking his fingers into the spongy turf. He lay there for a second, trying to collect himself. Then, just as he started to stand, he heard more noises, new noises. Darwin listened closely to the rapid clicks and tones that went up and down, bubbling noises like those made by a scuba diver breathing through a tank.

He noticed a crevice in the ground, which looked to be five feet wide, splitting the spongy terrain in two. The crevice was about fifty feet in front of him. As he slowly approached it, the noises became louder. Two separate voices seemed to be speaking and answering, almost as if they were communicating in some strange, indecipherable language. Darwin was now five feet from the crevice, four feet, three feet . . . Darwin peered over the edge to look inside, but just as he was close to seeing the bottom, he felt himself falling rapidly into space.

Darwin woke in his bed, panting loudly, his hands clammy, and his sheets soaked in sweat. He lay on his bed for a second to collect himself. What had he just seen? He recognized the mountains and the plains from previous visions, but he'd never heard those sounds before, and he'd never noticed the beautiful sky above him, either.

"Darwin! Come on, you'll be late for school!" his mother shouted from downstairs.

"Be right there," Darwin yelled back, trying to clear his head.

The dream was still imprinted on his mind like a film of soap scum he couldn't wipe away, no matter how hard he scrubbed. He looked down and noticed that he was already dressed for school in a collared shirt and jeans. When had he gotten dressed, he wondered. Before the vision? In the middle of it? It was strange to have no recollection of these events. Often, Darwin wouldn't remember what he was doing right before or immediately after these visions. These things were lost to the blackness, irretrievable. It made him feel uneasy to know his body was moving and working all on its own, without his knowledge.

As he got out of bed, he noticed his book sitting on the floor halfway underneath the bed, and then remembered the argument that he had gotten into with his father the night before, before kicking the book under the bed so that it disappeared from sight entirely. In a way, going to bed right after the argument somehow allowed him to forget the yelling and shouting that had rung loudly in his ears, until he put the pillow over his head and drifted off into oblivion.

Except it hadn't been. Not blissful. Not welcoming. Not exactly. He'd had another dream, "a vision," whatever the hell they were—and they were happening more often. A violent shiver wrenched his shoulders, and he shrugged off the thought, hurrying to grab his books and rush downstairs.

His mother was sitting at the kitchen table, gazing out the window, and didn't even hear Darwin as he raced down the stairs. "Morning, Mom," Darwin said with a little cough, so she would break her fixation on whatever she was staring at outside and snap back into the present.

"Oh! Good morning, dear. Sorry, you scared me." His mother sat up quickly, wiping her eyes, which were dark and a little red, as if she had been crying. Her hair was disheveled, the waves matted into snarls, which was uncharacteristic. For as long as Darwin could remember, his mom had always looked put together, no matter what time of day it was. "Did you sleep all right?"

"I slept fine, thanks. You know, you don't always have to make me breakfast. I'm old enough to feed myself," he said quietly, hoping she wouldn't take offense to what he'd said.

His mom was always so sensitive—too sensitive, sometimes—and whenever he inadvertently hurt her feelings, he always felt guilty afterward, which is why he hardly ever spoke up. But, as usual, his mom's mouth fell open in protest before she closed it quickly, getting up from the table and bustling around the kitchen like some kind of mad bird, wings flapping, as if the very idea caused her stress.

"Oh, it's fine, Darwin. I don't mind doing it," she responded in an injured voice.

She looked exhausted, her face pale and her eyes ringed with dark circles that made her look drawn and tired, and suddenly much older than her years, the skin beneath her eyes crepey and lined. At the kitchen counter, his mother poured herself some tea, her hand shaking a little as she did so.

"Are you okay, Mom?" Darwin asked tentatively, as he

watched her struggle to pour the amber liquid into a china teacup. It was the one she always used, the thin porcelain ringed with festive garlands of small pink roses.

"I'm fine, honey. I'm fine," she replied, her eyes darting around the room nervously, as if she were waiting for something or someone to interrupt the quiet calm of the morning. "You just eat your breakfast, and I'll take you to school."

Jane dropped Darwin off at the usual spot about ten minutes before the first bell rang, and Darwin made his way up to the third floor, to Ms. Edmond's class. When he walked in the room, he noticed that Tyler wasn't there, his stomach sinking a little in disappointment. The bell rang, and Ms. Edmond began her lecture for the day, which featured topics on the Civil War.

About five minutes into her lecture, a stomping sound could be heard in the hallway. The stomps began to get louder and louder, to the point where Ms. Edmond stopped speaking entirely as the heavy footsteps approached the classroom door. The stomps halted suddenly outside the door, and the door slowly opened, squeaking softly. Tyler's dark head came into view first, as he peeped around the door with a nervous look on his face. Ms. Edmond glared at Tyler, her hands on her hips, and looked up at the clock above the door. "Sorry, Ms. Edmond, I was . . . just running a little late this morning," Tyler said with a grin as he power walked toward his seat in the class.

"Punctuality is an important part of the rules in my class, Mr. Barros. I expect this won't happen again," Ms. Edmond said as she turned back toward the projector to continue her presentation.

"It won't," Tyler said as he looked toward Darwin with a little smirk on his face, clearly amused by her strictness. "Geez, you didn't tell me she was this uptight," Tyler whispered.

"Why were you late?" Darwin whispered back.

"I overslept, still getting used to this schedule after summer break," Tyler replied, while opening his backpack to take out his notebook.

The day went by pretty quickly and was fairly routine. Darwin went to each of his classes and had lunch with Tyler on the steps again. He learned more about Tyler and his family, and also about his life in Washington, DC. Tyler told him that his parents actually met in Mongolia while serving in the Peace Corps; his mother was of Mongolian decent, while his dad grew up in California. Tyler had been to Mongolia multiple times to visit family, and assured Darwin that Mongolian food was better than any other food he'd ever had.

As the final bell for the end of the day rang, Darwin and Tyler left class together to make their way to the parking lot.

"You want a ride home?" Tyler asked Darwin as he searched for his keys in his backpack.

"Oh, that's all right, my mom's coming to get me, anyway. Thanks, though."

"No problem. Maybe some other time," Tyler said.

"Yeah, maybe. My mom doesn't usually like me taking rides from other people, especially—" Darwin stopped midsentence as he turned the corner and saw Billy James laughing with his buddies, Charlie Harrington and Luke Randall. "Uh, let's go out this way," Darwin said to Tyler, moving in the direction of the stairs that led to a side door, hoping that Billy and his crew wouldn't see him.

"But why?" Tyler asked, looking confused. "My car is in the student lot that way." Tyler pointed in the direction where Billy and his friends stood.

"Um, yeah. Well, my mom usually parks outside here, through the side entrance," Darwin said, trying not to look in the direction where Billy stood.

"I thought you said she usually picks you up and drops you off at the front entrance, by the student lot," Tyler said, still looking perplexed.

"Look, I'm just going to go this way," Darwin said sternly, hoping that Tyler wouldn't push the issue any further.

"Okay, okay, no problem, I guess I can just walk a little farther," Tyler said, his easy smile disappearing, replaced by a frown that crinkled his otherwise smooth forehead, clearly taken aback by Darwin's tone. Without another word, they made their way down the stairs, heading toward the side entrance.

"You all right, man?" Tyler asked, as he looked at Darwin.

"Yeah, I'm fine, I just . . . those guys that you saw up there laughing with one another, they, uh, give me a hard time, and I try to avoid them when I can." Darwin exhaled heavily. Just telling Tyler had released some of the weight off his shoulders. But in reality, nothing was quite that easy.

"I know how that goes, I was bullied when I was younger," Tyler said in a low, reassuring voice.

"Younger?" Darwin said, with no small degree of confusion. "You mean like back in elementary school or something?"

Tyler's face froze for a moment, as if he'd somehow said something wrong. He took a deep breath before continuing. "Yeah, I was a little small for my age between third and fifth grade, and other kids gave me a hard time for it. It was no big deal," Tyler said flippantly, flashing Darwin a quick smile.

Looking at his friend, Darwin couldn't see how that could have been possible, since Tyler basically towered over him. But since Darwin was so short, everyone kind of did.

"I mean, I grew pretty quickly once I started high school a couple years back," Tyler added, noticing Darwin's confused expression.

"So, what did you do about it?" Darwin asked.

"About what? Getting bullied?"

"Yeah, I mean, did you just ignore them? Or did you get revenge later, when you finally grew?" Darwin asked.

"I generally just ignored them. Well, every now and then I would try and defend myself, but it always ended with me getting thrown into a garbage can or getting a chocolate-milk shower, which was *not* pleasant, let me tell you." Tyler let out a small laugh, as if the memory just amused him now, something Darwin found pretty hard to believe.

"The teachers never did anything?" Darwin asked, surprised that something like that could happen without any sort of punishment.

"They would get detention sometimes, but it didn't stop them," Tyler said. "Anyway, when I got older and bigger, I thought about beating them senseless, but the more I thought about it, the more I realized that it was pointless to sink to their level. Even though I really wanted to smash their faces in, I somehow managed to restrain myself," Tyler continued with a short laugh that came out so staccato that it was almost a bark. "Besides, we all grew up, you know? And I couldn't really still be mad about something they did when they were, like, nine years old," Tyler said as he shrugged his shoulders.

Darwin nodded. Although he found it hard to not want to seek revenge on Billy James and his crew, Tyler was right—he knew that he'd be no better, if he stooped to their level. But still, Darwin couldn't help thinking that Tyler's response was so mature. Most high school kids would've started punching in retaliation the second they were able to fight back successfully. Darwin himself had spent many a night fantasizing about the day when he'd be bigger, stronger, able to make his tormentors feel the same kind of pain they'd inflicted on him for years. The day he'd finally get even. All of them—everyone who had once laughed at him—would have to eat their words. But at the same time, he knew he'd never do it, no matter how much he managed to grow, or if his vitiligo suddenly vanished. He just didn't have it in him.

Tyler went off his separate way to the parking lot, and Darwin waited in his usual spot for his mom to pick him up. She hadn't arrived yet, and from time to time she would be late in picking up Darwin from school, if there were any emergencies at the hospital that would keep her past her shift. Darwin, aware of this, figured this might be one of those days and decided to sit on the steps and begin working on his homework to kill time. He pulled out his calculus assignment and began putting together the formula for the first problem.

As he worked, he felt a prickling on his skin, the sensation of being watched heavy upon him. He looked up and saw a man across the parking lot, near some bushes, looking at him. His blood ran cold as he remembered the man waiting outside his house the other night, looking up at him in the dark. Darwin stared back at the man, who, despite the hot summer weather they were currently enduring, was wearing a long black trench coat and a gray hat. The man was tall, imposingly so, and looked way older than a high school student. Just then, the man noticed Darwin staring back at him and turned his attention elsewhere, but stayed where he was. The man looked back at Darwin again, but looked away when he saw Darwin was still staring at him.

Darwin's heart sped up and his ears seemed to go spontaneously deaf, the noise of cars and students still streaming from the doors of the school, disappearing in a rush of white noise. Was . . . it possible? Could it be the same man from the other night, here in broad daylight, watching him? *That's crazy*, Darwin told himself sternly, trying to shrug off the thought. It continued to gnaw at him nonetheless, needling him like an itch he couldn't quite scratch. *But what if it is*, a little voice inside Darwin piped up. *What if it's him, and he's watching me—again.*

Just then, his mom pulled up in the lot, and Darwin saw the man start to walk away, looking back at him one last time before departing from the school parking lot. Darwin watched as the man tilted his chin downward, almost in greeting, before turning and walking away. The man shoved his hands into the pockets of his coat, hunched his shoulders as he strode until he rounded the corner, and moved out of sight.

"Hi, Mom." He got into the car. Darwin turned around, craning his neck to look off into the distance, where the man had been standing, but he was gone.

"Everything all right, dear?" she asked. Darwin didn't respond, still looking off in the direction where the man had gone out of sight. "Darwin?" she asked again.

"Oh, sorry, I was just . . . looking for someone," Darwin said, his mouth slightly open, brow wrinkled as he stared at the spot where the man had stood.

"Who?" his mom inquired. She looked around the parking lot, her eyes sweeping the perimeter.

"Um, no one, just a friend. It was the guy I was telling you about, Tyler," Darwin said, finally turning away and making eye contact with his mom, his nerve endings jangling like bells.

"Oh, well, okay, honey. I'm sure you'll see him tomorrow," Jane said as she started to drive off.

"Yeah, you're right," Darwin said in a voice that he hoped sounded nonchalant. He didn't want her to worry over something that was likely nothing. For all he knew, the man was simply looking at him for the same reason other people would stare at him. But he couldn't shake the feeling that it was more than that—much more. Darwin's palms began to sweat as he remembered that this kind of thing had happened once before—before the other night, even.

In fifth grade, he'd noticed a man watching him, a man dressed in dark clothing and wearing a hat that shadowed his face. The man had stood across the street from the playground, silently watching Darwin for close to an hour. When he mentioned it to his parents that night at dinner, they'd told him to forget about it and to never bring it up again, his father's face closing as suddenly as a book slamming shut, his eyes hooded and impenetrable.

Darwin began to sweat, thinking about it, a tight feeling invading his chest, as if some invisible force was pulling him across the room. *Maybe it wasn't even real*, Darwin had told himself at the time. In the safety of his house, in his room with his posters on the walls and the soft, yellow glow of his desk lamp, the thought made him feel a little better, even though he couldn't quite shake the feeling that it wasn't true. He'd seen the man. And the man had seen him. And now it seemed, all these years later, that the man was back. Had he been watching Darwin the whole time, just out of view? And if so, why was he showing himself now?

Sitting next to his mother in the car, listening to her hum cheerfully but tunelessly along with the radio, he felt the same sense of creeping dread. *Stop thinking about it*, he told himself with a shake of his head, trying to wipe his memory clean. *It isn't real*, he insisted stubbornly. But just like in fifth grade, there was that same nagging suspicion, that tugging feeling in the center of his chest, coupled with the sensation of pins and needles in his hands. He balled them into fists. These things told him that he wasn't so sure. *The man in the hat is back*, Darwin thought, and doubt was erased by near certainty. *He's really back*. But what did he want? As they pulled into the driveway, Darwin knew that no matter what it took, he had to find out.

CHAPTER 5

The next morning, Darwin walked into Social Studies class to find Tyler sitting at his desk, his dark head streaked with thin strands of silver bent over his notebook as his pen scratched furiously against a sheet of paper. Tyler was habitually late to first period, and Darwin's eyes widened in surprise to see that his friend had somehow managed to arrive before him.

"Well, well, well. Look who decided to show up," Tyler said, looking up with a grin, pointing to his watch with a big smirk on his face. Darwin shook his head good-naturedly, laughing a little under his breath as he shrugged off his backpack and slid into his seat.

"I'm not even late, there's still ten minutes before class starts," he protested amicably.

"How come you're so early?" Darwin asked. "Shouldn't you be strolling in twenty minutes from now?"

"My car is in the shop, so my parents had to drop me off on their way to work, and they work early. I've already been here for an hour."

"An hour?" Darwin asked, raising an eyebrow. "What have you been doing here all morning?"

"Oh, just some reading. A little writing. It was kind of nice, actually, no one was around to bother me."

"So, what happened to your car?" Darwin asked.

"Oh, um, I guess the alternator is broken? No idea how that happened. What sucks is that I'm going to have to come up with the money to pay for it," Tyler replied. "And I'll likely have to start walking home from school, since my parents both work late."

Darwin noticed that Tyler was fidgeting with his hands a little as he spoke, not looking up or making eye contact, which was unusual for Tyler.

"Well, my mom could give you a ride home, if you wanted. I don't think she would mind," Darwin said with a shrug.

"Really? You don't think that would be weird, I don't know your parents at all," Tyler said, looking up with a surprised look on his face that quickly turned to happiness as his mouth stretched into a wide smile.

"It's no big deal. I mean, she's taken kids who I barely know home from school before," Darwin said, while taking his notepad and books out of his backpack.

Just then, Ms. Edmond walked in the room and the class began to quickly move to their seats. She walked to the front of the classroom, toward the projector, and displayed a pie chart for the class to see. The chart wasn't titled or labeled in any way; just two large slices that fit into the pie, with five other smaller slices.

"Can anyone tell me what this pie chart represents?" Ms. Edmond asked. The class looked around at one another blankly, while Ms. Edmond waited for a response.

"A pie chart," Tommy Fieldstone shouted as the class laughed. Ms. Edmond didn't seem amused. She even crossed her arms over her chest before she spoke again, her voice a bit tenser.

"Yes, it's a pie chart. But does anyone know what it depicts?" she asked. Silence again. "What have we been talking about over the last two weeks, since school has started? What are some of the topics we addressed?"

Edwin Jones, another student in the class, raised his hand.

"Yes, Edwin."

"Well, we've talked a lot about American history and how we've grown as a country," Edwin said.

"Yes, that's correct. But in what way specifically have we grown as a country?" Ms. Edmond asked.

"Um, well, we've had a lot of people immigrate here from other countries, so that's a part of the growth," Edwin said, a little more bashful this time, as he wasn't sure this was the answer Ms. Edmond was looking for.

"Yes . . . true, true. But I'm talking more about growth from a financial standpoint." Ms. Edmond began to pace in front of the class. Then Julia Straken raised her hand. "Yes?"

"We've talked about how the United States has grown to be one of the biggest economies in the world," she said confidently. Julia was a total brownnoser. Always had the right answer, and raised her hand incessantly, shooting it up in the air like a flag five or six times during each class.

"Exactly! So, up until now we've talked about the benefits of what the economy has done for the industrialization of our country. But there are also downsides to the way our economic system is designed to favor a few, while leaving others at a disadvantage. And that's what this chart is all about." Ms. Edmond then went to the next slide, which now displayed the labels and percentages of the pie chart, which depicted the distribution of wealth in the United States.

"Socioeconomic inequality, one of the biggest problems that affects our country, but is rarely talked about or has taken action on. Now, what is socioeconomic inequality, you ask. Well, you're looking at it right now, in this pie chart. It's the concept of the extremes of social and economic wealth disruption among the population. Extremes of wealth and poverty, with wealth being controlled in the hands of few, is really what this chart is all about.

"Now, can anyone tell me why this distribution of wealth could potentially be a problem in the United States?" Ms. Edmond continued.

The class stayed silent, and after a long pause, Darwin raised his hand slowly.

"Yes, Darwin?" Ms. Edmond asked.

"Well, if wealth and power are controlled by a few, then the rest are disadvantaged and unlikely to move out of that socioeconomic category. Which creates more division among class, age, and even across racial lines," Darwin finished, and looked over at Tyler, who gave him a congratulatory nod. Some of the other students rolled their eyes.

"Right! See, when you have such a large divide in wealth in any country, it creates division among the population, and, most importantly, it makes it very difficult for those at the bottom to move out of that class. Now, some might view this as inaccurate, because our economic system is designed for all to prosper and succeed, given the proper motivation. But at the end of the day, those who do not have the money and resources to prosper and succeed will be unable to," Ms. Edmond finished as she turned off the projector.

"That's a bunch of crap!" someone shouted from the back in a loud, imperious voice.

Darwin looked around and saw that it was none other than Billy James, the boy who often bullied Darwin for his appearance.

"If you're lazy and can't work your way up to the top 1 percent, then that's your own fault," Billy added with a snort and a roll of his eyes.

Some of the class nodded in agreement. Darwin sighed loudly. It was known that Billy came from a wealthy family, and he often liked to flaunt it with his nice clothes, car, and other accessories. How could he possibly understand or empathize with those who had nothing—less than nothing?

"Uh-huh, now why do you think that, Billy?" Ms. Edmond asked patiently.

"Well, if you apply yourself and work hard, it doesn't matter who you are or where you come from, you can work your way up," Billy added with a shrug, as if he had it all figured out, and it was so obvious that it was pitiful that Ms. Edmond, or anyone else for that matter, couldn't see it.

"Right, but what if those people who work really hard and apply themselves to the best of their ability don't have access to the resources to get them to the top?" Darwin asked, without bothering to raise his hand this time.

Billy looked a little sheepish, as he didn't know how to respond.

"You may not be aware of this, but there's a large portion of the population who can't afford things like higher education, and who have been disadvantaged their whole lives, be it because of income, race, or gender, which doesn't allow them the same opportunities to succeed."

Billy opened his mouth, then closed it quickly, like a fish on land, gasping for air. It was obvious that he didn't know what to say, and he sat there with a frustrated look on his face, his cheeks flushing a bright red in indignation.

"Well, my family was able to work their way up just by working hard and being smart about the business decisions they made," Billy finally said, crossing his arms over his chest defensively.

Darwin rolled his eyes again. Everyone knew this wasn't true, as Billy's father had inherited a large sum of money, along with the family's real estate company, from his grandfather when he passed away.

Ms. Edmond paused for a moment, trying to choose her next words wisely. "That may be true, but some people don't have access to the necessary resources that would help them prosper, even in a free-market system," she added.

Billy just sat there, red-faced and confused at her words.

"Not everyone can to go to college, some simply can't afford it, and a history of oppression through generations hasn't allowed them to break out of their socioeconomic status. Does that make sense?" Ms. Edmond admonished him gently.

"Meh, I guess for people who are poor, it's easy to say that," Billy said dismissively, rolling his eyes again, as if the whole conversation was beneath him.

But before anyone could respond, the final bell for dismissal rang with a loud clang. Maybe the discussion, or Billy's annoying commentary, had taken the air out of him, but Darwin was suddenly so tired it took nearly all his energy just to stuff his books back into his backpack. *Maybe I need more potassium*, he thought through the static in his brain. His limbs felt heavy and dense, as if they were made of bricks.

Darwin spent most of the day slowly making his way to his classes using all of the energy he could. He tried to act normal as he and Tyler made their way out to the front parking lot at the end of the day to wait for Darwin's mom. Darwin already knew that most people found him weird because of his appearance. The last thing he wanted was to tell Tyler about his potassium deficiency. Like there needed to be another thing wrong with him.

"You sure she won't mind?" Tyler asked anxiously, as his eyes darted across the parking lot.

"Of course not, she'll be happy to take you," Darwin said reassuringly, the words slow and thick on his tongue.

Just then, Jane pulled up from around the corner to enter the parking lot. Darwin and Tyler walked over, and Darwin saw that his mom had a somewhat bewildered look on her usually sunny and open face. Jane pulled up right next to the boys. Darwin opened the door and asked, "Mom, can we take Tyler home from school today? His car is in the shop, and his parents work late."

"Oh, why certainly, dear," his mom said with a wide smile.

"Hi, Mrs. Sanders. It's nice to meet you," Tyler said, before getting into the backseat of the car while Darwin took the front seat. Jane smiled brightly.

"Well, it's nice to meet you, too, Tyler," she said as she began to drive out of the parking lot. "So, are you new to the area?"

"I am. I just moved here from Washington DC," Tyler said in a friendly tone. "My dad got a job out here, so we moved here a couple months ago."

"Oh! DC, that's a nice area," Darwin's mom said absentmindedly as she turned out of the lot and onto Main Street.

"Yeah, I miss it. But here in Crimson isn't too bad."

"Well, I'm sure it was tough moving to a new area and starting at a new school," his mom added pragmatically, as was her way.

"It hasn't been too bad—especially since I started hanging with Darwin," Tyler said matter-of-factly.

"Oh! That's very nice of you," his mother said, her voice filled with such surprise and happiness that Darwin was momentarily taken aback by it. "Did you hear that, Darwin?" His mom nudged Darwin playfully with her elbow, kind of like the way Tyler did, now that Darwin was thinking about it.

"I haven't really done much. I just know how it feels to be an outsider, and how mean some people can be if they don't know you," Darwin said, trying to deflect the attention away from himself. Praise, even if it was deserved, always made him nervous and uncomfortable, as if he were on display.

"He's a bit shy, but I'm trying to break him out of his shell," Tyler said with a little laugh. Darwin laughed a little under his breath.

"So, what do you do, Mrs. Sanders?" Tyler asked.

"Oh, please," his mom said, laughing off Tyler's formality with a wave of her hand. "You can call me Jane. But I do appreciate the politeness. I'm a nurse at one of the hospitals nearby."

"Tyler's scared of blood," Darwin said mischievously, his mouth curling into a grin.

"Is that right?" his mom mused as she turned the corner. "I've found over the years that blood's like anything else in life—after a while, you get used to it."

"I'll take your word for it," Tyler said with a grimace, and they all laughed.

Tyler and Jane talked the majority of the way home, while Tyler occasionally gave directions to his house. Darwin didn't say much, but instead just listened. As time went on, he was feeling even weaker, as if all the energy was being drained from his body slowly, and talking only made it worse. He learned new things about Tyler he hadn't known before, that his parents had also served in the Peace Corps in Algeria, before their time in Mongolia, way before Tyler was even born. Like Darwin, Tyler was an only child, although his parents had pretty much planned it that way.

"Yeah, for some reason my parents didn't want to have any more kids after me. I guess I was too much of a handful for them as a toddler, and they decided against it," Tyler said with a laugh.

"Oh! Well, Darwin was a bit of a rambunctious toddler himself, but then he mellowed out as he got a little older," his mom said thoughtfully. Darwin knew that she'd always wanted more children, and the fact that she wasn't able to have them would always be upsetting to her, but she never let it show. But even so, Darwin had always believed that it was his fault she hadn't been able to conceive more children.

Jane pulled up to Tyler's place after an approximate fifteen-minute drive from the school. It was at an apartment complex, which wasn't in the nicest shape. The complex was worn down, and looked like it hadn't been updated in the last thirty years. The shingles and siding of the building were falling off, and the sidewalks were cracked, with pot holes all over the pavement. The lawn around the apartments was buried beneath a tangle of overgrown grass and weeds.

Darwin blinked a few times in surprise. He'd assumed that Tyler and his family lived in a house, not an apartment. After all, they had moved down to Crimson for work, and surely they had enough money to afford something better than a run-down apartment. But then Darwin took a step back, ashamed that he had not only jumped to conclusions, but been so judgmental. Maybe they were saving money to buy a place since they had just moved here, or maybe they'd had a family crisis, which had eaten the majority of their income.

Whatever it was, Darwin respected the fact that Tyler came from a humble background. Most kids at his school came from a land of privilege, a fact that most of them took for granted, rich idiots like Billy among them. Darwin also admired the fact that Tyler didn't seem at all embarrassed by his home, as most other kids likely would have been. Most people at his school were always so concerned with their appearance and their status in life. Tyler didn't seem to care about any of that stuff at all.

"Well, thanks for the ride! Really appreciate it," Tyler said, making his way out of the car and slinging his backpack over one shoulder.

"No problem, and if you need a ride any other day while your car is being fixed, don't hesitate to ask. I pick up Darwin every day," Jane said pleasantly.

"Sounds good! See you tomorrow, Darwin," Tyler called out as he closed his door and made his way up to his apartment, unlocking it, and then quickly closing the worn, red-painted door behind him.

"Well, he's certainly a nice young man, isn't he?" his mom said admiringly as they pulled back onto the road.

"Yeah, he's a good guy," Darwin replied. "I like that he doesn't really care about what people think of him. He's different from all the other kids at school, including myself."

"Well, some people come from humbler backgrounds and just appreciate life and what they have. I hope I've taught you that as well, Darwin," his mother said as she turned left onto Main Street.

"You have, I just shouldn't worry so much about my appearance, I guess." Darwin sighed. He knew that his mom had taught him to enjoy life and to be thankful for everything he'd received. But even so, it was hard to fathom why he had been born with skin that drew nervous glances from almost everyone he passed, when other people just got to sail through life being, well, normal.

When they arrived home, Darwin immediately took his potassium. At this point, he was so depleted that he actually had difficulty lifting the glass of water to swallow the pills. It felt incredibly heavy in his hand, like it was made of lead. Darwin sat there for a moment, waiting for the pills to kick in so he could get his energy back, even though he knew that the potassium often took twenty minutes to a half-hour before it would take effect.

His father walked in about ten minutes later and, without saying hi to Darwin or his wife, headed straight for the TV to turn on the news. Darwin, who had almost fallen asleep on the kitchen table, raised himself up and thought about saying hi to his dad, but then decided there was no point. Once his father was into the news, he didn't like to be disturbed.

Darwin sat there at the kitchen table, looking at the TV, watching as his dad clicked the channels around impatiently until he stumbled upon sports, settling on a basketball game. As he sat there, Darwin started to feel a little better, the surge of potassium in his bloodstream lifting the horrid feeling of fatigue he'd been experiencing just moments before. He dreaded that feeling, his limbs heavy and aching, his head filled with incomprehensible noise. It was almost like coming down with the flu. The aches and weakness would get worse the longer he went without taking his pills, and it eventually would get to a point where he wouldn't be able to hold himself up and, if he wasn't careful, he'd eventually pass out.

After dinner, Darwin went straight to his room, as he didn't feel like being around his dad, who still refused to give him more than just one-word answers. Darwin fell facedown on his bed, then turned around to look up at the ceiling and think about how nice it would have been to have a sibling; that way, he wouldn't feel so alone at night when his parents did their own thing. He liked that he had made a friend in Tyler, but didn't feel comfortable spending time with him outside of school just yet. He couldn't even think about what they would do, if they were to hang out.

On top of that, Darwin wished more than anything that a girl could be a part of his life, even though he knew it was impossible. It didn't stop him from hoping for it in secret—especially every time Mindy Simmons walked by him in the hall. He usually got nervous when talking to girls, and the thought of dating one would give him even more anxiety. His interactions usually ended in awkward silences, or with him bringing up odd topics that most kids his age weren't interested in, such as the life expectancy of a centipede or the literacy rate in Lesotho. A player, he was decidedly not. He had, as he'd heard other kids say from time to time in the halls, no game. None at all.

Darwin had started to accept the fact that he was awkward not only in appearance, but also in personality. Plain and simple, he was a nerd. He liked math and science and reading books about social justice. He knew he wanted this year to be the one where he would break out of his shell and be more confident and comfortable in his own spotted skin, but it was a lot easier said than done. He knew that Tyler could help, but only so much. Darwin knew that this year he'd either soar or sink, but the burden was on him and him alone.

Just as he was beginning the slow slide into sleep, he heard the familiar sound of his parents arguing downstairs. His father's voice was brittle and measured as he made his point in staccato syllables; his mother's voice pleaded dimly, seeping into Darwin's half-awake brain. He could only make out snatches of conversation, words and phrases, but they were garbled, as if transmitted from some distant galaxy.

"You didn't get it?" his mother said, her voice animated with shock and surprise. "The promotion? But they . . . you told me they couldn't . . . you worked so hard!"

He heard his dad grumble in return, his words unintelligible but the anger in his voice transmitting clearly. "Passed me over . . . The agency specifically—" His father's voice was a low growl, even as he shouted, the words guttural, almost as if they were being torn from his throat.

His mother answered, high-pitched, pleading, like a bird twittering nervously in the trees outside. "But you . . . to reason . . . they can't make us . . . forever."

As Darwin lay there listening, he strained to stay awake; he fought the veil of darkness dropping over him, threatening to sweep him under. *The agency?* he mumbled, just before drifting off completely.

What agency?

CHAPTER 6

The next day, when Darwin arrived at school, he took his usual route to class by going the long way, to avoid Billy James and his posse. This required him to take the eastside walking bridge to get to the third floor. As he moved through the halls, he couldn't shake the little he'd heard last night of his parents' conversation. Darwin furrowed his brow, lost in thought, the excited chatter of passing classmates registering dimly in his ears.

As he made his way across the bridge, he spotted Mindy a little way off in the distance. She had a handful of freckles on her face, like a sprinkling of cinnamon, which Darwin always found cute and unique. She strolled over closer in Darwin's direction, in her red dress that flattered her petite figure, her red hair flaring suddenly in the sunlight, like an open flame. Darwin immediately felt a surge of heat in his chest and a flock of butterflies take up residence in his stomach, flapping their wings furiously. Should he say hi, should he stop and catch up with her for a bit, or should he just keep walking, looking the other way to avoid a guaranteed awkward interaction, he wondered frantically as he slowly started making his way closer to her, aware that he was quickly running out of time.

Just as Darwin made the decision to simply look away and avoid eye contact, Mindy shouted out, "Hey Darwin!" while approaching in what clearly was an invitation to chat for a bit before heading to class. She stopped in front of him and smiled, her teeth blindingly white and straight, her pale skin clear, her green eyes the color of damp leaves in the deepest part of the forest.

"Oh! Uh, hey Mindy," Darwin said nonchalantly, trying to make it seem like he hadn't noticed her until just now. Wasn't that what the cool guys did? Darwin had no idea, but that's always what seemed to work on TV, so he was rolling with it.

"How's it going? I feel like I never see you anymore, now that we aren't in the same Spanish class together like last year," Mindy exclaimed, adjusting the stack of books she held against her chest. Darwin froze for a moment, unsure of what to say back.

"Yeah, well, I've been good, re-really good," Darwin said, stuttering slightly. "Um, how have you been?" *Keep the focus on her*, he admonished himself. *As long as she does most of the talking, you'll be okay.*

"Oh, I'm good. I've got some decent classes this year, but I really can't stand my Spanish teacher, Mr. Reyes," she said, rolling her eyes. "He's super strict and has no sense of humor whatsoever. I wish I had Mrs. Youngman, like you."

"Ha-ha, yeah. I hear he's a bit much," Darwin said, not really quite sure what to say next, his mind suddenly as blank as paper. He kept asking himself over and over, *Why are you being so weird! Just talk to her like a normal person!*

"Yeah, well, anyway, it was good to see you. Maybe we could meet up sometime and study Spanish together like last year, you know, since you'll probably need help," Mindy said jokingly. Out of all of his classes, Spanish was the only one he struggled in, a fact that Mindy knew all too well, since they'd been in the same Spanish class last year.

"Um, yeah, definitely!" Darwin said enthusiastically. He then realized that maybe he sounded a little *too* excited, judging by Mindy's reaction—a slightly embarrassed smile. "Yeah, that would be . . . cool," he said, this time in a softer, more measured tone.

"All right, well, we'll work something out, then. See you around!" Mindy said as she made her way across the east-walk bridge.

"Yeah, see ya!" Darwin said again; this time his voice cracked slightly as he waved. Darwin turned around and exhaled loudly in exasperation. He felt like punching the first available wall. Instead he looked down at the floor, his feet frozen in place, even though he

knew he should be getting to class. Why couldn't he act like a normal person with her? Based on that awkward interaction, there was
no way she'd want to study with him, he thought dejectedly, unless
it was out of pity. Darwin took a deep breath and looked up to find
Tyler standing there with a big smirk on his face.

"Well, well, well, look at what we have here. Darwin was having a nice little conversation with his 'friend,'" Tyler said, while air
quoting the word.

Darwin forced himself to roll his eyes in exasperation, even
though he felt more like lying down on the dirty linoleum and dropping dead.

"She *is* just a friend! Although I'm sure after that interaction
she probably just thinks I'm a complete freak now," Darwin said,
while they made their way toward Social Studies.

"Ha! Why?" Tyler asked with a short laugh.

"I don't know, I could, like, barely talk to her. I kept getting
weird and overthinking things. I was stuttering some of my words,
my voice cracked . . ." Darwin's voice drifted off into nothingness.
Just remembering how disastrously it all went down was enough to
make him momentarily lose the power of speech.

"Hmm, sounds like an indication that you like her," Tyler said
teasingly.

"I don't like her any more than just as a friend," Darwin protested, knowing full well that it was a lie. He didn't even buy it himself. How could he expect Tyler to?

"Okay, okay. No need to convince me," Tyler said with a grin,
throwing up his hands in surrender.

The morning went by fairly quickly and before Darwin knew it,
it was time for lunch. Darwin and Tyler made their way to the cafeteria, Darwin with his usual sack lunch in hand. Tyler grabbed
chicken fingers with fries, and they started making their way outside. As they passed by the café lunch tables to go downstairs toward the parking lot, Tyler noticed Mindy sitting at the far end,
eating with one of her friends, the light streaming in through the
long bank of windows behind her turning her hair a burnished cop-
per. *Stop with the poetry*, Darwin admonished himself silently.
She's just a regular girl. The problem, Darwin knew, was that she

wasn't. Nor would she ever be. At least, not to him.

"Hey, hey, look! She's sitting over there," Tyler said in a hushed whisper, as he nudged Darwin again with his elbow.

"Yeah, so?" Darwin asked, looking slightly confused. "And quit that. Your goddamn elbows hurt," he grumbled.

"Sorry, I didn't realize you were such a delicate flower." Tyler smirked. "Let's go sit with them."

"What?" Darwin said in a tone that bordered on horror. "No way. She's talking to someone else anyway," Darwin said, as he turned around to keep heading toward the stairs. But before he could reach them, Tyler extended a hand and stopped him.

"Wait, wait. Let's just go sit with them for a bit, you can introduce me!" Tyler said, smiling broadly, as though this was the greatest idea in the world.

"What? No! I don't want to do that," Darwin said, shaking his head vehemently.

"Oh, come on! It'll be fun, besides, then you guys can plan your Spanish study session," Tyler said convincingly.

"I doubt she even wants to study together," he said, watching as she laughed with the girl sitting next to her. "She was probably just being nice."

"You don't know that, let's just give it a try!" Tyler said, looking at Darwin and waiting for a response.

Darwin stood there for a second, not really knowing what to do. On one hand, he wanted to socialize with the girl he had a crush on, get to know her better, but at the same time he didn't want to be awkward and embarrass himself the way he had that morning.

"Ugh, all right. But let's not stay for too long, especially if we start getting the feeling that they want us to leave," Darwin said grudgingly.

"Of course, no problem!" Tyler said jovially—maybe a little too jovially, Darwin thought with no small degree of suspicion.

Despite his fears, Darwin forced himself to take a deep breath as they made their way over to the far-end table of the cafeteria, where Mindy and her friend were sitting. Darwin could feel it in his stomach—that flock of demented birds. He was getting nervous again. He kept reminding himself to just talk to her like he would any other person. Mindy looked over once she noticed Darwin and Tyler approaching. She smiled, her teeth so straight and white, and waved as they came closer.

"Hey, Mindy. Do you, uh, mind if we sit with you guys?" Darwin asked tentatively, ready for her to say, "Hell NO!" so he could go slinking out of the cafeteria, red-faced and ashamed.

"Oh! Of course," Mindy said. Darwin could tell that her friend didn't seem too happy about it. She looked like someone had overturned a trash can all over their table, and her body language, as she moved over grudgingly in order to allow them to sit, said it all. *Maybe they were just having a private conversation and we interrupted*, Darwin thought as he tried to smile. *Maybe it has nothing to do with me at all.* But inside, he didn't quite buy it. For one, this kind of thing happened more than Darwin even liked to admit. Whether most kids didn't want to associate with him because of his status at the school, or because they were afraid of contracting his "disease," he wasn't sure. He suspected it was likely both.

"This is my friend, Tracy," Mindy said, motioning to the girl.

Tracy was beautiful, with long blond hair and deep brown eyes. Unlike Mindy, she was very tall, which she had to be, given the fact that she was the captain of the volleyball team. Darwin knew who Tracy was, but had never spoken to her. Tracy, with her golden hair and slim, athletic physique, got more than her fair share of attention from the guys at school. Yet, even though she didn't know him, it was clear that Tracy was treating Darwin like something she'd scraped off the bottom of her shoe. But Mindy didn't judge him or treat him like a freak. It was almost as if his appearance didn't faze her at all the way it did other people, like Tracy.

"This is my friend, Tyler. He's new to the school," Darwin said as they sat down.

"Hey guys! Nice to meet you," Tyler said with a slow smile, pushing back his sheaf of dark hair with one hand, until it stood charmingly on end.

"Nice to meet you, too!" Mindy replied. Tracy didn't say anything, but instead just half-smiled with a judgmental look on her face as Tyler sat down next to her. Darwin sat down on the other side of table next to Mindy, jiggling one leg nervously up and down.

"So where are you from, Tyler?" Mindy asked as she took a sip of her water.

"DC. My parents moved here for work," Tyler said as he started eating his chicken fingers. Darwin had learned this was sort of Tyler's go-to response when first meeting people.

"Oh, that's cool! I've never been there before. What's it like there?" Mindy asked, her face lighting up with genuine interest.

"Um, it's not too bad. There's a lot to do around the area, with the Smithsonian museums and all. Also, a lot of historical sites to see like the White House, Washington Monument, the Capitol Building," Tyler added.

"Museums? That's supposed to be fun?" Tracy chimed in, in a sarcastic tone.

"Well, I guess it depends on what you're into," Tyler responded, brushing off the rude sarcasm. "There's a decent night life there, too, some good sixteen-and-over clubs."

"Pshh," Tracy scoffed. "Clearly you don't party," she said, disdain dripping from every syllable. Mindy looked over at Tracy, rolling her eyes, exasperated with her friend's behavior.

"And you do?" Tyler asked, raising one eyebrow skeptically.

"Yeah, I do. But I can barely keep up with this one," Tracy said, tilting her chin in Mindy's direction. "She's a wild child."

"Oh, please," Mindy scoffed, taking a sip from the bottle of water in front of her. "So I like to go out once in a while. So what?"

"If you call every weekend once in a while, then sure, okay," Tracy retorted dryly, spearing a leaf of salad with her fork and bringing it to her lips. "If that's the game we're playing."

Mindy blushed, then crossed her arms over her chest, sitting back in her chair and giving Darwin an apologetic smile. Darwin could see the faint outline of a tattoo on her wrist every time the sleeve of her soft white shirt slid back a bit, and he was mesmerized by the gold hoops she wore in her ears, shining against her crimson hair. He was trying his best not to stare, to act more like Tyler, but it was hard when all he wanted to do was look at her, drink in every detail.

Over the past year, Darwin had heard the rumors about Mindy—that she studied hard and partied even harder. But he'd pretty much ignored them. After all, what she did was none of his business, and Darwin knew that if he'd been born with unblemished skin like every other kid at school, he'd probably be out every weekend, too—maybe even every night, if he thought he could get away with it. Sure, he knew there were parties almost every weekend, where kids were getting drunk, having sex, and getting high, but he was never invited. He'd always tried to pretend that everyone else was home studying on a Friday night, just like him, even though he knew it was just wishful thinking, that he was deluding himself. Somehow, it hurt less that way.

"Except I was grounded last weekend," Mindy said dryly. "So, I stayed home studying calculus and watching bad TV, which was *super* exciting. Ugh, I can't wait to get out of this town and do something worthwhile," she said, shaking her head with disdain.

"Oh yeah, like what?" Darwin asked curiously.

"Um, I don't know yet. I really want to go into public administration, manage a nonprofit one day or something. I also like journalism, being a reporter would be cool." Mindy flashed him a smile.

"Oh, that would be cool! I've always wanted to be a sports broadcaster. I probably won't go into that, though." Tyler polished off another chicken finger. Tracy looked disgusted as Tyler talked and ate with his mouth open. In truth, it was kind of revolting; not that Tyler seemed to care. "So, what's going on this weekend anyway?" Tyler asked after he swallowed, draining the remainder of his can of Coke and setting it on the table with a hollow clink.

Darwin's eyes widened. Where was Tyler going with this? Nowhere good, he suspected.

"I hear there's a party at Chase's house," Tracy said, looking down at the glossy red polish on her nails, spreading her fingers out in a fan to inspect her handiwork.

"Sounds awesome. Right, Darwin?" Tyler motioned with his eyes to Darwin, as if asking him to agree, without saying it.

"Um, yeah. That would be cool . . . I guess." Darwin swallowed hard, his pulse racing so quickly that he wondered if he might pass out right there at the table. Him? At a party? Everyone would stare, whisper, wonder just what the hell he was doing there. And there was no way his parents would let him out of the house, unless he made up some story. And what if they found out? Then what? Darwin's head spun with the possibilities.

"I think I'm busy," Tracy said in a voice as frosty as an icicle.

"Me too," Darwin said quickly, before anyone else could jump in. He felt a sharp kick on his shin from under the table; when he looked up in surprise, Tyler stared back, incredulous, his blue eyes wide in disbelief, his mouth slightly open.

"Your loss," Mindy said with a tight smile, balling up a napkin and tossing it onto her empty tray. Was he imagining it, or did she almost look . . . disappointed? *Say something*, Darwin admonished himself. *Make up some excuse for why you can't go!* But before Darwin could bring himself to speak, Tracy finally looked up from her fingernails and glared at Tyler.

"You really don't like me, huh?" Tyler said, a teasing smile playing at the corners of his lips. Mindy rolled her eyes in response, gathering up her trash and piling it onto her own tray, before standing up and pushing her chair back with a screech.

"What do you have next period?" Darwin blurted, while looking at Mindy, knowing that if he didn't speak to her now he'd lose his nerve altogether.

"Spanish," Mindy said, smiling. "You?" She slung her black leather satchel over one arm.

"Um, Tyler and I both have English, ironically," Darwin said with a laugh. Mindy smiled uncertainly, her expression quizzical, as if she were trying her best to get the joke but somehow couldn't. "Ha -a, bad joke, I guess. You know, since you're going to Spanish and we're going to English," Darwin said awkwardly.

"Oh, ha-ha. Gotcha," Mindy said, after a long moment.

I am such a loser, Darwin thought to himself darkly, as he fought the impulse to run away and hide, and from what seemed like very far away, he could hear Tyler chuckle under his breath a little, almost as if the entire situation amused him.

"Anyway, we'll see you guys later. Have fun in English!" Mindy and Tracy walked away, heading off in the opposite direction. Darwin closed his eyes in embarrassment, once the girls turned around.

"That was brutal," Darwin said dejectedly.

"Eh, it wasn't that bad. You even cracked a joke! I think in the last two weeks that I've known you, you've never made a joke or a wisecrack," Tyler said with a laugh.

"It was . . . stupid, I couldn't think of anything. Girls like guys who are funny, so I thought I would try."

"Oh, so now you care about what she thinks?" Tyler said, about to nudge Darwin again, but refraining. Darwin scoffed. "But why the hell didn't you want to go to that party?" Tyler asked, unable to stifle his confusion. "It was the perfect opportunity!"

"For *what*?" Darwin asked edgily as they walked into the main hallway, which was full of students making a pit stop at their lockers before heading off to afternoon classes.

"I dunno, dude," Tyler said, as if the answer was obvious. "To get to *know* her better, maybe?"

"I told you—she's just a friend," Darwin said with obvious irritation, his tone clipped, aware of how much he was protesting and how transparent it must seem to Tyler. His friend had what seemed like eons of experience with girls, in contrast to Darwin, who'd had approximately none. As they left his lips, the words sounded hollow and fake, even to Darwin himself. Tyler laughed and ran his hand through his already tousled hair.

"Right, buddy. You just keep telling yourself that," Tyler said, giving Darwin a wink. He stopped at the next doorway and headed into class. Darwin stood outside, not ready to go in just yet. He might have been able to lie to Tyler, but it was impossible to deny his feelings to himself. Despite the excuses he made and the lies he told about it, deep down Darwin wanted nothing more than for Mindy to be his girlfriend. But he also knew with a sinking sensation every time he thought of her clear, open face, and her wide, inquisitive green eyes, that the beautiful girls of the world would always be out of reach for guys like him. No matter how nice Mindy was or how much she treated him like he was another one of the guys, she was still way out of his league.

CHAPTER 7

Suddenly, it was winter, Darwin's favorite season, and snow had fallen twice already. Darwin loved the snow, the bracing cold that made his lungs feel as if they were on the brink of collapse every time he breathed in deeply. He loved the snow covering the ground in powdery heaps that resembled piles of pristine, white feathers from a distance. The small town of Crimson always expected two or three significant snows every winter. This wasn't one of them, though, as so far, this winter had only delivered about a half-inch, the white flakes already starting to melt into puddles of dirty gray slush that collected at the curb. Darwin's mom was always a nervous driver in the winter, even if there wasn't much snow on the ground. She'd been in a car accident in a blizzard when she was a little girl, and had been scared of driving in the winter ever since.

Darwin could see the tense look on his mother's face as she white-knuckled the steering wheel.

"Mom?" Darwin asked tentatively, not wanting to distract her too much.

"Yes, dear?" his mother replied, not taking her eyes off the road or her grip off the steering wheel.

"Why can't I get my driver's license yet?" Darwin asked, unable to keep the edge from his voice. He knew it probably wasn't the best time to bring up this subject—one his parents had already discussed with him before—but he thought maybe it would take some stress off his mom, if she didn't have to drive him to school every day, or at least not have to drive in the snow.

"Darwin, we talked about this, dear," Jane said, still not losing her focus on the road. "You're not ready."

"I'm sixteen, Mom, and I'm going to be seventeen in January. Most kids my age already have their license—and a car. Look at Tyler," Darwin said tersely.

"Darwin, I don't think you realize how dangerous driving is," his mother said, this time looking over at him before quickly returning her gaze to the road.

"I know it's dangerous. But you're not even giving me a chance. You can't keep sheltering me my whole life and then expect me to succeed in the outside world."

"Outside world?" his mother replied in astonishment. "You're not even an adult yet! And besides, you have us to help you become successful as an adult."

"Look, I'm going to be on my own soon, when I go to college in a couple of years," Darwin said practically, trying to keep his cool. "How am I going to get by when I can't even drive, and you guys won't even let me watch the news to see what's going on around the world?"

"When the time is right, you'll be able to get your driver's license," his mother said after a moment, her tone soft and careful, the kind one would use with a child, something that drove Darwin nuts. So maybe he wasn't an adult yet, but he wasn't a little kid either. It was time his parents stopped treating him like one.

"It's not even about that, Mom," Darwin snapped, unable to keep the irritation from his voice. "You guys need to let me grow up and do my own thing sometimes. At least, let me start walking to school again!"

"It's out of the question!" his mother said sharply, her hands gripping the steering wheel so tightly that her knuckles went pale and bloodless. "We can't risk you running into the same situation you did years ago," she finished, hitting the steering wheel with the flat of one palm for emphasis.

Darwin's eyes widened. His mother hardly ever raised her voice, and she definitely never hit things. That was his father's territory, generally speaking.

"That was eight years ago," he said, a little more gently this time. "What makes you think the same thing is going to happen again?"

"Honey, I understand this doesn't make sense to you," his mother said after a long pause, her tone even and measured again. "When you get older and become a parent, you'll understand." Darwin thought he'd be a millionaire if he had a dollar for every time one of his parents had said that to him throughout his life.

Knowing that continuing the argument would be futile, Darwin gave up and turned the other way to look out the window. He was tired of always being treated like a child. His parents needed to recognize that although he was still young, he was becoming an adult and needed to be treated like one. A heavy silence hung between them as his mother drove through the snow-swept streets and into the high school parking lot. She stopped at the curb in front of the main entrance, where she sat for a moment, her hands still gripping the wheel tightly. She released it and turned to him.

"Look, dear, tell you what," she said slowly, finding her words as she spoke them. "As soon as the winter is over, you can start walking to school again, BUT only if you are vigilant and be sure to call me when you arrive at school every day. And, after the winter, we'll start teaching you how to drive, you can get your permit then."

Darwin couldn't believe his ears. This was the first time ever his mom had agreed to a specified time of when he could start driving. Before, it was always, "When you're ready," which was really, "When *we're* ready."

"Really? Thanks, Mom!" Darwin said. "I promise you won't regret it."

His mom nodded with a nervous look on her face. Even though she'd relinquished some control and admitted that Darwin had to grow up sooner or later, it was clear that she still wasn't quite ready for it.

A few minutes later, Darwin walked into Social Studies and saw Tyler sitting in his usual spot, his head bent over, reading something in a newspaper.

"Hey Darwin. What's up, buddy?" Tyler said without looking up as Darwin approached, clearly engaged with whatever he was reading.

"Whatcha reading there?" Darwin asked, craning his neck to

look over Tyler's shoulder as he sat in the chair beside him.

"Oh, nothing, just seeing what's going on in the world." Tyler looked up with a grin. "I mean, ever since you started talking my ear off about social and economic issues, I thought I'd get myself up to speed on what's going on. After all, it's probably a good idea to start following this kind of stuff." Tyler folded up his newspaper.

Darwin had learned a lot in this class during the fall semester, everything from the history of American society to social-exchange theory, and the more he learned about social sciences, the more he became fascinated with them. Darwin spent much of his time over the fall in the library reading books on sociology and philosophy. He knew he wouldn't be able to read these sorts of books at home, with his dad's rules and temperament, so instead he'd devour them at the library, after school, on weekends, whenever he had free time. He'd tell his parents he was studying at the library, which they weren't too fond of at first, but then slowly got used to since the library was so close to home anyway.

"So, what were you reading about?" Darwin asked curiously.

"How the government is trying to control our borders more, you know, since they built the Liberty Wall south of the border to reduce illegal immigration. Now they want to do something similar for any immigrants who want to come into the country, even legally," Tyler said solemnly.

"Are you serious?" Darwin asked in disbelief.

"Yeah, something about just because they are legal doesn't mean they won't come into our country and become criminals. Especially if they don't have the means to survive on their own here," Tyler replied. "Apparently, they're going to increase security and control at all ports and airports for people traveling into the country with a visa."

Darwin was baffled by this news. In his view, we were all a part of the same world, all human beings; why was there a need to have any borders, period? Illegal, legal, whatever! Why couldn't every person travel the earth as freely as they liked? Maybe there was something larger at stake that he couldn't quite comprehend at his age, which would justify this type of initiative.

"Why would they want to do that? Don't they want people visiting and spending money here to help the economy? I thought this was supposed to be a nation that values its diversity?" Darwin asked.

"Ha, I thought so, too," Tyler said with a small laugh. "I guess not so much anymore, after all of these terror attacks, shootings, and violent crimes. Looks like they're trying to keep these people out, even though the majority of these crimes weren't committed by immigrants." Crime had risen in the United States by 16 percent in the last two years, in particular hate crimes. The mix of diversity and a growing population due to increased immigration had caused fear in a lot of American citizens, and some felt the need to take matters into their own hands when dealing with those they feared. Just then, Ms. Edmond walked in the door and the rest of the class settled in their seats, but not before Billy James waltzed by and knocked Darwin's notepad off his desk. It hit the ground with a loud *thwacking* sound. The class turned around to see what all the commotion was, and the room fell silent.

"What's your problem, man?" Tyler said in a low but menacing voice as he pushed his chair back abruptly and stood up, his face turning red.

"Oh, is the new guy coming to defend the freak?" Billy laughed nastily, his eyes wide and innocent-looking. His buddies, who were seated at their desks behind Darwin, snickered.

"Don't worry about it, it's not worth it," Darwin said to Tyler under his breath, hoping Tyler would just drop it before things got any worse.

"What's going on back there?" Ms. Edmond said in a stern voice. "Tyler, Billy, knock it off!" Tyler glared at Billy, while he sat back down in his chair.

"Yeah, that's what I thought, dude thinks he's tough," Billy added with a sneer.

"Billy! One more word and you're out of here, you understand?" Ms. Edmond yelled.

Billy smiled and went back to his desk. Billy was athletic and pretty strong for his age, which he had to be in order to be captain of the football team—his shoulders were as wide as the doorway—but Tyler was big as well, and he certainly was taller than Billy. Unlike the rest of the kids at school, Tyler didn't seem to be scared of Billy at all. Darwin respected that about him a great deal.

As the class ended, Tyler got up and stared Billy down, almost as if it was an invitation to go outside and fight in the hallway. Darwin looked at Tyler and asked for him to not make anything of it. Tyler didn't respond, just watched Billy leave the classroom, his eyes narrowing as he watched Billy walk out of the room, laughing as if he didn't have a care in the world.

When Tyler and Darwin walked out in the hallway, they found Billy heading toward his locker to meet up with his other football friends. Tyler slowed down his purposeful walk when he saw the sheer number of people surrounding Billy. It was clear that Tyler knew that if he were going to call out Billy in any way, it wouldn't be wise to do it in front of all of his buddies, who would clearly outnumber them.

"Come on, let's go," Darwin whispered to Tyler. Tyler still had an angry look on his face, his eyes hard as he turned around to go with Darwin to second period. "Don't let them get to you," Darwin said. "That's what they want. Trust me, I've been dealing with it for years," he said bitterly.

"You shouldn't have to put up with that," Tyler said, still glaring at Billy. "Can I ask you something?" He looked over at Darwin, his expression softening a bit.

"Yes?" Darwin asked curiously.

"I probably should have asked a long time ago, but I didn't know if you would be offended by it." Darwin looked very concerned, wondering what Tyler was referring to. "How did you get those . . . you know . . . spots on your skin?"

Darwin couldn't keep the look of surprise from his face. He hadn't seen that coming, not at all. He liked the fact that he'd known Tyler for three months and Tyler had never brought up the thing he was most insecure about.

"I have a skin condition," Darwin said, looking down at the ground. "I've had it ever since I was born, it's called vitiligo, but it's not contagious."

"So, will you have it for life?" Tyler asked curiously.

"Apparently. It hasn't gotten any better or worse since the day I was born," Darwin said sarcastically.

"Do you think if you didn't have it, guys like Billy James wouldn't give you a hard time?" Tyler asked.

"Maybe, though Billy and his crew tend to bully a lot of people, so who knows, they might still bully me even if I looked like everyone else."

"I just never understood why people have the need to do that," Tyler said, shaking his head in disapproval.

"Well, I guess people always fear what's different," Darwin said with a shrug of his shoulders.

Tyler looked over at him, a sad, faraway look on his face, as if a curtain had suddenly come down between them.

After that, the day proceeded normally, with Darwin and Tyler going to their respective classes. Darwin had seen Mindy in the hall twice on his way to class, but didn't say anything to her. He hadn't seen her much over the last couple of months, and he wondered if she still remembered that she'd invited him to study Spanish together, but then again, he also figured it was somewhat his fault for not trying to initiate it.

The final bell rang, and Darwin and Tyler made their way to the parking lot. Tyler went on his way to the student parking lot while Darwin headed toward the pickup line.

"See you tomorrow?" Tyler said.

"Yeah, sounds good," Darwin replied.

Tyler walked off and Darwin waited for his mom in the parking lot. The snow from the morning had already melted, but the weather was still very chilly. He sat there for a moment reflecting, wondering what could be done to change his image, his very skin. He had been putting up with strange looks his whole life, and was tired of it. He wanted to be normal, like any other kid, to have normal, unmottled skin. Why had God given him this appearance? He couldn't help wondering. Was it to punish him or test him? Either way, he figured there had to be a reason for it. He just wished he knew why, so he could better cope with the fact that he was the way he was for a particular reason instead of it feeling random and cruel.

Darwin thought about taking out his homework assignments and working on them until his mom arrived, but didn't feel like it. It was cold outside, and he wanted to keep his hands in his pockets for warmth and not unpack everything to work on his assignments. As Darwin sat there, he noticed a figure out of the corner of his eye, off in the distance. The hair rose up on his arms as Darwin quickly realized that it was the same man he had seen earlier outside his house, and again in the parking lot at school. He was in the same area as the last time Darwin had seen him months ago, when the school year first started. He wore the same black coat and gray hat. More pointedly, and just like the times before, he was staring right at Darwin.

Darwin noticed that the man was holding something about the size of a football. He squinted his eyes, but he couldn't quite make out what it was. The man then took the object and put it toward his face, with the end of it facing in Darwin's direction. All at once Darwin knew: it was a camera. He stood up quickly, and as he did so, the man lowered his camera quickly and looked off in another direction, acting like he was just taking pictures of the scenery, which was ridiculous as they were in a school parking lot, not standing in a field of wildflowers. It wasn't exactly a pastoral scene.

Darwin kept looking at the man, who was pretending to take pictures of trees nearby, to his right. Darwin started walking in the direction of the man, his blood thudding in his ears. He wasn't quite sure what he was going to do or why he was even approaching this man, who was likely crazy and potentially dangerous. The thought of the kidnappers from his childhood kept entering his head as he approached, the way they'd grabbed him roughly by the arm, throwing him into the van. The man was still pretending to take pictures of the trees, and hadn't noticed Darwin walking in his direction. Darwin began moving faster toward him, thinking about what he would say.

Suddenly, the man turned around to see where Darwin was. When the man noticed that Darwin was power walking in his direction, he quickly started walking away, holding his camera by his side. Darwin started walking faster.

Normally, Darwin would have been afraid to pursue such a potentially dangerous situation, but something was telling him that he needed to find out what this man was doing and what he wanted from him. The man quickly looked behind him to see if Darwin was still following, and picked up his speed as Darwin moved closer. Darwin started running, and the man then began to run, too, his camera swinging back and forth with every stride. He ran down the hill of the other side of the parking lot and started making his way off into the forest behind the school. Darwin picked up his speed, as he didn't want to lose him. The man entered the forest, and Darwin shortly followed behind.

The chase now began to be treacherous, as the thick trees were making it difficult to maneuver. Darwin was still on the man's tail, moving quickly with every stride, jumping over fallen branches and ducking the ones that hung low.

He was nearly thirty feet away, and started shouting, "HEY! Stop!" But the man continued to run, making twists and turns to try and lose Darwin.

As the chase continued, the two reached a small creek. The man jumped right in and crossed it, his legs soaked to the knees when he came out on the other side. Darwin stopped and hesitated, looking around to see if there was an easier way to cross. He didn't want to get wet in this cold weather, and if he did, he would surely have to explain to his mom why his legs were soaked. He was wasting time contemplating, and when he looked up he realized the man was getting farther and farther away.

Without another thought, Darwin leaped into the creek, trying to jump over as much water as possible. He landed in the middle, about knee-high in depth, taking three steps through the water as he made his way to the other side.

The water was ice-cold, and he could feel his socks become soaking wet immediately. Darwin's adrenaline made him numb to the shock of the freezing water, and he made his way to the other side quickly. By this time, the man had already gotten so far ahead that he was almost out of sight. Darwin ran as quickly as he could, despite the heavy weight of the water in his shoes, but it wasn't enough. He slowly saw the man disappear, as he came to a halt to catch his breath. Darwin thought about continuing to run after the man, but he knew it was going to get colder and dark soon, and he knew his mother was likely waiting for him in the parking lot, wondering where he was. He placed his hands on his side, and leaned down to try and catch his breath. The cold in his feet started to become painful, now that he had stopped, like tiny needles in his toes, the soles of his feet so cold they were giving off a burning sensation. His adrenaline was no longer pumping, his heartbeat slowing down in his chest. Darwin took one last look in the direction that the man had disappeared, and turned around and made his way back to the school.

When Darwin got back to the creek, he started to regret that he'd even attempted to cross it in the first place. He made his way through the water again, and this time the piercing, ice-cold water throbbed in his already burning and sore feet. Darwin got to the other side and tried to kick off the excess water that was dripping from his pants and shoes.

Walking back through the forest seemed like an eternity, as every step became more painful as the icy water numbed his feet and legs. He didn't realize how far he had run after the man, given the fact that his focus wasn't on the distance he was traveling, but rather, on catching up to the man. His fingers began to go numb as well, despite keeping his hands in his coat pockets. He tried warming them up by blowing into his hands and circling them around and around, but it was no use. The cold had started setting in, and Darwin needed to make sure he got back to safety quickly, before he froze to death.

As he neared the top of the hill to enter the parking lot, he saw his mom waiting in her car, the engine idling. Darwin made his way around the north side of the school, so it would look like he was coming out of the entrance. He made the long walk around the brick building, entering from the back side, toward the track field. The school was virtually empty, now that it was nearly an hour after school had ended. He started walking quickly, as he wasn't sure how long his mother had been waiting for him. With every step Darwin could hear his wet shoes squeaking and echoing through the hallway.

Right as Darwin turned the corner to make his way to the parking lot, Ms. Edmond appeared and nearly ran into him. "Oh! Darwin, what are you still doing here?" she asked with a startled expression, her eyes wide.

"Um, I just came back to get something out of my locker," Darwin responded. Ms. Edmond looked down at Darwin, her eyes taking in his soaked pant legs and shoes, the small puddle that was forming on the linoleum beneath his feet.

"Why are you all wet?" she asked suspiciously, peering at him more closely.

"Oh, um, I fell into a creek on my way back to school to get the . . . thing out of my locker," Darwin said.

Ms. Edmond didn't look wholly convinced. She looked down at his pant legs again, and Darwin knew that she wasn't sure whether to believe him.

"Are you okay? How did this even happen?" Ms. Edmond asked curiously.

"Well, I was walking home from school," Darwin started, "and when I realized I forgot my homework, I ran back super quickly, and because I was rushing I wasn't really paying attention to where I was going, so I fell into the creek—you know, the one behind the school? Don't worry, it's not too bad," he said in a rush, before she could get a word in edgewise.

Ms. Edmond still looked unconvinced.

"Um, sorry, Ms. Edmond, but I really have to run before it gets dark out," he said, panicking a little inside. What would he do if she didn't believe him?

"Well, Darwin," she said slowly, finally deciding to give him the benefit of the doubt, "you shouldn't walk home soaking wet in the freezing cold, you could catch something. Do you want . . ."

"Oh, my mom is here to pick me up," Darwin said, cutting Ms. Edmond off. "I-I called her, so I wouldn't have to walk back in the cold." Darwin was beginning to shiver now from his cold, soaking pants and shoes.

"All right, so then I'll see you tomorrow morning?" Ms. Edmond asked with a tentative smile. She bit her bottom lip as she looked at his wet clothes once more, her face still filled with concern.

"Yes, definitely," Darwin said, trying to end the conversation as quickly as he could. Before she could say another word, he jogged toward the front door and made his way out to the parking lot. He saw his mom looking out the car window from the driver's side, her face creased with worry. Darwin tried to think of what story he could possibly come up with that wouldn't frighten her. There was no way he could tell her the real reason he was soaking wet.

Darwin opened the door. "Hey Mom," he said quietly.

"What on earth happened? Why are you all wet?" she said with no small degree of alarm. Her eyes and mouth were wide open, and she was speechless, waiting for Darwin's response.

"Um, well . . . I was hanging out behind the school . . . and there were some large puddles back there from all the melted snow, I guess," Darwin started mumbling, not quite sure where he was going with this story, but silently praying that she didn't realize that he was making it up as he went along. "And I'm not quite sure what happened, but I was walking with Tyler and wasn't paying attention, and I fell into one of them."

Darwin knew that this story likely wasn't going to fly, but it was the best he could come up with off the top of his head. He'd always been a terrible liar.

"So, you fell into a *puddle*?" his mother said slowly, her forehead drawn into deep wrinkles, her gaze moving down to take in the clothes he wore. "Why would your pants be wet then?"

"Well, see," Darwin said quickly, "when I first stumbled, and my feet went into the puddle, I didn't expect it to be so deep, so I feel down to my knees." He could tell that just like Ms. Edmond, she was unconvinced. She blinked her eyes a few times and looked forward through the windshield. It was as if she knew Darwin was lying. She always did. When she didn't immediately respond, Darwin got into the car, sitting down in the passenger seat.

"No, no! You're too wet!" she exclaimed the minute Darwin's butt touched the smooth leather seat. "I think I've got a towel or an old blanket in the trunk, let me check," she said, unbuckling her seatbelt and getting out of the car. As he heard her open the trunk and begin to rummage around in there, Darwin knew he had to think of something else that would make the story more believable. Perhaps he could say he was accidently pushed into the puddle; maybe that Tyler was messing around and had nudged him, causing him to fall? It all sounded so dumb, so made up.

Before he could think of anything better, his mom came around to the passenger's side. She handed Darwin a towel to sit on and placed an old blanket on the floor below him. Darwin didn't say anything quite yet, as she still wasn't speaking. He noticed that as she made her way around to the driver's side again, her face had fallen. She turned to him the moment she got back into the car and shut the door, her eyes hazy with confusion. "Darwin, I . . ." But even as she tried to speak, her voice drifted off.

"It was just an accident, Mom," he said, in what he hoped was a reassuring voice. "Tyler nudged me when we were joking around, and that's how I fell in," Darwin interrupted.

"Darwin, you know I love you, but nothing makes me sadder than when you lie to me," his mom said, putting her hand on his head. "What happened?" she asked, looking at Darwin, her face suddenly turning very serious. Darwin knew he wasn't going to be able to get out of this; his mother always knew when he was lying. Darwin always joked that she could apply for a job as a CIA agent, and get hired instantly as a human lie detector.

"You're probably going to be mad," Darwin said, looking down.

"I'll try not to be," she said evenly.

Darwin proceeded to tell her about the man he had been seeing after school and outside their house, watching him, and even taking pictures of him in the most recent encounter. He explained that he didn't know what overcame him, but he decided to chase the man to find out who he was and why he was following him. During every step of the story, his mother looked at him in a kind of silent horror. He admitted to her that the first day of school was the first time he'd seen the man in the long black coat at school, and the day before at home. When Darwin finished, his mom sat there with her mouth open for a few seconds, before beginning to ask questions.

"You're sure you've never seen this man before?" she asked.

"No. At least, I'm pretty sure."

"Do you remember what day and time he was outside our house?"

"Um, I don't remember the date specifically, it was the day before school started. But it was night, I remember that. It was before dinner."

His mother sat there for a moment, lost in thought, her gaze faraway and unfocused. She shook her head and looked like she was about to start crying, tears welling up in her blue eyes.

"Darwin, did this man look anything at all like one of the men who tried to kidnap you?" she asked nervously.

"I never really got a good look at those guys back when I was a kid. Besides, I've only seen this guy off in the distance or looked at the back of his head when I was chasing him," Darwin replied.

"Do you know which direction he went?" his mother asked intently.

"I'm not sure specifically, but it was toward the south of the forest. He's likely long gone, Mom," Darwin said, looking at her, lost in thought for a moment. "Do we have to tell Dad?"

The thought made Darwin's stomach tighten with dread. His father would be furious—he knew that already. And furious at Darwin too. It wouldn't matter that it wasn't his fault. According to his father, *everything* was Darwin's fault, even the things that were out of his control. Maybe especially those.

"He needs to know about this, Darwin. Maybe he can help somehow, too."

Darwin let out a deep sigh. He figured he would have to tell his dad, but thought it was worth asking. Then his mother asked one last question.

"Honey, are you sure it wasn't your thoughts getting the best of you again?" she asked hesitantly.

"Mom, I'm telling you, this was real. This was different than before, I could feel the man and his footsteps running through the forest. I saw leaves and branches move as he stumbled while trying to run away. This was *real*," Darwin said defensively.

"Okay, dear, okay. I just want to make sure. Because you know we've been in this situation before," she said, her voice full of trepidation. It was clear from her reaction that she still didn't quite believe him, that she was at least a bit worried still that everything was all in his head.

"That was real, too," Darwin muttered under his breath.

"What was that?" she asked.

"Ugh, nothing. I-I just know this was real, Mom. I'll prove it to you. I'll bring a camera to school and take a picture of the guy next time I see him."

His mother looked at him and sighed deeply. "Okay, honey, I believe you. Really, I do." She reached out and placed one hand on his arm, patting gently. "We still need to talk to your dad about it though," she said, as she finally started the car.

As they made their way home in silence, without his mom's usual absentminded humming, Darwin could only think about the future. The man would come back, Darwin knew, even after their chase today. *And when he does, I'll get him on film*, Darwin thought to himself, crossing his arms over his chest. *And then, they'll have to believe me.*

CHAPTER 8

That afternoon, when Darwin returned home from school, the first thing he knew he needed to do was change his clothes. They were still soaking wet from his unexpected dip in the creek, particularly his pant legs, which were plastered to his calves. He went up to his room and changed into a soft pair of gray sweatpants and a black T-shirt. He could smell the intoxicating aroma of browning meat and roasting potatoes rising from downstairs, and his stomach seized with hunger. Dinner would be ready when his dad got home, in a little under an hour, but he was ravenous. All he could think about was a turkey sandwich on whole wheat with lots and lots of mustard.

"Darwin?" his mother called from downstairs. "I need to run to the store—I just realized we're out of salt!"

"Okay," he called back. *Perfect*, he thought. Now he could make his sandwich without having to deal with his mom. She would undoubtedly start worrying that he'd ruin his appetite, eating a sandwich this close to dinnertime. He padded downstairs in his socks, and grabbed the bread, meat, and mustard from the fridge. After topping one of the slices of bread with lettuce and turkey, he grabbed the mustard to finish it off.

He squeezed the mustard bottle hard, but nothing came out. It was almost empty. He gave it another squeeze, with both hands this time, and the remaining mustard spewed out in a direct line all over his sandwich as well as on the counter. Some of it made a lurid yellow smear on the tiled backsplash on the wall.

"Shoot!" Darwin muttered. His mom was a bit of a clean freak, and he didn't want her to notice when she got home that he'd spilled mustard all over her counter. He grabbed a paper towel and started wiping the counter, then the backsplash. As he applied pressure to the tile, he noticed a small block of tile pushed inward, almost as if he had created a dent in the wall merely by pushing on it lightly.

Darwin's heart beat faster. *Ugh. There's no way I could've pushed hard enough to break it*, he mused as he moved his hand back. But oddly enough, the crack in the tiled wall swelled out a bit, protruding from the rest.

Without thinking, he pushed in again, and this time it fell back into its place, making a sharp click. Darwin, bewildered now, pushed on the tile again. Just as before, it sunk in momentarily, and then popped out about a quarter of an inch from the other tiles. Darwin looked around him, making sure he wasn't imagining things, then looked back at the backsplash. With his, finger he lifted the misplaced tile.

His brain flooded with confusion as he looked down at what he'd found—a keypad of numbers that ranged from one to nine, with three colored buttons at the bottom of the numbers: one green, one blue, and one red. It had to be a PIN code for something in the kitchen, but what could it be?

He looked around to see if there was anything that might require a code. Was it a burglar alarm? If so, why was it hidden? At first, he thought maybe the keypad was connected to the fridge. Maybe this was a way to control the temperature inside? *No, no*, he thought. That couldn't be it. He would have known, if that were the case.

The only thing Darwin was sure of, as he stared at the mysterious device, was that whatever it was, it was something his parents didn't want him to know about.

Darwin pressed some of the numbers and the colored buttons, but nothing happened. The code could be anything; there were so many different possible combinations of numbers, and of course he didn't even know exactly how many numbers were required to complete the code.

He couldn't believe that this thing had been in his house this whole time. All these years, and he'd never known about it. What else was his family keeping from him? What other secrets didn't he know about, he wondered, as he ran a hand over the keypad. The buttons felt slick beneath the pads of his fingers.

His mom would be back any minute, so Darwin cleaned up the rest of the mustard and took the sandwich up to his room. He devoured it, sitting at his desk. As he ate, he brainstormed ways to crack the code.

There were really only a few options, as he saw it. He could either spend hours upon hours trying every single combination possibility for a three-, four-, five- or six-code PIN. But that would take way too long—years, maybe. Another way would be to hide out and wait for his dad to open the tile and watch him enter the code himself. He knew this option was unlikely as well, given that it would be virtually impossible to hide well enough to be imperceptible, yet still be able to see the code being entered. Besides, Darwin knew his dad would never do it when he was around. So he would have to make up a story, a reason why he had to get out of the house, leave the house, and then hide *inside* the house and wait for his dad to make his way over to the tile to punch in the code.

And who knew how often the keypad was actually used? He couldn't count on his dad activating the PIN pad every time Darwin was out of the house.

He knew it was also possible—but not likely—that his parents might not even know this device was hidden behind the backsplash tile. For all Darwin knew, they'd bought the house this way. Or maybe they knew about the PIN pad, but it was for something the previous owner had used, and it no longer functioned. But all these ideas struck him as highly unlikely.

Darwin had read about crime-scene investigations where investigators used black lights to determine if blood might have been cleaned up at a crime scene. He remembered that the chemical they used was called luminol.

He didn't need luminol, but what he did need was a way for fingerprints to become visible under a black light. If he could do this, he would be able to see what numbers were being pushed on the PIN pad.

Darwin had learned in chemistry class that using fluorescent ink from highlighter markers was often used to identify fingerprints, which could be seen under black lights. The highlighter fluid had to be extracted by opening the marker, and then put into a spray bottle. The image being investigated was then sprayed for fingerprints, and a black light was shone over it to make the fingerprints visible.

He needed to go to the store. He needed a bunch of highlighter fluid, and who knew what else? He'd have to do some Internet searches, make a list . . .

Darwin heard the garage door open; the sound of it jolted him out of his thoughts. Moments later, he heard his mother's voice, cheery as ever, floating up through the air. "Darwin? I'm back!"

As Darwin sat at his desk, the numbers on the PIN pad flashed across his mind. He'd go to the store tomorrow, or as soon as he could. He had to. He could think of nothing now, except for what was behind the tile in the kitchen, and what it might unlock.

CHAPTER 9

Darwin sat in the waiting room of Dr. Lewsky's office, waiting for his name to be called. He was the only person in the room, and as he looked around at the bland beige and tan décor, the potted plants in the corners and the Persian rugs strewn across the shiny wood floors, he wondered what could possibly be taking so long. The receptionist sat at her desk, typing on the computer and every now and then looking up at Darwin to see if he was still there.

Finally, a middle-aged woman with red hair the color of dark autumn leaves opened the door and called Darwin's name, peering over a pair of rectangular black glasses. She had a big, fake smile plastered across her face. Darwin disliked her immediately.

"How are you?" the woman said in a patronizing voice, as if Darwin was a child.

"I'm good, thanks," he said brusquely as he got to his feet.

"We're going to be right this way." She led Darwin through a hallway with a bunch of closed doors he assumed were other offices. "And you're going to be right in here, now the doctor will be right in, he just needed to use the restroom real quick, okay?" she said, still talking to Darwin like he had never been to a doctor's office before.

"Yeah, okay, thanks," he said as she closed the door behind him. Darwin took a seat on one of the couches.

He looked around the room and saw the doctor had a bookshelf filled with books, and the kind of artwork you might find in a cheesy hotel room, pictures of scenic mountain views; one a painting of a duck alone in a pond; and another was a picture of the Golden Gate Bridge, clearly a stock photo, which Darwin was pretty sure he had seen at IKEA. Right above the doctor's desk he saw a diploma from Princeton University, a medical degree in psychiatry.

Darwin wondered how long the doctor would be; he didn't have anything to keep himself entertained. Perhaps he should go over to the bookshelf and start reading one of the doctor's books, but then thought the doctor might not like for his things to be touched without permission. Two months ago, Darwin had heard that the psychiatrist he'd seen as a child had passed away from a heart attack. Darwin was sorry the man was dead, but he'd never really cared for him as his doctor. He was just another in a handful of doctors who hadn't believed Darwin about the visions; worse yet, they were always borderline accusing Darwin of making things up. Which was nothing new for Darwin, really, but weren't psychiatrists supposed to believe their patients? Be on their side, with things? At least, sometimes?

Darwin sighed loudly, looking around the room. He didn't want to be sitting there, but he'd been forced to by his parents, as a result of his encounter with the man. His mother claimed that she believed Darwin, that the man was real, but predictably, his father didn't believe Darwin. He was adamant that Darwin needed to see someone right away, and that all of this nonsense was a product of his overactive imagination—or a paranoid delusion, just like he had believed years ago when Darwin was a child. All Darwin could think about was the PIN pad, and getting to the store to buy the necessary ingredients to uncover the fingerprints that he knew were imprinted upon the smooth plastic keys. Sitting here and talking about his feelings with yet another doctor, who would smile at him patronizingly without believing him, was a total waste of time.

Dr. Lewsky walked into the room and closed the door behind him. He was tall and athletic-looking, with a full head of dark brown hair. He looked younger than most doctors Darwin had come into contact with, and if he didn't know any better, Darwin would have thought Dr. Lewsky had just finished medical school.

"Sorry about the wait, Darwin, I've just been in back-to-back appointments all day and needed a quick break," he said.

"That's fine, no problem."

"Now, let me get your file." Dr. Lewsky started rummaging through his filing cabinets in his desk, and pulled out a portfolio. "Ah, here it is!" He made his way over to the couch, sitting on the opposite side of Darwin, and began reading through the files. "So Darwin, it looks like you were previously seeing Dr. Lin?"

"Yes, it was some time ago."

"Right, I see the last visit you made was about seven or so years ago." The doctor continued to dig through the files. "So, how are things going? Why come back after so many years?"

"Well, it wasn't really my decision. I was kind of forced to by my parents." Darwin shrugged.

"Is there any reason they should be concerned?" Dr. Lewsky added, while starting to jot down notes.

"Well, a man's been following me. I've seen him outside my school twice, and once at night outside our house."

"What does he look like?" Dr. Lewsky said, looking up expectantly.

"I've never gotten a good look at him, he's always been at a distance. But every time I've seen him, he's wearing a long black coat and gray hat."

"What else can you tell me about this man, about his overall appearance, that is?" Dr. Lewsky continued to write in his notepad, without looking up at Darwin.

"Well, he seems to be fairly tall, slender. His hair is brown. Other than that, I don't really know anything else about the guy."

"Hmm, I see." He continued to write in his booklet. He paused for a moment and looked out the window. "Now, Darwin, you've had this same type of situation happen before, correct?"

"Yes, back when I was much younger."

"You felt that someone was watching you or following you?"

"I only saw him once, but he was definitely watching me outside of my elementary school, and then I saw him follow me at a distance on my way home. I never saw him again after that," Darwin said, squeezing his hands together tightly. He was getting nervous, his hands shaking. He hated talking about this stuff, hated remembering it altogether. He untangled his tightly squeezed hands and began to massage his neck with one hand to calm himself down.

"Did this man you saw back when you were younger have any similarities to the man you've seen recently?"

"I don't know. I can't remember. He was tall and slender, I guess, but he didn't wear the same thing. I don't really remember anything else about the guy. I've tried to block it out of my memory."

Dr. Lewsky said nothing for a moment, and continued writing down notes, which made Darwin feel even more nervous.

"So, Darwin, I'm also seeing from Dr. Lin's notes that you'd been having visions? Are these still happening?" he asked curiously, looking up from his pad.

"They don't happen as frequently as they used to, but I did have one recently," Darwin said, trying to keep his tone nonchalant, hoping that he didn't sound completely nuts.

"What happened in this most recent vision?" The doctor's pen was poised over his pad, his face open and expectant. If he thought Darwin was completely crazy, he sure was hiding it better than any of the others.

"I don't know, they're always hard to explain. It . . . it just feels like I'm in some sort of alternate world. There aren't people around, just plant life and mountains that I've never seen before."

Dr. Lewsky looked at Darwin curiously and continued writing. "What do you think these visions mean?" he asked.

"I don't know, I'm not sure why they happen. Maybe it's just a way for my mind to take a break from reality?" Darwin could tell the doctor was a bit confused. The expression of his scrunched forehead and furrowed brow made it apparent that he was looking for clarity. "But it feels so real, almost as if this has happened to me before, like a previous experience."

"You mean like experiencing a flashback?"

"Yeah, I mean, I'm not really sure what else to call it."

The doctor finished up writing some notes and there was silence for a good twenty seconds before he proceeded.

"Well, Darwin, based on the way you've described this, I would characterize this as a temporary loss of consciousness, which is often referred to as syncope."

Darwin wrinkled his brow in confusion. He'd never heard the term before. "What's that?"

"Well, it essentially means you faint or collapse. It's very common in those who experience a reduction in blood flow."

"But I don't actually faint or collapse. I wake up still sitting or even standing sometimes, and not on the ground," Darwin said, still looking confused.

"Well, that's the tricky part," Dr. Lewsky said patiently. "What may be happening is that you actually get up while still under a loss of consciousness, and by the time you regain consciousness you're already fully up and ready to move. It's almost like a blackout, if you will."

Darwin didn't know what to say. He knew that these moments weren't simply a result of fainting or from a loss of consciousness. He was clearly in another state of mind in these visions, an alternate reality. As he saw it, there wasn't a complete loss of consciousness, because he was still conscious—just in an alternate state.

"Darwin, do you ever feel scared that people might be after you?" Dr. Lewsky asked.

"I mean . . . maybe a little. At least after what happened recently." Darwin shrugged, aware that they were entering dangerous territory. This was how the questions always began, and things always ended the same way—with yet another doctor not believing him.

"Does this have anything to do with the attempted kidnapping that happened back when you were in the third grade?"

Darwin looked down, not really wanting to speak anymore. He didn't like to think about that day, and lately it had been coming up more and more, back from the past and into the present, where it most definitely didn't belong.

"I don't know. I guess it could," Darwin mumbled, hoping that Dr. Lewsky would quit this line of questioning and move on to something else.

Dr. Lewsky continued to look at Darwin, despite the fact that Darwin wouldn't make eye contact with him.

"Darwin, it's okay," he said in a soft voice. So soft that Darwin looked up and met the doctor's gaze. "You can talk to me about it. That's what I'm here for."

Darwin started clenching his hands together even tighter. "Sorry, I'm just not in the mood," he responded.

"I understand, I know that events such as these can be very traumatic, especially at a young age."

Darwin didn't respond, but instead continued to clench his hands together ever-so-tightly.

"So, what do you like to do for fun?" Dr. Lewsky asked, finally changing the subject.

"Umm, well, I like to read," Darwin said quietly.

"Yeah? What do you like to read?" Dr. Lewsky asked, with what sounded like real interest.

"Mainly nonfiction. I like reading stories on history, sociology, any social science, really," Darwin said, now looking up at the doctor and feeling a little more comfortable. "I do like some fiction, though. But I most like reading about how our society works, and how it's evolved over time. The concept of so many people working together and building cultures is fascinating to me."

"You know, I have to agree," Dr. Lewsky said, nodding his head sagely. "It's fascinating, when you think about how we've managed to build everything on this earth, and the kind of teamwork and cooperation it took to get there."

Darwin smiled back, nodding his head in agreement.

"That's a part of the reason why I went into psychology," Dr. Lewsky said. He leaned back in his chair a bit, crossing one leg over the other. "I loved the social sciences as well. The MD part of my degree was interesting, but for me it really couldn't compare to the study of our minds and how they are shaped by the environment we live in."

Darwin was beginning to kind of like Dr. Lewsky. There was something more genuine and open about him than about Dr. Lin. And even though Darwin didn't agree that he was suffering from some kind of temporary memory loss during his visions, he knew that what he was going through was strange, and that he needed treatment for it.

Dr. Lewsky suggested some simple cognitive behavioral therapy techniques for Darwin to practice before their next meeting. Darwin was instructed to always keep his mind in the present, and to distinguish reality from fantasy. Lewsky asked for him to start refocusing his mind elsewhere, such as on outdoor activities, exercise, or even reading something that he enjoyed when he felt that there was someone watching or following him. The point was to get his mind to accept that he was suffering from schizophrenia, and to understand that his thoughts needed to be refocused elsewhere to improve his condition. Dr. Lewsky also prescribed an antipsychotic medication to take daily, but emphasized that Darwin's primary focus should be on the cognitive behavioral therapy exercises they had discussed.

Darwin agreed, nodding his head at Lewsky's suggestions. But deep down inside, Darwin didn't believe he was paranoid, or that he was constantly thinking someone was watching him. He only felt it in the moment when it was actually happening. Even though he liked Dr. Lewsky, he didn't agree with his diagnosis any more than he had with the rest of the psychiatrists who'd examined him over the years.

On the way home, Darwin didn't talk much and instead gazed out the window. He wondered if in fact he had been crazy, if he was imagining all of these things: the man, the visions, all of it. He was almost certain that these were real occurrences, but he couldn't be sure.

And if it was a mental illness, why was it happening to him? *Well, I guess things could always get worse*, Darwin thought with a small smile. *Or better.* After all, there were good things in his life, like being friends with Tyler, having a loving and supportive mother. And even though things hadn't gone the way he would've liked, at least he'd managed to talk to Mindy that day in the cafeteria without turning red or stuttering in her presence. That had to count for something, right?

But the doctor's diagnosis paled in comparison to what Darwin had discovered yesterday: the PIN pad, the secret behind the tile; the secret that had been there like a cancer, growing all along, permeating the house, his family. As they rode home, it was all he could think about, and he knew he couldn't wait much longer to figure out the mystery—or, at least, he knew he had to try.

"Can we stop by Target on the way home?" Darwin asked.

His mom was humming along with the radio. She reached out and turned the volume down before answering.

"Sure, hon. Why?" His mom glanced over at him as she turned the car right, giving him a small, absentminded smile.

"I just need to pick up some highlighters," Darwin said. "A new notebook, too." He didn't really need a notebook, but he figured it made the whole thing sound more credible.

When they reached the store, Darwin unbuckled his seatbelt quickly, and opened the door before his mother could say anything or follow him.

"I'll just be a few minutes," he said, closing the door. He walked quickly toward the red sign overhead.

In the store, the bright lights glared from above. He strode over to the school supplies section, found the highlighters, and estimated how many he would need. Based on the instructions he'd read online, and from what he'd learned in Chemistry, he knew he would have to buy quite a few to get enough fluid.

Darwin grabbed a box of twenty highlighters. *That should be enough*, he thought. He also needed some fluorescent ultraviolet goggles, in order to see the fingerprints, which weirdly enough he found in the hardware section; not just one pair, but three—and they were on sale.

Darwin went up to the cashier quickly. When he set down the box of highlighters, the tall and gangly cashier looked at him with an odd expression, picking up the box and examining it carefully.

"Hmm, that's a lot of highlighters. Are you studying for something?" the cashier asked. After ringing them up, he placed the highlighters in a plastic bag.

"Umm, yeah. Lots of studying to do." Darwin's voice shook a little; he couldn't hide his nervousness. He didn't dare make eye contact, and he couldn't wait to get out of there. He was probably taking too long, as it was. Any minute now his mom would come walking through the double doors, looking for him.

"That's cool, what are you studying for?" the cashier asked inquisitively. *Maybe a bit too inquisitively*, Darwin thought. Since when did people ask this many questions? Had he just never noticed?

"Uh, the SAT," he blurted. It was the first thing that popped into his head, even though he had already taken it.

"Oh yeah, I totally failed that test. Guess it's why I'm working here, huh?" the cashier giggled. Darwin chuckled nervously and pushed the goggles toward the register, as they were still sitting forgotten on the counter, waiting for the clerk to ring them up.

"So, when are you taking the SAT?" the clerk asked as he lazily scanned the goggles, as if they had all the time in the world.

"Umm . . ." Darwin was scrambling in his head think of a date. "I'm taking it in . . ." Darwin stopped midsentence and froze completely, and the cashier looked around to see where Darwin was looking. It was the man in the long black coat and gray hat he had seen outside his school and home. He wasn't looking at Darwin, though—he appeared to be shopping. The man strolled down one of the aisles, with Darwin's gaze still fixed upon him.

"Umm . . . are you okay?" the cashier asked. Darwin had completely forgotten he was in mid-conversation with the clerk, who was now peering at Darwin in something not unlike concern, maybe even alarm.

"Yeah, yeah. I'm fine. I thought I saw someone I knew," Darwin stammered, turning around to see where the man had gone.

"Well, whoever it was, you definitely didn't look happy to see them," the cashier quipped, handing over the receipt.

Darwin grabbed the thin paper and his bag of highlighters and goggles, watching as the man headed toward the back of the store.

"It's not real, it's not real," he said to himself over and over as he rushed for the exit.

He knew it was best to ignore these hallucinations when they happened; wasn't that what Dr. Lewsky had said? But he couldn't help thinking there was a possibility that he wasn't imagining this, and that both his doctor and parents were wrong. That everyone had always been wrong about this. That maybe Darwin should trust his gut, which told him insistently that these visions were real.

Darwin stopped right before reaching the doors, and did an about-face. There was no way he was going to leave without confronting this man. He had to know once and for all if what was happening to him was real, if he should trust his own instincts, or if they were faulty. Darwin returned to the back of the store, passing the women's clothing and aisles of groceries until finally he came to the hardware section, right where he'd found his goggles. He looked around the nearby aisles, but there was no sign of the man. Then, as he looked up toward the cash registers, he saw him. The man in the hat, motionless, looking at the candy display.

Darwin's heart beat quickly. He took a deep breath and walked over. He inched closer, until the man was within reach. Should he touch him? Darwin wondered, his heart beating so loudly that he was afraid it might just jump out of his chest. Should he say something? The man still didn't notice Darwin coming up behind him.

Darwin coughed. "Excuse me," he said in what he hoped was an authoritative voice.

The man turned around slowly, and his bright blue eyes widened when he realized it was Darwin who had approached him.

"Who are you? I've seen you around, looking at me, following me near my school." Darwin couldn't keep the accusatory tone from his voice.

The man didn't respond, but continued to stare at Darwin, his face white with shock.

"What do you want from me?" Darwin asked. Without answering, the man replaced a Snickers bar he'd been holding in one hand back on the shelf. Darwin noticed that the man's hands were shaking a bit. But before Darwin could accuse him of anything else, the man began walking away.

"Hey! Hey, I asked you a question!" Darwin said, raising his voice now. Bystanders looked over in concern, but Darwin didn't care. He ran in front of the man and blocked his way, forcing him to stop walking. "Who are you?"

The man paused, took a breath, and said quietly, "Please move."

"Everything all right here?" one of the store clerks asked.

He's real, Darwin thought excitedly. He wasn't just a figment of Darwin's imagination. The doctors had insisted that the man who had been following him wasn't real. They were wrong.

The man paused and stated bluntly, "We're fine," in a flat tone. The clerk looked at Darwin inquisitively. "I'm sorry, there has been some sort of mistake," the man said, before walking quickly toward the exit.

"Hey! Hey!" Darwin shouted as the man walked out of the store without looking back. Darwin watched him leave. He tried to see where he was going, but the man quickly turned the corner around the store and was gone. Darwin took a deep breath, his heart still hammering in his chest. He'd known the man was real all along, and in the future, he wasn't going to let anyone tell him otherwise. He took a deep breath and exhaled loudly, returning to the car.

When he opened the door and slid inside, his mom was in the midst of a phone conversation with his dad, which was a relief, as she clearly hadn't registered how long he'd been gone. Whatever they were talking about, it was heated enough to keep her from noticing much of anything at all. His mother's tone was sharper and more clipped than Darwin had ever heard it when she addressed his father, and after a few one-word answers she ended the call, putting her phone back in her pocket and starting the engine.

"Your dad has to work late tonight," she said with a tight smile. "So, it's just you and me for dinner. And I have my book club later on—we're meeting at Sarah's. Will you be okay alone for a few hours?" she asked worriedly, pulling out of the lot.

"Mom, I'm sixteen, not six," Darwin said impatiently, flooded with relief that he'd be alone in the house. He'd forgotten it was book-club night. Maybe if he worked quickly, he could figure the whole thing out before they got home.

"Good," she answered. "We're discussing *Fifty Shades of Grey* tonight, and I wouldn't want to miss it," she said mischievously.

"Gross," Darwin muttered under his breath, laughing a little in spite of himself.

When they got home, Darwin wolfed down some pot roast his mom heated up for both of them, and then went up to his room, ostensibly to start his homework. When he heard his mom open the garage door to leave, he grabbed the bag of highlighters and got to work.

Making the fluorescent solution was hard work, and opening the pens was a chore in itself. Every time he managed to break one open, some of the liquid spilled out onto his desk. He quickly realized that, whenever it appeared he was close to cracking the sides, he should hold the highlighter over the cup to catch the solution.

After breaking through five pens, it occurred to him to start using a hammer to create the initial cracks, and then extract the solution by squeezing the marker with his hands.

After going through half of the highlighters, he realized he had possibly underestimated the amount he needed. Twenty markers might not be enough. The last thing he wanted to do was go back to the store and buy more. The journey alone would take much too long, and he would be forced to wait until tomorrow to start over.

After extracting all of the highlighter ink, he had about half an inch worth of florescent solution in his cup. Would it be enough? He wasn't sure. He contemplated whether he should wait to buy more highlighters and start all over again tomorrow. *But why not give it a go?* he thought.

Darwin filled one of his mother's spray bottles with the florescent solution. Looking at the spray bottle, he knew it couldn't be enough. He made his way over to the backsplash tile, which hid the PIN-code pad, opened it, and sprayed the solution on the keys. Not much came out at first, but Darwin sprayed until the entire PIN code was covered in the nearly invisible solution.

He dimmed the lights and went to get his UV goggles. He took a deep breath and turned on the handheld black light he had borrowed from his chemistry class, and shone it on the keypad. The solution glowed brightly under the black light, until the whole keypad was a beaming fluorescent yellow. But unlike the rest of the keypad, four numbers showed consistent fingerprints, with partial fingerprints on the numbers around them. The numbers that had the most prominent fingerprint marks were one, five, seven, and eight. Numbers two and four had some partial fingerprints, but this was likely due to inaccurate touching when typing in the code. *These have to be the four numbers*, Darwin thought. The question now was how to crack the code.

Darwin knew it would take hours, if not days, to enter all the possible codes. His mom would probably be home soon, along with his dad. But he could work till he heard the garage door open, couldn't he? With that, he wrote down the numbers with the fingerprints, and started listing combinations of potential four-digit codes.

Quickly he realized this wasn't going to work, either. He needed a spreadsheet, as there would be thousands of combinations, and he needed all of them to be clearly organized, so that when it came time to try all of the codes, he could do it in a succinct fashion.

Darwin wiped the solution off the keypad, then headed upstairs to his computer to start typing the combinations. He had gotten through 547 of them, when he heard the low rumble of the garage door.

"Darwin! I'm home," his mom said cheerfully as she called up the stairs.

Darwin saved his Excel spreadsheet and put his computer on sleep mode, in case she was thinking about coming to his room. "Hey, Mom. Just finishing up some homework," he shouted back down the stairs, before walking over and closing the bedroom door. He didn't think his mom would think anything of seeing him working on an Excel sheet, but he also didn't want her asking questions. He wasn't the best liar.

After completing around 8,700 potential codes, Darwin checked the clock. It was already midnight. He was close to completing all the possible combinations, but he was too tired to finish. He fell asleep at his desk, his head cradled in his arms.

The next morning was Saturday, and Darwin woke to the sounds of his parents bustling around downstairs. His dad must've come home really late. Darwin stood, stretching his back after a night spent sleeping at his desk. He winced when he put his hands over his head, his back cramping. When he went downstairs, his mom and dad were already dressed and just finishing up breakfast, both dressed in jeans and light sweaters.

"Morning, sleepyhead," his mom called out cheerily from the kitchen sink, where she was rinsing the breakfast dishes. "It's after ten. You must've been exhausted last night." His dad sat at the table munching on a piece of toast, which he waved at Darwin in greeting, his mouth full.

"We're going to the botanical gardens today," his mom said excitedly as she turned around to look at him, drying her hands on a yellow kitchen towel. His mom was an amateur gardener, with the unfortunate habit of killing nearly everything she touched. Still, there was nothing she liked more than to spend a Saturday looking at plants. "Want to join us?"

Darwin coughed a few times, hoping it sounded believable, then sniffed and said, "I think I'm coming down with a cold. Better stay home, so I don't have to miss school on Monday."

Darwin's dad grunted as he pushed his chair back. He stood and took his plate to the sink.

Darwin's mom walked over and placed the flat of her palm on Darwin's forehead, checking his temperature, her blue eyes crinkled with worry. "You feel pretty cool," she said with relief. "But best to stay home if you feel like you're coming down with something."

She released him and walked over to the front door, where she found her sneakers on the floor and slipped them on. "We'll be home around three or so," she said as she bent down to tie the laces.

After they left, and the house was silent, Darwin went back up to his room. There, he immediately began completing the rest of the combinations list. By the time he finished, it was nearly noon and he had only three hours to test out the nearly ten thousand possible combinations. With luck, he would identify which one it was within the first hundred tries.

It was wishful thinking. His first hundred attempts resulted in nothing but a red flashing *Denied* message displayed above the numbers. Two hundred yielded nothing; three hundred, still nothing. Entering the numbers over and over was mentally taxing, not to mention tiring to his hand, which was constantly lifted in trying possible combinations of numbers over and over. He had to take breaks frequently to stop the aching that radiated from his fingers down to the bones in his wrist.

Two hours went by, with over five hundred combinations attempted, none of which worked. Darwin began to feel a little defeated. He looked down at the printed Excel sheet, and realized there was a possibility that the code could have a five- or six-number combination, if any of the numbers he found with fingerprints were entered twice.

Darwin pounded his fist on the counter, annoyed at himself for not realizing this before. He took a deep breath, returned to the keypad, and continued his attempts. Six hundred attempts; still nothing. Then, as he typed the combination 1785, the keypad flashed green above the numbers: *Granted.*

Darwin stared incomprehensibly at the PIN pad. He couldn't believe his eyes. Had he really cracked the code? There was no way he could be that lucky. He waited, and nothing happened. He looked around to see if anything had moved or opened. Then, a soft noise like a refrigerator door opening slowly sounded from behind him. Darwin spun around to see what it was.

One side of the wall inside the pantry was ajar. The wall had come undone about five inches, and Darwin realized that beyond the door, there were steps leading down. His stomach plummeted, and his heart raced. How had he lived in this house for so many years, without knowing about a hidden passageway? How could he have grown up here oblivious, trusting his parents, who had clearly been keeping this from him? And if they'd kept the knowledge of a secret passageway in his childhood home from him, what else were they hiding? Darwin shivered, his shoulders spasming at the thought. Of course, there was the possibility that his parents were as clueless as he had been all these years. But that just didn't seem very likely.

Darwin knew he had only a short while before his parents came home. He stood inside the pantry, in the semi-darkness, looking at the door and contemplating whether he should explore what was down there. His watch read 2:15, which would give him roughly forty-five minutes to check things out. If it wasn't enough time, he could always try to find some way to get back in tomorrow. Or the next day.

He took one deep breath, opened the door, and made his way down the stairs and into the darkness.

CHAPTER 10

It was dark. The smell of wood, which only grew stronger with every step, tingled Darwin's nose. He couldn't see anything, as the kitchen light shining through the open door of the pantry faded the lower he went. He reached out, trying to feel a light switch, but could feel nothing along the walls. After a couple more steps down, Darwin reached the bottom. The smell of wood was still strong in the blackness. Then, after moving his hands a little higher, his fingers snagged something protruding from the wall. Darwin grasped his two fingers on the switch and pulled upward.

The bright light overpowered Darwin's eyes and forced him to close them for a few seconds. As he opened his eyes slowly, he was surprised to see a desk with a chair, both made of solid wood. He looked around the walls and noticed pictures of his father, dressed in a suit, standing alongside groups of other men. When Darwin leaned closer to get a better look at the pictures, he realized they were photographs of prominent political figures: senators and other elected officials. There were snapshots of well-known sites in Washington, DC, and photos of his father standing by the Washington Monument, the Lincoln Memorial, and the Capitol. Darwin's head began to spin. What was his father doing in pictures with these political figures? And why had he never mentioned it?

Darwin tried to remember if his dad had ever gone to DC, but couldn't think of any times when that might have happened—none he'd heard about. It must have been back when he was too young to remember, given that his dad did look much younger in the pictures.

But then, why did Darwin have a sneaking suspicion that wasn't it at all? That his dad had been hiding some whole other secret life from him, and maybe from his mother, too? As Darwin stood there, his mind racing, he tried to make sense of it. But he only ended up more confused.

Walking over to the desk, Darwin noticed some plaques hanging directly above it. One of the glossy wooden surfaces with gold lettering read: *Dave Sanders: For most outstanding work in the field of international security.* There were three of these awards, all for the same accomplishment. But what struck Darwin most was the crest on each award in the bottom-right corner—a crest he'd seen before. It was from the Central Intelligence Agency.

Darwin looked closely at the crest to make sure he was reading it correctly. His heart beat rapidly as he read it three times; each time he only fell further into a sea of disbelief. Had his father formerly worked for the CIA? And if so, then why hadn't he told Darwin about this before? Did his mother even know? Or had his dad been keeping secrets all these years?

Darwin pushed the chair aside and started frantically searching through the desk drawers to see what else he could find. When he opened the first drawer, he found stacks of photos, pictures of what appeared to be people wearing white coats and working in a lab. There were men dressed in white protective suits alongside test tubes and petri dishes on a lab table. There was no sign of his father in these photos. Darwin turned one photograph around to find the phrase *Specimen B from Florana* written on the back side.

"Florana?" Darwin said to himself. What was *that*?

He put the photograph down and noticed others with similar images on the back, each stating a different specimen from Florana. Darwin kept going through the photos until he came across one of his father shaking hands with a man and holding up what appeared to be a bug inside a test tube.

Darwin didn't know what to make of all of this. He stashed the photos away in the order he'd found them, and went to the next drawer.

The second drawer didn't have much in it, only a few test tubes and what looked like some cleaning material, and a bottle of WD-

40. The last drawer held a binder of papers, which contained graphics of patterns and designs that were like nothing Darwin had seen before. The graphics were displayed in straight lines, with formations inside the lines that resembled the shapes one might find inside a kaleidoscope. At the bottom right of each paper was written *Florana, page 3.2,* and each page had a separate number. Darwin assumed this had to be someone's name, but why were all of these records stored in a hidden room?

Suddenly, Darwin heard the squeak of the garage door opening. Someone had come home early. He closed the binder and placed it back in the drawer, in its exact position, so his father wouldn't notice any changes. He raced to the stairs, as he could hear the garage door stop and the engine of a slowly entering car. He slammed the light switch off and sprinted up the stairs, but just as he got halfway up the steps he stopped. He hadn't put the chair back in its place, tucked neatly beneath the desk. This was something his father would definitely notice—he was always reminding Darwin to tuck in his chair before leaving the dinner table. Darwin rushed back down the steps in a panic, flicked on the light, and scrambled to push the chair back under the desk.

He made it up the stairs just in time, stepping out of the pantry and into the bright light of the kitchen. He heard the door to the garage close sharply, and then the sound of his father's sneakers—the Nikes he wore on weekends—squeaking against the wood floors as he made his way to the kitchen.

Darwin wiped his brow with a kitchen towel quickly, trying to catch his breath and act normally. His heart was hammering, and he felt like he was about to implode, both from frantically running up the stairs and from trying to make sense of what he'd just discovered. As his father entered the room, his jeans and navy sweatshirt spotted with raindrops, Darwin noticed that his dad's expression was dark, as if a cloud were passing across it, his gaze steely and impassive. Dave looked over at the pantry door, which, in his haste, Darwin had left ajar.

"Hey Dad," Darwin said, moving over to the refrigerator and hoping he didn't still sound out of breath. He pulled out a jug of orange juice and carried it over to the counter, taking a glass down from the cabinet. *Act normally*, he told himself sternly, pouring juice into the glass and lifting it to his lips. *It's like any other normal day, where you didn't just find some secret barracks underneath you.* "Is it raining out?" Darwin asked, raising the glass to his lips, trying his best to stop his hand from shaking.

"It was at the gardens," his dad said gruffly. "So we left."

"Oh," Darwin said, swallowing hard, the taste of the juice more bitter than sweet. "Where's Mom?"

"Out front," his dad said. "Fussing with those flowers she planted last week."

Darwin nodded, the tension in the room settling around them in a thick haze. Darwin could hear his heart knocking against his ribs, his pulse thudding in his ears. He prayed his father couldn't hear it.

"You look flushed," his dad said, looking Darwin over carefully, his dark eyes narrowing.

"Oh, yeah?" Darwin said, trying to sound nonchalant. But when the blank and stony expression on his father's face failed to relax, Darwin suspected that he was failing miserably.

"Did you take your potassium today?" his dad inquired in a sharp voice, crossing his arms over his chest, as if he was ready for a fight.

"Yep," Darwin said as he put the glass down on the counter and wiped his mouth with the back of his hand. "At lunch."

"Why is the pantry door open?" his dad said, his gaze moving from Darwin to the door, which was still standing ajar.

"Uh . . . I was getting a snack," Darwin said, trying his best to keep his voice from shaking. He was so nervous, it felt as if his nerve endings were on fire.

"Of *what*," his dad asked, his tone stern.

"Some c-crackers," Darwin stammered, willing himself to stop stuttering.

His dad nodded slowly, his eyes still fixed on Darwin. And standing there, Darwin had the sneaking suspicion that no matter what he said or how convincing his answers might be, his dad didn't quite believe him.

"Make sure you clean up after yourself when you're through in here," his father said, finally breaking eye contact and walking over to the refrigerator. He pulled out a bottle of beer, twisting off the top before walking out of the room. Darwin heard the TV being switched on and the announcer's voice on a sports broadcast his father was watching on ESPN. He exhaled loudly, gulping the remainder of the orange juice before placing the glass in the dishwasher.

That night, he lay in his bed, restless, unable to sleep. The sheets wound themselves around his legs like a nest of snakes, until Darwin had to push them to the foot of the bed in a heap. He lay on his back, staring up into the darkness of the room, unable to stop the images of what he'd seen in that secret room from flooding his mind. He had the scary feeling that his dad was someone he had never really known. A stranger. That he'd been sharing a house with a person who had more secrets than he could count, who needed a whole extra room to store them. There hadn't been a photo of the man Darwin had seen following him, watching him, but he couldn't help thinking that maybe, just maybe, in some inexplicable way, the two were connected.

CHAPTER 11

The holidays had come and gone before Darwin knew it. Darwin arrived at school after being dropped off by his mother, pulling his jacket more tightly around him as he walked to the front doors. Christmas had arrived in a flurry of gifts and holiday meals. Darwin suffered through most of the meals uncomfortably, his father's gaze boring into him every time Darwin raised a fork to his lips and tried to swallow. No matter what Darwin did or didn't do, since that afternoon his dad had found him in the kitchen out of breath with the pantry door left open, it seemed like he was suspicious of Darwin's every move. Even though Darwin knew logically that it was unlikely his father could know that he had gotten into the secret room, he couldn't shake the idea that his dad knew exactly what he'd been up to. Darwin had been sure to put everything back where he'd found it, and was careful not to leave any markings on the items he had touched. But still, every time Darwin looked up at Christmas dinner, he met the eyes of his father, watchful, distrustful. Darwin could hardly bring himself to swallow the turkey and dressing at what, under normal circumstances, was his favorite meal of the year.

But as hard as it was, Darwin tried his best to set his sights on the future. It was a new year, and his mom had promised to teach him to drive, though she'd shown no signs of actually wanting to do so, and hadn't mentioned it since that day they'd discussed it on the way to school. If Darwin really wanted his license, he'd probably have to take matters into his own hands. It wasn't going to magically happen—not if his parents had any say in it.

That morning, as Darwin and Tyler were walking through the hall across the east bridge, Mindy approached them, her long red hair flaring in the sunlight, causing Darwin's heart to lurch in his chest.

"Hey guys!" Mindy said, as she stopped in front of them, clutching her books to her chest. She was wearing faded jeans and a loose black sweater, and when she smiled, Darwin swallowed hard. He tried his best to return her grin, though it came out as more of a grimace. He wondered if he would ever be comfortable around girls—especially girls he liked—as he shifted his weight nervously from one foot to the other.

"Oh, hey Mindy!" Darwin said, shoving his hands in his pockets, aware that his face was hot, his cheeks reddened.

"How's it going, Mindy?" added Tyler with his usual lazy grin, as if they had all the time in the world to stand around and chat.

"How was your break? Do anything fun?" Mindy asked brightly.

"Umm, it was good." Darwin shrugged. "We didn't really go anywhere . . ." Darwin mentally kicked himself. He knew he should've come up with something a little more exciting than that. "How about you?"

"Oh, my family and I went to Hawaii, it was amazing. My first time there." Mindy's face was flushed with excitement, her white skin turned strawberry pink, and Darwin had never seen her look prettier than she did in that moment.

"Oh, that sounds great! I've always wanted to go to Hawaii," Darwin said, which wasn't actually true, but he didn't really know what else to say. He hated hot weather and he wasn't much of a beach guy, mainly due to his skin condition. He could barely deal with Texas summers.

"The weather is great," Mindy said excitedly, "and there's so much to do and see."

Darwin nodded his head, unsure of what else to add to the conversation.

"That's cool. I was in DC," Tyler interjected, noticing that Darwin was struggling to keep the conversation going. "It was pretty uneventful, though."

"Oh, were you back there to see friends or family?" Mindy asked.

"Yeah, my grandparents still live there, and I got to see some of my old friends from school."

"I bet you miss it there."

"Meh, not really, I'm starting to like it here more and more. Small towns are starting to become my thing," Tyler said with a little laugh. Mindy chuckled a little.

"So hey, the reason I wanted to talk to you guys is that I've started volunteering at a nursing home!"

Before they could respond, Mindy rushed on, her words coming so fast they were practically falling over one another.

"Oh yeah?" Tyler said, nodding with approval. "The one just down the other block from here, over on Third Street?"

"Yep, it's called Sun Parks. It's actually an assisted-living facility, but they still need a lot of volunteers."

"What's the difference?" Tyler asked.

"Well, an assisted-living facility is basically a home for seniors who need help dressing, eating, bathing, and stuff, but don't necessarily need a ton of medical care—well, not yet anyway."

"Gotcha. So how long have you been doing this?" Tyler asked with interest.

"Just a few weeks—I started right before break, but I really like it so far, and I was wondering if maybe you guys wanted to volunteer, too?" she said, looking right at Darwin. "It's great for college apps, no doubt, which is why I originally started doing it. But honestly, it's so much more than that. It's just really cool to help people, to feel like I'm making a difference, you know?"

Darwin nodded, unsure of what to say. He watched as Mindy's cheeks grew even more flushed, and she looked away for a moment, before returning his gaze with a smile. There was nothing he'd like more than to spend time with Mindy outside of school, but why was she asking him, he wondered? Why him, out of all the other guys in school? Cooler guys. Guys with actual social lives.

"Yeah, for sure! That would be awesome. Right, Darwin?" Tyler said, slapping Darwin on the back.

"Um, yeah. Of course," Darwin said, trying to sound more confident than he felt.

"I mean, no pressure," Mindy said quickly, noticing the lack of excitement on Darwin's face.

"No, no. That sounds like a lot of fun, really!" Darwin said quickly with a smile, not wanting to offend her. "And I like the idea of helping people," he finished, surprised he wasn't stuttering like he usually did around Mindy.

"Okay, great!" Mindy said excitedly, her eyes shining with happiness.

"Is your friend Tracy going to volunteer, too?" Tyler asked.

"Yeah, I think so. I'm going to see if she wants to, at least."

"Oh goody! Can't wait to hear how enthusiastic she is about cleaning rooms and serving meals to old people," Tyler said sarcastically.

"Hey! I mean, she might have fun, you never know," Mindy said with a little chuckle.

"Okay, well, anyway, I'll tell the director that you're interested and text you guys the info later on," she said breathlessly as the first bell rang. "Guess that's my cue," she said with a smile as she made her way down the hallway and off to class.

"See ya!" Darwin and Tyler both said at the same time.

"There you go, that's what I'm talking about!" Tyler said jovially, putting his arm around Darwin's shoulder. "And you thought she was just being nice. She actually wants to hang out with you!"

"I guess, but what if I'm not any good at it," Darwin said, a note of worry creeping into his voice.

"Listen, Darwin, it's volunteer work, how hard can it be? I still think it'll be pretty cool. I mean, at the very least you'll probably learn something, right?" Tyler added. "For a girl that you really like, you learn to like and appreciate the things she enjoys," he said, slapping his hand on Darwin's shoulder.

"How do you know this stuff?"

"What do you mean? You think I've never had a girlfriend before?"

Darwin thought for a second, and realized they had never actually talked about it.

"I mean, I'm not that vocal about it," Tyler said with a shrug as they moved down the hall, "but I know how girls think."

"You had a girlfriend in DC?" Darwin asked.

"Yeah, we'd been together a couple years."

"Why did you guys break up?" Darwin wondered aloud, hoping that he wasn't getting too personal.

"Well, when I moved away from DC, we basically knew that a long-distance relationship wasn't going to work, and we were both too young to make any type of long-term commitment, so we decided to break it off, at least for now anyway."

"Do you miss her?" Darwin asked.

"Of course, but we're still friends and everything."

"Do you think you'll ever get back together?" Darwin asked. Tyler stood there for a second, contemplating the question.

"I don't know, probably not, given her career," he said thoughtfully.

"Her career?" Darwin couldn't help but be confused. What kind of a career could a sixteen-year-old possibly have that would get in the way of dating?

"Oh!" Tyler said as if a light bulb had just gone off inside his brain. "I mean, like her *academic* career," he said quickly. "She goes to a private school, and she wouldn't be able to transfer without losing her credits."

"Well, you guys might be able to make it work at college or something," Darwin offered up hopefully.

"Yeah . . . maybe," Tyler said, while continuing to walk in the direction of their social studies class.

After school let out, Darwin and Tyler made their way to the parking lot; Darwin to the pickup area to wait for his mom, and Tyler, who normally went to the students' parking to get his car, to the main parking lot, which was designated as staff parking.

"You sure you're not going to get a ticket for parking in the staff lot?" Darwin asked.

"Nah, I've done it before. I don't think they monitor it. Besides, if they do, I'll just explain I had a doctor's appointment and the lot was full when I got here. And if they still have a problem with it, I'll tell them they should make the parking lot bigger. I mean, what school doesn't have enough parking spots for its students? Kind of ridiculous, if you ask me."

"Yeah, I think it's to encourage kids to carpool, help the environment," Darwin said with a shrug.

"Psh," Tyler scoffed. "I mean, if that was the real reason, then fine, but I think it's because the school is too cheap to expand the parking lot. Or I guess I should say the federal government is too cheap. They're too busy spending way too much money on the military and not enough on our public-education systems."

"Yeah, I guess." Darwin looked around for his mom.

"You sure you don't want me to just give you a ride? I mean, your parents know me better now, wouldn't they be okay with it?"

"No, it's fine. Thanks for offering, but my mom will be here soon, any—" Darwin stopped midsentence. He looked off in the distance, across the lot, and spotted the man in the long black coat and gray hat, in the same place he had been the last two times. This time, the man wasn't holding a camera, but he *was* making direct eye contact with Darwin.

"You okay, man?" Tyler said, reaching out to touch Darwin's shoulder gently. Darwin didn't respond at first, and he watched as the man looked off to his right, now avoiding eye contact with Darwin, but staying in the same location.

"Uh . . . yeah. Yeah . . . I'm fine," Darwin said, still staring in the direction of the man. Tyler glanced over to see what Darwin was looking at.

"What is it? What do you see?" Tyler asked.

Should I tell him? Darwin wondered. While it was probably best to ignore the man, as his psychiatrist had recommended, the trouble was that after the incident at Target, Darwin was surer than ever that the man was real. And he was definitely following Darwin. If, by some strange twist of fate, though, Darwin was imagining everything, the last thing he'd want was for Tyler to prove it by saying, "*What* man?" Then he'd jump to the conclusion that Darwin was in fact crazy.

Before he could decide what to do, the man walked off toward the same hill Darwin had chased him down the last time. Darwin desperately wanted to follow him, to see where he was going. As he decided to get moving, he noticed Tyler's hands waving in front of his face, fingers waggling in a vain effort to get his attention.

"Dude, are you even *listening* to me?" Tyler asked, snapping his fingers before Darwin's eyes. The sound jolted Darwin out of his thoughts.

"Sorry, yeah. I'm fine," Darwin said distractedly. "Just daydreaming."

"So, you mean you don't respond to people when they ask you five times what's going on, when you daydream?" Tyler asked, clearly annoyed.

"Sorry, I don't know what happened. Sometimes I daydream, and I just . . . tune everything out, I guess."

"Well, that's kind of weird. I mean, sure, I've been known to daydream every now and then, but if someone was shouting my name repeatedly, I would snap out of it," Tyler said, chuckling a little.

Tyler's words rang hollow in Darwin's ears. He couldn't stop squinting off in the direction, fixated on the spot, where the man had been standing.

"What are you looking at, anyway?" Tyler asked.

"Don't worry about it," Darwin said, turning back to Tyler with an apologetic smile. "I'll see you tomorrow, all right?"

"Oh . . . uh, okay. See you tomorrow."

Just then, his mom pulled up in the car, all smiles, and Darwin gratefully slid into the warmth and comfort of the front seat. He couldn't shake the feeling that the man was still out there somewhere, watching, waiting. He said hello to his mother, but immediately turned to look out the window.

What if the man had something to do with his father's secret room? Darwin's eyes widened at the thought. He had to get back down there, as soon as he could, to look around more thoroughly. Could the man want information that was down there? Did he want to hurt Darwin—or was he protecting him? His brain swam with the possibilities.

"How about tomorrow we start teaching you how to drive?" his mom asked, breaking into his thoughts and trying to lighten the mood.

"Really?" Darwin asked, turning to look at her, his voice colored with surprise.

"Yeah, really. I'll take you out to the abandoned parking lot up by the old college, and we can drive around a bit. In the meantime, you can start studying for your permit."

"Oh, I've already been studying the book. I'm ready."

"Oh, you have, have you? And where might I ask did you get the driver's manual to study?" his mom asked, clearly bemused.

Darwin gave her a small smile. "I just went to the DMV one day while I was waiting for you to finish grocery shopping."

"Ha! I see," she laughed. "Well, you're quite the sneaky one, aren't you? Well, okay then, tomorrow we'll start practicing at the abandoned parking lot, and if I feel like you've made good progress and look comfortable behind the wheel, we'll go to the DMV so you can take your permit test. How does that sound?"

"Great!" Darwin said. His mom always knew how to cheer him up. Despite the fact that she was pretty much the definition of over-bearing at times.

That night, as promised, Mindy called with info on the nursing-home job. She relayed that the director wanted Darwin and Tyler to come around the next day, after school, if he could make it. "If you're still interested, I mean," Mindy said, with a nervous laugh. Darwin wanted more than anything to tell her he was more than in-terested; he was flattered that she'd even asked. He needed to figure out a way to keep Mindy talking, to keep her on the line. But pre-dictably he drew a blank, and the conversation grew heavy with long pauses and awkward silences, before they finally hung up.

Tomorrow will be different, Darwin told himself firmly as he heard his mom calling him to take out the garbage. *If I see her there, we'll talk.* But as he walked down the stairs, his heart was heavy. As much as he wanted to believe it just might happen, despite every-thing, deep down he was scared she'd reject him, scared to leave himself as vulnerable as she made him feel every time he looked into her open, cheerful face, and those brilliant green eyes.

CHAPTER 12

The next afternoon, after the final bell rang, the boys headed to Sun Parks. As they walked the streets in the overcast January afternoon, the sky darkened with clouds, as if the sun had disappeared completely. It was only a few short blocks to the nursing home, an imposing brick building with two glass double doors in the front, the entrance graced by an elaborate green-and-white striped awning. When they went inside, the lobby was quiet. Residents sat in groups near long banks of windows, chatting or playing cards. Tyler walked up to the receptionist behind a cubicle, smiling confidently, as always. Darwin shook his head good-naturedly. He still had no idea where Tyler got his seemingly endless confidence, but it never failed to amuse him.

"Hey," Tyler said with a nod. "I'm Tyler Barros. My friend Darwin and I are supposed to volunteer today."

The receptionist, a young woman in her early thirties with long dark hair, smiled, handing Tyler a sheaf of papers across the partition. "You'll both need to fill out these forms. Someone will be out to get you in a few minutes."

After a portly man named Ben took them to a conference room where they watched a brief orientation video, Darwin and Tyler were split up. Tyler was assigned to kitchen duty, while Darwin was given a yellow bucket full of cleaning supplies and a vacuum, and asked to help clean the rooms of the residents. There were over forty-five units in the facility, so Darwin figured it would probably take forever. Darwin kept craning his neck as they walked through the facility, hoping to get a glimpse of Mindy's crimson hair. His heart sank a bit every time he turned a corner, only to find it empty.

He went into his first room, a tidy space with gray painted walls and a narrow twin bed, and started vacuuming the floor while the resident, an older gentleman probably in his seventies, with a thick head of white hair and a beard that looked like it hadn't been trimmed in a while, appeared to be asleep in his bed. Darwin winced at the roar of the vacuum, but kept going, as he'd been instructed to clean the rooms even if the residents were sleeping inside them.

"Who are you?" the old man asked abruptly as he woke up from the sound of the vacuum, clutching the gray woolen blanket to his chest.

"Oh, sorry, sir. I'm Darwin. I'm a new volunteer here," Darwin said nervously, walking over to shake the man's hand. "I'm here to clean your room."

"Oh! Well, that's good because it's starting to get pretty dusty around here," the old man said, visibly relaxing a little and letting go of his tight grip on the blanket.

"Yeah, I'll also be cleaning your bathroom, if that's all right with you?"

"Oh sure, sure. No problem," the man answered. With that, Darwin flipped the switch again and continued to vacuum the floor.

"SO, WHERE ARE YOU FROM?" the man shouted over the wall of noise. Darwin turned it off to hear what the man was saying.

"Sorry, sir, what was that?"

"I said, where are you from?"

"I live just about a mile or so away. I go to the high school just up the street."

"Oh! I actually went there myself, back when they first built the place."

"Really, no kidding?" Darwin said, wondering how he'd never known that his school was that old. Darwin made his way over to the bathroom to start cleaning that first, so he could continue his conversation with the man without the vacuum interfering.

"Well, that's good that you're here," the man said, sitting up in bed and propping himself up on the pillows. "We need more kids like you. Most people are so busy with their lives nowadays that they forget about giving back," the man said as Darwin scrubbed out the bathroom sink. "Did you know that this facility is subsidized by the government?" The man went on, "That means we don't have to pay much to stay at this place, but because of that we also don't have enough funding to hire the resources to take care of the residents. So we always advertise for volunteers, but we hardly ever get any."

"My friend Mindy told me about this place," Darwin said as he cleaned the mirror with Windex, filling the tiny space with the antiseptic smell.

"Oh, Mindy!" the old man said with obvious pleasure. "She's a real peach, that one, isn't she? Always comes to see me when she's working." Darwin finished with the mirror and wiped his hands on one of the rags he'd brought in with him.

"Say, what are those spots all over your face?" the man asked, not unkindly, but even so, Darwin wasn't really quite sure how to respond. Most people just stared at his skin, but rarely asked so bluntly what was wrong with him.

"Oh, I was born with a skin condition where I don't have any pigmentation on certain parts of my body," Darwin answered, noticing that talking about it really never got any easier, no matter how many times he said the words out loud.

"And they're just round circles like that?" the man asked inquisitively, leaning forward to peer at Darwin more closely.

"Yep, they've been there since I was born," Darwin said, kneeling down and shaking a can of Ajax into the tub, before wetting the sponge and scrubbing in vigorous circles.

"Oh, well, I'm sorry to hear that. You know, I lost my hand back in the war, so I know how it feels to be different. It wasn't until I was around forty or so that I got a prosthetic." At this, Darwin stopped cleaning and turned around to face the man, who raised his right hand in the air. Darwin hadn't noticed it at all initially, but could now clearly see that the hand was prosthetic, as it resembled a shiny, flesh-colored plastic.

"I'm so sorry. What happened?" Darwin asked quietly, not wanting to upset the man.

"I was running through the fields with one of my fellow privates—we were running from the enemy on the other side, the North Vietnamese—and the next thing I knew they started firing at us. Two bullets were direct hits to my hand. It was so ripped up that by the time we got back to camp, I had to have it removed," the man finished, looking down at the prosthetic.

"What was it like, being in the war?" Darwin said, sitting back on his heels for a moment, the scrubbing forgotten.

"Well, I didn't go there by choice, I got drafted. At first it wasn't too bad, you had a place to sleep, people to spend time with, free food. But then as we soon started to realize that we weren't winning the war and that we really had no business being there, things got tough. Lost a lot of friends, spent nights listening to explosions off in the distance, wondering if I was going to make it to morning." The man's face clouded over, and his eyes grew misty, unfocused.

"That must have been awful," Darwin said quietly. "I'm so sorry."

"Well, that's all right," the man said, waving one hand in the air as if he were shooing away a pesky fly. "I'm still alive, and for the most part, I still have my health," he said, turning to look out the window. "Although I'm not too sure the world is in a much better place since then. People are still fighting one another, fighting for power and land. Some are fighting just purely out of hate. I wonder if they'll ever learn."

"Learn what?" Darwin asked curiously.

"Learn that we are all one, that unless we get along, work together, and help one another, we'll never be able to succeed as a society."

Darwin nodded wordlessly, as the man continued to look out the window at the bare trees off in the distance, swaying in the breeze. He seemed lost in his own thoughts. Darwin took this as his cue to finish the cleaning, turning back to the task at hand. When he was finished, Darwin gathered up his bucket of supplies and approached the bed.

"I'm sorry, but I don't think I ever got your name," Darwin said softly, as the man turned to face him again. Now that they were close-up, Darwin took in the man's wizened face, the leathery skin, but noticed that the man's blue eyes were still bright and full of life.

"Oh! It's Ted, a lot of people call me Teddy," he said with a smile, as if Darwin had somehow made his day, simply by asking.

"Well, nice to meet you, Ted."

"Very nice to meet you, as well," Ted said as he shook Darwin's hand.

Darwin made his way through all of the other units. Most of the residents either weren't home or were asleep on their bed. Darwin talked to a few others who were home and awake, but most seemed to suffer from dementia and had a hard time maintaining a conversation.

After Darwin finished, he made his way to the kitchen to find Tyler elbow-deep in a sink full of suds, finishing the last of a stack of dirty plates, scrubbing them clean while sweating profusely.

"Man! That was some hard work. They need things to move so fast around here, and it's so hot I feel like I can barely breathe," Tyler said, wiping his forehead with the back of one wet hand. "How was the cleaning?"

"It wasn't too bad. I talked to one guy who was pretty interesting," Darwin said as he sat down on a nearby chair close to the stove. "He said they don't get volunteers too often around here."

"I could see that, not a lot of people willing to just give away their time for free," Tyler said with a wry smile.

"Right, but how can we change that?"

"Change what?"

"Change the mentality of always just doing what you want to do?"

"Well, don't get me wrong, Darwin, this is nice and all, but I prefer my free time," Tyler said as he started cleaning the last plate.

"Of course, we all do. But don't you think the more people help others, they'll want to give back to someone else?"

"I mean, sure. But most people don't really care about anyone other than themselves."

Darwin stood there for a moment. He knew that Tyler was right, and that only so much could be done to change anyone else's views.

"Anyway," Tyler said, turning around to wipe his hands on a dishtowel, "I'm done now. Should we head out?"

"Yeah, sounds good," Darwin said, moving toward the door. "I'm scheduled to come back next week. Do you want to do the same?"

"I guess . . . but can I not do the kitchen duty next time? It's so dang hot in here," Tyler said with a smirk.

"Sure, no problem. But then again, it's not really up to me." Darwin chuckled.

CHAPTER 13

An enormous flash of light shined across Darwin's closed eyelids. He opened them to find himself standing in a jungle of trees with multicolored leaves, the same jungle he'd witnessed before, and instantly he realized he was in another one of his visions. He recognized the tree in front of him, its bright blue trunk and spiral branches. The rest of the trees around him had the same brightly colored leaves as before, and were blowing slightly in the cool breeze.

Darwin started walking quickly, unsure of where to go other than in the direction he'd gone last time. Suddenly, the siren-like noise went off again in the distance, and Darwin began jogging in the direction of the noise, as he didn't want this vision to end before finding out what it was. He pushed and shoved his way through the twisted branches hanging low to the ground, the colored leaves rustling with every step he took.

The sirens went off again, this time much louder, as Darwin was nearer to their apparent location. Darwin picked up his speed. He finally passed through the trees and could see the large mountains he had been seeing in his visions since he was a kid. Again, the sirens went off, this time to his right.

Darwin quickly turned to his right and started running again. Suddenly, he approached the crevasse he had come upon before. He stopped quickly and slowly peered over. The weird clicking noises that he had heard coming from the bottom of the crevasse in his previous vision were no longer occurring. He peered over a little farther, cautiously, not sure what to expect below. He realized the crevasse was only about six feet deep. This was farther than he had seen before. Not sure of what to do next, he looked around him to see if the sirens would potentially go off again.

Just then, the clicking noises started, different pitches of clicks going back and forth. The noises were coming from inside the crevasse, but nothing could be seen on the crevasse floor. Darwin knew he needed to make his way down to the bottom. It wasn't deep enough down there, but doing a straight jump would likely hurt.

He sat down and started pushing his legs over the side, slowly pushing himself down along the side of the wall, digging his hands into the soft soil. Darwin sunk his foot into the side of the crevasse wall while holding onto the top with his arms. Plop! Success on the first try, his foot fitting into the wall nicely. He moved down to put his other foot into the wall a little lower. As he jammed his foot in, he noticed that the texture was much softer, almost like mud. His foot fell out and Darwin tumbled, falling back-first into the crevasse.

"Ahh!" Darwin said, holding onto the bottom of his back. "Oww," Darwin said to himself.

He looked around, along the floor of the crevasse. There was nothing to see except the cold wet floor he was lying on. He noticed a dark area up ahead that almost resembled a cave. He slowly got to his feet and started making his way toward it. As he neared it, he realized it wasn't a cave, but rather a part of the wall from the crevasse that was missing and was creating what resembled an awning that provided shade over the floor.

Darwin couldn't tell how deep-backed it was, as it was impossible to see in the pitch darkness. He slowly made his way into the shaded area, his footsteps making loud noises with every step through the wet, muddy floor. As he made his way farther under the sheltered area, Darwin started hearing the clicking noises again, moving rapidly and much louder than they had before, when he was peering over the top of the crevasse.

He backed away quickly to where he could see, again looking into the shaded area. He squinted his eyes, trying to see what was possibly creating that clicking noise. The clicking started slowing down,

still moving in a particular pattern and pitch. Darwin was frightened,
but had to find out what this noise was. He slowly started making his
way into the shaded area again, until he was completely covered by
darkness and couldn't see anything in front of him.

The clicking noises began to sound off rapidly in chaotic pitch-
es, this time with no semblance of a pattern whatsoever. The noises
were getting louder, and they were approaching. Louder, louder,
faster, faster, clicking on both sides of him now; he could hear it
piercing through his ears. The piercing was so loud that Darwin
was forced to plug his ears with his fingers, when suddenly another
large flash of light shined over Darwin's eyes, and he opened them
to find himself in his room.

Darwin was breathing quickly, his forehead and back coated in
sweat. His back was still hurting like it had in the vision, almost as
if he had fallen in real life. When he scanned his surroundings, he
realized he may have actually fallen, as he was lying on the floor,
right next to his bed. He took some deep breaths slowly, to calm
himself down. "Breathe, breathe," he said to himself. He looked
over at the clock and realized he was late for school. He was surprised his mother hadn't called for him yet.

"Darwin! Come on, you're going to be late for school!" he
heard his mom yell.

There it was; Darwin half-smiled to himself.

"Coming, Mom!" Darwin shouted back. He packed his stuff,
got dressed quickly while wincing from the pain in his back, and
went off to school, his mom handing him a blueberry muffin for
breakfast on their way out.

Two weeks had passed since Tyler and Darwin had started volunteering at the nursing home. Darwin had since been twice again
by himself, once again cleaning the rooms as he did the first time,
and once working in the kitchen. He had spent more time with Ted,
and even took him for a walk in his wheelchair around the grounds
of the home. The residents had started recognizing him, not just because of his skin, but rather because of the fact that he always
seemed so willing and thrilled to help out with whatever the residents needed: food, clothing, or just helping to push their wheel-

chairs to the dining area. They were becoming fond of Darwin, and he was becoming fond of them.

Over the past two weeks, Darwin and Tyler had been brainstorming ways they could get their fellow students involved with volunteering. They had put together flyers calling for volunteers for the nursing home, but so far no one had responded. Darwin also found a couple of other organizations that would be great volunteer opportunities: one was a food bank that provided food for the homeless, and the other was a program that helped children learn to read. Darwin had sent out an email to some of the school staff to see if they would be willing to circulate these opportunities around to the student body. They did, but again, no responses.

"What if we have Mindy appeal to them?" Darwin asked suddenly. Tyler was sitting next to him in Health class.

"Huh?" Tyler looked over, clearly not paying attention.

"The other kids. Think about it—she's nice, caring, and a lot of people here like her. They'd probably listen to her. And, after all, if she's doing it, then everyone else will think it's cool, too."

"Listen, Darwin," Tyler began, "I think it's great that you have this passion to volunteer, really I do. But shouldn't you be focusing on stuff like school and work—your future?"

"Why can't I do both? I don't even work anyway, not yet at least."

Tyler shrugged, clearly not knowing what to say. "I mean, hey, if it's that important to you, I'm happy to help out, just don't get too discouraged when you don't get the best responses from people."

Darwin looked up at the clock and realized class was almost out. He quickly started packing up his bags. "Okay, so I think Mindy's locker is right around the corner. Once the period ends, let's go over there and wait for her," Darwin said.

"You *think* her locker is over there?" Tyler said, smiling.

"Okay, okay. I *know* her locker is over there," Darwin said. The bell rang and he and Tyler made their way out into the hallway.

Students were frantically running by one another, trying to get to their next classes, some taking their time and chitchatting with one another. Darwin could see Billy James off in the distance, but thankfully he was walking in the other direction. Just then, Mindy came around the corner and started making her way toward her locker. Darwin stood there for a second, nervous about what to say or how to phrase it. Tyler looked up at Darwin, waiting for him to move.

"So, are you going to go over there and talk to her?" he asked.

"Yeah . . . yeah, just give me a second," Darwin said, taking a deep breath.

Tyler chuckled, as if he thought it was cute, seeing Darwin muster up the courage to talk to Mindy. Darwin made his way over to Mindy's locker, but not before almost running into someone, as he wasn't paying attention to where he was going.

"Watch it!" a boy shouted as he passed by Darwin, shaking his head. This noise got Mindy's attention, and she looked over.

"Oh . . . uh, hey Mindy!" Darwin waved nervously as he made his way toward her.

"Oh, hi Darwin!" Mindy replied with a smile. Darwin loved Mindy's smile. *It could brighten up anybody's day*, he thought. "So, how's volunteering been going? I thought I'd run into you by now, but no such luck! What days do you guys usually go?"

"I've been going on Tuesdays and Thursdays. Tyler comes on Thursdays, too."

"Okay, well, what about if I go on Tuesdays? That way, you always have someone to go with," Mindy said, smiling. "You know, since I got you into this in the first place? It's probably the least I can do."

Darwin could feel his face getting red from blushing. "Oh . . . well . . . g-great!" Darwin said, struggling to find the right words to say back. "So, next Tuesday, then, d-do you want to meet around here after school and then we c-can go together?" Darwin was embarrassed that he was stuttering slightly, but Mindy just chuckled back, not at him but with him.

"Yeah, that sounds good," she said, tossing her long red hair from one shoulder as if it annoyed her.

"I've been trying to get other people interested in volunteering, too," Darwin said quickly, before he lost his nerve. "But it's not going too well." He took a deep breath before continuing, "I was thinking that maybe if *you* got the word out, people might be more receptive?"

"Why me?" Mindy said with a slow smile.

"Well . . ." Darwin's face was now beet red, but he knew that be couldn't stop now. Not if he wanted to have any chance at all with this girl. "You're smart. And nice. And people really like you. I think they'd listen to what you have to say."

"People like you, too, Darwin," Mindy said after a long pause. For a moment, they just stared at each other. Darwin forced himself to maintain eye contact, though all he wanted was to look away, anywhere safe.

"Maybe," he finally conceded. "But you know I'm . . ." His words trailed off helplessly.

"You're what?" Mindy asked, raising one eyebrow, her lips cocked in a half-smile.

"Different," he breathed, shrugging his shoulders.

"I think we all feel that way inside," Mindy said knowingly, shifting her weight from one foot to the other and readjusting the load of books in her arm. "But if it means that much to you, I'll try to talk to some people, get them interested."

Darwin smiled back, a little sheepishly this time, unable to keep his eyes off her. "That would be great. I better get to class," he said reluctantly. "But I'll see you later then?"

"Later," Mindy said as she walked off, waving goodbye to Darwin and smiling broadly. But then again, she was usually smiling, wasn't she? Darwin, on the other hand, was so uncharacteristically happy it was impossible to hide his beaming face from Tyler, who was still standing off on the side, watching him.

"Well, that seemed like a good talk," Tyler said with a grin.

"Yeah." Darwin chuckled a little. "She said she would come on Tuesdays, so that I don't have to go alone." Darwin's eyes were positively glowing.

"Okay, okay, easy there, chief. Don't get all weird on me now."

"I know, I know. It's just that no girl has ever really wanted to do something with me before, I mean outside of studying. It's just not something I'm used to."

"Yeah, I'm happy for you, man. You deserve it."

"Thanks," Darwin said, looking up at Tyler. He took a deep

breath before continuing, hoping Tyler wouldn't think he was a sap for what he was about to say. "You know, I'm sure you've noticed, but you were too nice to say anything, but most kids won't even come near me. They think they'll catch some sort of disease. But you don't seem to care about any of that at all. You're not scared of me. And I know it's hard for kids our age to go against something that is a popular idea, even if it is mean."

"I'm just treating you like I would any other person," Tyler said, while patting Darwin on the shoulder. "It's not a big deal, you know?"

But Darwin knew that it was. And he knew that if he and Tyler had somehow become friends, he could make other friends, too, if he wanted. Like Mindy.

CHAPTER 14

Tuesday rolled around before Darwin knew it, and that afternoon, after the last bell rang, he and Mindy met up by her locker to make their way toward the nursing home. Initially, Tyler was going to come, too, but he ended up not feeling so well after lunch and went home early from school. Darwin suspected that Tyler was feeling fine—he just wanted to give Darwin the opportunity to be alone with Mindy, something that made Darwin both elated and more nervous than he'd ever been in his short life.

Darwin and Mindy walked together and talked about school, college plans, and what they wanted to do when they grew up. Darwin was fairly nervous the whole time, but managed not to stutter while talking to her like he usually did. He learned that Mindy's first choice was to go to Brown University and study economics or public administration.

"So, what do you want to do after graduation?" Mindy asked. Darwin thought about it, and realized he actually wasn't sure of what he wanted to do with his life. He knew he wanted to go to college, but there were so many areas of study that he was interested in, it was hard to choose just one to focus on for the rest of his life.

"Well, ideally I'd like to go to Princeton, but I don't know if that's realistic," Darwin replied.

"Oh yeah? What makes you think Princeton is unrealistic?" Mindy asked, looking over at him with one eyebrow raised.

"Well, it's a hard school to get into, and on top of that it'll be a school that will require interviews most likely, and I know as soon as they see me, they'll check me off the list."

"All schools have interviews these days, Darwin," Mindy replied with a laugh. "But why do you say that?"

Darwin hesitated for a moment to see if Mindy was joking. "Are you serious? I mean, just look at me."

"They can't discriminate, Darwin. Besides, there is nothing wrong with the way you look. If you have the brains to get in, they'll let you in." Mindy shrugged, as if it was as simple as that.

Darwin could feel his cheeks getting red again. It was the first time anybody other than his family had told him that there was nothing wrong with the way he looked. So many nights Darwin would stare at himself in the mirror, looking at his spotted skin, and wishing somehow it would magically go away. Looking at his smaller-than-average head, wishing he was born with a normal-sized skull.

"Thanks, that's nice of you. I guess I could be a little more optimistic," Darwin said, trying to hold back his nerves. Mindy just smiled warmly and kept walking.

The two arrived at the nursing home around 3:30. The rooms had just been cleaned, so Darwin was off the hook on that front, but they were in desperate need of help in the kitchen, as their main chef was out sick and one of the dishwashers had walked out on the job the day before.

When they were asked to help prepare dinner for the residents, Mindy and Darwin happily accepted. They chopped carrots, broccoli, celery, potatoes, and even chicken into small pieces. Everything had to be cut and prepared properly, so that the residents could both chew and consume the food comfortably.

As he worked, Darwin was pleased to look over from time to time and see Mindy enjoying herself. It was hard work, especially at the pace they were expected to work, but Mindy never seemed to be bothered by it and kept a smile on her face the whole time. Somehow, the job went faster with her there.

After the dinner was prepared and served, they stayed an extra hour and a half to help clean up, given they were short on a dishwasher. Darwin and Mindy worked together in washing and drying the dishes; Darwin washing and Mindy drying. The volunteer coordinator, a short, silver-haired woman in her sixties, was so thankful and appreciative of all their work that she gave them a big box of cookies to take home.

"Who knows where we would have been tonight, without all of your help!" she said, beaming at both of them. "The more volunteers the better!"

"Of course, no problem, ma'am," Mindy replied.

"Aw . . . and aren't you just so cute," the woman said, resting her hand on Mindy's shoulder. "So, are you two a couple?"

Darwin nearly choked on his own saliva.

"Oh, ha-ha. Umm, not like that, but we're good friends," Mindy replied, clearly looking uncomfortable as well.

"Yeah . . . y-yeah. Just friends," Darwin added hastily.

"Oh! Sorry, didn't mean to make things awkward. Just thought since you two worked so well together that you might be an item," the woman said, making the situation even more awkward. "He's a really good guy, though, always willing to help out and never complains," she added.

Mindy, smiling, looked over at Darwin, seeing how uncomfortable he was. "Yeah, he really is."

Darwin looked over at Mindy to see her smiling at him intently. He half-smiled back, not sure what to say. He laughed a little, nervously, before the woman came to the rescue and changed the subject.

"So, Darwin, I hope to see you back here soon."

"O-of course. I'll be coming by Thursday, at my usual time."

"Wonderful. You two get home safe, now. I'll see you all next time."

Darwin and Mindy walked out of the nursing home and made their way back to the school, since Mindy's car was parked there. Darwin's mother was going to be picking him up from the nursing home, but he figured he would walk Mindy back to her car first, since it was dark out now.

They didn't speak much on the way back to school. The volunteer coordinator's comment had created a heaviness between them, an awkwardness. Darwin kicked the piles of snow lining the sidewalk and thought about bringing it up, making a joke out of it, but didn't know whether it would upset her.

"So, did you have fun tonight?" he asked as they arrived back in the student parking lot, which was empty except for Mindy's lone red car, the paint shining cherry red under the streetlights.

"Yeah, it was actually a lot of fun, it always feels nice to give back."

"Oh yeah?"

"Yeah, I mean I have grandparents who are at that stage in their lives where they need a lot of help. They're far away, though, so the least I can do is pay it forward," Mindy said, a bashful expression on her face, as if her kindness was slightly embarrassing in some way.

Mindy and Darwin nodded at each other, trying to figure out what else to say now that they had reached her car.

"All right, well, thanks for going with me. Maybe we can do it again sometime—if you want," Darwin said.

"I'd like that," Mindy replied, looking at Darwin with that beautiful smile that always made him smile back helplessly. She then opened her car door and got inside, flipping on the headlights and starting the engine. Sure, there'd been a bit of awkwardness at the end of the night, but it had been the first time in his life when he felt his appearance really didn't matter to a girl. She'd treated him just like anyone else. It was a new feeling for Darwin, one he wanted more of.

As she drove away, she waved at him, still smiling brightly. After her car drove out of the lot and disappeared, Darwin stood in the parking lot, which was suddenly quiet and still, realizing that even though she'd barely driven out of sight, he already missed her.

CHAPTER 15

A few months later, spring arrived in Crimson, and after all of the snow from the winter, the leaves had started covering the bare branches of the trees again. Flowers were blooming, the days were getting longer, and every now and then you could smell the smoky scent of roasting meat from the neighbors' BBQs. Darwin always enjoyed spring, and not just because of the way the plants came back into full bloom, covering the bare branches of the trees with tender green leaves, but rather that the weather was exactly how he preferred it, not too hot—as it would get in summer months—and yet not too cold.

Darwin was continuing to volunteer on a consistent basis at the nursing home, with both Mindy and Tyler. Mindy had also gotten many students involved in volunteering at Sun Parks, and she'd begun volunteering at a local shelter, preparing and serving food to the homeless. She got Darwin involved in that as well, and both of them started volunteering there once a week, sometimes working the same shifts, companionably side by side.

In addition, Darwin had also received his driver's permit at the end of the winter, once the snow thawed. His mom had finally come around to teaching him how to drive, and it would only be four more months before he could take the driving test. Every day, whenever his mom needed to run an errand, Darwin asked to drive her there. The more he drove, the better he got at it, and the more his mother gained confidence in him.

Darwin and Tyler began spending more and more time together, both at school and outside of it. After school, Darwin and Tyler would go downtown and hang out at the local ice cream shop, called Ginger. It was a popular place to hang out for most students after school, especially now that the weather was getting warmer and the thought of ice cream didn't make everyone shiver.

After a long day at school, which featured Darwin getting spit wads spat at him by Billy James in their Social Studies class, Tyler suggested they grab some ice cream at Ginger. Of course, Darwin agreed, and they made the short walk to their small downtown area. Ginger had been around for some time, but Darwin had never really gone there until this past year, as it would have been embarrassing to go by himself.

Darwin and Tyler entered the shop, which was relatively slow given the fact that it was right after school. The place didn't usually get busy until around 4:00 or 4:30.

"Can I get a strawberry shake, please?" Darwin asked the cashier. "What do you want?" he asked Tyler.

"Hmmm, I think I'm just going to go with a good old-fashioned root beer float," Tyler replied. Darwin reached for his wallet to pay for both of them.

"Oh man, no worries. I've got this. It's been a long day for you with that jerk, Billy James, harassing you."

Tyler jumped in front of Darwin with his credit card in hand and gave it quickly to the cashier, before Darwin could try and swat it away.

"Thanks man, I owe you one," Darwin said.

"You don't owe me anything. Just enjoy your shake and get your mind off things."

The two went to the upstairs area, to find some seating. Luckily for them, the whole upstairs was practically empty. The upstairs seating was usually packed, and one would often have to wait at the stairwell until someone left in order to find a seat.

As Darwin reached the top of the stairs, he quickly became out of breath and started feeling a little dizzy. This was unusual, as Darwin walked up stairs to his room every day, which were more steps than these, and he never felt winded by any means. He shrugged it off and made sure Tyler, who was walking up in front of him, didn't notice. As they sat down in the chair, Darwin began to feel a little better. He was no longer dizzy, but he did feel quite exhausted.

"How's your shake?" Tyler asked after taking a spoonful of his root beer float.

"Oh . . . fine. Thanks again for getting it for me."

"No problem. So hey, this weekend, do you want to go out and shoot some hoops? There's apparently this new indoor spot that just opened up across town, supposed to be pretty cool."

"Yeah, sure, that sounds like fun," Darwin said, taking another swig of his shake. "But I'm supposed to help my dad build some tables and other furniture this weekend or something."

"Oh really? What kind of furniture?"

"I don't know, I don't even think *he* knows. He says I need to learn how to be more of a 'man' and not a little kid anymore, that my mom has been babying me my whole life and I need to be more disciplined since I'm turning seventeen in a few months."

"Man, why is your dad so strict?"

"I don't know, he's just always been that way. I have my theories, but I don't know if they're true."

"What kind of theories?"

Darwin hesitated for a second, but then figured he and Tyler were close enough now that he could share this kind of stuff with him. He told Tyler all about his mother having complications at his birth, and as result never being able to have more children. He also mentioned how it had been his dad's dream to have a large family, since he grew up as one of six kids.

"You think your dad is strict because of that?" Tyler asked in a sarcastic tone, clearly unconvinced by Darwin's explanation.

"Well, I don't know. I just feel like he resents me for it. Like it was my fault my mom couldn't have kids anymore."

"No way, dude, it has to be something else," Tyler said emphatically.

Darwin shrugged, it was the only reason he could really come up with as to why his dad was always so strict and so angry with him. That, and the fact that his dad had been raised by a strict father himself.

146

"Oh no . . . don't look," Tyler said, a note of disgust coloring his voice.

Darwin turned his head around to see Billy James walk into the shop, followed by his posse of cretins. Darwin turned around with an annoyed look on his face; the last person he wanted to see right then was Billy. "Just please, don't say anything," Darwin said to Tyler, imploring him.

But before Tyler could respond, Billy caught sight of them above, shouting out, "Oh! Is that the freak I see over there? Kinda easy to tell with all those giant warts on the back of his head." Billy's crew all laughed out loud. "You know, I wonder if he even eats real human food like the rest of us." Billy started walking up the stairs with the rest of his crew following behind him, laughing. Darwin just sat there, not turning around, looking down at his shake. He was used to this type of bullying, but it was slowly wearing on him. "I knew it," Billy said, standing directly behind Darwin. "I can spot a diseased freak from a mile away."

"Cut it out, man," Tyler said to Billy.

"Oh, you've got something to say again, I see. Always sticking up for your little freak friend. Why don't you let him defend himself, huh?"

"Five guys surrounding you, making fun of a guy much smaller than you, very brave of you. You must feel great about yourself," Tyler said as he started to clap slowly in Billy's direction. Darwin tried to get Tyler's attention to tell him stop, but he kept clapping.

Billy let out a high-pitched laugh. "Oh, we've got a comedian over here, guys. You won't be laughing when I'm done with you, clown. No teachers around to help you now."

"You think I'm afraid of some insecure prick who tries to prove his strength through bullying?" Tyler sneered.

"Well, why don't you get up, then," Billy said through gritted teeth, about a foot away from Tyler's face now.

"Nah, I'm good. You're not worth it."

"Oh! The dude claims he's not scared, but is too scared to do anything about it."

Billy's crew started roaring with laughter. "I mean, what do you expect, he hangs out with the freak, no threat there!" one of Billy's friends shouted over the laughter.

Darwin could see the anger building on Tyler's face. The last thing he wanted was for Tyler to give in to their bullying. Darwin started becoming short of breath again, as if he had just run up the stairs. His hands and arms started to ache, and his chest became painful. *Potassium!* Darwin thought quickly. He needed his potassium. He'd felt this feeling before the last time he'd suffered from low potassium levels and eventually collapsed, when he was a kid.

"I don't waste my time on guys like you. Now, why don't you girls run along and go get something to eat with your daddy's money," Tyler said, waving his hand away from Billy, who suddenly slammed his hands on the table.

"Nobody tells me what to do, bitch!" Billy shouted loudly, to the point where other guests were beginning to get alarmed.

"What's going on up there?" the cashier shouted from underneath.

"Well, maybe people *ought* to start telling you what to do," Tyler said, smiling back at Billy. "Then maybe one day you'll amount to more than just being a parasite to society."

Darwin's breathing became more and more labored, sticking in his chest like glue. He needed his potassium. He started rummaging through his bag to take out his pills. Billy looked over to see what Darwin was looking for.

"And what is this?" Billy said, now distracted by Darwin's pills. "Is this what you take to make those ugly spots go away?" Billy ripped the bottle right out of Darwin's hand. "Well, I'll tell you this much, buddy, it doesn't look like it's working."

"No . . . no, please, I-I need those," Darwin said quietly, gasping for air.

"What . . . what? I can't hear you through your squeaky voice, freak!" Billy said, bringing his face close to Darwin's. Darwin started to slowly make his way to the ground, to maintain his balance. The room spun dizzily before his eyes, and Darwin tried putting his hands to the ground to compose himself, but his palms were sweating profusely. He could hear Billy and his friends laughing at the top of their lungs. The laughter then suddenly turned to shouting and the scuffling of footsteps. Darwin looked up to see that Tyler had tackled Billy to the floor, and was punching him over and over. Billy's friends then started pulling Tyler off him while kicking and punching him at the same time.

"No . . . no, stop," Darwin said weakly, but he couldn't be heard over the commotion taking place in front of him.

"Hey, hey! What the hell is going on up here?" the cashier shouted, running up the stairs. Darwin was slowly fading out of consciousness as his breathing began to slow. The room was spinning, moving like a Nickelodeon movie, slide after slide in slow motion. Darwin could feel his breathing starting to slow down even further and the sound of the shouting drifting away as he slid into blackness.

CHAPTER 16

Darwin was lying on the sand. He could hear waves crashing off in the distance and the sound of the wind blowing through his ears. He looked up to see where he was, but didn't recognize anything. He was obviously at some sort of ocean, but the terrain looked much different than what he had seen of oceans on TV. Darwin had never been to the beach before; in fact, he had barely even traveled outside of Crimson.

The sand was a dark red color, and blue crystal-like rocks were scattered across the deep red sand. He had never seen anything like it before in his life, and it was remarkable. He looked up at the sky and despite the fact that it was light out, he could see the darkness of space and the stars overhead. It was as if the sun was shining on the land, but there was no atmosphere between space and the earth. Darwin was mesmerized by the beautiful sky, and he had never seen so many stars before in his life; some that were so bright, he had to squint when he looked directly at them.

Darwin looked around as he suddenly heard a noise coming from behind him. Way off in the distance he could see a shadowy figure roaming on the sand. The figure was dark, and was moving slowly in Darwin's direction. As it got closer, Darwin could make out the figure, and realized it was indeed walking on what appeared to be two legs. Darwin stood up quickly, frightened by what he was seeing. As the figure drew closer, Darwin could make out arms, and if he looked hard enough, it appeared to have eyes as well. Darwin thought about running, but something was telling him to stay put, that this thing he was seeing wasn't going to harm him, and that there was a purpose for why it was coming toward him.

As the figure approached closer, walking along the red sand, Darwin couldn't believe his eyes. His mouth dropped at the sight of it, and he didn't even know how to react. It was now just about twenty feet from him when it suddenly stopped and stared back at Darwin. The person had green eyes, long brown hair, but most importantly, its skin was spotted all over in circles, just like Darwin's, and on top of that, it had an unusually small head in proportion to the rest of its body. Darwin couldn't tell exactly if this individual was male or female, but based on the long hair and shape of the body, he assumed it was female. She was clothed in what appeared to be a single sheet covering her body all the way down to her knees.

She made direct eye contact with Darwin. They both stood there and stared at each other, for what seemed like a good fifteen seconds. Darwin's heart was beating rapidly. Where was he and who was this person, he thought. Was he in danger? Should he speak? A number of thoughts raced through Darwin's mind, and all he could do was simply stand there and stare back at this . . . whatever she was.

The girl started walking closer after making eye contact. Darwin initially flinched, almost instinctually to protect himself. The girl froze, Darwin's sudden movement startling her. They both continued to look at each other, and again she started making her way closer to Darwin. She was about ten feet away now, and Darwin could clearly see her deep green eyes and even the wrinkles on her face. He was breathing heavily now, incredibly nervous and unsure of what to anticipate. She stopped directly in front of Darwin. He was mesmerized by what he was seeing; she looked just like him, something he had never seen before. He knew that he should be afraid, but for whatever reason there was something incredibly tranquil about this interaction, as if Darwin had nothing to fear. It was almost like seeing a long-lost friend.

The two just stared at each other. Darwin could see that her eyes had started to water, what for he didn't know, but the thought of seeing her emotional made him a bit emotional, too. Darwin couldn't just stand there any longer without saying anything; he knew he had to speak up.

"Who are you?" he asked. The girl didn't respond; instead, she just looked at him with a confused look on her face, her eyes still watery. "Can, can you hear me?"

Still nothing from the girl.

"My name's Darwin . . . do you, do you have a name?"

He wasn't getting anything out of this girl. He was quite certain that perhaps she couldn't understand him. He reached out his hand to shake hers, to see if perhaps body language would work. She looked down at Darwin's hand and back up again at him with the same confused look. "Where are we, what is this place?" The girl looked behind her quickly, as if something from afar had distracted her, but Darwin didn't hear anything. She looked back at him, still not making any noise. She lifted up her hand the same way Darwin had done to shake hers. Darwin looked down at her hand and hesitated for a moment, before extending his hand forward and clasping it in hers.

Darwin felt a surge of energy go through his body; it was a connection he had never felt before in his life. He wasn't sure, but it almost felt like his body was rising up into the sky, a feeling so relaxed and calm he couldn't quite describe it. He looked back at the girl, who was now closing her eyes. She started to squeeze his hand even tighter, and then she spoke.

She started making clicking noises in different notes and tones, just like the clicking noises Darwin had heard in the crevasse in his previous visions but could never find the source of. Darwin's eyes grew big and wide. Could it have been her that he was hearing in his dreams this whole time? Was he finally connecting with the person he'd been seeking? Was it real? Another vision? Or something else? The girl continued to make clicking noises while Darwin stared in disbelief back at her. She then began to loosen her grip, and he could feel himself coming back down to the ground. She opened her eyes, looking back at Darwin, and raised her hand to touch his cheek. The warmth of her hand was so soothing and relaxing that Darwin could feel his eyelids getting heavier, like he was about to fall asleep. She made a few more clicking sounds as Darwin slowly faded out of consciousness. He didn't want to sleep right now; he wanted to stay in this place for as long as he could and continue to have this feeling, this connection. But he couldn't fight it; the clicking noise slowly started to fade, and Darwin was out.

Darwin opened his eyes to find himself sitting in a hospital bed. He looked over to his right and saw his mom with her eyes closed, praying with her hands clenched together. He looked around the room, not quite sure how he got there. He looked at his arm to see he had been given an IV, and there was also a heart monitor attached to his chest.

Darwin tried to think hard about how he could have ended up in this predicament. Then, it hit him, all rushing back in a wave of images. Losing consciousness at Ginger. Tyler punching Billy James. *Tyler!* he thought, his eyes now opening wide. The last thing he saw was Billy's crew trying to break up the fight, all ganging up on Tyler, throwing punches and kicking him as he lay on the ground.

"Oh my God! Baby, are you okay?" his mother whispered, bending over him as she realized Darwin was awake. Darwin took a second to respond, his throat dry, mouth thick with spit.

"Yeah . . . yeah, I'm fine, Mom," Darwin said, breathing slowly. "What happened? How long have I been out?"

"You've only been out for a few hours, it's around midnight now," she said as she stroked Darwin's head. "You passed out. The doctor said it was from the lack of potassium. Tyler called an ambulance when he saw that you were unconscious."

"What happened to Tyler, where is he?" Darwin asked frantically, sitting up in bed. His mother gently placed a hand on his shoulder and took a deep breath before responding.

"Well, he's at the police station right now."

Darwin hesitated. "But . . . but why? He didn't do anything, it was Billy James causing all of the trouble."

"Well, that may be, but what Tyler did also wasn't good either, Darwin. You can't let your emotions get the best of you."

"Is he okay? Was he hurt? The last thing I remember was the guys jumping on him to get him off Billy."

His mom hesitated, a concerned look on her face, which made Darwin that much more worried. "He's fine, he'll be okay," she said, looking at Darwin. "Although, because of the incident, he's going to be in some legal trouble."

"What do you mean?" Darwin asked uncomprehendingly.

"Well, he hurt that boy Billy pretty bad. In fact, Billy's here in the hospital, too, recovering."

"Well, Billy initiated the whole thing," Darwin said defiantly. "Tyler was provoked. Do they know that?"

"I'm sure they know that, dear, but the fact of the matter is that he put a kid in the hospital."

"So, what happens now?"

"Well, he was arrested and is currently at the police station being processed. We're not quite sure what's going to happen, but I don't know if the school is going to take this lightly."

"What does the school have to do with it? It didn't happen on school grounds or even during school hours."

"I know, dear, but . . . it's a little more complicated than that."

Darwin sat there in frustration, not knowing what to say. He knew it wasn't Tyler's fault. Billy had a knack for provoking people, and this time he got what was coming to him. The only good thing about this situation was the embarrassment Billy would have to face by admitting that someone had wiped the floor with him, something that had never happened in Billy's life.

Just then, his dad walked in the door with an angry look on his face. Darwin had almost forgotten that his dad wasn't there when he'd woken up. "Why the hell weren't you taking your potassium? You know that this kind of thing happens when you don't!" he barked, throwing his hands in the air in exasperation.

"It wasn't my fault, Dad. I was doing fine the whole day, and then suddenly lost a lot of energy when we got to Ginger. And when I tried to take more, Billy James took the pills away from me."

"Pshh," his father scoffed.

"Dave, give him a break, he's been through a lot today," his mother said imploringly, her blue eyes watery and pleading.

"Oh, he's been through a lot?" his dad said in a mocking tone of voice. "How do you think I feel, sitting in the middle of a meeting, slammed at work all day, and I get a call saying I need to come to the hospital right away, all because my son couldn't remember to take his pills? Do you not realize, Darwin, that something like this can kill you?"

Darwin could feel his face burning and knew his cheeks must be bright red. He was angrier than he'd been in a long time. He usually bit his tongue in moments like this, but he couldn't hold back any longer.

"Shut up! Just shut up!" he shouted. His father turned around quickly to look at Darwin, almost like he wasn't sure he'd heard him correctly. "I'm sick of it! You're always blaming me and Mom for all of your problems. When are you going to finally take responsibility for something in your life?"

"Responsibility? You don't know a thing about responsibility," his dad said through gritted teeth. "I take care of this family, provide for you both, I raised you . . ."

"You didn't raise me, Mom did!" Darwin interrupted. "The only thing you've ever done is complain about everything. Mom does everything she can to make you happy, and this is how you repay her? It's bullshit!"

"You watch your mouth, young man!" his father thundered, pointing his finger at Darwin.

"No! I'm tired of it. It wasn't my or Mom's fault that she wasn't able to have more children, and it wasn't our fault that you had a rough childhood. Be grateful for what you have, and stop blaming us for everything that goes wrong."

His dad stood there looking back at Darwin, breathing heavily, not saying a word. In an attempt to compose himself, Darwin watched as his father rolled up his sleeves methodically, one sleeve at a time, and then walked out of the room. His mother was silent, her eyes wide and frightened. After his outburst, Darwin wasn't sure if she was more scared of him or of his father.

"Sorry that you had to see that, Mom. I just . . . I just couldn't take it anymore," he said, aware now that his hands were shaking.

"I know, honey, I understand. I think it was very brave what you said. You still have to respect your father, though, and you can't use language like that."

"Well, sometimes he needs to be put in his place," Darwin said.

"Just remember that he's your father and he loves you very

much," his mother said. Darwin rolled his eyes. *How many times have I heard that before?* he thought. "Anyway, the doctor has been giving you potassium through your IV. He expects that you'll be out by tomorrow morning, but he wanted to make sure you woke up first, which you have now," she added, smiling.

Darwin spent the night in the hospital, his mother sleeping in a chair by the side of the bed the entire time. He didn't know where his dad had gone or if he was planning on coming back in the morning. Around 2 a.m., the doctor entered the room to speak to Darwin's mother. The sound of the doctor's voice penetrated his dreams, which were chaotic and hazy, waking him from slumber. Instinctively, though, he kept his eyes tightly closed.

"How's he doing?" the doctor asked in a low voice.

"Okay, I guess. He's just been sleeping for the past hour or so," he heard his mother reply nervously.

"Listen, I don't know how much longer we can keep this quiet, the visions, his thoughts, what happened tonight with Tyler, all of it, he's going to find out sooner or later." Darwin's ears perked up but he remained motionless, so they wouldn't suspect that he was awake.

"Not yet, he's not ready," his mother whispered.

"Well, it's not really up to us, is it? I've got to run it by Greer."

"Let's talk about this outside," his mother said, and Darwin heard the sound of the chair scraping against the linoleum as she got to her feet. "I don't want to wake him."

Darwin rolled over as soon as he heard the door close. What could they possibly be talking about? Find out what? Who was Greer?

Darwin lay there in thought for a few minutes when he heard the doorknob turn slightly, and he quickly turned around, to the direction he was in before they had left the room. He closed his eyes quickly and remained that way until he fell back asleep again.

The doctor observed Darwin the following morning, clearing him for release around nine. Darwin knew that he was going to be late, but the second he mentioned going to school to his mom, she flatly refused, stating that he needed to take the day off. It was Friday after all, and he would have the whole weekend to recover.

When his mom pulled into the driveway, Darwin quickly got

out of the car and made his way into the house, to the phone. The only thing he could think about was that he needed to see if Tyler was okay and find out how he was doing. "Easy, dear! You literally just got out of the hospital. Let's just take it easy today, all right?" his mother said cautiously.

"Sure thing, Mom," Darwin said, not really paying attention as he began dialing Tyler's number. The phone rang once, twice, and then a third time before going to voicemail. Darwin thought he must be at school. "Mom!" Darwin shouted across the room. "Are you sure I can't go to school today?"

"No! You just got out of the hospital, besides, it's too late in the day now. Don't worry, I've notified your teachers, they'll give you what you missed on Monday."

Darwin sighed. He wanted to know what had happened last night. If Tyler had seriously hurt Billy, he could be in a lot of trouble with the law, even if he was a minor. Darwin went up to his room to rest for a bit and read some of his textbooks, since he knew he would be missing school that day.

Darwin called Tyler again at noon, thinking he might have come home for lunch; no answer. He tried calling again at 3:30, figuring he would be home by then after school; no answer. 5:30; no answer. 8:00; no answer. It was strange that Tyler wasn't home at all, and that he hadn't tried to contact Darwin since the incident—unless he was in major trouble. The thought made Darwin's stomach twist with nervousness, as if his insides were being wrung out.

Darwin went into the kitchen, where his mom was sitting at the table doing a crossword puzzle and listening to the radio.

"Can we call the police station to try and find out what happened to Tyler?" Darwin asked.

His mother looked up, and Darwin saw for the first time how exhausted she looked, how the skin beneath her eyes was dark and almost crumpled. "Let me see what I can find out," she said as she got up, making her way to the phone on the counter and beginning to dial. Just then, the local news began broadcasting a breaking news story, and Darwin leaned forward, listening carefully.

"In other news, the police have arrested a boy in connection with a fight at Ginger café last night, involving a number of high school students. Two students were hospitalized due to the incident, and the boy accused of instigating the fight could face criminal charges of felony assault. The two boys who were hospitalized are recovering and in stable condition, and doctors expect they will make a full recovery."

"Two boys?" Darwin wondered aloud. "Is one of them me?"

"I assume so, dear."

"But I didn't go to the hospital because of injuries from the fight! They're trying to say that Tyler beat the crap out of two people?"

"Well, they didn't really say that," his mother replied evenly, trying to diffuse Darwin's anger.

"And I'm not in the hospital, still recovering. They're trying to paint Tyler as the bad guy!" Darwin said heatedly.

"Easy, honey, I'm sure everything will get sorted out."

"Felony assault? That could mean jail time, Mom."

Darwin began pacing back and forth in the living room, when his dad walked in the door. He looked at Darwin impassively, and passed through to their bedroom, without saying a word to Darwin or his wife. Darwin wasn't about to go apologize after what had gone down last night at the hospital. *If anybody is going to apologize, it should be him*, thought Darwin.

Darwin didn't know what to do about the Tyler situation. But he knew this likely meant that Tyler wouldn't be able to come back to school for a bit.

"Well, what do we do, Mom?" Darwin asked, still pacing.

"Let's just be patient and see how things pan out. You never know. After all, you said yourself that it wasn't his fault. There's a possibility he won't be found guilty."

"I wonder what happened to Billy," Darwin said with disdain.

Although Darwin had never liked Billy and had always hoped that karma would somehow even the scales for the way he'd bullied Darwin all these years, he couldn't seem to stop himself from hoping that, despite everything, Billy was all right. From what he could remember before passing out, Tyler had been wailing on him pretty good . . .

CHAPTER 17

The next morning, Darwin woke to the sound of the phone ringing loudly in his ears. When he picked up the receiver, the police were on the other end of the line, asking for him to come down to the station to discuss what had happened. Darwin said he wasn't feeling up to it, given that he had just gotten out of the hospital a day ago, but that was a lie. He was back to his normal self again, but for whatever reason, he just couldn't bring himself to go. The incident was still too fresh in his memory, too traumatic for him, not the fight between Tyler and Billy, but rather what he had seen while he was unconscious. He wanted to go back to that state so badly, as he had so many questions, and even just a day later he was already forgetting what felt like crucial details.

That first Monday back at school went by very slowly. Darwin had a hard time concentrating in the aftermath of all that had happened, and on top of it, he was forced to deal with the whispers as he walked down the hall, the prying eyes of the students, who seemed to stare at him more than usual. As the story had been in the local news, naturally everyone in the school knew what had happened, or at least they *thought* they knew what had happened. Rumors were going around that Darwin had initiated the whole fight, and that Billy had knocked Darwin out before Tyler beat Billy to a pulp. He wished Tyler's temper hadn't gotten the best of him, especially against a known instigator like Billy.

The final bell rang, and Darwin slowly walked out to the parking lot by himself. His mother was waiting for him in the car, which was unusual, as she was always a little late in picking him up, given her work schedule.

"Tyler called today," she said, the minute he got into the car. "And he wants you to call him back when you get home."

"What? Seriously? What did he say?" Darwin asked, raising his voice anxiously.

"He didn't say much. Just that he wanted you to call him back. He's out of jail now."

"Since when? Does that mean he's not in trouble anymore? Have the charges been dropped?"

"Oh, I wouldn't go that far. He's still in a lot of trouble, but he was released on bail."

Darwin slouched back into his seat. "He didn't say anything else, anything about what happened that night?"

"You're just going to have to call him back," his mother said, impatiently now. "He couldn't talk for long." Darwin could tell something was wrong by her tone, and by the way her mouth turned down sharply at the corners, as if the sadness of the situation itself was pulling it downward. Maybe, Darwin thought, she was just worried about him, and about everything that had happened at Ginger. Maybe it was all now just sinking in.

Darwin rushed inside the house the second they parked the car in the garage. He made his way right to the kitchen and picked up the phone immediately to call Tyler. The phone rang three times; no answer. Four times; still no answer.

"Hello?" Finally, Tyler picked up.

"Hey! It's me," Darwin said with relief at the sound of Tyler's voice.

"Darwin, how's it going, buddy?" Tyler said warmly, almost as if nothing had happened.

"I'm doing okay, how about you?"

"Same." Tyler didn't know what to say or how to start the conversation. "Listen, I'm sorry about what happened the other night."

"Dude, don't be sorry. It wasn't your fault."

"Well, whether it was my fault or not is neither here nor there at this point. Point is, I shouldn't have lost my cool like that. You even warned me to not let Billy get to me."

"I know, but sometimes it's hard not to with that guy. A part of me is glad that he finally got what was coming to him."

"Yeah, but I shouldn't have resorted to violence."

"So . . . what happens now?" Darwin asked.

Tyler took a deep breath and paused before answering. "It might be better for me to talk about this with you in person. Can I come over to your house real quick?"

Darwin looked really concerned. It appeared to be more serious than he had initially thought, if Tyler preferred to have the conversation in person. "Umm . . . yeah, sure. I'll be here."

When Tyler arrived about fifteen minutes after they got off the phone, Darwin was first at the door as soon as he heard the knock, his mother right behind him.

"Oh . . . uh, hey, Mrs. Sanders," Tyler said first, noticing Darwin's mom, who was standing behind Darwin, her arms crossed over her chest.

"Hi Tyler," Darwin's mother said with an uncomfortable look on her face, refusing to make eye contact. Instead she gazed off in the distance, somewhere beyond Tyler's left shoulder.

"Do you mind, uh . . . if I speak with Darwin alone for a second?" Tyler asked. Darwin's mom paused, as if she wanted to say something but thought better of it, and then walked away toward the living room. "Can we go outside?" he asked Darwin in a low voice.

"Yeah, sure," Darwin said as they walked out and he closed the door behind them. "Sorry about that, I'm not sure what's going on with my mom. She's been acting strange all day," Darwin said with a nervous smile.

"It's fine, don't worry about it," Tyler said with a smile, though the smile seemed forced.

The boys took a seat on the front lawn. "Listen, Darwin . . . I'm not really sure how to tell you this." Darwin's heart started beating quickly, not knowing what Tyler was about to say. "I guess I'll just come out with it. Given everything that happened the other night at Ginger, I'm not going to be able to come back to school."

Darwin sat there for a moment, looking back at Tyler in confusion. "You mean, you've been suspended or something?"

"No, Darwin, I'm . . . I'm just not coming back."

"But, but why?" Darwin asked, his confusion rising inside him and nearly blotting out rational thought. "It didn't even happen on campus! They can't kick you out of school for good!"

"It's . . . more complicated than that, I guess."

"How?"

"Well . . . it's tricky. Billy was hurt pretty badly and his family is threatening to sue."

"That's ridiculous. For once in Billy's life something didn't go his way, so his family feels the need to retaliate," Darwin said angrily. "But again, though, what does that have to do with the school kicking you out? I could see them trying to expel you if it had happened on school property, but it didn't." Darwin got up and started pacing back and forth, unable to sit still any longer. "So, what, are you just going to start going to Hawthorne High now?" Hawthorne High was the nearest high school in their town, about a twenty-minute drive from Crimson High.

Tyler paused and looked down, taking a deep breath. "I'm moving back to DC," he said.

Darwin stopped in his tracks and stood there silently, his mouth falling open, and in that one moment all the words he'd wanted to say moments earlier suddenly disappeared.

"My dad's being transferred back to his old job. And, I mean, if we move back to DC, all of this will blow over eventually, and we'll never see these people again."

Darwin simply stood there and stared at Tyler. It didn't make sense to him; it seemed like everything was being blown out of proportion, and all because of one fight, one mistake, Tyler had to move back to where he'd come from after not even living in Crimson for a year?

"So just like that? Just because your parents are worried about their reputation, you're going back to DC? After what, being here all of seven or eight months?" Darwin finally said.

"Look, Darwin. I know it sucks, you don't think I'm pissed about it either? I like it here, but this is something I've got to do," Tyler said, his tone almost pleading now.

Darwin still couldn't make sense of it; the whole thing seemed so drastic. Tyler was exiling himself from the community by choice? It wasn't like he'd committed a heinous crime or anything. There was no way this was it. There had to be something Tyler wasn't telling him.

"Anyway, I'll be here for another week or so packing up all of my stuff," Tyler said breezily. "We'll hang out this week I'm sure, and obviously you can always visit me in DC."

"Wait," Darwin said quickly, unwilling to let the matter go, "but if you're being charged here, won't there be a trial? You can't just take off, right? Leave the state? Wouldn't there be a warrant out for your arrest or something?"

Tyler paused for a second, and it looked as if he was trying to find the right words to say.

"Well, I told you, man, it's complicated. I can't get into any of the specifics, but yes, they know that I'm moving back to DC. They're letting me go. In lieu of a trial. It's a crappy deal, but I'm taking it."

Darwin started shaking his head. "The whole thing, it just, it isn't fair."

"What's not fair?"

"That you're being charged for this when you were provoked."

"I should have controlled myself better," Tyler said. "Anyway, you're going to be fine. You'll go back to school, you're almost done with your junior year, and then you'll only have one more year until you're out of this town."

"I still have to live with the way I look, though, people constantly staring at me, pointing at me, wondering if I have some contagious disease," Darwin said darkly.

"Who cares about that? You're stronger than them. You can do anything they can do—probably more. Don't let it get to you when you notice people looking at you, discriminating against you. People are always scared of what's different."

Darwin took a deep sigh and sat back down next to Tyler. "I just wish that for one day I could be normal, look normal, like anyone else. I think about it all the time. Every day I ask myself why I was born this way, why did it have to happen to me?"

Tyler stared down at the ground, looking really sad. It was clear that he wanted to say something, but he didn't know how or even if he should. Darwin could sense that Tyler was trying to get something out. "What is it?" he asked.

Tyler still didn't respond. He looked back at Darwin. "Don't worry about it," he finally said. "Everything happens for a reason."

Over the next week, Darwin and Tyler spent as much time together as they could, playing basketball, walking around town, and even going to the movies one night. Mindy also joined up with them one day to volunteer at the nursing home. She was sad to see Tyler go, too—she knew that he was Darwin's closest friend, and could only imagine how upset he must be. In truth, Tyler's impending departure *was* hard for Darwin, but he tried to remain positive as best he could, and to remind himself that what Tyler had said was mostly true; that everything did happen for a reason, no matter how crummy the reason really was. Throughout his whole life, Darwin had never really had a person he could truly call a friend. He had some acquaintances here and there who weren't mean to him like most other kids, but none he would consider close enough to call a real friend. Tyler was that guy, his only friend. And if it wasn't for Tyler, he would have never become as close to Mindy. He'd gone from barely being able to speak to girls to making lasting friendships with them, and it was all due to the way that Tyler had gently and good-naturedly pushed Darwin outside of his comfort zone. Tyler never treated Darwin as if he were different, and would routinely stick up for him when Darwin needed it most, which unfortunately had led to his departure from the great town of Crimson.

On Tyler's last day, he stopped by Darwin's house after helping his parents pack the U-Haul, to say one last goodbye. They walked slowly down the driveway, where the truck was waiting. Darwin knew that this was likely the last time he would ever see Tyler again, since the chances of Darwin ever going up to DC were slim to none, given the fact that his family rarely traveled and he didn't have the money to finance the trip himself.

"Well, I guess this is it, man," Tyler said, looking at the red-and-white truck parked at the curb. "Where are your parents?" Darwin asked curiously, wondering if Tyler was going to head back to the now-empty apartment to pick them up before hitting the road.

"Oh," Tyler said, running one hand through his hair. "Well, they agreed to let me drive the truck back to DC. My mom hates road trips, so they're going to catch a flight. Should be fun, though," Tyler said brightly. "Road trips usually are."

Darwin shrugged. He couldn't help feeling a little envious of Tyler. His parents gave him so much freedom, even when he messed up and got in trouble, while Darwin practically had to stage a coup in order to even learn how to drive.

"You know what's weird?" Darwin said slowly, "I just realized that I never met your parents."

"You're not missing much." Tyler laughed. "They're just like yours. Overbearing mother, strict father, pretty standard stuff."

Darwin had always assumed there was something about Tyler's parents or home life that made him so adamant about never hanging out at his place. Darwin hadn't wanted to press Tyler any further, in case the reason was something really personal that he didn't want to explain to Darwin. The last thing he ever wanted to do was make Tyler uncomfortable. After all, he had never made Darwin feel that way himself.

"You know," Tyler said, "I know things are going to be hard for you for a while, Darwin. But you're stronger than you think, and one day you'll show all of the idiots here in Crimson what you're made of."

"Thanks, Tyler," Darwin said gratefully. "You know, I owe you a lot of credit for pushing me out of my comfort zone. If you hadn't, I'd probably still be afraid to talk to girls, letting those guys walk all over me, and staying quiet just so they'd leave me alone."

"That was all you, buddy," Tyler said quietly. "I didn't have anything to do with that, really. Don't sell yourself short."

The two boys stood there, not knowing what else to say. It felt weird saying goodbye and having it be so final. They hadn't known each other for that long, but it had felt like a long time for both of them.

"You know, I still could've helped you pack. You didn't need to say no just because you felt bad about leaving," Darwin said.

Tyler laughed. "I know, but moving is always a pain. No reason to put you through that, when I got myself into this whole mess to begin with. Besides, my parents did most of the packing, I just helped." Tyler shrugged.

"Well, good luck back in DC. Try to come back and visit every now and then, huh?" Darwin said, slapping Tyler on the back.

"Thanks, will do, man. Will do," Tyler said, smiling. "And look, don't let your dad get to you, you'll be on your own soon enough."

Darwin nodded his head in acknowledgment. Tyler opened the door to the U-Haul and hopped in.

"Tyler?" Darwin said.

"Yeah?" Tyler replied, before closing the door.

"What was it that you wanted to say the other day, when you first told me you were moving back to DC?" Darwin was remembering when Tyler looked upset sitting on their front lawn, looking as if he was trying to get something out but didn't know how.

Tyler sat there for a second, seemingly lost in thought. "It's important that you . . . well, you'll hopefully find out in good time," he said cryptically, his gaze suddenly serious and a bit distant, miles away from his usual easy-going manner.

Before Darwin could respond, Tyler closed the door, started the engine of the truck, and gave a quick wave before driving off. Darwin stood there for a bit, watching the truck as it reached the end of the road, growing smaller, until it was just a small dot in the distance. *Find out in good time?* he thought. *What does that mean?*

CHAPTER 18

The weather was becoming warmer with every passing day, as the students neared the end of the school year. The local pool had finally opened, and a lot of young children and adults would often go there on the weekends and after school. Darwin had continued to volunteer at the nursing home with Mindy, and with the weather being warmer, most of the tasks that needed to be done occurred outside in the gardens or pressure washing the siding of the building.

Mindy was still volunteering three times a week at Sun Parks, and even started bringing some of her friends, who were becoming regular volunteers. Given Mindy's popularity, it was easy for her to influence other students to spend time serving their community, and because she was well-liked, these friends naturally treated Darwin well, out of respect for Mindy. They didn't act like he was some infectious disease, walking around and waiting to claim his next victim, or think he was a clueless nerd, like most of the other students.

It was one of the happiest times in Darwin's life. He felt included for the first time since he'd met Tyler. The sharp uptick in community service wasn't going unnoticed either. The city hall started taking note of the increase in student volunteers at the various nonprofit organizations in town, and as such, they agreed to provide funding for food and transportation services to and from the volunteer sites.

Now that they had a decent amount of participation in community activities, Darwin had also begun a volunteer club at school. They currently had nine members, with Mindy acting as president, and Darwin was glad to have her take the lead. She was better at mobilizing the masses than he was, and more comfortable speaking in large groups.

With two weeks of school left to go before summer break, the volunteer club organized a lunch to celebrate the starting of their club and all the work they had contributed over the past few months. They were meeting at Terry's, a local diner, which was walking distance from the school. Students often grabbed lunch there because the food was delicious and cheap, besides being so close to campus.

That morning, Darwin woke up with a bit of a sore throat and a heavy cough. He figured he would push through it, and took some cough drops before heading out the door with a bottle of orange juice. By the time Darwin got to Ms. Edmond's class, he could tell that his throat was already getting worse. It was becoming harder to swallow without feeling like his throat was packed with razor blades. He sat down in his chair and coughed a few times while painfully swallowing his saliva. He grimaced with every swallow, and even other students noticed that he wasn't doing well. One of the students in the volunteer club, Justin Diaz, a short, dark-haired junior, came over and asked if he was okay.

"I'm fine. Thanks, though," Darwin said, now sniffling, as he could feel his nose starting to become congested. Darwin looked over at Tyler's desk, which was now being occupied by a new student. He wondered how Tyler was doing back in DC. He was surprised that he hadn't heard from him in the two-and-a-half months since he'd left. No calls, no emails, nothing. Darwin had tried to contact him from time to time, but was never able to reach him.

By the time class was dismissed, it was clear Darwin was in bad shape. He was sneezing, coughing, and every swallow was accompanied with extreme pain. Ms. Edmond approached him and asked if he wanted to go see the nurse.

"Oh no, no. I'm fine, really," Darwin said in a congested voice.

"Are you sure? I would feel more comfortable if you went," Ms. Edmond said.

Darwin obliged and made his way to the nurse's office instead of to his next class. He waited a good thirty minutes or so before the nurse even showed up, and he considered leaving and going back to class against Ms. Edmond's wishes, but just as he was about to get up, the nurse, a frizzy blonde in her late thirties wearing a white sweatshirt with a picture of a panda bear on the front, entered the room.

"Well, hello there! How are we doing?" she asked. Darwin had never been to the school nurse before, and didn't even know what her name was.

"I'm fine, Ms. Edmond asked me to come see you. I think I might be coming down with something," he said while coughing profusely.

"Hmm, that's a strong cough, you must have been practicing that for a while, doesn't sound as fake as some of the other kids'," the nurse said jovially, her blue eyes crinkling at the corners whenever she smiled.

"Sorry?" he asked, unsure if she was joking.

"Well, you know, a lot of kids come into my office faking some kind of illness to try and get sent home, but I'm quick to spot false symptoms. But you sound like the real deal. Let's take a look at your vitals and see how you're doing. Also, I'm going to take a quick look into your mouth to see what's going on with your throat." The nurse opened one her cupboards and pulled out a light and a popsicle stick. "Now, open up and say ahh."

"Ahh," Darwin said, as she put the stick on his tongue.

"Hmmm." She hummed, pulling the stick out of Darwin's mouth. She probed the glands on his neck, then placed one hand on his forehead. "Let me take your temperature while I do the rest of your vitals, okay?"

Darwin reluctantly agreed. He knew that if he was really sick, he'd likely miss the group lunch. His stomach sank at the thought.

"100.4! Well, it looks like you have a fever," she said happily, almost as if she'd won the lottery. "My recommendation would be for you to go home and rest, so you don't spread it around." Darwin nodded slowly in disappointment. He wanted to push back, but didn't have the energy to argue with his throat throbbing in pain. "Drink some tea with honey, and make sure you get plenty of fluids to keep you hydrated. Now, do you want me to call your parents to have them come pick you up?"

"No, no. That's all right. I'll just walk home," Darwin said quickly. He didn't want his mom to worry about him, and he knew that it was hard for her to leave her shift on such short notice. Besides, it wasn't like he was so sick that he couldn't take care of himself. He was seventeen, for crying out loud—he wasn't a child. "Really, I'll be fine," he reiterated, as he saw the unconvinced look on the nurse's face.

"Well, all right, if you say so," she said in an unsure tone.

"My mom will be getting off around three, so I'll be fine until then." Darwin then realized he would need to call his mom eventually and tell her, so she didn't come to the school to pick him up. He figured he would do that after he got home later in the afternoon. Before he left the building, Darwin wrote Mindy a note and slipped it through the vent of her locker, telling her that he was sick and wouldn't be able to make it to the lunch.

The walk home seemed like an eternity for Darwin. He was coughing and sniffling the whole time, and was now starting to feel shivery from the fever. Every step that he took was short and slow. When he finally arrived at his house shortly before noon, coughing all the way up the driveway, he could barely make it to the front door, and opening it seemed to take all his effort. As he started making his way up the stairs to his bedroom, he suddenly stopped when he heard a noise in the kitchen, like footsteps padding across the tile floor. But just as quickly as it had started, the noise stopped, and Darwin continued walking up the stairs to his bedroom, where he threw off his backpack and flopped onto his bed face first. He lay there for a couple of minutes, trying to muster up the energy to go make himself some tea. Then, he could hear the movement again. This time it was louder, or at least it seemed much closer. Darwin lifted up his head quickly and looked out of his bedroom door. The noise now sounded like a cupboard door shuffling open, and then he could hear someone talking. It was his dad's voice.

"How many times do I have to tell you, he's making progress!" It sounded at first like his father was talking to himself, but then it quickly became apparent he was having a conversation over the phone.

"I told you, I'll be there in the morning to give you an update," his dad continued. "Well, that's not what Dr. Greer instructed me to do." There was that name again: Dr. Greer. The same name Darwin had overheard the doctor say to his mother at the hospital.

Darwin slowly got off his bed and made his way to the bedroom door, trying not to make any noise and almost forgetting that he was sick. He peered out into the hallway and stopped at the top of the staircase. He didn't know why his dad was home and not at work, and who could he be talking to and what about? Whatever it was, Darwin knew that his dad would be furious, if he found out that he had been listening in on his conversation.

"Listen, I've been doing this for years, you think you know him better than me?" his dad said forcefully. "All right, all right, fine. I'll see you in the morning," his dad barked as he hung up the phone and started pacing around the kitchen.

Darwin stood there, unsure of what to do. Eventually he needed to go downstairs and acknowledge his father's presence, but he couldn't do it now, not after his dad had just finished what seemed like a heated phone call. Should he just stay in his room until later that night, so his dad wouldn't know he'd come home early? *No, that won't work,* Darwin thought. He knew that he needed to call his mom at some point before three, so she knew not to pick him up, and when he did, she would tell his dad that he had come home early anyway. He had to act quickly, but Darwin couldn't stop thinking about the conversation he'd overhead, a conversation clearly not meant for his ears. Who had his father been talking to? And did it have anything to do with the things Darwin had seen in his father's secret room? *He's making progress,* Darwin thought to himself, turning the words over in his mind obsessively. Who was his dad referring to?

Darwin tiptoed slowly back to his room and just as he approached the doorway, he stepped on the soft part of the floor right outside his room. It was a spot he always avoided walking over, as the floorboard below the carpet always made a loud creak. The board squeaked for what seemed like an eternity. He stopped and listened to see if there was any movement from downstairs. He could hear his dad stop his frantic pacing and then walk toward the stairs. Darwin knew he was caught, and there was nothing he could do about it. He couldn't believe that out of all the times he'd walked into his bedroom avoiding that small spot, he'd forgotten to do it the time he'd actually tried to move quietly. Darwin turned around, as he could hear his father approaching the bottom of the stairs.

"Darwin?" Dave asked, looking perplexed. He was still dressed in his usual work attire of crisp white dress shirt and dark slacks. His black shoes were so shiny that Darwin bet he could probably see his own reflection in them, if he leaned over and examined them more closely. "What are you doing home from school?" he asked angrily, his cheeks reddening.

"Sorry, Dad, I . . . I didn't mean to startle you," Darwin stammered, caught off guard. "The school nurse sent me home, I'm not feeling well."

"What do you mean?" his dad said suspiciously, his eyes narrowing. "Come here." Darwin walked down the stairs slowly, coughing as he went. When he reached the bottom, his father reached out and placed a hand over Darwin's forehead.

"Doesn't feel like you have a fever," he said dismissively.

"The nurse she said it was 100.4."

"Hmm, well, that's barely a temperature, you know. And why didn't you call your mom and have her come get you?"

"I don't know . . . I just didn't want to worry her." Darwin shrugged. "It's not a big deal, Dad. I'll be fine, I'm just going to make some tea," Darwin said as he tried to squeeze past his dad to get to the kitchen.

"No!" his father shouted as Darwin stopped dead in his tracks. "No . . . I mean, don't worry about it. I'll get it for you." His father's eyes were wide and panicked, and Darwin was dumbstruck, unable to say a word.

"O . . . kay," Darwin responded slowly. He knew why his dad didn't want him in the kitchen—it was obvious. Ever since his father had caught Darwin in the kitchen that day he had unlocked the secret room, things had been tense between them. More than tense. Every night, at dinner, his father watched him like a hawk. He hardly ever took his eyes off Darwin's face, waiting for that moment when Darwin might inadvertently look past the dining-room table and into the kitchen, where the pantry lay in wait. Those dinners were excruciating. More so than usual. Darwin would attempt to answer his mother's chitchat, asking about his day, while all the while trying to ignore that his father was looking at his own son like he was something to be wary of. But even without his dad's obvious suspicion, his insistence on making Darwin a cup of tea was strange—his dad hardly ever did anything to take care of Darwin—not physically, at least. That had always been his mother's territory. *Maybe he feels guilty*, Darwin thought, as he watched his dad walk over to the stove, turning the burner on beneath the kettle.

"Why don't you go upstairs? I'll be right there with it," his father said.

Darwin made his way to his room and lay down on his bed, but before he could really get comfortable, his father appeared, a few minutes later, holding a steaming cup of herbal tea, setting it down on the nightstand. "Feel better, now," his father said in a tone that almost resembled a threat.

"Right, thanks, Dad," Darwin answered, trying to smile as if nothing was wrong.

Darwin wanted to ask why his dad was home so early, but figured asking would only anger him and wasn't worth an argument, especially when he wasn't feeling well.

"I'll call your mom and let her know you're here," his father said with a grunt before turning and walking out the door. He closed it behind him with a sharp click.

After his mom arrived home from work later that afternoon, Darwin heard her light, quick footsteps on the stairs as she hurried up to check on him. As soon as she entered the room, her training as a nurse took over. She placed one soft, cool hand on Darwin's head, then took his temperature. The thermometer read 101.2.

"You stay here and rest, I'll bring you some food and plenty of orange juice," his mother said reassuringly.

"Thanks, Mom," Darwin said in a muffled voice, his nose so congested that he felt as if he could barely breathe, much less talk.

"I think it would be best if you stayed home from school tomorrow."

"Okay," Darwin said. He couldn't argue with that, as he was feeling even worse than he had just a couple hours ago. Darwin wanted to tell his mom what he'd heard when he first arrived at home, but he didn't want to upset her, especially when he wasn't sure who or what his dad was talking about.

The next day Darwin stayed at home, still recovering. He lay in his bed, bored, with nothing to do. He had already read all of the books in his room and the only other books in the house were his dad's old accounting textbooks from school, which didn't interest him. By afternoon, Darwin slowly grew tired from boredom and could feel himself slipping into sleep. His eyes were heavy, refusing to stay open, no matter how hard he tried. He didn't want to drift into sleep because he knew that if he did, he would have a hard time falling asleep that night. He could hear the birds chirping outside his window, so peacefully and melodically that he couldn't help but sink further into his pillow, tuning out everything around him with the exception of the birds and their melodious, cheerful tweeting.

Darwin awoke to find himself yet again in the colorful jungle he'd seen before in his dreams. He was in the exact location he always started out in. He looked around for the opening in the trees that would lead him to the mountains, and started power walking in that direction as soon as he heard the sirens' wail. The sirens went off two more times before Darwin made it to the opening, where he could see the large mountains and open land.

Like he did the other times before, he made his way toward the crevasse, where he had previously heard noises coming from the floor. He slowly climbed down the wall of the crevasse to get to the bottom, which was roughly six feet below. He didn't want to slip and fall like he had the last time, so he took his time making his way down while the sirens wailed in the background.

By the time Darwin reached the crevasse floor, he could already hear the clicking noises coming from the same cave-like area to his right. He cautiously started making his way over in the direction of the noises, which sounded incredibly similar to the clicking he'd heard in his unconscious state after passing out at Ginger.

The clicking continued back and forth, but just as he approached the cave, it stopped. Darwin, too, stopped dead in his tracks, waiting to see if the noise would start up again. The last time he had gotten to this point, the clicking had grown louder and louder, as if he was nearing whatever was making the noise.

Darwin slowly stepped into the cave, into complete darkness.

He took one, two, three steps, and then heard a loud crack! He stopped and looked around, though it was pointless, as he couldn't see anything but the light he had walked in from. He started walking again, and just as he took another step closer, he could hear the clicking sound, louder than he had ever heard it. It was right in front of him. Darwin, shaking with fear, stood there frozen as the clicking continued.

He slowly reached out to see if he could touch anything, his arm extending farther and farther and then, he touched it. It felt like flesh, but was very cold and brittle. The clicking noise became frantic, going at fast speeds and in multiple tones. The sound became so loud that Darwin had to cover his ears with his hands. He ran outside the cave, scared that he had done something wrong.

The clicking noises stopped. Darwin looked back into the cave, but he couldn't see anything in the pitch darkness. Then suddenly, a figure appeared, walking closer to him. Darwin stood there with his mouth open. He couldn't believe his eyes. It was the same figure that had appeared in his vision when he was unconscious after the fight at Ginger. She had the same skin patterns and big green eyes. Her hair was exactly the same as before, and she was wearing the same plain white sheet over her body. She stared back at him, silent and unmoving. Darwin, who was afraid yet curious at the same time, finally spoke.

"It's you again," he said. The girl didn't move at all, but instead just continued to stare at Darwin from the edge of the cave. "Come on out, I won't hurt you." He reached out his hand to her to indicate that she should come forward. She slowly approached, still keeping her eyes on Darwin, and as she got closer to his hand, she reached out to hold onto it.

Darwin felt a wave of emotion come over him as they stood there holding each other's hands. He began to tear up, and he wiped his eyes quickly with his free hand so she wouldn't notice. She then grabbed it and pulled it down, raising her own hand to gently wipe the tears from his eyes for him. She smiled, still not making any noise.

Darwin, shaking a bit, said in a quavering voice, "Who are you?" The girl responded by making slight, slow clicking noises.

Darwin pointed to his chest, "My name is Darwin. What is your name?" he asked as he pointed back at her, as he had done the first time he saw her. Darwin could tell that she didn't understand, but he knew that he couldn't just give up. "Look, look. My name is Darwin." He pointed at his chest again. "What is your name?" The girl then pointed at herself, making a few clicking noises, then pointed at Darwin and did the same.

Darwin smiled; it was clear to him that whoever she was, she didn't speak a normal vocal language like he was used to. No matter what he said, they wouldn't be able to communicate verbally. His only hope was to use body language to understand each other.

Darwin waved to her in an attempt to say hello. She stood there looking confused. He held up two fingers in a peace sign, but that didn't work either. He scratched his head, thinking of what he could do to try to communicate with her. But as he stood there, she approached him and slowly placed her hand on his heart. Darwin's body was overcome with a cooling sensation. It was hard to describe, but it was almost like they were connected, in sync, despite the fact that they could not communicate directly with each other. Darwin could feel so many different sentiments all at once: joy, sadness, excitement—everything. He looked at the girl, who was fixated on her hand touching his heart, and just as she looked up, making eye contact with Darwin, he woke from his slumber.

Darwin's body was all sweaty, which he was used to, as he often experienced night sweats, even when he didn't have visions. But unlike times before, his whole body felt tingly—similar to the feeling one gets when their foot falls asleep, except this was all over his body. He lay there for a moment, so the tingling sensation would wear off. He struggled to move his body. It took about a whole minute for the feeling to go away, and even after that he lay in his bed for a good twenty minutes contemplating the dream he'd just had. After a while, Darwin sat up and noticed with no small degree of surprise that his illness was completely gone: no more sore throat, no more cold feeling, not even a stuffy nose. He'd been cured, just like that.

Later that night, at dinner, Darwin pushed his food around on his plate like he was still sick. He grimaced painfully every time he drank from his water glass. But it was only for show. The truth was that ever since waking up from his dream hours earlier, he felt fine. Like the sickness had never even happened. After dinner, Darwin went up to his room to read for a while, wanting to be out of sight in case his parents figured out that he was mysteriously no longer coughing. A few minutes later, Darwin heard raised voices coming through the floorboards, rising up into the air. His parents were arguing, which usually consisted of his father yelling at his mom. However, unlike most of their arguments, Darwin started to hear his mom raising her voice back at his father, the sound catching him off guard.

"No, no!" his mother shouted as Darwin made his way over to the door so that he could hear them more clearly.

"Would you keep it down! He's right up there!" his dad whispered loudly. It was hard for Darwin to hear through his closed door, so he opened it slowly, being careful to not make the door creak as it swung open.

"We are NOT doing that! Do you hear me?" his mother said back, this time in a lower voice, an almost growl.

"How many times do I have to tell you? The agency requires us to do this," his father replied in exasperation.

"I don't care what the agency says, it's not right!" his mom hissed. "How do you know for sure he's found out?"

"Jane, my photographs were out of order, and there are handprints all over the walls. And I saw him coming out of the pantry. What more proof do you want?"

Darwin's heart dropped to the bottom of his stomach. His dad knew that Darwin had found out he had once worked for the CIA. *How could I have been so stupid?* Darwin thought. Did he really think his dad wouldn't find out that someone had been down there, tinkering around with his stuff? He didn't even think about the handprints on the wall, but it made sense, given that he was fumbling to find a light switch.

"Well, it doesn't matter, we're not doing it," his mother added again. This time a bit more firmly.

"Don't you remember the contract we signed? Are you somehow forgetting that little detail? We agreed eighteen years ago that if he was ever to find out, or if that information was compromised, we'd have to terminate the whole operation, as the potential repercussions that it would have on all of us would be serious," his father added.

Darwin shuddered at the sound of this. What was his dad talking about, and what did he mean by the word 'terminate?' He started walking back into his bedroom, and once inside, he leaned against the wall for a moment, his heart racing. He could still hear his parents arguing, but the words weren't as clear, as they were now speaking in very low voices. All of the new information he'd discovered was more than he could handle: the secret office, the photographs, the awards from the CIA, and now overhearing his parents arguing about what to do, now that he had found out? It was all too much for him. His face crumpled, and a lone tear slid down his cheek. He couldn't bear to face the punishment for breaking into his father's secret office and rummaging through all of his documents. He knew that no matter how much his mom stood up for him, his dad wouldn't hear any of it.

Darwin thought about Tyler and wondered what he'd do in this situation. Tyler had always told him that his parents were strict, and that he had learned how to handle it. He wished that Tyler still lived near him; it had been over two and a half months since they'd talked, and Darwin had started to wonder if he would ever see Tyler again.

Just then, the arguing between his parents stopped abruptly. Darwin lifted up his head and made his way toward the door, which was still open.

"Go talk to him," Darwin could hear his dad whispering to his mom. Darwin closed his door quickly but quietly, as he could hear his mom making her way up to his room. Darwin darted over to his bed and opened a book to pretend he was reading.

His mom knocked softly on the door. "Come in," Darwin said. As soon as she entered the room, wearing the soft, pink bathrobe she changed into every night before bed, Darwin could see that his mother was visibly upset, and looked as if she were about to cry, her blue eyes red around the rims.

"Hi, dear, how are you?" she said softly, closing the door behind her.

"Mom, what's wrong?" Darwin replied, alarmed by the grave look on her face.

"Oh, nothing! I just came to check on you," she said unconvincingly, with a bright, fake smile. "You barely ate anything at dinner, Darwin," she said.

"Sorry, Mom, it was good, I'm just not very hungry."

"Oh . . . I see. Well, is there anything I can get you?"

"No, that's okay. I'm fine."

His mother nodded her head, and it appeared as if she was trying to hold back tears. She wouldn't look Darwin in the eye, but instead placed her hand on his leg. "You know, dear, we love you very much."

Darwin, in a confused tone, responded, "Yeah, I know, Mom. I love you, too."

"And you know that sometimes when your dad is stern with you, it's because he wants what's best for you."

Darwin didn't know how to respond; he couldn't figure out where all of this was coming from.

"Just remember that, okay?" she said as she looked up at Darwin for the first time since walking into his room. Darwin put his hand over his mom's and nodded his head. Without another word, she then got up and left the room, closing the door behind her. Darwin made his way over to the door to see if his parents were going to continue their conversation.

"So?" Darwin heard his father ask.

"He's fine, just leave me alone," his mom snapped.

"You know we have to do this," his father said in a low, urgent tone of voice.

"But what if I never see him again?" His mother started crying. "This is different from what we signed and agreed to eighteen years ago. He's our boy."

There was a quick pause and then his father responded, "It's not up to us now."

Darwin had heard just about enough. The fact that his mom indicated that she might never see him again was enough cause for concern. He ducked underneath his bed to find his suitcase, and started packing. Shirts, socks, boxers, pants; he placed as many clothes as he could in the suitcase. In addition to this, he threw in some books, along with some photos of him and his mom.

Turning the doorknob to his bedroom door softly and slowly, Darwin made his way to the bathroom to gather his toiletries. As he walked to the bathroom, he could hear his mom crying. It sounded like she was on her own, as he couldn't hear any other noise but the sound of her sniffling. Darwin stood there and paused for a moment. He didn't want to leave his mom; he knew he was responding to everything in the heat of the moment, but he couldn't stay and wait to find out what his dad had in store for him, either.

He got back to his room and tucked his toothbrush and tooth- paste into the side pocket of the suitcase. He took a look around, trying to figure out if there was anything else he needed. He then spotted, sitting on his desk, a piece of limestone his mother had giv- en to him on his tenth birthday. She'd called it a "good luck rock," one that he could take with him whenever he felt alone or scared. Darwin grabbed the rock and looked at it for a bit—he missed those days when he was younger, when his mother and father got along and he didn't have any cares in the world.

The back door of the house swung open and then shut again. Darwin figured his dad had gone outside to take a breather and col- lect himself, and was now back in, as Darwin could hear heavy footsteps along the kitchen floor. Darwin knew that it was unlikely he would be able to run away from home tonight, with both of his parents downstairs; that it would be wise to wait until the morning, after they went off to work. They wouldn't notice he was missing until they came home in the evening, and by then Darwin would be long gone.

Darwin ripped a piece of paper from one of his notebooks and started writing down his plan for where he would go and how he would get there. He didn't have much money, but he also knew where his parents stored cash for emergencies. He didn't know how much was in there, as he'd never used any of it, but he hoped that it would be enough to get him to where he wanted to go: Washington, DC.

CHAPTER 19

The next morning, Darwin awoke early, as he was anxious and nervous about running away from home. He went back and forth in the middle of the night on whether it was a good idea. After all, school wasn't out yet, and there were still two weeks left of classes, but Darwin knew they were just a formality, since he'd already earned enough credits to complete his junior year.

Darwin had to wait for a good hour or so as his parents got ready to head off to work. His parents rarely said bye to him before leaving, even when he was home sick, but the thought of leaving without saying anything to his mother tortured Darwin inside.

When he heard his mom down in the kitchen making a quick breakfast, he ran downstairs to say goodbye.

"Mom?"

"Oh! Darwin, dear, what are you doing up so early?" his mom said while she scooped her eggs onto a plate. She was ready for work and dressed in her usual attire of light blue scrubs and sensible shoes. "Are you feeling better?" Darwin had almost forgotten that his parents still thought he was sick, which was his excuse for not going to school today.

"I . . . I just wanted to tell you to have a good day. And that I love you."

She looked at Darwin with a smile, as her eyes started to tear up. She set her eggs down and walked over to Darwin and gave him a hug. "I love you, too, dear." She kissed Darwin on the forehead, then made her way back to the stove to retrieve her eggs.

Darwin made his way back up the stairs slowly, sad and heart-broken, thinking of how upset his mother would be when she found out he had left the house for good. His mom had always been so protective, and he knew it would kill her to wonder where he was and if he was all right.

As soon as Darwin heard the front door close and the cars pull out of the garage, he made himself a quick plate of toast and eggs, but not before grabbing a handful of money from the chest in his parents' room. The chest had $280 in it, which Darwin felt was enough to start him on his way—this was in addition to the $40 Darwin had saved up from shoveling snow for some of his elderly neighbors in the winter. He wasn't sure how much the bus ride to DC would be, but it couldn't be that much, he thought. The most expensive thing would likely be a hotel, if he needed to stay in one for a night. Admittedly, Darwin knew that his overall plan to run away was not well-thought-out and could likely lead to disaster, and contrary to how he usually conducted his life, he was winging it for the first time and anxious at the idea of being on his own and making his own decisions.

Darwin grabbed his belongings and made his way out the door. He took one last look at the house, remembering all of the memories he had there, the good and the bad. He remembered the days when his parents still loved each other and rarely fought. He remembered his grandmother coming to visit and living with them before she was put in a nursing home. Of course, he couldn't forget all of the times his father shouted at him or ignored him when he'd needed him the most. But he also knew that it was best to try and remember the happy times over the heartbreak, and that the good in his life had mostly outweighed the bad. One last look, and he was off.

Around 10 a.m., Darwin arrived at the Greyhound bus station in Crimson, which was about a ten-minute walk from the house. He made his way up to the call window, where an attendant was waiting. The middle-aged attendant, wearing his uniform and large glasses, looked Darwin up and down and asked, "Can I help you?" in a monotone voice, as if he was bored out of his mind.

"I need a bus ticket to Washington, DC."

"DC, huh? You want to do a direct trip or an overnight stop?"

the man continued in his monotone voice.

"Well, what's the difference in price?" Darwin asked nervously.

"No difference, you just have to pay your own fare for the cost of a hotel. Bus goes to Richmond, Virginia, and arrives around 10 p.m. Then starts up again the next morning at 7 a.m. Otherwise, it's a straight shot to DC, which is a twenty-hour drive, with stops along the way, of course."

"Got it, okay, I'll do the direct trip," Darwin said firmly. It was probably best, given his limited supply of cash. "How much?"

The man made a few clicks on his computer and in the same monotone voice said, "Comes to a total of $97.72, after fees and taxes."

Darwin was a little taken aback, as he hadn't anticipated it being that much. It was a bus, not a plane, for goodness sake. He took the cash out of his pocket and the man printed his ticket.

"Next bus off to DC leaves at 11:30," the man said, handing him the slim piece of paper.

Since Darwin had an hour and a half to himself, he started mapping out what he was going to do when he got to DC. He knew that running away was just the beginning of the battle. Finding out where he was going to stay and how he was going to take care of himself was the hard part. He was hoping to look Tyler up when he got to DC and see if he could somehow help out, either with finding him a place to stay or maybe helping him find a job, figuring out how Darwin could get himself enrolled in school. He knew he could count on Tyler—the only thing he worried about was if Tyler or Tyler's parents might report him to the police. After all, Darwin was still technically a minor. There was no getting around it.

The bus arrived around 11:15, and when Darwin boarded he was surprised to see so many people already on the bus who had come from different locations. The bus smelled stale, like a room with the shades drawn and windows closed tightly. He was nervous, as most of the people on board looked like they had just walked out of a horror film. Most of the passengers were tatted up all over their bodies, some with holes in their clothes, others wearing clothes that looked like they hadn't been washed in months. Darwin was the only young person on the bus and, given the fact that it was his first time traveling alone, he wanted to make sure he didn't draw any attention to himself or cause any trouble.

This was wishful thinking, as most of the passengers stared at him, partially because he looked so young, and partially because of his skin. Darwin nervously made his way to the back of the bus without making eye contact. He went all the way down to the back row, next to the bathroom, which smelled of urine and cleaning products. He sat down next to a woman who was probably in her mid- to late thirties. Her hair was disheveled, and she had a sleeve of black and gray tattoos on one arm. She looked at Darwin, annoyed to see that he had sat down next to her.

"Just don't talk to me or lean on me," she said in a raspy voice. Darwin nodded and didn't respond as the woman leaned her head back on the seat and closed her eyes, forgetting all about him.

It was a long journey to DC. They'd been on the bus for four hours, and Darwin didn't have anything to do but read the books he'd read before, and of course he couldn't speak to the person sitting next to him, per her request. Not that she was awake, anyway. Darwin looked around and noticed a newspaper sitting on one of the chairs diagonal from him. The person sitting in the window seat was asleep, so Darwin slowly went over and picked up the paper, figuring he would give it back as soon as the man woke up.

Darwin skimmed over some articles on politics, and found an article on a shooting that had taken place the night before in Chicago, Illinois. This was the fifth shooting in that city alone in the past two weeks. The article described how the shootings were likely caused by gang activity or drug deals gone wrong. Seven people in total had been shot and killed, as well as one child, who had been an innocent bystander. Darwin shook his head, thinking of the pain some of these families were going through.

He continued reading and found other similar articles with disturbing news, one on another shooting in Atlanta, this one motivated by racism, and another article on refugees fleeing their countries due to religious persecution. These were the kind of things Darwin's parents always hid him from and never wanted him to know about. He could see why they were keeping world affairs away from him for so long, as the constant negative events seen in the media would take a toll on anyone's mental stability. The world was in a bad state. If you looked too long and too hard at every new atrocity, you might well go mad.

The sun started setting, and Darwin realized his parents would be home by now and were probably frantically looking for him. He imagined his mom's reaction. He knew she would be devastated and somehow would blame herself for it. He wished he could let her know that it wasn't her fault. As he turned to stare at the golden glow of the sun, turning fiery shades of red and orange as it neared the ground, he swallowed hard, choking back his tears. It felt like there was a golf ball stuck in his throat, and no matter how many times he swallowed, it wouldn't go away.

As it grew dark, the bus made a pit stop at a nearby rest area for a bathroom break. This was the third stop the bus had made since starting its journey, once for lunch and once for dinner. Darwin dismounted the bus and did a long stretch, accompanied with a yawn, as he made his way to the men's bathroom. The long trip with nothing to do made him very tired, and he decided he would take a nap when getting back on the bus; he just needed to make sure he didn't fall asleep on the woman sitting next to him who had yet to speak since their first interaction.

The men's bathroom was an absolute mess, but then again, what else could you expect from a rest-area bathroom, Darwin figured. There was what appeared to be water all over the ground, mixed with toilet-paper chunks. The smell of urine and feces assaulted him the minute he stepped inside, and he grimaced, trying to hold his breath.

Just as he opened the door to the stall, a bag was quickly thrown over his head from behind him, and through the thick fabric he could feel someone grabbing him and covering his mouth. Darwin shouted at the top of his lungs, but only so much sound could be made, as the hand covering his mouth muffled his screams. As he continued to shout, whoever was holding him started dragging him backward, out of the bathroom.

"WHAT ARE YOU DOING?" Darwin continued to scream, even though he couldn't even make out what he was saying himself through the muffled noise. Darwin kicked and swung his body around, trying to free himself, doing anything that he could, but the person had such a strong grip that it only made Darwin more exhausted.

The temperature changed; he felt cold air on his hands. He knew they were now outside. He could hear the cars on the freeway zooming by in the distance, and the sound of traffic made him more determined than ever and stiffened his resolve. He kept screaming as loud and as hard as he could. It was dark inside the bag, and as he yelled, flashes of the attempted kidnapping years ago came back to him. How eerily similar this was. Another person grabbed his legs to stop him from kicking, and the two started carrying him off in a direction Darwin was unable to identify, given his disorientation. Then, Darwin felt a slight pricking sensation in his neck and within seconds his vision started fading and he was out cold.

Darwin woke up groggy and disoriented; his vision was blurry and his mouth completely dry, so dry that it felt like he had swallowed sand. He could barely make out what appeared to be two men in the front seat of a vehicle. His memory was fuzzy, filled with holes. The last thing he remembered was standing in the bathroom, that awful smell, the dirty floor . . . He looked down at his hands, noticing they were tied together, and all at once it came flooding back, the bag over his head, his screams, his throat raw and dry from them. His eyes widened, and he immediately began to scream again, but as he did so, he realized that a gag was covering his mouth to prevent him from making any noise. Then, a voice said in his right ear, "Relax . . . relax." But the last thing Darwin wanted to do was relax. For all he knew, these men were about to kill him and throw him in a dumpster somewhere.

"Relax, no one is going to hurt you," the man said again. Darwin still shouted, as he could hear other cars driving by, hoping he would be able to draw attention from outside.

"Shut up!" the man behind the wheel shouted. "Get him to shut up!"

"Stop yelling, we're not going to hurt you. Understand?" His voice was deep and calm; he sounded like a radio broadcaster. Darwin finally stopped shouting, partially because he was exhausted from all the yelling, not to mention the fact that he was still a bit drowsy from whatever they'd used to sedate him.

The man lifted the gag off Darwin's mouth, once he noticed Darwin had calmed down a bit. He was in his late forties, Darwin guessed, with a full head of salt-and-pepper hair. He was dressed in all black, and his leather jacket shone slickly in the darkness of the interior. He couldn't see the other man in the front seat clearly—it was too dark—and Darwin was still too disoriented. Everything swam before his eyes hazily, the headlights shining out and illuminating the parking lot, the shadowy figures of the men. The leather seats felt cool beneath him.

"You ready to calm down?" he asked. Darwin was still breathing heavily, like he'd just run a 100-meter dash.

"What do you want?" Darwin asked, his voice raspy from screaming so hard.

"We don't want anything, we're taking you somewhere," the man said calmly.

"Yeah, I figured that part, but why, and where?" Darwin asked, stuttering slightly.

"Just sit back, it'll be a while," the man said with an air of finality, as if it would be futile to ask more questions.

"What do you mean? What do you want from me?" Darwin said, still breathing quickly.

"You'll see soon enough."

"Well, can you untie me?"

"Can't do that," the driver responded in his deep voice as they pulled out of the lot. The car now started driving quickly—it was clear they had just entered a freeway. Darwin was still trembling, wondering where these three men could possibly be taking him and why. No one knew who Darwin was, so what did they want with him, of all people? Then it occurred to him that perhaps they were bringing him back to his parents? That couldn't be it, though. Otherwise, they wouldn't have taken him as roughly as they did, and they probably would have told him who they were and what they were doing.

Two hours went by, or at least it felt like two hours. He had no idea where they were, and this made his stomach cramp with fear. They were on a freeway this whole time, judging by the speed of the car. Even two hours in, the men still wouldn't tell Darwin anything; in fact, they had barely spoken at all—even to each other. The car ride was punctuated with nothing but more silence.

Another two hours went by, and the only interaction they had was asking if Darwin needed to go to the bathroom. When he said yes, they pulled off on a side road and took him out to the middle of nowhere, in a thick grove of trees so he could empty his bladder without being seen.

At this point, Darwin was so tired that he could barely keep his eyes open. The leather seats of the car were starting to get uncomfortable after sitting in them for so long. Darwin estimated that it was around two or three in the morning, given that he was abducted around 10 p.m., and it felt like they had been driving for at least four or five hours.

After what seemed like another three hours of driving in complete silence, the car suddenly started to slow down and turned off the freeway. The men still didn't speak to each other, but it was clear they both knew where to go nonetheless.

The car slowly came to a stop, and the window was rolled down on the driver's side.

A man spoke from outside, "Hey Tim."

Darwin immediately started shouting at the top of his lungs, "HELP, HELP, HELP!" His voice was still so hoarse that he could barely shout above a whisper, but he gave it everything he had.

"Shut up!" the driver yelled. But the man in the back wasn't covering Darwin's mouth; weren't they worried he would cause a scene to the person outside? Why weren't they worried? Unless they were in a location that was so isolated that they didn't *have* to worry about it. The very thought made Darwin scream even louder.

"HELP, HELP! THESE MEN HAVE ABDUCTED ME!" Darwin yelled.

"I'm not going to tell you again, shut up!" the driver said heatedly.

"Just relax," the deep voice from the man in the back said calmly.

"Don't worry, we got him. Taking him to the boss now," the driver said authoritatively.

"Sounds good, I'll open the gate."

The boss? Who is the boss? Darwin's mind started racing. He was convinced that these were going to be his last hours on Earth. Even the man outside was in on it and couldn't care less that a teenager had been kidnapped.

Darwin couldn't think of anything else to do but shout over and over, "HELP, PLEASE, SOMEBODY HELP ME!"

He kicked his feet, which weren't tied, and thrashed around in the backseat until he was coated in sweat.

The men didn't say anything this time—it was as if they were tired of telling him to calm down and decided it was no use anymore. Just then, the vehicle came to a complete stop and the man in the back grabbed Darwin and swung the side door open. "Are you going to stay calm? We're not going to hurt you," the deep voice echoed.

"Yes," Darwin said through heavy breathing. The man guided Darwin out of the vehicle and started walking him toward a huge brick building. After entering, they led him down a series of brightly lit hallways, the walls painted white, the floors so clean that every squeak from their shoes echoed through the narrow passageway.

They stopped in front of a metal door. "Wait here," the man said, as he opened the door with a crack, and then Darwin heard the voice of another man asking him to enter. The man pushed Darwin through the half-open door and said, "Sit here," as he guided Darwin down into a hard folding chair. Darwin started trembling in anticipation of what might happen, and his breath started accelerating to the point where he was close to hyperventilating. The room was dimly lit, and Darwin could see a large desk in front of him, a small brass desk lamp placed on the top, shining on the wooden surface.

Darwin felt the man's hand still resting on his shoulder and he closed his eyes tightly, uncertain of what might happen. He heard footsteps edging toward him and stopping suddenly in front of him. Darwin opened his eyes slowly. A man he had never seen before was standing in front of him, smiling, his eyes kind, crinkled at the corners, and somehow strangely familiar. He looked at Darwin and said, "Hello, Darwin. It's good to see you again."

CHAPTER 20

Darwin stared at the man, stunned and confused. He didn't recognize this man at all. He was older, with gray curly hair and round glasses. He was dressed neatly in a gray vest with a clean white dress shirt underneath, a tie, and a pair of dark slacks. The man looked back at Darwin, with his hands in his pockets, that smile still hovering on his lips, and when he noticed Darwin's confusion, he spoke again.

"You probably don't remember me, do you?" the man asked. "Well, it's probably been around fifteen years since the last time I saw you. You were just a little tyke then."

His voice trembling, Darwin managed to get out, "What do you want from me?"

The man chuckled a little and walked closer to Darwin. "I don't want anything from you. The question is, what do you want from me?"

Darwin gave the man a perplexed look. "I don't understand, I don't know who you are, what could I possibly want from you, other than an explanation for why I'm here and why you've kidnapped me?" The anger rose up again, engulfing him. This was the second time in his life that men had tried to take him away, maybe to hurt him. There was no way he was going down without a fight.

The man looked up at the ceiling, still smiling, and started to pace. "Have you ever wondered, Darwin, why we are here?"

"Yes, I'd *really* like to understand why I'm here right now," Darwin replied sarcastically.

"No, no. I mean why we are here on this earth, what life means, and what our purpose is?"

Darwin frowned, unable to figure out what this man was getting at. Was he trying to be clever and come up with some deep meaning, some bogus reasoning as to why he kidnapped young children? Darwin simply shrugged his shoulders in response, annoyed that the man wasn't getting to the point more quickly.

"Have you ever considered whether we are alone in this universe?"

Still struggling to make sense of the man's line of thinking, Darwin shrugged his shoulders once again, not only irritated, but dejected now.

The man looked at Darwin and laughed a little. "Darwin, have you ever wondered why you look the way you do?" Darwin looked up sharply, giving the man his full attention. He looked at the man intently, his eyes narrowing as he considered the question.

"What do you mean?" Darwin asked.

"Come, follow me," the man said, still smiling as he beckoned for Darwin to follow him, which Darwin did, reluctantly. But Darwin still didn't trust him. For all he knew, he was some creep who was about to show him the room where he kept his other victims.

They walked toward a glass wall, which abruptly opened down the middle, sliding both ways as they approached. It led to another room, this one much larger, with no windows in sight. The ceilings were tall, and the walls were covered with photographs of planets and galaxies as well as spaceships. Some of the photos were old and in black and white. A long table stood in the center of the room, its polished wooden surface shining under the lights above.

The man walked alongside Darwin, looking at him while Darwin looked around the room, craning his neck to take it all in. "In 1977, NASA sent out two spacecraft that would travel beyond the depths of our solar system," the man said. "The spacecraft were called Voyager 1 and Voyager 2. Both crafts carried with them a 12-inch golden phonograph record that contained pictures and sounds of Earth. In addition, we also provided data detailing the location of our world, a sort of galactic map, if you will. This was designed to illustrate how to locate us, should either Voyager ever come into contact with an alien life form or civilization. Now, when we launched this, we didn't know how long it would take to ever reach the edge of our solar system. The initial mission of Voyager 2 was to do a fly-by of our outer planets—Jupiter, Saturn, Uranus, and Neptune. Voyager 1, on the other hand, was designed to travel out and explore our outer solar system. The Voyagers traveled at a speed of 11 miles per second, which sounds pretty fast, but our solar system is massive."

Darwin was listening intently. He'd heard of the Voyager program before in one of his science classes, but didn't know much about it. Nevertheless, he didn't know what this had to do with him, or why he was here in this room.

"After we launched Voyager 1 into space, fourteen years after its launch," the man continued, "it had finally reached the Kuiper Belt and was ready to become the first spacecraft that would travel outside of our solar system." He stopped at one of the photos on the wall and pointed at a picture of Voyager 1 before it was launched into space. "But after it exited our solar system, a mere two months later, it disappeared. We had no record of it in our systems. Then when using our Hubble telescope we looked a little more closely at the area where it was last seen before it disappeared, we noticed a strange, dark, circular sphere just outside of the Kuiper Belt."

The man smiled encouragingly at Darwin, as if this was exciting him.

"Sorry, but Mr. . . . ." Darwin's voice trailed off as he waited for the man to finish his sentence for him.

"Greer. You can call me Dr. Greer."

Darwin stopped dead in his tracks, his mouth dryer than ever.

"Dr. Greer, you said?"

"Yes."

Darwin tried to wrap his brain around what was happening. It couldn't have been a coincidence that the name that both the doctor in the hospital and his father had said when he'd overheard him on the phone was the name of this man standing in front of him.

"Dr. Greer, I'm sorry, but I still don't get what's going on, and what all of this has to do with why I look the way I do. And why you've kidnapped me."

"Darwin, you were running away from home, were you not?" Dr. Greer asked in a contemplative voice.

Darwin, taken aback, looked at the man with a stunned look on his face. "How . . . how, d-did you know that?"

"It was something your father said, right? How a matter needed to be taken care of, should you ever find out? Ring a bell?"

Darwin stood there in silence. How could this man possibly know all of this? Was he a spy of some sort? Did his dad hire him to come find him and teach him some kind of lesson to never run away from home again? Was that why the man in the gray hat had been following him all of this time? Did he work for Dr. Greer?

"Well, this is what your dad didn't want you to know about," said Dr. Greer.

"What is?" Darwin asked, so confused now that he thought his brain might explode if he didn't get some real answers—and quick.

"The story I'm telling you," Dr. Greer said patiently.

Darwin stopped and listened intently without asking any questions, despite the fact that he had hundreds. Dr. Greer waited for Darwin to collect himself before proceeding. "Now, you might be asking yourself, what was this black sphere you found in space just outside of our solar system and why is this significant?"

Darwin didn't have an answer.

"Have you ever heard of something called a black hole, Darwin?"

"Umm, well, I've read about it here and there. Something about gravitational mass being compressed in one area, which causes it to suck anything up in its path."

"Exactly!" Dr. Greer said excitedly. "So, as soon as we saw this black hole, we figured Voyager had to have been sucked up by it completely. If that was, in fact, the case, we knew we had lost it forever." Dr. Greer started making his way over to the wall, and pointed at another photo of a spacecraft that looked similar to the last. "When we lost Voyager 1, we started building another similar spacecraft that would have the same mission. Basically, to repeat what we'd already done, but this time bypassing the black hole completely. We were going to name this spacecraft Civic 1. But, in the days leading up to the launch of Civic, something incredible happened."

"What was it?" Darwin asked, genuinely interested now, and moving closer to look at the spacecraft more carefully.

"One of our scientists who was monitoring and researching the black hole found a small spacecraft entering our solar system. It looked almost as if it had come out of the black hole, and it was a craft we'd never seen before." Dr. Greer now walked over to another picture and pointed at the spacecraft, which looked very different from the previous two Voyagers. This ship was shaped like a rectangle with an antenna on the top and a flattened-out back that almost formed a tail.

"Is that it?" Darwin asked.

"Yep, not too big, about the size of a small house, but boy was it something."

"So, what was it?" Darwin asked, staring at the photo. "Was it one of ours?"

Dr. Greer smiled and laughed a little. "No, no. This wasn't ours at all. Which is why our scientist who discovered it thought he was seeing things when he spotted it. We didn't know where it had come from or why it all of a sudden showed up out of nowhere." Dr. Greer paused and looked at Darwin.

"So, then what?" Darwin asked, intrigued, and wondering why Dr. Greer hadn't continued.

"Well, we didn't do anything first but simply track its whereabouts, it was too far away to really do anything but just watch. But as we began tracking the ship, we noticed that it started traveling in closer and closer to the center of our solar system. And then we soon realized it was heading in our direction . . . toward Earth."

"Toward Earth?"

"Uh-huh, toward Earth."

"How is it that nobody ever knew about this, why wasn't it covered in the media, wouldn't it have been huge news?" Darwin wondered a bit skeptically.

"Well, yes, it would have been big news, but you'd be surprised by the number of things that are kept secret by either the CIA or NASA—mostly for the good of the people."

"But I don't understand," Darwin said slowly. "How could keeping something like that be for the good of the people? Don't they have the right to know?"

Greer shoved his hands in his pockets and looked at Darwin, a benevolent expression on his face, which was sharply lined, as though the last few years had taken a toll on him physically. "Darwin, if there was anything you could change about yourself, what would it be?"

Darwin struggled to understand the relevance here, but he muttered an answer anyway. "I wish I looked different . . . I wish I didn't have this stupid skin condition." He shrugged, inexplicably embarrassed.

"Uh-huh, and why is that?"

"Because I always stand out wherever I go, and people think I have some sort of contagious disease. I just want to look normal. Like everyone else."

"But you're not like everyone else, Darwin," Greer said, his dark, weary eyes boring into Darwin's own tired blue orbs.

"I'm not?"

"No," Dr. Greer said, his tone clipped as he continued on. "There's a good reason why you feel the way you do, Darwin. Society, more often than not, tends to fear what's different or what is perceived as a threat." Dr. Greer started walking along the wall again. "Just look at our history, for example. What we did to the Native Americans when we first embarked on this new land; what we did to slaves, and then even when they were freed, what we did to them to ensure they didn't have the same rights as we did. We persecuted, executed, and discriminated against people, and why? All because they were considered 'different.' Not like us, they didn't talk the same way we did, they had different thoughts, different beliefs, and yet no one stopped to consider that they were human beings, just like every person on this earth."

Darwin stood there nodding his head in agreement. What Dr. Greer was saying reminded him of what Tyler had told him, that people always feared what was different.

"Now, knowing the history of our society and how it reacts to things that might pose a threat to it or its existence, can you imagine the reaction most people would have when finding out that a foreign spacecraft that we had never seen before was heading toward our planet?" Dr. Greer said. He then turned his attention to another pho-to, this one of open space with galaxies scattered all around. "Of course, not everyone would view something like this in a negative or threatening way; there are, of course, others who would embrace it. But without knowing what this spacecraft was or what it wanted, we couldn't take that risk and let it get out to the public."

"But . . . but how were you able to keep it a secret? I mean, wouldn't any astronomer or scientist who happened to be using a telescope notice it?" Darwin wondered aloud, looking at the photos more carefully.

"Well, technically, yes, it's possible. But you have to think about the size of this spacecraft relative to the vast universe around us. Anybody looking at a telescope would have to have pinpoint precision and accuracy to notice it. They would have to come upon it through sheer luck by using a sophisticated telescope, and even then, the chances of them being able to find it, if they didn't know where it was or where it was going, were very slim. Besides, let's say somebody did find it and made a fuss about it—do you think people would treat them any differently than all of the others who've claimed to have seen UFOs or interacted with alien life forms? Those kind of stories end up in the *Enquirer*," Dr. Greer said, chuckling a little.

"So, did the ship eventually land on Earth?"

Dr. Greer scratched his head. "Well, not the ship, no," he said. "The ship remained just outside our atmosphere and we sent a team up to explore it."

"And what did they find?" Darwin asked, his voice barely above a whisper. He couldn't believe that something like this had actually occurred in his lifetime, something out of science-fiction books, the kind of discovery that astronomers dreamed about for their entire careers.

"Come with me," Dr. Greer said, directing Darwin through a side door adjacent to the large room they stood in. When they walked in, the first things Darwin noticed were a bunch of shapes and figures plastered against the wall, squiggly lines that went around in a rectangular shape. The other lines were linear, with shapes inside them. Within the rectangles were dashes and other signs that Darwin couldn't make out because they were so small. They were similar to the graphics he had found in his dad's desk drawer, along with the pictures titling specimens from Florana.

The room they had entered was a small one, not much larger than Darwin's living room. There weren't any pictures on these walls, just the markings of the shapes and figures. There were desks around the room and a long wooden table in the middle.

"What are those markings on the wall, Dr. Greer?" Darwin asked curiously.

"That? That's a written language."

Darwin hesitated before responding, looking confused. "But . . . what language is it?"

"It's not from our planet. When we finally were able to get into the ship, we found a multitude of these markings and shapes displayed all over the walls of the spacecraft."

Darwin stood there with his mouth open, struggling to find the words to speak. "So . . . so, th-this is from a *different* planet, another living life form?"

Dr. Greer smiled. "That's correct." He walked over to the long table, which was actually a large digital flat screen. He pointed at the screen, which was displaying a large blue planet. "And not just any living life form, an intelligent living life form, much more advanced than our own civilization."

Darwin looked more closely. The large blue planet resembled Earth, but with much more water than land.

"How do you know that?"

"Well, as you can imagine, it took years for us to be able to decode all of their writing. We had over two hundred people specializing in linguistics and coding, who spent nearly five years just cracking the code. It was hard work, but we eventually got around to what they were trying to communicate to us."

"And? What did they want? Why did they come here?"

Dr. Greer laughed a little. "They found our Voyager."

Darwin stood there in disbelief. "But, how?" Darwin said, confused. "I thought you said Voyager disappeared into a black hole?"

"Right, that's exactly right. And it traveled through that black hole to another location in our universe, an area that we had discovered before, but didn't know much about. A galaxy much larger than our own: Andromeda. The planet itself that Voyager came into contact with after being flung through the black hole was also much larger than Earth. A planet named Florana."

Darwin stood there dumbfounded. He had heard this name before. It was written in his father's notebooks in the hidden room he had found. "I've heard of that before . . . it, I saw it in my father's office. I just thought it was someone's name." But deep down, Darwin knew that wasn't exactly true. He'd known even then that it was so much more than just a name. He'd had that feeling, that feeling that there was something important about that name, something he needed to remember when the time came. And that time was now. "So then they sent a ship here, but how did they know how to find us?" Darwin asked.

"Don't you remember?" Dr. Greer said, picking up speed. "On Voyager we had left instructions for where we were located, based on the positioning of the stars and our location inside the Milky Way galaxy. Now, for the Floranian people, they likely knew that black hole existed but didn't dare go near it, and who would, if they knew anything about black holes? But when they saw the Voyager come out of the black hole, and when they received it on their planet intact, they likely, or at least we speculate, were able to put their spacecraft back through it. They always had complete control of their ship—unlike us, with Voyager, after it disappeared. Their technology is far more advanced than ours and so complex that we still haven't even been able to duplicate their work to improve our space technology."

"So, when you figured out what they were saying, or what they had displayed in their spaceship in their language, what was it that they wanted? Were they hostile?" Darwin now paced back and forth at the front of the long table, filled with curiosity about what they'd uncovered. He forced himself to stop pacing for a moment and looked at Dr. Greer, waiting for him to answer.

Dr. Greer smiled at Darwin. "Not all creatures are fearful or threatened by what's different from them, Darwin. On the contrary, they gave us a very precious gift, a little peace offering if you will, to see if we were worthy."

"What was the gift?"

Dr. Greer paused, looked deeply into Darwin's eyes through his round glasses, and said, "It was you, Darwin."

CHAPTER 21

Darwin sat on his bed staring at the wall in front of him, his mind racing. Dr. Greer and his team had provided Darwin with a room in which he could stay inside the facility. The room was small, not much bigger than a prison cell, with a desk and a personal TV. Darwin was still trying to wrap his mind around everything he'd just heard. It was overwhelming enough to find out that an alien species had contacted Earth by sending a ship just outside of our atmosphere, but to find out that his life and everything that he knew about it was a lie was almost incomprehensible.

The memory kept playing over and over in Darwin's head. Dr. Greer telling him that he was the gift this species had given to the world, with specific instructions on how to create one of their own species on Earth. Darwin was no longer who he thought he was. All his life he'd thought he was just another kid, a human like any other who happened to suffer from a rare skin condition and who, every so often, had weird visions. But Darwin had just discovered that he wasn't human at all. He was a creation, not born from parents, but rather made using various chromosomes and DNA to form what Dr. Greer called a "Floranian."

Florana, as Dr. Greer described it, was the planet that these alien life forms came from. They were a part of the galaxy of Andromeda, which was roughly 2.5 million light years away from Earth. Normally it would be impossible to reach this galaxy through normal means of space travel, but by being connected through the black hole at the edge of the Kuiper Belt, Darwin learned that humans could be connected to them in just twelve years in Earth time.

By the time Voyager 1 had reached them and their ship returned to us, just shy of twenty-four years had passed. Once the ship was discovered outside our atmosphere, it then took NASA, with some two hundred resources, five years to decode the Floranian language. The ship had a host of information on it, which included photographs of their species and their civilization, how long their world had existed, their advanced technology, and above all, instructions for how to create one of their own using stem cells and DNA chromosomes. The purpose of doing this was to see how one of their own species would adapt to our world, to determine if Earth was safe enough for more Floranians to reside on, and hopefully for both populations to work together and exchange resources. Essentially, they wanted to see if Floranians would be accepted by the general population and treated fairly, and to ensure the earth wouldn't be a hostile environment before sending others there.

Darwin was that test. He was the man-made creation of a Floranian that NASA had spent over two years meticulously putting together cell by cell, created from a test tube. In fact, it had taken NASA nine attempts to finally complete him. It was all too much information for Darwin to handle, and he had to sit and clear his head for a bit in order to take in everything Dr. Greer had just divulged to him. He concentrated on taking deep breaths, filling his lungs with air and then releasing it in order to calm himself.

Dr. Greer, noticing Darwin's deep breathing and slightly overwhelmed state, said he'd be back in a little while to walk Darwin through some further information. As Darwin watched Dr. Greer slip quietly out the door, he wondered what else there could be?

The question that Darwin wanted to know most was, why? Why didn't they tell him about this earlier? Why did he have to go through his entire childhood believing he was something he wasn't? Why didn't his parents tell him? Did they even know? They had to, Darwin thought; he wasn't their biological child, so clearly, they knew. So many questions were racing through Darwin's mind that he could barely keep track of them. All he could do was hope that the answers would all be revealed to him in due time.

A knock came on the door, which was then slowly opened.

Darwin could see Dr. Greer's curly gray head sticking out, his friendly face peering around the door frame. "You doing all right?" he asked kindly. Darwin didn't say anything but nodded his head. "I know it's a lot to take in, but I promise you, everything you'll need to know will be given to you when you're ready to receive it."

"I think I'm ready to receive it now," Darwin said, unsure if the words he'd just spoken were really true.

"Well . . . maybe not everything, but come with me, I want to show you something."

Dr. Greer walked Darwin down a long corridor. Lined up against the walls were doors that led to rooms very similar to the one Darwin was staying in. No windows could be found around these parts; everything was encased in dark gray walls, and Darwin wondered how Dr. Greer could work down here without any natural sunlight.

"You hungry?" Dr. Greer asked. "I just realized that we haven't offered you anything since your arrival." Darwin wasn't really hungry; in fact, he felt a little queasy. A day on the run from his parents, to then being stopped and presumably kidnapped by masked assailants, to now finding out that he was a creation from another planet hadn't exactly helped his anxiety levels. Or his appetite.

"Not really?" Darwin said quietly, his answer more of a question than a statement.

"I know a lot has happened in the last twenty-four hours, but don't worry, you're in good hands with my team here." Just then, it occurred to Darwin that he still hadn't met anyone from Dr. Greer's team. They weren't around, and Dr. Greer referred to them quite often. Perhaps they were based somewhere else?

Dr. Greer reached a door at the end of the corridor, which was labeled *Conference*, and opened the door to a large room filled with people who were all chatting and laughing with one another. A spread of pastries, doughnuts, fruit, and coffee nearly covered the entire conference table. They all looked up as soon as the door opened, and their talking slowly died down. Those who were sitting stood up, looking at Darwin intently. Initially, Darwin thought they were staring at his skin, just the way everyone else usually did. Then he noticed that they almost seemed happy to see him, their faces uniformly beaming with smiles and some even nodding approvingly when Darwin made eye contact.

"Darwin, meet the team," Dr. Greer said, motioning his hand across the room. "This is the Floranian Special Services team, these are the people who are responsible for everything relating to Florana. Most of the team is here, some are located elsewhere or are traveling on business."

Darwin looked around the room slowly, with a nervous smile on his face. The team members varied in age, with some appearing to be in their late sixties while others were in their early thirties. A few people started coming up to Darwin to introduce themselves.

"Darwin!" one man said as he approached him. "I can't believe we're meeting you, at last. Rick Mantis, I work in linguistics and coding. I'm one of the people who translates all of the symbols and graphics that make the Floranian language."

Rick was one of the older men, perhaps in his late fifties to early sixties. He was bald and had glasses so thick they looked like twin magnifying glasses perched on the end of his nose.

"Nice to meet you," Darwin said, still nervous and feeling slightly uneasy from all of the people looking at him.

"Boy, you sure grew up fast. I haven't seen you since you were just a few months old," Rick marveled.

"Rick's been with the department for over twenty years, he assisted on translating the instructions for how to create you," Dr. Greer said. Darwin nodded to acknowledge Rick, but his thoughts swam in his brain too quickly to grab onto any one of them. The whole thing was still too much. As curious as he was to know everything, he knew that obtaining such information so quickly could have a psychological effect on him, too, and he wasn't sure it would be wholly positive.

Darwin began to breathe rapidly; he couldn't seem to catch his breath, and every inhale was faint, as if he had just gotten the wind knocked out of him. Both Rick and Dr. Greer immediately switched from smiling to expressing extreme concern. They held Darwin by the arms as he stumbled forward. The rest of the crew slowly stopped talking as they noticed what was going on.

"Darwin, Darwin . . . you all right?" Dr. Greer asked. Darwin did everything he could to respond, but no words came out; only gasps for air. "Come with me," Dr. Greer said as he looked back at the team, who by now all looked concerned, as Darwin could barely breathe. "Okay, folks, let's get back to work, huh?" Dr. Greer said briskly as he held on to Darwin, leading him out of the room.

Dr. Greer brought Darwin back to his room, as he was still gasping for air. "Darwin, Darwin, relax. Just try and breathe normally."

Darwin felt his whole body twitching; he was gasping for air, his heart was racing, and there was nothing he could do to control it. Was he going to die, right here in this strange place? Without his parents, with these people he didn't know? He had never had these feelings or thoughts of being close to death before, and they terrified him.

"I think he's having a panic attack," Dr. Greer said to Rick, who had followed them back to Darwin's room and was looking around at Darwin from behind Dr. Greer. Dr. Greer quickly started looking around the room and pulled a brown paper bag out from the desk. "Darwin, I need you to breathe into this, just try and breathe normally." Dr. Greer gently led Darwin over to his bed and motioned for him to sit down, then handed Darwin the paper bag.

Darwin put the bag over his mouth and tried breathing as normally as he could. He was still struggling to inhale, and continued to gasp for air through the paper bag. Then, after about thirty seconds or so, Darwin's breathing began to slow down. He could feel air finally entering his lungs properly, without much struggle.

Another minute went by, and Darwin was starting to resume normal breathing, still blowing into the bag. "Is that better?" Dr. Greer asked. Darwin looked up at Rick and could see that his facial expression had calmed down a bit. "You were hyperventilating. I think all of this has been a bit of a shock to your nervous system. Not to mention the fact that you haven't gotten much sleep. Might be best if we retire for the day. You can rest up and we'll chat tomorrow morning."

Darwin pulled the paper bag away from his mouth, and he looked around his room, not making eye contact with either Dr. Greer or Rick. "Have you all kidnapped me? Why are you locking me up here, is this some sort of trick? Where are my parents?" Darwin's voice cracked as he spoke, then started to rise.

"Darwin," Dr. Greer paused. "You're not being kidnapped. We need you to remain here for your own security. We need to ensure that we can trust you. Everything that has been revealed to you is highly classified information, and could be incredibly dangerous if it were to get out to the public. Do you understand?"

"No, no . . . my parents are going to worry about me. Where are they, I want to talk to my mom," Darwin said, looking back and forth at both Dr. Greer and Rick. He began to shout, "What do you guys want from me, huh? Are you after my family? What is this place, really? Is Dr. Greer even your real name?"

Dr. Greer slowly walked over to the chair sitting at the desk and pulled it over to the bed, where Darwin was sitting. "Listen, Darwin. I know this all sounds crazy and it would only be natural for you to not want to believe it, but let me ask you something. Did you ever think it was strange when you caught your dad talking on the phone about something that clearly didn't have anything to do with his job? Or how about when you found his little office? Something didn't add up, right?"

Darwin stared at Dr. Greer in surprise. "How did you know that?"

"Your dad was never an accountant," Dr. Greer said, sitting down on the bed beside him. "Darwin, he's been working for the CIA, and a has been a liaison with NASA, specifically with my team, for the past twenty-five years." Darwin sat there in shock, his face blank and impassive. He felt as if he could literally feel the blood draining from it. How could he have been deceived by his parents this whole time, he wondered. They had lied to him his whole life, and they had always known. They'd always known who he was. *What* he was. "You see, your dad joined the department when he was twenty-seven. He was young, ambitious, and looking for an opportunity to move up at the Agency. He joined the Floranian Special Services team around the time the Floranian spaceship came into our orbit. Now, at the time, the team wasn't called that, and we didn't know what the Floranians had on their spacecraft. Five years passed, after we decoded their language, and then sure enough we had the blueprint of how to make you. We spent a good three months deliberating on how we should approach it; should we make this discovery public and let the world know that an alien life form would soon be living among us? Or should we have the child raised with a family like anyone else, keeping your identity and everything about you confidential? This was, after all, what the Floranian people wanted. They wanted to see if one of their own would be treated fairly, before coming to visit our world. Naturally, we thought making you public would only cause you to become a celebrity in the eyes of the world, and you wouldn't truly be brought up organically in our society."

Darwin didn't want to believe it. There were too many factors that didn't support everything Dr. Greer claimed. Then, he remembered what his psychiatrist had told him. Schizophrenia, he'd been diagnosed with schizophrenia. Could he be in the middle of a dream? Another one of his visions?

"No!" Darwin shouted, jumping to his feet. "This isn't real, you're not real. I need my medication . . . I have to go home."

Dr. Greer got up and walked over to the desk, opened the top drawer, and pulled a bottle out from under the desk along with what looked like a prescription. "You mean, this medication?" Dr. Greer held the bottle up so Darwin could see it clearly. It was a prescription drug, all right, Darwin's medication, the same one that had been given to him by the psychiatrist. The label even listed his name and the dosage instructions.

"How . . . how do you have it? That's my medication," Darwin said, looking at Dr. Greer with a stunned look on his face, his eyes wide, his mouth falling open.

"Abilify, a common antipsychotic used to treat schizophrenia, yes. But this isn't Abilify, and you've never taken Abilify in your life." Dr. Greer popped open the bottle and poured one of the pills into his hand. "These are sugar tablets, a placebo, if you will." He then popped the pill into his mouth and began to chew. "See, they're quite good, actually. Have a taste." Dr. Greer handed one of the tablets to Darwin.

Darwin stared at the tablet in his hand, looked up, and said, "You mean . . . I've been taking candy my whole life?"

Dr. Greer nodded.

"But, how was that supposed to treat my schizophrenia?" Darwin sputtered, aware that he'd never felt so close to losing it completely.

Dr. Greer smiled. "You never had it, Darwin. All of those visions, dreams, that you had, those were all real. It's a part of the mind of a Floranian. It comes with the territory."

"But . . . but what about the people I saw, the people who weren't supposed to be real? There was a man, who was following me, my doctor said it was just my imagination."

"That man's name is Mark Leverne, and he works on my team. He was assigned with keeping an eye on you, to make sure you were progressing well. He probably didn't do the best job since you caught him multiple times, but maybe you're just a clever kid."

Darwin was shaking his head. The whole thing was ludicrous. "What about my doctor?" he asked.

"Hired by the government as well, he was given specific instructions to tell you that you had been imagining these people, we couldn't let your curiosity run wild and have you try to find out why this man was watching you, following you. The risk of you finding out what was going on before you were ready wasn't something we wanted to chance."

Darwin paused for a moment; he remembered the two men who had tried to kidnap him, when he was in third grade. "The men who tried to kidnap me when I was younger, that was your team, too?"

Dr. Greer looked down, a little hesitant, before responding, "Well, not exactly. They used to be members of our team, but they were fixated on exposing you to the world. They felt it wasn't right to keep this type of information hidden from people, and to also keep it hidden from you—who you really are."

"Then why would they kidnap me?"

"Well, their desire to expose you to the world naturally led to their termination at NASA. Once they were fired, they took matters into their own hands and wanted to show the world what they knew, that NASA had created a Floranian." Dr. Greer stood up from his chair and began to pace. "They knew that no credible news outlet would believe them without proof. They knew where you were, where you went to school, and so they tried to capture you so they could prove to the media that their information was both accurate and credible."

Darwin remained silent, and his eyes were wide with confusion. Dr. Greer could see that this was enough information thrown at Darwin for the day. "Let's turn in for the day, shall we? Get some rest, it'll be a big day tomorrow, I've got someone coming to visit you," Dr. Greer said as he made his way to the door.

"Is it my parents?" Darwin looked up intently at Dr. Greer.

"No, not your parents, we've notified them, and they'll be coming soon as well. Your dad is in a bit of trouble for letting his assignment run away," Dr. Greer said, a hint of a smile playing at the corners of his lips.

"Is he going to be okay?" Darwin asked, concerned. Despite the fact that he and his dad had never gotten along, he didn't want anything bad to happen to him.

"Oh yes, he'll be fine. He just might have to face some questioning from the department, and to be quite frank, it looks like he'll be reassigned, since you now know who you are. It was always the protocol to have you brought to NASA and to tell you everything, should you ever have the slightest inkling. We needed to ensure that you understood the importance of keeping something like this confidential."

Darwin sat there for a second and looked at Dr. Greer, who was making his way out the door of his room. "That's the thing, I don't know who I am at all now. Everything that I thought I was—it was all a lie. My whole life."

Dr. Greer turned around and looked at Darwin. "Don't view it that way, Darwin. Look at it as a new beginning, a new avenue for you to explore who you really are. Your creation and the discovery of it could have a profound impact on the world. Do you understand that? With you, we have finally discovered that we are no longer alone in this vast universe, and maybe, just maybe, the people of this world will come to understand and recognize our purpose on this planet."

Dr. Greer rested his hand lightly on Darwin's shoulder. Maybe Dr. Greer was right. Darwin didn't know for sure, but he knew that he wanted to believe him. Darwin looked up at Dr. Greer's kind, benevolent face, and Darwin felt his panic attack receding, the adrenaline fading to a faint buzzing in his veins, and for the first time he felt almost hopeful that there might be some optimism in the situation he currently found himself in.

CHAPTER 22

Darwin awoke the next morning to the sound of knocking on his door. He squeezed his eyes tightly and rubbed them with his palms. He had almost forgotten where he was. He slowly made his way over to the door, stumbling a little. He didn't know what time it was but knew that it had to be early, as he was still exhausted. Of course, he hadn't slept well at all, given everything that was on his mind.

Darwin opened the door slowly and saw a man in his sixties with close-cropped silver hair, dressed in a carefully pressed dark suit. He was holding a tray with a lid over it. "Sorry, I don't mean to bother you, but I have your breakfast," the man said in a British accent.

"Oh . . . of course, thank you. Please come in," Darwin said, opening the door widely so the man could enter.

The man walked inside and set the tray down on the desk. "Anything else I can help you with? You know where the bathroom and showers are?"

"Yeah, I do. And no, this should be fine. Thank you."

The man exited the room, closing the door behind him. Darwin then made his way over to his breakfast. He opened the lid to find a stack of pancakes with a side of fruit and eggs. Up in the right-hand corner of the tray was a potassium tablet. He chuckled a little and thought to himself, *Of course*. He remembered why he in fact needed to take the potassium, not because of a condition he had been told he was born with, but rather because it was a vital mineral needed for the Floranian body, which required four times the amount of potassium a human body needed. Rick Mantis had provided him this tidbit of information last night. Unlike the Abilify, the potassium wasn't a placebo.

As Darwin sank his teeth into the pancakes, he heard another quick knock on the door, followed by the door being opened slowly. Darwin looked up to see who it was. His mouth dropped open, with half-eaten pancakes sitting inside. His mind was racing, trying to put together how this could possibly be. The door closed, and Tyler Barros stood in front of the door, looking at Darwin with a slight grin on his face. At first, Darwin almost didn't even recognize him. He was wearing a dark suit and had a full thick beard. His hair was also much longer than Darwin remembered it. It was almost as if Tyler hadn't cut his hair since the last time they'd seen each other.

"How's it going, buddy?" Tyler asked. Darwin didn't know what to say; he still had the half-eaten pancakes in his mouth, trying to understand why on earth Tyler was here and how he could have gotten into the building. Finally, after chewing his pancakes quickly, Darwin struggled to get some words out.

"Wh . . . what . . . what are you d-doing here?"

"Well, Dr. Greer thought that it would be good for me to come spend some time with you. Guess he wants to make sure you don't get homesick or anything," Tyler said with that old familiar grin.

"But . . . but how do you know Dr. Greer? Why would he contact you? What's going on?" Darwin asked, the questions falling from his lips in staccato bursts, like machine-gun fire.

"Easy, buddy, easy," Tyler said, seeing Darwin's agitation. "Listen, I know what Dr. Greer told you, and I know that it can't be easy, finding out everything he told you yesterday. I'm sure you feel betrayed and deceived, but I want to let you know that it was all for your own good." Darwin wasn't following; he was still confused as to how Tyler could know what he was and where he had come from, and be so calm about it. Any other human being, outside of those at NASA, would be in a state of shock—just like Darwin. Why was Tyler so calm?

"What are you trying to get at? How long have you known about all of this?" Darwin asked.

"Darwin, remember when I told you around the time when we first met that I was always interested in law enforcement or government work?"

Darwin nodded, still nervous as to what Tyler's point was.

"Well, the reason I was interested in government work is because that's what I actually do."

"But . . . you're in high school. How could you get a job like that?"

Tyler looked at him, his expression grave, and Darwin could tell that whatever Tyler had to say wasn't going to be easy to hear. "I'm not who you think I am."

Darwin's head moved back, waiting for Tyler to finish.

"I'm not seventeen, I'm twenty-eight, and I work for Dr. Greer on NASA's Floranian Special Services team."

Darwin's breath and heart rate started to increase rapidly. Not only had he been lied to by his parents for his whole life about what he was, but now he found out his only friend from school was in fact a part of this NASA organization that was most likely responsible for his creation and development.

"What . . . what do you mean? Are you saying you're in on all of this? You knew this whole time, and you never told me? I really thought you were my friend." Darwin's voice started to rise slowly.

"I was your friend, Darwin. I am. You're a good kid, and you didn't deserve to be treated the way you were at school. It reminded me of myself back when I was in high school. I was a late bloomer, and very small for my age. Kids picked on me all the time, and I hated it."

Darwin rolled his eyes in disbelief. Why should he believe Tyler when he had deceived him into believing they were actually friends? Darwin crossed his arms over his chest and stared at the floor, refusing to make eye contact.

"Look," Tyler continued, taking a step toward Darwin, "when I was asked to take on this assignment, I wanted to do more than just see you as a social experiment, I wanted to *help* you. I wanted to help boost your confidence, urge you to stand up for yourself, and to realize that there are people in this world who treat one another with kindness and respect." Tyler waved one hand in front of Darwin's face, urging Darwin to look over at him. "Listen, if I could do it all over again, I wouldn't have taken the assignment. The closer we got, the more terrible I felt keeping all of this from you. But you have to understand, I was working undercover on a highly secretive mission, and if I'd told you, it could've had huge consequences, not only for you and me, but for the world."

Despite the anger he still felt about being lied to, Darwin felt his resolve starting to thaw. As angry as he was, Darwin knew that he couldn't stay mad at Tyler for long—he was the only friend he'd ever really had.

"What else do I not know?" Darwin asked wearily, the adrenaline still pumping through his veins.

"I'm afraid there is quite a bit still, but you got the big stuff from Dr. Greer." Tyler started making his way out of the room, resting one hand on the doorknob before looking back at Darwin. "Come on, I'll fill you in. Let's take a walk and I'll show you around."

It was the first time Darwin had been outside since he was abducted by Dr. Greer's men a couple of days prior. It was early enough in the morning that the birds outside were still chirping in the trees. It was a beautiful campus, with long winding pathways that stretched across large fields, which had little gardens littered throughout the grounds. The sun was out and shining brightly as they walked down the concrete pathways of the campus. The humidity felt like a wave of mist was constantly being sprayed upon them. Darwin could tell it was going to be a warm summer day.

They had walked around the facility for about an hour before it started to become too hot and humid to remain outdoors. Darwin had asked a lot of questions and received a lot of answers, but still wanted to know more; namely, what came next. The department had always known there would be a time when Darwin would discover who he was, but what was the plan after that?

"Do you think they'll come visit us now?" Darwin asked as the two entered back inside the facility.

"Who?" Tyler said, turning to shoot him a quizzical glance.

"The Floranians. Now that they know I was taken care of properly and that there is no danger or threat to them, wouldn't they come? Wasn't that the whole point of even sending me?"

"Well, you have to understand that just because you are okay doesn't mean they would be safe here. The public doesn't even know that we've made contact with other life forms. We have no idea what kind of reaction we would get from the world, knowing that we aren't alone, and that our Floranian brothers and sisters want to visit Earth."

"You think people here would be hostile toward them?" Darwin wondered aloud as they walked down the brightly lit, silent hallway.

"We don't want to jump to conclusions, but if the way we currently treat others who aren't like us is any indication how we would behave toward such a thing, then I would say there is likely going to be some backlash. Look at our nation for example—we've built walls and borders to keep people out of our country. Keeping people of their own kind, human beings who inhabit this earth, away from our land. And why? Because they look different? They speak a different language? Imagine what that would be on a scale of a completely different species they know nothing about?"

Darwin nodded his head. He had to admit Tyler was right, just judging by the way kids treated him at school.

"So, what I am supposed to do? Just go back home and live my life? How can I do that now, knowing what I know?" Darwin sighed in frustration. It didn't even feel possible to return to that old life. It was gone. As they stopped in front of a large set of double doors, Darwin knew that as much as he may have wanted to, there was no going back now.

"Don't worry, we'll figure something out. Honestly, you weren't supposed to find any of this out now. The plan was to do it once you fully became an adult, around your mid-twenties. But then when you discovered your dad's hidden office and tried to run away from home, we clearly had to intervene."

Tyler pushed open the doors and led Darwin inside a large room with a pool table, two ping-pong tables, and two foosball tables. There was a large flat-screen TV and a huge sectional couch. Snacks and soft drinks were also stored behind a bar next to the pool table.

"THIS is where you guys work?" Darwin asked with his eyes wide, taking in the room.

Tyler laughed. "No, no. This is our recreation room, just a place to take a break from time to time."

"This is great. I wish I worked for you guys," Darwin said wistfully, as he looked around the room.

"Well, in a way you do. You're like an ambassador to the planet of Florana," Tyler said with a smile.

Darwin snickered. "I guess so. Even though I just found out about the job two days ago." Darwin paused, wanting to ask Tyler something that had been on his mind. "Tyler, what happened to you after that fight with Billy? I mean, since you weren't really a student, you couldn't have been suspended. Why did you have to leave?"

Tyler nodded his head and his face fell slightly, as though it distressed him to think of the incident. "Well, Dr. Greer felt that it would be best for me to remove myself from the assignment, given what had happened. I shouldn't have let my emotions get the best of me there, because that's a part of my job, to be detached. To be honest, I was lucky I didn't get fired. I lost my cool, and I should have been more professional, knowing that I was on the job. Obviously, the principal knew I wasn't really a student, but he thought I was working undercover as a law-enforcement agent. When he heard about the incident, he said he had no choice but to dismiss me. Dr. Greer felt that I wasn't ready for this type of assignment, so he brought me back here to work on Floranian coding."

"Coding? What do you mean, I thought you guys already decoded their language?" Darwin asked, walking over to the ping-pong table and picking up a small white ball. He held it in his palm.

"Well, yes, we have. But they left thousands of scriptures that still need to be translated. Aside from creating you, we want to know what their message is for us."

"What have you uncovered so far?" Darwin asked, releasing the ball back onto the table, where it rolled across the green top.

"Some of it is pretty basic stuff right now: where their planet is, what it's made of, how many people inhabit it. Obviously, much of the information they've provided to us could've changed, since this was over ten years ago and the fact that their planet is some 2.5 million light years away from us."

"So, what is their planet made of, how many of them are there?" Darwin asked excitedly.

"Tell you what, we've compiled all of this information into a document, I'll print it out and you can read through it, that way you can get all of your questions answered."

Darwin nodded in agreement and instead of talking about Florana like they had done over the past hour, they decided to take a break and play some ping-pong.

"I figured you might need a mental break from everything that has happened over the past two days. The rec room is just the place to do that."

"Cool," Darwin said, picking up a paddle. "You up for a match?" he asked with a smile.

"Thought you'd never ask." Tyler grinned as he removed his suit jacket, throwing it over on the couch nearby, and stepping to the other side of the table.

CHAPTER 23

The writing on the whiteboard was scribbled all over, with so many different options and ideas, but none of them seemed to be ideal. Dr. Greer and fifteen members of his team whom he'd previously selected sat in their conference room, all looking at the board without saying a word to one another. They had been there for two hours, trying to decide the best course of action going forward. Darwin's future, and the future of the world, depended on whatever solution they came up with.

"I like the approach of wait and see," a tall and gangly man with a dark beard, who went by the name of Lionel Stark, said after a good thirty seconds of silence from the group staring at the board. The wait-and-see tactic was an approach to keep everything quiet, the way they had for the last seventeen years of Darwin's life, with the hope that in five to ten years it would be an appropriate time to divulge the information to the public. But the team worried that given the current state of the United States and the world, being so divided, violent, and apathetic, introducing a new alien life form on Earth would only cause chaos, which would have an extremely negative impact on Darwin and would obviously deter the Floranians from ever wanting to visit Earth at all.

"We really can't wait that long, though. Darwin already knows who he is and it's imperative to prove to the Floranians that we aren't a hostile world. This is the next step in advancing our civilization. There's so much we don't know about their world, their society, or even what they know about this universe that we don't. It's critical that we maintain a good relationship with them," Alina Rans, the head of the linguistics coding team, blurted out, her green eyes ablaze with emotion. She tossed her head. Her brunette hair was streaked with subtle strands of blond highlights; tight curls fell in ringlets to her shoulders, a high contrast against the dark suit she wore.

"How is waiting another five to ten years a bad thing?" Lionel asked.

"Because the Floranians have already waited seventeen years for Darwin to grow up. We know that they have been monitoring him and his environment since he was created, based on the scriptures they have sent to us. Keeping it a secret from him for this long, then telling him and asking him to continue on with his life like nothing has happened, isn't going to bode well with the Floranians, and especially not for Darwin."

"Then what do you suggest, Alina?" Dr. Greer asked.

"I still think our best option is to inform the public immediately," she said. "And ensure that he's set up with the proper security and protection."

"The problem with that is that we don't have sufficient resources to protect Darwin 24/7. We already know Dave is useless—he could barely even be a father for the child. Jane is still an option, but she's too attached and emotional for an assignment like this. They've both been with NASA for too long. The fact is that we need someone new."

"Then we need to find more resources, increase our budget, make a proposal to the executive branch," Alina added.

"You want to get the president involved?" Lionel asked incredulously, shooting Dr. Greer a look of disbelief.

"Why not, he's already aware of the situation," Alina pointed out. "He's known ever since he took office."

"It's not that simple, Alina," Dr. Greer noted with a sigh. "We need to figure out where Darwin would stay, where he would go to school. No amount of protection will make everything okay for Darwin, once this news becomes public. His whole life is going to change."

Alina paused for a moment and tried to wrap her head around this. She knew that keeping the Floranians private from the people of the world was not what humankind needed at this time.

"Dr. Greer, you're concerned with the current state of the world, correct?" Alina asked.

Dr. Greer paused for a moment before answering, "Of course."

"And you're worried that exposing Darwin and the world to what we have discovered could have a negative impact on the population, and make things even worse?"

Dr. Greer nodded his head. "Go on."

"What if this is what the world needs right now? To be blunt, we are suffering, afflicted, and in pain. With every passing day there is more violence and more individuals losing their livelihood. The United States is becoming segregated again from the increasing levels of crime. To make matters worse, other countries around the world are following suit. The gap between the rich and poor is widening every day, and the poor are routinely used as a scapegoat for the world's problems. We need a unifying source, someone to look up to, something that tells our citizens that they're not alone. I understand the concern, the ramifications that it could have on both you and the department by making this public, it could cause chaos, the world could be more fearful than it's ever been. But I firmly believe that announcing that we are no longer alone, that we share a common bond with others in this universe, would have a profoundly positive impact on this earth." Alina took a deep breath, aware that the room had fallen silent and the men seated at the table were now looking at her quietly and intently. She just hoped it had been enough.

Dr. Greer sat quietly, considering all she had said, a solemn look on his face, as if his heart was heavy. "All right," he said finally. "If you can come up with a concrete plan, and it's feasible for the well-being of both Darwin and this world, I will entertain it," he said slowly.

Alina smiled with joy; she knew the task would be difficult, a lot of responsibility would be placed on her shoulders, but she was ready for the challenge.

"Yes, Dr. Greer, it'll be my priority. I'll leave Tyler Barros in charge of the translation team while I focus on this."

"Let's try and turn a solution around quickly, though," Dr.

Greer said as he pushed back his chair and stood up, signaling that the meeting was now over. "We don't want to leave Darwin in the dark forever. He has to know what the next steps are."

The next day, Tyler came barreling into Darwin's room, out of breath as if he had just run a long-distance race. Today, instead of the dark suit he'd worn the previous morning, he was dressed a bit more informally in a pair of dark jeans and a pale blue dress shirt. He crouched down, placing his hands on his knees and trying to catch his breath as he took in great noisy gulps of air.

"What's wrong?" Darwin asked, his adrenaline suddenly pumping at the sign of seeing Tyler gasping for air. He was sitting up in bed, which was made, and was fully dressed in jeans and a black T-shirt he'd found in the closet.

"They . . . made me . . . head of translation," Tyler replied, inhaling after each word.

"That's great!" Darwin exclaimed. "Isn't that what you wanted?"

Tyler started waiving his hand and shaking his head *no*, along with the heavy inhales and exhales.

"No, I mean, yeah, it's great, but it's just an interim role while Mrs. Rans heads up another assignment." Tyler was now starting to catch his breath. "The reason I rushed over here, though, was to tell you that she's been tasked with coming up with a plan of attack for how to make your creation and the discovery of Florana public to the world."

Darwin stood up, unable to fully process what he'd just heard. It seemed too good to be true. "Really? They . . . they want to do that?"

"Well, if they can come up with a good plan, then yeah. But it makes sense, we can't just keep hiding this from the world, it's an amazing discovery that could shape our future." Tyler had now caught his breath back, and had stood up to his full height. "Do you have any water or something, I'm dying over here."

Darwin motioned over to the mini-refrigerator in his room, and Tyler strode over and, grabbing one, screwed the top off and proceeded to chug the contents faster than anyone Darwin had ever seen.

"Where did you come from that you're so out of breath?"

Tyler took a final gulp of water and exhaled with an "Ahh." He then gained some breath and spoke loudly. "From the archives room where all of the Floranian writing is housed, it's about a half-mile away from here, and I ran the whole way." Darwin looked uneasily at Tyler, opening his mouth as if to say something, then closed it. "What is it? You're excited, right?" Tyler said encouragingly. "Now the whole world will know who you are, you'll be respected, honored, an inspiration. You realize you'll be treated like a celebrity?"

Darwin scratched his head and stood up. Before he knew it, he had started pacing, the way he'd always done when he was upset or angry. The same pacing he'd seen his father do for years. "I don't know. I mean . . . what if I get ridiculed even more?

"How so?" Tyler asked patiently, sitting on top of the mini-fridge.

"I mean, my whole life, kids at school would make fun of me, thinking I was an alien or something because of the way I looked, and it turns out that they were right—I'm an alien, after all! Don't you think people will be freaked out? You always said that people fear what's different."

Tyler sat there for a moment, contemplating Darwin's words, before lifting a hand to scratch his forehead. "Well, there will obviously be people who won't be accepting of you." He then waved his hand to show he disagreed with his previous statement. "No, you know what, who cares what those people think? This is an historic moment for humankind. We've made contact with an outside world, and the implications that it could have on our future, the level of intergalactic communication that will result from it, will have so much weight on how we live as a society, moving forward. There is simply no way people will have any opposition to this. I'm sure of it," he said decisively, as if the matter was now closed.

Darwin sighed, sitting back down on the bed, needing to catch his breath after his frantic pacing. He hoped Tyler was right, but he couldn't help but think that Tyler's opinion was rather biased, to say the least, as he worked for NASA. Naturally, he would assume most people would think like him and embrace the idea of making contact with another life form. Tyler had been working with NASA for almost four years, and most others on the team had been working with the department for their whole career. This is what they dreamed of, a day when humanity would find intelligent life in the universe, proving we weren't alone. But was it the dream shared by the rest of the population who lived on Earth, Darwin wondered. And if it wasn't, what would happen to him as a result?

Alina spent the next forty-eight hours tirelessly working on a strategy to inform the world of the Floranian discovery. She'd barely slept, only taking two-hour naps in the early morning, spending countless hours drafting proposals, budgeting numbers for additional resources for security, and an overall timeline. She looked up at the clock mounted on the wall, noticing it was nearly midnight. She looked down at all of her notes and spreadsheets and sighed out loud, as she knew there was still a great deal of work to be done before Dr. Greer would approve the plan to inform the world of Florana.

Another two hours went by, and Alina was desperately trying to keep her eyes open. No amount of coffee was helping after the lack of sleep she'd had over the last two days. She opened one of the desk drawers and pulled out a sleeping bag she'd stored there for the past week, given the long nights she'd been enduring. She moved her chair to the corner of the office and rolled out the bag right next to her desk. She thought about going to the bathroom to brush her teeth and wash her face, but then rejected that idea quickly when she lay down on top of her sleeping bag, her limbs so heavy they felt like they were made of lead.

Just as she was starting to fall asleep, she heard a noise outside her office that sounded like a clattering of dishes. She peered up slowly over the top of her desk and looked outside the clear glass walls of her office. Nothing was there. She heard the noise again. There was definitely someone in the kitchenette nearby, a few doors down from her office. But who would still be here working at this time of night, she thought. Besides the security guards who patrolled the campus, it was unlikely that anyone else would still be working at 2:00 a.m.

Alina opened the door to her office and walked down to the kitchenette, the noise growing louder with her approach. She slowly glanced around the corner into the kitchenette and spotted someone standing there, his back toward her. Alina's mouth opened when she realized it was Darwin. He appeared to be making a sandwich, and she watched as he methodically layered slices of turkey breast atop the bread, adding slices of cheese in between the layers. Alina wondered how on earth he could have found this area at all. It wasn't close to his room, and technically Darwin wasn't allowed to walk around the facility at night unsupervised.

"Ahem." Alina cleared her throat to get Darwin's attention. Darwin swung around quickly, his eyes widening. "Oh, it's okay." Alina reached out with her hand. "Sorry, I didn't mean to scare you. My name is Alina, I work on Dr. Greer's team." Darwin stood there motionless, still looking a little wary and holding a bottle of mustard in one hand like a makeshift weapon. In the fluorescent light of the kitchenette, she could see his spotted skin clearly, his skin pale beneath it, as if he'd been terrified by her unexpected presence. This was actually the first time Alina had ever seen Darwin up close, and she couldn't help but be surprised by, well, how normal he looked. There was the vitiligo, sure, but other than that he was a teenage boy, making himself a midnight snack. Just like millions of teenage boys all over the world.

"Sorry . . . I didn't know anybody was here," Darwin said, relaxing his grip on the mustard bottle and taking a deep breath.

"My name is Alina, Alina Rans," she said as she walked slowly toward him, reaching out her hand to shake his.

"I'm Darwin. Nice to meet you." Darwin shook her hand, his palm cool and dry against her own. "Are you the same Alina that Tyler reports to for translation and coding?"

"Yep! That's me," Alina said with a smile. "I heard you two became pretty close when Tyler was assigned to accompany you at school."

Darwin chuckled, turning back to his sandwich and adding a pile of lettuce to the bread and meat. "You mean when he was assigned to be my friend out of pity?"

Alina laughed for a moment, despite herself. "Well, I wouldn't characterize it quite like that. We wanted to make sure that you had someone there for you, someone you could trust and confide in other than your mom."

"Ha!" Darwin scoffed, placing his now-finished sandwich on a plate. "Trust. And yet he was keeping a secret from me the whole time, wasn't he," Darwin mused, shaking his head.

"He had to, Darwin," Alina said quietly. "Everything about his assignment was confidential. I'm sure if he was given the green light to tell you who he really was, he would have. Anyway, you guys are friends again now, right?"

Darwin nodded, shrugging his shoulders. "I mean, I get why he didn't say anything. I just don't appreciate being lied to for nearly a year."

Alina nodded. As much as she didn't want to admit it, she doubted she'd have liked it much either, if their positions had been reversed. Best thing to do, she knew now, was to change the subject. "But what are you doing out here anyway?"

"Dr. Greer told me I could use the kitchen if I ever got hungry," Darwin said, gesturing at his sandwich, still untouched on the plate.

Alina looked at him curiously. "But why are you up so late? Or early, I guess I should say," she added with a small smile.

"I couldn't sleep," Darwin said, his gaze dropping to the floor. "Actually, I haven't been sleeping well for the past few days."

Alina could sympathize. She knew there had to be a lot on Darwin's mind, given everything that had happened over the past few weeks, and, of course, she herself had been struggling with sleep due to the pressure of being tasked with coming up with a plan to inform the public of their discovery.

"Why don't you come back to my office and eat?" she said impulsively, though she wasn't sure it was the greatest idea. Still, she wanted to talk to Darwin to get to know him better, to understand where his head was at, and more importantly, maybe she could gain some kind of understanding of what he would like in regards to his future.

Darwin walked into Alina's office and looked around, clearly impressed and admiring the setup. Alina had to admit that it was a very nice office, with a solid-oak desk and two leather chairs on the other side. A gleaming mahogany bookshelf was placed along the left side of the office, containing a multitude of books on astronomy, aerodynamics, and linguistics.

"Why do you have books on aerodynamics?" Darwin asked, walking over to the bookshelf and examining the titles, still holding his plate in both hands.

"Oh, it used to be a passion of mine. I always wanted to be a pilot, growing up, or perhaps an engineer for airplanes," Alina replied with a smile. Those days all seemed so long ago, so far away now that it was almost as if they'd happened to someone else entirely.

"Why didn't you?" Darwin asked curiously.

"Well, I gained a new interest in linguistics when I went to college, and I also found astronomy fascinating. So working for NASA in the translations department fit for me."

Darwin turned away from the bookcase and sat down on one of the leather chairs in front of Alina's desk.

"So, how are you feeling about everything?" Alina asked as she sat on the adjacent leather chair.

"A bit confused," Darwin said. "I don't know what all of this means and what I should do now. Can you imagine growing up your whole life thinking you were someone you weren't, or that your parents were never really your parents at all?"

Alina looked at Darwin intently. "Yes," she said in a sympathetic tone. "Maybe not to the extent that you have, but when I turned sixteen, I found out I was adopted. Growing up, I'd never suspected that my parents weren't my true biological family, and finding out that I was adopted was a shock. I hated them for it, and I felt deceived. Like, all of a sudden, I couldn't trust them anymore, that they weren't family. I was so angry at what they had done that I actually ran away from home."

"Where did you go?" Darwin asked, looking very curiously at Alina.

"Well, I didn't get far. I went to a friend's house. I stayed there that night, and before the sun rose the next day, I came to the realization that it didn't matter. They had raised me with love and compassion. I couldn't forgive them for lying to me, but I was grateful that they'd decided to take care of and raise a child that wasn't their own all those years ago. The sacrifices they made for me outweighed the gravity of the secret they'd kept from me."

Darwin nodded. His sandwich still rested on his lap. Alina could tell by the way his eyes glazed over, his expression suddenly far away, that he was thinking about his family, about the mother he'd left behind, the secrets his parents had kept from him, too, for all these years. Years he'd thought he was someone else entirely.

"Darwin, given what you know now about yourself, what is it you want to do, moving forward?" Alina asked gently.

"I want to help people," Darwin finally said. "That's when I'm the happiest."

"Help people?" Alina responded, a bit taken aback. "Help people in what way?"

"Those who are in need: the elderly, the homeless, kids who are disadvantaged, people with disabilities. Sometimes people just need a friend," Darwin said quietly. "My friends and I used to volunteer at a retirement home back in Crimson, and sometimes we'd volunteer at a local homeless shelter, too."

"Hmm, that's very admirable of you," Alina said, nodding.

"Not really." Darwin smiled. "Sometimes I feel like I do it just because I know it makes me happy. But if I can bring joy to others in the process, then I know I've done my job." Darwin finally reached down and picked up the sandwich, biting into it and chewing thoughtfully.

Alina looked at Darwin and smiled when he wasn't looking. She couldn't help but be impressed by how mature he was. It was in that moment that Alina knew what she needed to do to finalize her plan. She liked the idea of Darwin bringing the people of the world together, but how? Maybe she had been thinking about things the wrong way. Maybe it would be possible for Darwin *himself* to bring the world together, to unite the planet in one healing force, working for change. She just needed to figure out the right recipe to set him up for success.

CHAPTER 24

After another grueling three days of work and a combined seven hours of sleep, Alina finally had everything all put together to announce NASA's discovery of Florana and the next steps for Darwin to the public. She had everything outlined, from the president's address to the nation and world to follow-up articles and press releases containing more information on the discovery. People on the team would be delegated to interview with the press, as it was very likely news outlets would be all over this story and would need some answers from those working inside. In addition, she was able to find resources internally to act as security guards for Darwin at all times for his first few months, until they could receive additional budget from the government. His residence had been reserved with the help of some government-owned properties in the DC area, a nice one-bedroom place that would have everything Darwin needed. Of course, his education would be highly important for what Alina had in mind for Darwin. Now it was just a matter of getting the plan approved by Dr. Greer.

Alina knocked three times softly on the door of Dr. Greer's office. "Come in!" Greer's voice shouted through the door. Alina opened the door and made her way into the office. Dr. Greer had the nicest office in the building, with a nearly 360-degree view of the campus, with dark leather seats, his own bar and kitchenette. "Ahh, Alina! Great to see you. How have you been?"

Alina smiled. "I'm doing well, Dr. Greer. Tired, but I'm excited to show you what I've put together."

"Now, Alina, before we get into that, I know you've put a great deal of time and effort into all of this and the department appreciates your sacrifices greatly."

"Thank you, sir." Alina nodded in appreciation.

"But, that being said, it doesn't mean I will approve your plan or that changes won't need to be made to it. I just don't want you to get your hopes up and then feel defeated. This plan . . . or strategy, is crucial to our future generations, its delivery to the public has to be done in a way that doesn't instill fear among people or leave them to doubt the credibility of our discovery."

Alina took a deep breath. "I know, I know." She knew that a lot was riding on this, not just for her career, but on a much larger level across the world.

"Well, all right, let's get to it."

The next day, Dr. Greer called a mandatory staff meeting for all of his direct reports to go over what they were now calling Operation Connect. The "connect" meaning to bring together two separate worlds for the first time in universal civilization. The people of Florana had known about Earth for some time when they discovered the Voyager some thirty years ago, but only a select few on Earth knew of the existence of a planet that was inhabited by not just life, but intelligent life. Dr. Greer had asked if Alina would be willing to present the overall operation to the rest of the team, just as she had done with him.

"I have confidence that you will do well, and presenting it myself won't give you the fair recognition that you deserve. This is your plan and I want everyone to know that," he'd told Alina during their meeting the previous afternoon. She was thrilled with his confidence in her, but truth be told, the thought of presenting the plan to the entire team made her more than a little nervous.

When Alina began her presentation, she could tell from the frowns and dubious looks on the faces of the team that they were a bit skeptical at first, but the further along she went into the details, the more the team started buying into the plan. The first thing that needed to be done was to announce Darwin's presence to the world. Alina had put together a speech, which would be read by the president of the United States at a press conference, which would take place as soon as possible.

Next, Alina outlined all of the necessary precautions that needed to be put in place following the press conference. She had identified the additional security that would be needed at all major government agencies, in particular, at NASA headquarters. Three people would need to keep watch over Darwin at all times, and Darwin was to remain at NASA HQ for the next two weeks while under protection, before he would occupy his own residence. Darwin's parents were scheduled to visit him for the first time since he'd run away, and would be with him during the press conference.

Once Darwin moved into his own residence, he would be provided with a security team to watch over him night and day. If he chose to be, Darwin could also be escorted to and from school as an additional precaution. Darwin still needed to finish his senior year of high school, so Alina had arranged for him to finish his last year at Sunridge High, which was about three miles from his apartment.

After that, Darwin would then have full autonomy to do what he wished. He would be a celebrity, known all over the word and highly recognizable, so of course he would need security and protection for the rest of his life, but he also needed to finish his education. Alina didn't want to force or demand that Darwin follow a particular field of study because, in her view, everything about Darwin's life had been controlled, and she wanted to allow him to make his own decisions and gain some independence.

Of course, no one knew what exactly would transpire when the world was informed that we had finally made contact with other life forms in the universe. Dr. Greer's team hoped that the world would embrace it, accept them, and finally understand that we were all one people living on the planet, living in this universe. Of course, there was always the possibility that it could backfire, causing a mountain of fear to spread across the globe. Would this fear then lead to people trying to profit off the emotions of others? How would a discovery like that affect industry and commerce, politics and religion?

It was this uncertainty that kept Alina up at night, staring into the darkness. She knew she would be the one responsible for whatever outcome came from publicizing the discovery. Once the plan was in place and the press release was sent to the president, all any of them could do was watch and wait . . . and hope for the best.

CHAPTER 25

Eight Years Later

The buzz of the doorbell rang just as Darwin was pouring himself a bowl of cereal in his sunny kitchen. Morning light streamed across the tiled floors. He made his way over to the front door, already knowing who it would be.

"Fifteen minutes before we head out, sir," said Darwin's bodyguard, Sid, before Darwin even had a chance to open the door the whole way. Sid was wearing his usual dark sunglasses and button-up shirt with slacks. He was always well-dressed, no matter the occasion. Darwin knew that Sid must have a good tailor, given how large he was. Sid's body resembled that of an offensive lineman, all broad shoulders, a barrel chest and tightly muscled biceps. His head was bald and shiny, as if he shaved it daily, and he always wore a cologne that reminded Darwin, inexplicably, of pencil shavings and raw wood.

"Oh, okay, Sid. I'll be down in a minute, just finishing up some breakfast," Darwin said. "And how many times do I have to tell you, you don't need to call me sir," he added with a chuckle. "Just call me by my name."

"S-Sorry, Darwin. I'll be down in the car waiting."

Sid had been Darwin's bodyguard ever since he had left NASA headquarters, eight years ago. By this point they were fairly comfortable with each other, but for some reason Sid couldn't bring himself to call Darwin by his name. Sid had worked as a security guard for the last thirty years, mostly for high-profile clients, and it was ingrained in him to address the people he worked for formally.

Darwin finished up his cereal and brushed his teeth quickly, but not before taking a look at himself in the mirror. He noticed the gray hairs in his sideburns were becoming more prominent, it seemed, with each passing day. The gray hairs were beginning to match the white hair of the spots on his head. He looked a little more closely at his skin, which had somewhat aged, with some slight wrinkles, since the day he found out about who he was, but of course the white spots mottling his skin still remained exactly as they had been.

Darwin finished up brushing his teeth and made his way down to the car to find Sid waiting for him outside the car. Darwin hopped in the vehicle while Sid went around the other side to sit beside him. The driver, Alfred, a portly man in his late sixties, who Darwin didn't know very well as he'd been recently hired, tipped his head to Darwin through the rearview mirror and said, "Morning!"

"Good morning, Alfred. How are you?" Darwin asked.

"Just great, going to be another beautiful day here." Darwin smiled back at the driver as he started making his way out of the apartment parking lot.

"So, what do you have on the agenda today, Darwin?" Sid asked.

Darwin gave him a little smirk, pleased with the fact that he had actually called him by his name.

"Well, I've got an event down at the homeless shelter followed by lunch with the kids at Boys & Girls club. Then I actually have a meeting with Dr. Greer later this afternoon."

"Oh, that's scheduled for today? I thought that was tomorrow?" Sid asked, clearly confused.

"No, Dr. Greer moved it up to today, sounded like whatever he needs to talk to me about is urgent."

Now twenty-five years old, Darwin worked independently as an activist for interplanetary exploration. NASA funded his program, but it wasn't enough for Darwin to sustain a living. The program was well-known throughout the world, simply because Darwin was a celebrity. But gaining support for the program was another thing entirely. Even those who supported interplanetary and intergalactic exploration rarely donated to the cause. Capitol Hill wouldn't pass bills to increase taxes that would specifically fund this program, especially since a good deal of tax dollars were going to NASA to fund other programs that were deemed worthier.

For this reason, Darwin was required to meet with Dr. Greer on a monthly basis, to report on the status of the program, discuss finances, and check in. Mainly the meetings were to monitor Darwin, so they could continue to learn more about Florana through his dreams and visions.

Dr. Greer knew that fame could often be overwhelming, especially in Darwin's case, as there was no one else in the world like him. As such, Dr. Greer wanted to see him every month to see how he was coping mentally.

So far, Darwin had taken on his role as ambassador to the world very well. He was always calm and collected, even though harsh words were routinely hurled against him by the anti-Neila movement. He felt a great deal of responsibility not only for the earth, but for the people of Florana as well. It was largely his responsibility, he felt, to bring the people of the world together in harmony, to embrace the idea of accepting and unifying those who lived elsewhere in the universe.

As the car made its way around the corner, the sounds of protesting could be heard. As they drew closer, the people started yelling louder, noticing that Darwin was passing by in the vehicle.

"Freak, you're not wanted here!" one person shouted at the car.

"Go back to your planet, Neila! Take your propaganda elsewhere," another shouted.

Darwin tried to ignore the yelling by not making eye contact and just looking forward at the back of the driver's seat.

Darwin was used to this. By now this had started to become a daily occurrence. Every day when he would leave his home and go beyond the confines of his apartment complex, protesters would be standing outside, waiting and shouting obscenities as he drove by. It wasn't all bad, though; Darwin would have a few supporters from time to time. But generally, outside of his place, it was the anti-Neila movement. Neila was beginning to become a derogatory term, which really only applied to Darwin, aside from all of the other Floranians not on Earth.

Neila was "alien" spelled backward. People who were opposed to the idea of an alien living on Earth used this term to refer to Darwin and other "non-humans." The idea stemmed from the fact that aliens and other life forms were a backward population, different from Earthlings and not as highly evolved. Because Darwin was small and had spotted skin, the anti-Nelia movement attributed this to Florana being a planet that wasn't as developed and evolved as Earth. The sentiment was that if they had evolved further or were more advanced than Earthlings, then Floranians would have been bigger, stronger, and more physically appealing. Not to mention the fact that hatred from the anti-Neila movement stemmed from the fundamental fear and distrust that Floranians only wanted to harm the human race.

Alfred apologized to Darwin after they passed the group of protesters outside his apartment complex, "S-sorry, sir."

"That's all right. It's not your fault," Darwin replied. "And call me Darwin, okay?" Alfred nodded his head in agreement, keeping his eyes on the road.

Darwin thought back to the time of the press announcement by the president that revealed the discovery of Florana eight years prior. He remembered it like it was yesterday.

"My fellow Americans and the people of the world," the president's voice echoed in Darwin's head. "Today we embark on a new chapter in human history." Overall, the speech was roughly fifteen minutes long and went into the details of the discovery and what it meant for the world and its people. "We announce today that NASA has discovered a new planet, which has been named 'Florana,' off in the galaxy of Andromeda."

Darwin remembered his mother squeezing his hand as they watched the press conference live on TV from NASA headquarters. It felt like with every sentence the president completed, his mother's grip on Darwin's hand became tighter. "But more important than the discovery of Florana itself, Floranians have sent us a very precious gift, but the gift would also in turn be a test. A test to see if our planet was worthy, safe, friendly, and unified." Right before the president announced his name, Darwin's heart was beating so fast he could swear it could be heard across the room. "The boy's name is Darwin Sanders."

That phrase repeated over and over in Darwin's head. Never in his life did he think his name would be on the lips of the president of the United States. At the time, he remembered the uncertainty of what could potentially happen, which frightened him greatly. The president explained how Florana had come into contact with Earth, the amount of time it took to decode the Floranians' language, and the instructions for how to create one of their people. The press, of course, had loads of questions, and the president was willing to answer what he could. Dr. Greer was at the press conference as well, and took specific questions relating to Florana and Darwin.

More than anything, Darwin remembered on that day seeing his parents again for the first time since running away from home. His mother cried the second she saw Darwin in his room at NASA headquarters. She hugged him so tightly that Darwin felt like he was about to burst. Even his father came in and shook Darwin's hand. Of course, they were mad at Darwin for running away. They had gone through a vigorous application process to be given the assignment of raising Darwin, and when he took off, it didn't look good for them, from a career standpoint.

Darwin snapped out of it when the car rolled up to the homeless shelter. Sure enough, there were more protesters standing outside. Some were holding signs that read, *Save our planet, keep Neila out!* Another read, *Humans only!*

Darwin ignored the signs and shouting from protesters and proceeded inside, where he was warmly greeted by the director of the shelter. Darwin and the director, Joe Hardy, knew each other quite well, as Darwin had been volunteering at the shelter for over five years now. Darwin didn't have any money to give, so he figured the least he could do was give his time to volunteer three days a week, serving the residents food, and helping out the staff with the dishes, just as he'd done back in Crimson.

Next stop was the Boys & Girls Club, where Darwin served lunch to the kids attending the summer program. He then read to the younger children and helped others with reading and math. At the end of the event, the staff had asked Darwin to give a speech. Many organizations supporting noble causes had reached out, asking him to speak at events. It wasn't just the fact that Darwin was a public figure, but rather how inspirational his words were to people, especially young people. Whether he fully realized it or not, Darwin made an impact on the young people he came in contact with—especially on young minds that were hungry for knowledge, for understanding, for the truth.

"Just a little speech, the kids would love it," Edwin Garcia, the director of this particular facility, said excitedly, leaning in to pat Darwin on the back encouragingly. Edwin was in his mid-forties, with a full head of dark hair. His deep brown skin contrasted beautifully against the white dress shirt he wore tucked into faded jeans. The kids all loved Edwin and followed him around adoringly, viewing him more as a big brother than as an authority figure.

Darwin had always been shy, partially because of his appearance, but over his years in college, he'd gained considerable confidence in his public-speaking abilities. After all, the people who were pro-Florana often wanted to hear from him, and as soon as he gave his first public speech, which was broadcast on live TV a few months after he moved from NASA headquarters, the expectation was then set to continue those types of appearances.

"Well," Darwin said as he leaned into the microphone set up at the front of the cafeteria where he had helped serve lunch. "I hope you all had a great time today. I know I did. Just coming here and seeing all you guys working together, working so hard, really made my day." Some of the kids cheered. "You know," Darwin continued, "a lot of you guys ask me what it's like to be from another planet. And I always respond that I'm not really from another planet, I'm from this universe. Just like all of you. We may look different or like different things, but we all live in this universe. Right?"

Some of the kids began to nod.

"Now, until we start to recognize that fact, we'll never be able to come together and try to understand the big question: why are we here? What is our purpose, and why are we living in this great universe? Just like you guys share the basketballs during gym class or work together to paint a mural, it takes cooperation from everyone, no matter who you are or what you look like, if we want to succeed in working together. It's on you guys, that's right, you guys, to make this world a better place. And the question you should always be asking yourself is, what am I doing to help others? How can I serve the people around me? Thank you so much, I had a great time, and hope to see you all again soon."

The kids erupted in cheers and applause. Darwin smiled and waved as he made his way toward the exit to get back in the car.

Later that afternoon, when Darwin arrived at NASA headquarters, he was pleased to see Tyler there to greet him. Tyler had aged well and looked just like he had eight years ago, with the exception that there were more gray hairs in his beard. His hair never seemed to go completely gray, and he was still fit and in shape. Tyler was now heading up the translation-services division of Project Florana, as Alina Rans had retired the previous year to spend more time with her family. Tyler and Darwin caught up for a bit while they walked to Dr. Greer's office. Tyler was a family man now, with two children, and he loved to show Darwin videos of them playing in their backyard.

"I'm telling you, man. She's going to be an astronaut someday," Tyler said, referring to his eldest daughter, Monique. "She's always asking me questions about the stars, how many galaxies there are in the universe. Who knows, maybe she'll be one of the first Earthlings to go to Florana!" he said, smiling in adoration at the video of Monique jumping on their trampoline, her long brown hair flying around her heart-shaped face.

"Maybe, it would be something," Darwin said.

"Anyway, thanks for coming today instead of tomorrow. Dr. Greer and I wanted to see you as soon as we could."

"Well, what's up?" Darwin said curiously.

"Greer will go into the details, but let's just say we cracked something big on some of the more recent content we translated from Florana's spacecraft," Tyler answered cryptically.

Both of them started power walking to Dr. Greer's office. *Cracked something big?* Darwin thought. It had been nearly thirty years since the spacecraft from Florana had entered the earth's atmosphere, and despite the mountains of documentation and scripture they found on board, he had thought that everything had been decoded and translated.

The two of them walked into Dr. Greer's office to find him analyzing a chart on his whiteboard. In recent years, Greer had lost a great deal of his hair and was hanging on to what he had left, as opposed to shaving it off completely. Every time Darwin saw Greer, he looked older and thinner, almost frail; his once smartly tailored suits now hung from his body. Perhaps the stress of the whole Florana project had finally started to weigh on him. Over the last eight years, sleep for him rarely occurred on a nightly basis. His health was slowly beginning to deteriorate, and many in the department wondered how much longer it would be before he would retire like Alina had.

"Ah, Darwin! Good to see you, thanks so much for coming early. How is everything?" Dr. Greer asked in a jolly voice.

"Um, good, good," Darwin said, not really in the mood for chitchat after what Tyler had just told him. He was hoping Dr. Greer would get to the point.

"Well, I suppose you're probably wondering what couldn't wait until tomorrow."

Darwin nodded in agreement.

"Darwin, when was the last time you had one of your dreams or visions where you interacted with Floranians?" Dr. Greer inquired, sitting down in a chair behind his cluttered desk and motioning for Darwin to sit across from him.

"Um, it's been a while. Probably about six months or so. I don't get them as often as I used to when I was younger."

"Uh-huh." Dr. Greer nodded. "And what happened in that most recent dream?"

"Well, it was a little different from most of the dreams that I've had. Unlike being on a different planet, I was on Earth, and the Floranians were there with me. There weren't any other Earthlings around, though." Darwin shifted uncomfortably in his chair, wondering where all of this was going.

"How can you be sure that you were on Earth?"

"We were close to my apartment, and it was just three of them. They talked in their normal clicking noises, which obviously I couldn't understand. Then we started hearing loud shouts from pro-testers, anti-Neila, they disappeared, and I woke up."

Dr. Greer turned to his left to look at Tyler, who was leaning against the glass of the office wall. Tyler nodded slightly.

"So, what's going on?" Darwin asked curiously.

Dr. Greer took a deep breath. "Darwin, we have reason to be-lieve that more Floranians may be coming to Earth."

Darwin, confused, looked at Dr. Greer and then at Tyler, who gave him a little nod in agreement. Darwin struggled to come up with any words, then finally he blurted out, "Wh-what makes you think that?"

"When we were reviewing some of the old documents that had previously been decoded, we noticed that there was a small amount of content under the description of your brain composition that wasn't picked up before. The reason it wasn't picked up was be-cause the print was so small, our translators simply thought they were just small markings on the parchment itself."

"Uh-huh," Darwin said as he motioned his hands for Dr. Greer to keep going.

"Anyway, over the last couple of days Tyler and his team have been translating that content, and what we found was that although most of your body composition they have described is very similar to ours, there is something special about the Floranian brain that is unlike anything we have as humans."

Darwin paused and leaned back in his chair. "And how do they differ?"

"It's hard to explain, because we don't fully understand it our-selves. Evidently your brain can sense the feeling of others . . . well, other Floranians," Dr. Greer said. "It also has the ability to predict the behaviors and needs of its fellow people."

"So, it's like what? Intuition?" Darwin said skeptically.

"In a way, but it seems a bit more than that. You're living 2.5 million light years away from any contact with Floranians, yet somehow you are able to channel this intuitive brain to predict the behaviors and desires of the Floranian people. That's much more than intuition, if you ask me."

Darwin, shaking his head, was trying to gather his thoughts.

"But how do you know that's actually the case?"

"Because the documentation from the Floranians supports it, and on top of that, you've been having these visions your whole life, which always have consisted of connecting with Floranians, never Earthlings."

"Yeah, but those could have just been dreams—all dreams are weird, they don't have any meaning or purpose," Darwin said with a shrug.

"What about those blackouts you have? Where you have those visions that happen suddenly, and you wake up and can't remember how you entered into that state? You don't find it odd that these have happened in the middle of the day, and not while sleeping at night?"

Darwin shrugged. He didn't really have a good answer for Dr. Greer. He'd been having these dreams and visions his whole life. So many of them that it had almost become normal for him. It didn't feel odd or out of the ordinary anymore. The visions had always been incredibly real when he was a kid, almost as if he were experiencing a memory, but as he got older and learned about Florana, he'd just assumed they were strange dreams that he had about his own people from time to time.

"Perhaps they're trying to connect to you or connect you to them," Tyler said, still leaning against the office wall.

"Okay, but wait. What does this have to do with the idea that Floranians are wanting to visit here?" Darwin asked, interrupting Tyler.

"Your most recent dream was being with them on Earth, correct?" said Dr. Greer.

"Right."

"If your brain is designed to have a mental connection with them and you can sense their feelings and behavior, that would lead us to believe that their desire or intention is to visit Earth one day, perhaps to see you."

"Yeah, but you don't know that. I don't know that. I couldn't tell what they were feeling in the last dream, for all I know they hated this place and disappeared the second they heard the sound of protesters in the distance."

"Yes, that's true, we don't know for sure. But we can assume, based on your brain composition and your last dream, that there is a possibility Floranians have an intention to visit the earth," Dr. Greer said, looking up at Tyler. "If you have more dreams or visions like that, please let us know, Darwin. It's very important that we start to track these now."

Darwin took his hands and rubbed them hard against his face, scrubbing his eyes with his fists as if he wanted to obliterate them. He was tired of being monitored in this way. It was enough. After leaving NASA eight years ago, he'd finally gained some independence, and having to report his life events to Dr. Greer made him feel like he was still being controlled.

"Yeah, I'll let you know," Darwin said reluctantly as he stood up.

"Thank you," Dr. Greer said with obvious relief. "Also, Darwin, I think this goes without saying, but please keep this matter secret. We don't want anything leaked to the press, given the political sensitivity of Florana."

"You mean because of the anti-Neilas?"

Dr. Green cringed. "Don't use that word, all right? Let's just say, 'the opposition.'"

"Right, right. Of course," Darwin replied quickly.

"And Darwin, I would maybe go easy on . . ." Dr. Greer struggled to come up with the right words.

"On what?"

"On your freedom of expression," Dr. Greer said with a pointed look, his dark eyes boring into Darwin's own.

Darwin was confused. Why should he have to tone anything down? Why couldn't he speak his mind, just like everyone else in the world?

"Darwin, you've essentially become an ambassador to the world and Florana. What you stand for and the struggles that you've overcome have made people love and support you," Dr. Greer said solemnly. "But you also have to understand that there are some people out there who aren't too keen on the idea of interplanetary exploration, especially the idea of other aliens visiting our world. We receive threats against you here at NASA on a daily basis from the opposition, and I'm not going to take those threats lightly. So, all I'm saying is to be mindful of what you say in your speeches and addresses."

Darwin opened his mouth in protest, but then shut it. He wanted to argue with Dr. Greer, but he knew from experience that it wasn't going to get him anywhere. Despite his annoyance at being warned to tone it down, he knew that Dr. Greer was only trying to keep him safe. So he kept his mouth shut, nodding his head briskly in agreement, and Tyler walked him out of the office.

As they walked silently together down the brightly lit hallway of NASA HQ, Darwin was lost in thought. He didn't care that the anti-Neilas were threatened by his cause, to connect and communicate with other planets and life forms, even if it meant that his own life would be in danger because of it. He knew that what was potentially at stake was far too important to be ignored by the world, even if there were a great deal of people who were opposed to it. After all, wasn't that how change happened? From a few people who were willing to buck the system by standing up for what they believed in? Darwin's jaw tightened in resolve as he put one foot in front of the other. As they made their way back to the front entrance and out into the sunlight, Darwin knew that there was no way he was going to give up his mission that easily—no matter what Dr. Greer had to say about it.

CHAPTER 26

The morning after Darwin's last meeting with Dr. Greer, Darwin was making some breakfast in his small, cheerful kitchen. The walls were painted a bright yellow that he always found uplifting, especially in the morning light. He began frying some eggs when all of a sudden he started to feel dizzy, almost as if he was going to pass out. The room spun violently, and he grabbed the side of the counter so that he didn't fall to the ground. His knees felt weak, and he leaned over the counter, taking deep gulps of air, willing himself to stay upright. The feeling went away for a bit and he stood up slowly, cautiously, then he went back to frying his eggs, sunny-side up, just how he liked them. He was sliding the eggs onto a white china plate when the feeling came roaring back again, and this time it was stronger. Darwin tried using the counter to stabilize himself again, but the room kept spinning faster and faster. His hand slipped off the counter and he slowly fell to the ground, sliding into darkness as he hit the floor.

When Darwin awoke, he instantly recognized that he was outside the house that he'd grown up in in Crimson. It looked just the same as it had the last time he saw it over a year ago, when he had visited his mom at Christmas. He looked around at the neighborhood and there was no one in sight, not even a car driving past. He walked up the patio steps to his front door, and opened it to see if anyone was inside.

"Hello?" he shouted, but there was no answer. He made his way through the living room and into the kitchen. It was as if noth-

ing had been touched or moved in over a year. He heard a soft creaking noise coming from one of the floorboards in the family room. He raced into the room quickly to see if it was his mom, but all he could see was the silhouette of a body against the bright sun shining through the window.

"Hello?" he said again, this time in a softer tone. The person turned around slowly, and he recognized her right away, his eyes widening in shock. It was the same girl he had been seeing in his visions, a Floranian, a girl who looked strikingly similar to himself in terms of body type and complexion. The girl he had first come into contact with all those years ago, when he was in high school, who had touched his cheek.

The girl didn't make her usual clicking noises to show that she was conveying some sort of dialogue. Instead, she simply stared into Darwin's eyes, without blinking. Her spotted skin seemed even more prominent than the last time Darwin had seen her in his dreams.

"Hi," Darwin said. "It's been a while."

The girl didn't move and continued to stare back at Darwin, her face expressionless.

"Listen, I don't know if this is true," Darwin said, taking a step closer to her, "but some of the people here who have been studying me for years feel that Floranians want to come to Earth." The girl still said nothing. "Is this true?" Darwin knew that she couldn't understand him, but he often spoke to her anyway, even just to demonstrate to her that he was trying to communicate.

Darwin started feeling a little frustrated when it became clear that she wasn't going to break her silence. If it was true that Floranians had the ability to sense the feelings of others and predict their behavior, then why did he have no idea what this girl in front of him was feeling? The thought made him anxious.

Then, she started walking toward him slowly. He stood there, unsure of what she was going to do. As she drew closer, she reached out her hand to grab Darwin's. She clasped his hand in hers and slowly lifted it toward her body. She guided his hand upward and placed it firmly on her heart, which was throbbing rapidly. Darwin's hand started shaking, and he could feel warmth in the palm of his hand—it was as if her heart was entering or being channeled into his body.

Darwin's legs started to buckle, and it was hard for him to maintain his balance. The warmth that had entered through his hand now started penetrating throughout his body. He slowly went down, sinking to his knees. The Floranian girl gently guided him down to the ground, where he lay motionless. He opened his mouth to try and speak, but nothing came out.

Even though his body was limp and weak, Darwin felt a sense of satisfaction he'd never felt before, a warmth that slowly radiated throughout his limbs, turning them as loose as pudding, his mind both content and peaceful. He lay there on the ground, a small smile gracing his lips, wishing he could stay in this state forever. But it was over all too soon. Just as Darwin started getting comfortable, the ground like a plush feather bed, he woke up with a thud, feeling the cold, hard tile pressed up against his face.

Darwin lay there for a while, but immediately jumped up when he smelled something burning—the eggs that he was cooking before he'd passed out. He quickly turned off the stove and scraped the charred eggs from the frying pan.

As he vigorously scraped the pan, he felt a strange tingling sensation in his right hand, the hand the girl in his dream had used to feel her heart. The sensation slowly progressed through his arms and into his chest, then traveled through the rest of his body. It was almost like he could feel, hear, smell, and see everything at the same time. All of his senses were being stimulated at once, but with what he couldn't describe.

Then, just as he was putting the frying pan into his sink, he felt a sense of joy and elation, as if he had just witnessed his first child being born or was walking down the aisle on his wedding day. He felt so much joy that he started to tear up, his chest filling with happiness. But why? Nothing had happened to create this sense of joy, and surely it wasn't normal to be this happy over cleaning a frying pan with burned eggs on it. Perhaps it was an aftereffect of the dream he just had with the girl from Florana, he thought. But this had never happened before. What made this dream so different, he wondered?

His mind went straight to what Dr. Greer had revealed to him a few days earlier. "They can sense the feelings of others and predict their behavior, and that's what distinguishes their brain from ours." He said Greer's words over and over in his head, pondering them. Was it possible that he was getting this joyous feeling from the Floranian girl he'd just seen in his dream?

Darwin still found it hard to believe that he could sense the feelings of those who were over 2.5 million light years away from him. After all, Dr. Greer and his team couldn't be one hundred percent sure that the Floranian brain operated this way. What would even be the benefit of being able to know what others around them were feeling or to predict their behavior? Feelings and behavior should be private to the individual. To Darwin, it seemed somewhat invasive.

The feeling of happiness soon wore off, ebbing away slowly until all that was left was a slight tingling sensation in his hands, and Darwin felt back to his normal self again. That night, he couldn't sleep for wondering what it all meant.

The next day, Tyler came over. Even after, or maybe because of, everything they'd been through, they were still good friends, and Tyler came over a few times a week just to hang out, watch TV, or go on hikes near Darwin's apartment. Darwin felt like he had to tell Tyler not only about his dream, but more importantly about the strange sensation he'd felt after coming out of it. The thing was, he didn't want Tyler to make a big deal out of it and tell Dr. Greer. For all Darwin knew, it could have been nothing, or something he'd dreamt after hearing he had the ability to understand the feelings of others. After all, the placebo effect had worked on him before with the Abilify.

Tyler and Darwin were sitting on his couch as Tyler flipped through the channels, looking for something to watch on TV. Tyler was dressed in shorts and a sweatshirt, in preparation for the hike they'd planned that day. But heavy rain was falling outside, drumming aggressively on the roof, and it seemed that some TV time was in order, at least until the weather cleared up. Darwin figured he would tell Tyler about the vision but downplay it a bit, so that he wouldn't be so alarmed. He didn't think it was necessary for Greer to jump to conclusions. The population was already weary of Darwin, and the idea of aliens communicating with the world or the thought of Floranians actually coming to Earth would have them up in arms in protest, and they would take whatever precautionary measures they felt were necessary for protection.

"What? Are you serious?" Tyler exclaimed, muting the volume on the TV after Darwin told him about the way his hands had started to tingle after the dream.

"I don't know what it means or if it was just a coincidence, but the feeling then moved throughout my body."

"Are you sure you've never felt anything like this before after one of your visions or dreams?"

Darwin sat there and thought for a moment. "I don't think so. I feel like I would remember it. It was like nothing I'd ever felt before."

"What did it feel like?" Tyler asked, now sitting at the edge of his seat.

"I don't know, I just felt an extreme amount of joy, it was almost as if I was connected to her in some way I can't really explain."

"Hmm," Tyler said as he nodded his head slowly.

"What do you think it could mean?" Darwin asked.

"Maybe you could feel her emotions. I mean, your brain is designed to do that," Tyler replied.

"Yeah, but you don't know that for sure yet."

"We're almost certain, Darwin."

Darwin sat back against his couch and let out a sharp breath.

"And you were here? Like, on Earth?" Tyler asked.

"Yeah, the last two times have been on Earth. Although this time was actually at my parents' home, where I grew up."

"Really? Interesting," Tyler said.

"Why is that interesting?"

"I don't know. I'm just trying to understand why it would have been there, of all places."

Darwin had asked Tyler not to tell Dr. Greer about this latest dream. Tyler said he wouldn't, but that eventually he would need to keep Dr. Greer in the loop. If Darwin could in fact feel their emotions and behavior, they would potentially be able to understand the wants and desires of Floranians, which could help connect Earthlings and Floranians on an emotional level, something that would be an unprecedented discovery. In addition to that, if Darwin were able to predict the behaviors of Floranians, they would be able to identify if the Floranians had any intention to visit Earth.

Darwin and Tyler had dinner together at his apartment. Darwin was starting to take an interest in cooking—in particular, in making desserts. Pies, cakes, cream puffs; week after week Darwin stood in his kitchen at night, stirring and measuring, filling the room with the homey scent of melting butter and caramelized sugar. Darwin pulled an apple pie with a lattice top from the oven and set it on the counter to cool, standing back to admire his handiwork. He figured if he acted distracted enough, Tyler might change the subject, which thankfully he did.

"How are your parents doing?" Tyler called out.

"Oh . . . uh, fine. They're doing fine, I suppose. I haven't seen my mom in a couple months, since she was here last."

"And what about your dad?" Tyler asked.

Darwin brought the pan of lasagna he'd made earlier over to the table. He cut them both large pieces and motioned to Tyler to come and eat. They sat down at Darwin's round, wooden kitchen table, and immediately attacked their food. The pasta was rich with ricotta cheese and parmesan, and a creamy tomato sauce Darwin made that called for almost a stick of butter. Truth be told, he hadn't seen his father in over three years. Two years after Darwin and Florana had been made public, his father had been fired from his position at NASA and had started running his own business designing telescopes, which had always been a hobby of his. His parents had split up three years ago, and ever since, his father hadn't made much of an effort to see Darwin. Of course, Darwin didn't care much to see his father either, but it did sadden him that his own dad didn't make any effort to connect with him, now that his mother was no longer in his father's life.

"I haven't heard from him," Darwin finally said, as he cut himself another piece of lasagna. It was ironic that Tyler had brought up his dad while they ate lasagna, his dad's favorite meal. "But you knew this, though, you know he basically hasn't spoken to me since he and my mom split up."

"I know, I know," Tyler said, waving his fork around as he

chewed. "I just haven't asked you in a while. Thought I'd see if anything had changed."

"Apparently not," Darwin said, taking another bite. "I mean, they're not even really my parents, anyway. They were assigned to take care of me." His fork hovered in midair as his mother's kind face flashed in front of his eyes. A jolt of pain went through his chest. Despite everything, she had loved him. That much, Darwin was sure of.

"Well, I wouldn't look at it that way," Tyler said, swallowing hard. "At least your mom took care of you and raised you like her own. That's more than some biological mothers do."

Darwin nodded his head in agreement, but the thought that his parents had lied to him all those years still pained him deeply. It was a wound that just wouldn't go away, needling him day in and day out. He could never forget it, and as a result, it had been hard to trust anybody since. After the boys finished the lasagna, Darwin brought out the apple pie that had now fully cooled, and they stuffed themselves until they couldn't fit another bite in their mouths.

The next morning, when Darwin was washing his face in the bathroom, his hands began tingling like they had the day before, millions of tiny pinpricks beneath the skin, running all over his hands like electricity. He paused with his hands in midair, and then stopped and dried them without fully rinsing the soap off, looking down and making a fist a few times to make sure that it wasn't all in his head. The tingling sensation started running through his arms and into his chest. However, unlike like last time, Darwin didn't have the same feeling of happiness or euphoria. This time, there was only a feeling of emptiness, as if there was a void, something missing that he needed to obtain.

Darwin sat down in a chair at the kitchen table and let the feeling consume him, trying his hardest to figure out what exactly was trying to be communicated. The feeling of emptiness quickly changed to a sense of desire, a craving of some kind. Initially it felt like hunger, and as Darwin went to grab an apple to satisfy the craving, he soon realized it was more of a longing, a desire to see someone or something, the feeling of emptiness settling in the middle of his chest.

Then, just like that, in a matter of seconds, the feeling went away. Darwin sat there trying to make out what had just happened, but came up blank. He grabbed his phone and called Tyler. After all, he was the head of translation services for project Florana. Maybe he could make sense of what had just happened, even if Darwin couldn't. After Darwin explained, Tyler was quiet for a moment, weighing his words carefully before finally speaking.

"Sounds like it means that whichever Floranian was trying to communicate with you felt empty, down, and longing for something to fill that void," Tyler said.

"But what could that be?" Darwin asked curiously, walking over to the couch and sinking into the soft cushions.

"Could be a number of things. It could be completely irrelevant, and just a feeling they had with one of their family members or loved ones. Then again, it could mean they have a longing or desire to visit you, to see you for the first time."

Darwin chuckled a bit. "I doubt that," he said.

"Think about it. You're famous here because of your discovery, right?" Tyler went on. "Maybe you're famous there, too. After all, you traveled through galaxies to be raised on another planet. You might be just as special to them, if not more than you are here."

Darwin didn't reply. He wanted to believe Tyler, but the whole thing just seemed too far-fetched. Why would the Floranians want to come here just to meet him? If they even cared about him at all, they wouldn't have sent him here all alone to be raised on a planet they were unfamiliar with. A world he considered to be in disarray.

CHAPTER 27

It was early Tuesday morning, and Darwin had been up and rehearsing his speech since 6 a.m. That day, he was scheduled to be the keynote speaker at another rally for the support of interplanetary research, which seemed to have gained more and more support over the past year. Darwin wanted to ensure that his speech really hit home with his audience and would promote more support from those who were still opposed to the movement.

"There was a time when we thought we were alone in this universe, and now that time is no more . . ." *No no*, Darwin said to himself. *Too cliché*. The buildup to the discovery of Florana and what it meant to Earthlings and their place in the universe needed to be way more creative. "There was a time when we were CERTAIN that we were alone in this universe. We initially thought the earth was flat, then we thought we were the only planet in the vast universe revolving around the sun. Then we discovered that we were not the only planet in our solar system, but there were, in fact, other planets rotating around the sun. Then we discovered that we were actually a part of a larger galaxy with a multitude of other suns. And then, of course, we later realized that our galaxy is just one of a billion galaxies in this vast universe." He paused and took a drink of water. "Now, how could we have thought that . . ." Darwin stopped abruptly. His focus turned to the TV, showing the news in the background.

He reached quickly for his remote to turn up the volume. "These images are coming in live from London, England, where there has been speculation that a bomb was detonated at a rally for interplanetary research," the news broadcaster said. The whole area on the screen was covered in a haze of smoke and debris. "Thousands of people came here today near Kings Cross to march in support of interplanetary research, and . . ." The broadcaster paused and put her finger over her earpiece. "And now, we're getting confirmation that the explosion was in fact a bomb, we're not sure if this was a suicide bomber, but the massive explosion that you're seeing was some sort of a bomb, whether or not this was aimed at the rally we don't know for sure, but one can assume it was directed at those supporting alien exploration."

Darwin couldn't believe his eyes, and he simply sat there and shook his head. This was the third terrorist attack in the last two months, and the seventh in just a year. Five of those seven were attacks made by anti-Neilas in their protest of Floranians coming to Earth. The other two were terror attacks that were racially and religiously motivated.

There was a knock at the door, and Darwin made his way over, looking through the peephole before answering. Obviously, attacks like these were motivated purely by Darwin's presence on this earth, and by his outspokenness toward space exploration. He couldn't be too careful.

It was Sid, his bodyguard. Darwin breathed a sigh of relief and opened the door. "Sir . . . I, I mean Darwin. There has been another attack," Sid said, removing the dark sunglasses that shielded his eyes, a grave expression on his face. Sid wore his customary dark suit with black dress shoes polished to a shine.

"I know, Sid. I know. Just saw it all over the news. Terrible, just terrible," Darwin said, motioning for Sid to come in. "The people who commit these atrocities will never understand the pain and suffering the families and friends of the victims will go through. I can't even imagine losing a loved one to something like this," Darwin said, shaking his head while looking back over at the TV. "Completely innocent people, whose lives are taken from them all because their views differed from someone else's."

"So, I think it's safe to say that the rally here will likely be cancelled," Sid said with a nod, looking disappointed.

Darwin was silent for a moment; he knew that the expectation would be to cancel the rally in DC out of respect for the families, and of course the protection of others in case other terror attacks were imminent. But was it more disrespectful to have the rally and honor those who were impacted by this attack, or cancel and let the anti-Neila movement think it was succeeding? A stand needed to be taken that the pro-Florana movement was not going to back down, no matter how much opposition it received.

"No," Darwin responded slowly to Sid. "No, don't cancel the rally. Tell Greer that we are moving forward with the rally, regardless."

"But, Darwin, it'll be dangerous after something like this just happened."

"We're not cancelling the rally, Sid," Darwin said firmly. "If we cancel, we let the anti-Neila win. And there are a lot of things I want to address to the public in the wake of yet another a terrorist attack. These atrocities need to stop. We can't have this if we're ever to become united, not just as Earthlings, but as any living life form in this universe."

Before Sid could respond, Darwin put on his blazer and made his way out to the car, Sid following closely behind. Darwin could already hear the protesters booing and chanting outside his complex, before he could even see them. The signs were even worse this time, as they came around the corner of the complex. *Burn in hell, Neila!* one of the signs read. Another read, *Protect our earth, our children, our future*. Darwin stared back at the protesters, his face impassive. They were screaming and shouting at him.

One woman yelled, "See what happens when you stick around?" referring to the attack that had just occurred in London.

Darwin ignored the screams and chants from the crowd; he knew he needed to remain focused on the rally downtown and the speech he was about to deliver.

When the car pulled up alongside Pennsylvania Avenue, near the White House, where the march would finish, he could already see protesters waiting with their signs. There were police and security guards as well, and security was on high alert given the attack that had just occurred in London hours earlier.

The march was to begin at the Lincoln Memorial at the end of the National Mall. A few speakers would welcome the group and introduce Darwin, before they would begin their nearly 1.5-mile march to the White House. Security guards and policemen on horses were stationed on every street corner, armed and prepared should any sort of riot or attack occur.

As Darwin looked out at the crowd of people waiting to begin the rally, he was disappointed to see that not as many people had showed up as he would have liked. Dr. Greer and his team had estimated some two thousand supporters would attend, but when he looked out it seemed like the crowd barely numbered a thousand.

Although he was disappointed by the turnout, he wasn't at all surprised. He suspected that a lot of supporters who'd intended to show up had most likely decided to stay home out of fear, due to the attack in London. To be fair, a good number of supporters had figured the rally would be canceled and, as a result, did not make their way to the rally that morning.

It was nearing 9:00 a.m., and it was time for the rally to begin. Darwin stood below the stage in front of the Lincoln Memorial, rehearsing in his head what he was going to say. He was nervous, his stomach fluttering, which was unusual, as Darwin had become so accustomed to public speaking that nerves rarely affected him these days. But then again, Darwin had never spoken in front of an audience this large before, and he knew that TV networks would be covering the rally, especially given what had occurred in London.

"Some, I'm sure are shocked to learn given the incident that occurred in London, thought that the rally on interplanetary research would be canceled this morning, but NASA, along with lead activist and ambassador to Florana, Darwin Sanders, have made the decision to continue with today's rally. One can only imagine the dangers that a rally like this poses just hours after the terrorist attack on London," one news broadcaster said.

"And now, it is my great pleasure to present to you our keynote speaker, Darwin Sanders," the emcee announced.

Darwin made his way up the stairs to the podium; a loud boom of cheers roared from the supporters. He was so nervous he could barely contain himself. His hands were shaking and every muscle in his stomach felt like it was moving up into his throat. The crowd quieted down as Darwin reached the lectern. He looked out, and for a brief moment, he forgot what he was going to say. *How did I want to start this?* he asked himself frantically. He'd always been so comfortable and confident when it came to public speaking, since college, so why did this feel so different?

"Ahem," he coughed into the microphone, which shrieked with a loud sound of feedback, and some of the audience in the front had to quickly cover their ears. "Sorry," Darwin said, tapping the microphone nervously. Then, he remembered how he wanted to start. "I want to thank you all for being here today, on such a great occasion to support a cause that has been so dear to me. A cause that I believe will help in the advancement of understanding our universe and provide us with the tools and—" Darwin paused for a moment. The crowd stood there staring, waiting for him to continue.

Darwin dropped his head down and placed his hands on the edges of the lectern, gripping it tightly. As much as he wanted to deliver the speech that he had prepared for this occasion, something just didn't seem right. He needed to address what was really on his mind. Darwin pushed his notes aside and continued, taking a deep breath before speaking.

"I came here today with a feeling of great optimism. I woke this morning excited to deliver the speech I'd prepared, as I mentioned, for such a great occasion. It's a day to be celebrated, to be excited about. We're living in a new age, where life on other planets is a reality." Darwin paused again. "But sadly, I cannot say that today is a day to be celebrated. Earlier this morning we witnessed yet another gruesome attack on our planet. An attack that was fueled by hate, fear, and prejudice. When we look back and reflect on our nation's history, even our world history, most people would say we've made progress in terms of race relations, equality between men and women, social inequality, and the advancement of education. But I ask you, have we really progressed as a society? Are we better now than we were twenty or thirty years ago? When I was growing up, I struggled to find meaning in life. Why was I born the way I was, with my skin mottled? Why couldn't I be just like everybody else? My insecurities and fear as a child and teenager all stemmed from the fact that I wasn't considered normal in the eyes of others, that people saw me as being different, and because of the way I looked, there had to be something wrong with me." Darwin looked up at the sky. In a rush, Darwin's nervousness melted away. There was the strangest sensation in his limbs, a prickling on the back of his neck, as if someone was watching him, silently telling him that everything would be all right.

"For thousands of years, we have fought with one another over differences of beliefs, opinions, land, and even based on physical appearances. There have been billions of people killed in wars, terrorist attacks, gang violence, and crimes of passion throughout our history. And, of course, we're human, right? We're not perfect. But despite our imperfections, we can't seem to learn from our mistakes. Mistakes that have had a critical impact on the development of our society."

"I want to take a step back and talk about this planet earth and its place in the overall universe. The Earth is one of eight planets in our very own solar system. Our sun is a hundred and nine times the size of Earth. Now, our solar system is located in the Milky Way galaxy, which is a hundred thousand light years across with over one hundred *billion* stars." He took a quick pause. "And the Milky Way galaxy is just *one* of some hundred billion galaxies in the observable universe.

"Now, you're probably asking why I'm even bringing up these figures at all. Well, if you can picture the magnitude and size of our entire universe relative to the size of our planet, which to us is extremely vast and large, you begin to understand the insignificance of our world compared to everything else out there. We, as people, are literally smaller than a speck of dust in this vast universe. Specks of dust that continue to fight, attack, and kill one another over the differences among us. And when you understand it from that perspective, you then have to ask yourself, is there more to this life than just living on this earth, something deeper, something higher? We'll never truly know the answer, but we might be able to gain a broader understanding by connecting with life on other planets. Perhaps they know more about this universe than we do; maybe they have been able to connect with other life from other planets, or perhaps they have the answer to that question we are all curious about: why?

Why are we here? What is our purpose in life? And how can we fulfill that purpose?"

Darwin looked around at the crowd. Some people were nodding in agreement, and most were fixated on Darwin, paying close attention.

"Before Florana came into contact with us," Darwin continued, "we shunned, persecuted, and even killed other human beings. We put borders up around countries to keep others out. In some instances, we even built walls to ensure security. The idea that someone of a different race, religion, or ethnic background could enter one's nation was an alarming idea to most. And yet, it never occurred to people that we are all humans living on this earth. One people, together, coexisting in one space. Though we may differ in appearance, differ in values and beliefs, we are all human, are we not?

"But then again, I'm not technically from this earth, so what does that make me? I walk, talk, think, and act just like any other human on this planet. And yes, my appearance differs from others, from all of you, really. I was created by NASA with specific instructions, and I turned out like this." Darwin motioned his hand up and down his body. "Obviously, my skin is interesting for some, others oftentimes find it unsettling or disturbing. But, it's a part of me." Darwin took a sip of water. "Floranians are the same way. They may be from a different planet, a different galaxy, but they are still beings living in this universe, just like all of us. We have no reason to believe that they would be hostile or violent. If they were, they would have attacked our planet years ago, when they sent their spacecraft to the outskirts of our atmosphere. They sent us a gift, to be able to connect us to their world and realize that life, intelligent life, in our universe exists outside of planet earth.

"This is why I firmly believe that it's incumbent upon all of us here on Earth to work together, serve one another, accept all people with open arms, and make this planet a place where other alien life would feel welcome when visiting, and would see us as a model for planetary peace and union. However, I'm sad to say that I'm not sure intelligent life would even want to visit our world. Not with the way we continue to destroy one another and ourselves. That's why I call on each of you to reflect every day, help others, and think about what you personally can do to make Earth a place where others would want to visit." Darwin took his hands off the lectern and finished by saying, "I want to thank all of you for joining me here today, and I look forward to marching in this rally for supporting interplanetary research and exploration. Thank you."

The crowd erupted in applause and stood up as Darwin walked away from the lectern. You could hear some slight boos from anti-Neila who were off in the distance listening to the speech, but the boos were drowned out by all of the clapping.

Tyler, who was standing behind the stage, came over and shook Darwin's hand, congratulating him. He was impressed by the poise and confidence Darwin had, speaking in front of so many people in person and through TV. "I thought you said you were nervous?" Tyler grinned.

"I've never been more nervous in my entire life. But as I started speaking, I don't know, something came over me and all of my nerves just washed away. It's like there was something there, helping me."

"Well, whatever it was, it sure as hell worked," Tyler said jokingly. "Anyway, I'm going to head back to headquarters, you going there after the rally?"

"Um, I guess? I don't have any plans."

"Okay, I'll see you there. Enjoy the walk and be safe!" Tyler said as he went off in the other direction. As he left, multiple people came crowding over to talk to Darwin and shake his hand for delivering such a wonderful speech.

"Excellent speech, Darwin. Really insightful!" a young woman wearing a red jacket said, her wide blue eyes appraising him, her smile friendly.

"Really makes you think about this world and our place in the whole universe. There's got to be something more than just this life, right?" said a middle-aged man with a dark ponytail streaked with gray, and a full beard.

Darwin didn't enjoy the attention that came with being the only non-Earthling living on Earth, but he also didn't want to come across as rude, so naturally he would answer people's questions from time to time, and even allow them to take pictures with him. To Darwin, he hadn't really done anything to deserve his celebrity status, and found that his fame was unwarranted.

The walk to the White House didn't take long, and although there were some protesters along the way, the majority of the people were cheering as the march went by. Darwin was a little nervous as he got to the end of the march, but the amount of security was overwhelming, which made him feel more at ease.

Darwin began taking more pictures with supporters waiting for him at the end of the walk. Everyone wanted to shake his hand, and Darwin thanked them for their support. Many people were shouting his name to get his attention for either a picture or a handshake, but Darwin noticed a particular voice that was calling out to him as he was in the middle of taking a picture with a Korean family.

He looked up to see who was calling his name, and why the voice sounded so familiar. The person called for him again. "Darwin!" she shouted. Darwin turned around, and his heart nearly skipped a beat when he realized who it was. He hadn't seen or heard from her in over eight years, but she still looked the same, despite some mild aging. She had the same beautiful smile, her red hair setting his heart alight, just as it had all those years ago in high school.

It was Mindy Simmons.

CHAPTER 28

Mindy rushed over to Darwin and embraced him tightly. Darwin still couldn't believe his eyes. It had been so long since he'd seen her, back in high school, but he had never forgotten about her. Every now and then he'd dream of seeing her again; he'd close his eyes and suddenly he'd be back in the halls of Crimson High, watching as she walked toward him, her smile wide, her hair like a sudden flame. He'd awaken with a smile on his lips, his heart light, until he looked around his bedroom and remembered that it had been a dream. It wasn't real. And Mindy was long gone. Except she wasn't. She was right here in front of him now, waiting for him to say something.

"How are you?" she shouted.

"I'm . . . I'm good." Darwin smiled, feeling those familiar birds take up residence in his gut at the sight of her. "How have you been?"

"I'm great! It's been so long since I've seen you. Well . . . seen you in person, anyway. Been seeing you on TV and whatnot." She blushed, her pale skin turning a delicate shade of rose. She hadn't changed much since high school. Her long legs were encased in dark jeans, the fitted white button-down she wore turning her already pale skin nearly translucent.

"Right? It's been a really long time. So, what brings you to DC?" Darwin asked. He still wasn't quite sure what to say to her. It had been so long since they'd interacted that he was beginning to feel a little awkward. He shifted his weight from one foot to the other, trying to think of what to say next, feeling the crush of bodies all around them draw closer. More people were trying to get near Darwin to introduce themselves, and some of them were clearly getting frustrated that Mindy, who seemed to be just another bystander, was getting all the attention.

"Darwin! Darwin! Darwin!" they kept shouting at him.

"Guys, can you give us a second?" Darwin yelled out good-naturedly. In response, the crowd backed off a bit, and reluctantly let Mindy proceed in her conversation with Darwin.

"Well, believe it or not, I just got a job here," she said excitedly.

"Really?" Darwin said, looking shocked. This was too much good news for him to handle.

"Yeah, I'm working for this nonprofit organization that runs homeless shelters throughout the city."

Darwin smiled. He always knew Mindy would end up helping others as a career path. "That's awesome! I'm so glad to hear it."

"Yeah, you know I kept thinking about what you said in one of your first public interviews about how we should always ask ourselves what we're doing for others. It reminded me of all the times you and I volunteered at the nursing home, and I wanted to be able to give back that way, like I used to."

"That's great, Mindy. Really, I couldn't be happier for you."

Mindy smiled and pulled the mass of her shining red hair back behind one ear. "So, listen, we should get together sometime soon and catch up. Maybe have lunch or something?"

Darwin's heart started to beat a little faster, and he could feel his palms starting to sweat. Why was he getting nervous, he thought. It wasn't like she was asking him out on a date; just to get together sometime.

"Yeah, absolutely. That would be great," Darwin said enthusiastically.

"Great! Are you free tomorrow?"

Darwin quickly tried to think if he had anything going on tomorrow.

"Yeah, tomorrow works," Darwin said happily as they exchanged phone numbers.

Mindy smiled back. "All right, then, sounds good. I've got to run back to work, just wanted to come by and say hi, since I knew you'd be here. Call me tomorrow and we'll figure something out for lunch! Here's my number," Mindy said. She recited her number while Darwin quickly jotted it down in his phone.

"Yeah, see you tomorrow!" Darwin said as Mindy turned around and walked off into the crowd. He stood there for a bit, watching her walk away, his heart jumping inside his chest.

The crowd was anxious to get Darwin back again. They began shouting his name again for photos, and Darwin came back to the present. He spent another two hours taking photos and shaking hands with supporters. By the end of it, he was so exhausted from being on his feet all day that he had to call and cancel meeting up with Tyler at NASA headquarters.

The next day, Darwin woke at ten, sleeping in a little later than he would've liked, particularly because he was getting lunch with Mindy at noon, and the traffic alone would mean it would take him roughly forty-five minutes to get to V Station, a new vegetarian place downtown that Mindy had chosen when he'd called her that morning. Since Darwin had last seen Mindy, she'd become vegetarian—not for health reasons but rather for animal-rights purposes, which she'd become an avid supporter of in recent years, after rescuing a German shepherd from the local pound in Crimson.

Darwin rolled out of bed slowly after hanging up the phone with Mindy, and it took him a good twenty minutes just to pick out his outfit. Darwin had never been known for his fashion sense, but he wanted to look good for Mindy. He never could quite figure out why she brought this out in him. Even in high school, he always seemed to get a little nervous around her.

Sid was waiting outside to escort Darwin to his car. Sid's place was the loft right across the hall from Darwin. He'd been guarding Darwin for the last eight years, ever since the announcement of the discovery of Florana. Sid had put on a good ten pounds over the past few years, which seemed to reside mostly in his middle. Other than that, he was exactly the same—big, muscled, and always with a wide smile.

He knocked on the door around 11, to see if Darwin was close to being ready.

"I'll be right there," Darwin shouted from his bathroom.

He quickly washed his face and made sure soap didn't spill on the shirt that had taken him nearly twenty minutes to pick out. He took one last look at himself in the mirror and smoothed his hair with his hands. He stared at himself, looking at the large white spots on his face, and couldn't help wishing that for just this one day they would disappear. But that was silly, wasn't it? Mindy had known him for years. She knew exactly what he looked like, and it had never seemed to matter to her at all. So why was he so worried now? Maybe it was because he was growing older, and after all these years he was still alone.

Darwin always hoped he would one day marry and have children of his own, but he knew that the chances of that happening were slim to none, given the fact that everyone knew he wasn't technically human. It was unlikely that anyone would want to conceive a child with him, not knowing what the result would be of an Earthling having a child with a Floranian, or more accurately an alien, as most people would say.

He took one last deep breath and made his way out of the apartment. It took nearly forty-five minutes to arrive at the restaurant, and even though Darwin felt awful that he was about ten minutes late, Mindy didn't seem to mind at all and looked just as happy to see him as she had yesterday. When he walked into the restaurant, he had to stop for a moment. His breath caught in his throat the second he laid eyes on her. She sat at a table by the window, illuminated in a large square of sunlight that made her hair glow like fire and her green eyes sparkle. She wore a fuzzy white sweater that clung to her every curve, and a pair of faded jeans. Her long legs ended in a pair of well-worn ankle boots that almost matched the russet shade of her hair.

She got up from the table where she was waiting patiently, and gave Darwin a hug.

"Hey! How's it going?" she asked. She smelled like lilacs, her body was warm and soft beneath the sweater, and all of a sudden Darwin was dizzy.

"Good, good. Sorry I'm late," he said, with a nervous smile.

"Oh, no problem at all, I was a little late myself," she added.

"Have a seat, I'm excited for you to try this place!"

"Yeah, me too. It looks nice," Darwin said nervously, looking around and taking in the white-painted walls. The room was decorated with lush plants, the tables made from recycled wood. "Can't believe I've never been here before."

Mindy ordered for them both, as Darwin wasn't sure what to get. She ordered all of her favorite things: kale sticks, avocado toast, quinoa bites, and a large strawberry salad for them to share. Darwin wasn't much of a healthy eater, but he ate all of his food regardless, so as not to offend Mindy. Truth be told, much of it was pretty tasty.

They talked mostly about high school, and how glad they were that it was over and in the past. Darwin obviously didn't have the best experience, but he was surprised to learn that Mindy hated high school as well. She had always seemed to be so happy, and was popular with mostly everyone. She claimed that it was mostly fake and that she'd spent most of her time putting up a front that she was happy. For her, she realized she was happiest when she was volunteering at the nursing home or the homeless shelter. "That's when I realized what it feels like to actually be happy," she said. "Before that, I think I always thought I was happy, but never truly felt that way. Something was just missing. My dad drank a lot," she said, her expression darkening as she looked down at the table. "And it really made things hard for my mom and me. That's why I went out so much—I couldn't stand being trapped in that house, watching him drink himself to death. Sometimes he'd get mad and start yelling at my mom, at me. It was just safer if I wasn't around too much, you know?"

Without thinking, Darwin reached across the table and took Mindy's hand in his own. She looked up, her green eyes locking onto his, glossy with unshed tears. They sat in silence for a moment, the din of the restaurant surrounding them in a hum of voices and the clattering of dishes. Darwin wished he could stay in this moment forever; make time stop. But he knew he couldn't. Reluctantly, he released Mindy's hand.

"Is he okay now?" Darwin asked, sitting back in his chair and picking up his fork again, scraping the last of the strawberry salad from his plate.

"My dad?" Mindy asked. "Yeah. He went to AA when I was a freshman in college. Hasn't had a drink in years."

When they finished their meal, they ordered a pot of ginger tea, as it was clear that they both wanted to keep the conversation going. Up until then, they'd only really talked about the past; because they enjoyed each other's company so much, neither of them wanted to leave and go their separate ways so quickly. Lunch felt like it flew by in barely a half-hour.

"So, do you like it here in DC?" Mindy asked.

"Yeah . . . yeah, I do," Darwin replied with a little hesitation in his voice.

"Ahh, you paused," Mindy said, with a knowing smile. "Come on, you can be honest with me."

Darwin smiled back. He hadn't realized he was so transparent with Mindy. "It's nothing against the city itself, it's a nice place to live. I just miss home sometimes. And I know it was never really my home and they were never really my parents, but from time to time I miss it. It's just nostalgia, I guess."

Mindy raised her eyebrows. "Not me. I was so sick of it that I just *had* to get out. But then again, I've only been away for a couple months, so I'm sure I'll miss it eventually," she said with a little laugh.

"I'm sure you'll like it here," Darwin replied with a smile.

The two of them took a sip of their tea, not quite sure what to say next.

"So, how do you decide what to talk about in your speeches?" Mindy asked to break the silence.

"Well, it depends." Darwin put his cup back down. "If the organization or event is sponsoring or promoting a particular initiative, then I try to talk about that subject. But then sometimes they give me free reign to say or talk about whatever I want."

"So, in those instances, how do you come up with whatever you want to talk about?"

Darwin paused for a moment and took another sip of tea. "Well, I often use what's going on in the world at that time as inspiration for material to use in my speech. The sad thing is, most of what's been going on in the world lately is so negative. Terrorist attacks, mass shootings, politicians fighting with one another, war. Because of this, my speeches are usually centered on bringing an awareness to these issues and hoping that it might inspire people to make a change for the better."

"That's great, Darwin." Mindy smiled warmly. "I hope things get better all the time, but the sad thing is that I don't know if they really will or if anything will ever change."

They looked at each other grimly. It wasn't the most positive subject, Darwin thought, but then again, she did ask how he came up with the topics for his speeches.

"Does it bother you?" Mindy asked.

"Does what bother me?" Darwin said, momentarily confused.

"You know, does it bother you that some people are so hateful in the way they treat you, and that their hatred has resulted in a lot of bloodshed over the last few years?"

"Of course, it bothers me," Darwin said with a sigh. "Sometimes I wish I could have just stayed that little awkward kid with spotted skin, and that what I am had never gone public." Darwin paused, taking another sip of his tea. "But at the same time, you have to face what's been given to you in life head-on, and do whatever you can to make the best of it. Given my position as a public figure, I thought the least I could do was inspire others to do something good for their fellow people, for this earth."

Mindy nodded her head, as if she couldn't agree more with that sentiment. They both sat there in silence, and then Darwin finally asked the question that had been on his mind for some time.

"Mindy," he said. She looked up from her tea. "How come you never contacted me in all of these years?"

Mindy looked down at the table, not quite sure how to respond. "It wasn't that I didn't want to . . . to reach out to you." She started tapping her fingers against the table nervously. "It was just hard for me at first. I had a hard time believing the whole thing, once it was announced publicly."

"What do you mean?" Darwin asked, wrinkling his brow in confusion.

"I mean, I had known you as Darwin Sanders, the kid I went to school with. I never would have imagined that you were the first alien the earth had come into contact with. I felt deceived, scared."

"And how do you think I felt?" Darwin's expression quickly changed to one of frustration. "You don't think I felt deceived all these years? My parents lied to me my whole childhood. Making up stories that I had some sort of skin condition, a mental-health problem, lying about what they actually did for a living, or not telling me the truth about why I was almost kidnapped in third grade. Hell, my best friend was even in on the whole thing," Darwin said with a short laugh. "He was only my friend, so he could watch over me. Because he was being paid to do it." Darwin took a deep breath, gulping air into his lungs. Then he swigged the rest of his tea, draining the cup. *Calm down*, he told himself sternly.

"You were almost kidnapped in third grade?" Mindy asked curiously, her green eyes widening.

"Yeah, it's a long story," Darwin said, trying to brush it off. "Some people who used to work for NASA were after me to prove to the press I was a government secret. Anyway, that's beside the point. What I mean is, you don't think I was scared? Being the only person in the world who didn't belong? I could have used a friend like you in those times, someone to talk to, someone I could confide in after I first found out what I was."

Mindy's jade-colored eyes welled with tears, glistening in the light, and she wiped them quickly. "I'm sorry that I wasn't there for you, Darwin. I was just confused and wasn't sure what to believe. And it made it even harder that my parents were very much against this whole idea of interplanetary communication or whatever."

"You parents are anti-Neila?" Darwin exclaimed.

Mindy sat back in her chair, a stunned look on her face. "Don't say that word. Doesn't it offend you?"

"Yes," Darwin said slowly, "but at the same time, I realize that people only say it because they are afraid of something that isn't in fact a threat to them."

Mindy took a deep breath, then exhaled loudly. "My parents wouldn't allow me to associate with you. I know you tried contacting me shortly after high school, but they always screened my calls and emails. They became very controlling after your announcement was made. The thought that their daughter had been going to school with some . . . alien." She hesitated for a moment, before continuing, "It infuriated them. At the time, I believed what they said because I was young and stupid. Now I know they were just ignorant and were unable to see the beauty in communicating with other forms of life in the universe."

Darwin paused with his mouth open slightly. He couldn't believe that the girl he knew and respected so much in high school had been an anti-Neila supporter. For all he knew, she could have been the type that picketed and protested outside his apartment complex, screaming obscenities. But she had changed—she had realized how hateful and ignorant it was to be against someone purely because of where they were from. Surely that had to count for something—a lot.

Mindy relayed that it had finally all sunk in for her when she witnessed two of her friends, exchange students from Nigeria who'd come to the United States to study biology, being attacked, beaten up until they were unconscious, by a group of white supremacists. How could anyone do that to someone they knew nothing about other than their physical appearance, she thought at the time.

This event, Mindy recalled, made her realize that the way the white supremacists rushed to judge her friends was exactly the same way she was judging Darwin. She had known him as an incredible, smart, and caring person, yet when she found out that he came from a different planet, she'd instantly turned her back on him.

"Darwin, I'm so sorry," she said, her face a mask of anguish.

"Sorry for what?" Darwin said quietly, looking into her beautiful face, which was full of pain and regret.

"For not being there for you, for never reaching out to you all these years. All because my parents had convinced me you were some kind of . . . I don't know, monster. It wasn't fair to you, and I'm sorry for that." Mindy sighed, reaching across the table to take his hand. At the touch of her warm fingers, Darwin felt something uncoil inside him and relax, what remained of his anger slowly dissolving.

"Do you want to go get some ice cream?" Mindy asked. "There's a great place around the corner from here."

The two of them walked over to the ice cream shop and grabbed two mint chocolate chip cones. This time Mindy paid, waving away the money he held out in protest. Perhaps she felt guilty for abandoning him all those years ago, Darwin thought. Or maybe it was just that she was still a kindhearted person, always ready to help others, to give back. He hoped, more than anything, that this was the case.

They decided to walk around for a bit while they ate. It was a nice summer day, the pale blue sky filled with puffy white clouds, and despite the normally stifling humidity that stretched across the DC area in the summer, this afternoon was mild, a light breeze riffling Mindy's hair, lifting it from her shoulders every now and then. They walked through downtown, past a series of tall brick buildings, and made their way through a park, lush and green, with children playing nearby in the playground filled with brightly colored climbing structures and swings.

"So, what's next for this whole Floranian thing?" Mindy asked as she took a bite of her ice cream.

"Do you mean, what are we planning to do as far as connecting with them?"

"Yeah, like what have we done in an attempt to make contact? I mean, they sent you to us, so they know where we are. Are we ever going to visit them?"

Darwin hesitated before responding. He knew that all of the information NASA had on Florana was strictly classified, unless it had already been publicly revealed. Despite the fact that there were many unanswered questions that even Darwin himself didn't know the answers to, there were matters on Florana that had not yet been shared with the public and were being kept confidential for safety reasons. The hypothesis that Floranians were looking to visit Earth, according to Dr. Greer and Tyler, was just one in a series of matters the public knew nothing about.

"Well, it's tricky," Darwin said, rubbing the back of his neck. The polo shirt he wore felt sticky due to the humidity, and all at once he remembered how he always seemed to break out in a sweat when Mindy was nearby. Clearly nothing had changed.

"What do you mean?" Mindy asked, looking confused.

"I mean that I can't tell you about it."

"But why not?" Mindy said, stopping in her tracks and turning to face him.

"It's confidential, for security reasons. If some of the information were to be leaked, it could have huge ramifications on the population as a whole."

Mindy stood there for a second and paused before taking her next bite of ice cream.

"So, you're saying NASA is actually keeping stuff from the public?"

"I wouldn't look at it that way," Darwin demurred, "it's just that there is a lot we still don't know about, and if the public were to find out . . ."

"We wouldn't be able to handle it?" Mindy finished his sentence, raising one eyebrow and then smiling.

"To an extent, yes, people might not be ready for it yet." Darwin thought of the things the public didn't know yet—the writings and scriptures that were found on the spacecraft where Darwin's DNA was found, the decoder and translation of Floranian writing, and Darwin's own dreams and visions. There was no way that the general public was ready to know all that had been kept from them. Sometimes secrets were kept for good reason. This was one of them.

Mindy rolled her eyes and started walking again. "Do we know where Florana is, at least? They've never mentioned its location on the news," Mindy asked.

"We don't, actually," Darwin said. "We know it's located somewhere in the Andromeda galaxy, based on location points they provided in their spacecraft, but we haven't been able to pin down the precise location."

Mindy looked a little disappointed upon hearing this news, and focused on her ice cream once again, taking small bites of the cone now.

"We've tried using the Hubble telescope to hone in on where Florana may potentially be, but the Andromeda galaxy is 2.5 million light years away and is a massive galaxy, twenty percent bigger than our own Milky Way, with over one trillion stars. It's almost like trying to find a needle in a haystack, twice."

"But if they gave you a general idea of where they are located, why wouldn't they just tell you their exact location? Why be vague about it?"

"Well, maybe they didn't want to give their exact whereabouts, in case we were a hostile world. For all they knew, we could have waged war against them and attempted to take all of their resources."

"Then why even visit us in the first place?" Mindy asked, taking the last bites of her cone and wiping her hands on a paper napkin.

Darwin thought about how he wanted to answer this question, before going right into it. He took a deep breath, and then began to explain. "Mindy, for the last fifty years or so, we've always wondered if there was life on other planets, and if there was life, was there intelligent life. Ever since we launched our first man into space, we thought, could it be possible?" Darwin continued, "Our goal had always been to discover life on other planets. But we never really thought about what the potential consequences were for discovering something like this, and we certainly never thought out what the next steps would be after such a discovery. What if Floranians were curious about the same thing we were—whether there was other intelligent life out there?" Darwin went on. "And then all of a sudden they came into contact with our Voyager spacecraft, showing them pictures of who we are, music that we've created, and a location on how to find us. You don't think they would be curious to know who we were and want to make contact with us?"

Mindy shrugged. "I mean, I guess, but that still doesn't explain why they wouldn't tell us where they are located. If they wanted to make contact with us, why not tell us where they are? After all, we told them where we are."

"Well, I'm sure they were just being cautious." Darwin shrugged, throwing the remainder of his cone in a trashcan as they passed by. "As friendly and peaceful as we probably looked in the photos they found on Voyager, they weren't sure how we would react to the idea that there was life on another planet. They wanted to test us out first, before telling us exactly where they were."

Mindy nodded her head in acknowledgment. "I guess it makes sense," she said almost grudgingly. "I mean, to be cautious and all."

They created me to see how I would be treated on Earth, and if the planet was worth visiting based on how they received me, that's how cautious they were."

"But how would they know if you were being treated well and had assimilated into our world?" Mindy asked, her tone filled with skepticism.

Darwin hesitated. He knew he didn't have any concrete proof, but he did feel connected to the Floranian people through his dreams and visions. But confessing these dreams to Mindy would be against NASA's security protocol.

"I can't quite say," Darwin said, aware that he sounded cryptic, as if he were dodging the question, "but I just have a feeling they're aware of what's going on."

"What does that mean?" Mindy asked, her green eyes lighting up with excitement the way they always had whenever she was intrigued.

"I just—I can't get into it," Darwin stammered, praying silently that she'd just let it go and wouldn't ask any other questions.

"Because of security reasons or something?"

"Exactly. I'm sure it will all be revealed in due time, but I can't go into any more details."

As they continued to walk through the park, Mindy looked straight ahead, a distant expression on her face. It felt like suddenly she was a million miles away. It was clear that she felt miffed that he wouldn't confide in her, at least not all the way, but even though he cared for and respected Mindy greatly, he couldn't forget the fact that she had willingly lost contact with him all of those years ago, out of fear. Sure, she had apologized and was making an effort to rekindle their friendship, but why should he trust her with classified information? It was asking too much, too soon, Darwin thought.

Darwin changed the subject back to high school and Crimson; Mindy's distant demeanor gradually warmed toward him again. They spent a few more hours roaming the streets of the nation's capital, and eventually parted ways so Darwin could meet Tyler for dinner.

They hugged goodbye and agreed to see each other more often now that Mindy was living in the area.

"I'm really glad we reconnected," Darwin said with a shy smile.

"Me too," Mindy answered softly, reaching down again and touching her hand to his, just for a moment. As Darwin walked away, he turned around and looked at Mindy walking in the other direction, marveling at her quick steps, how surely her feet touched the ground as she moved through the world. He wondered what would have happened between them, had it never been revealed that he was a life form from another planet.

CHAPTER 29

It was a chilly and overcast summer day, unusual weather for this time of year in DC. A week had passed since Darwin had reconnected with Mindy, and the clouds overhead looked as if they were about to start pouring down rain any second now. Darwin jogged quickly through one of the parking lots at NASA HQ, making his way toward one of the side entrances, but he wasn't running to avoid the inevitable rain or the misty, languid air, but rather because he needed to see Dr. Greer right away.

His heart was beating fast and his arms and hands were shaking so much that he had a bit of trouble opening the side door, his fingers slipping on the handle. Darwin didn't know what to make of what had just happened to him. He'd never experienced anything like it before, and if there was anyone who would have an explanation, it would be Dr. Greer.

Loud thumps echoed in the hallway with each of Darwin's strides. He made his way to Dr. Greer's office, ignoring the looks of concern people were giving him in the hallway.

"Are you all right?" one man asked as Darwin zoomed past without saying a word.

Some even started picking up their phones, whether to call security, Dr. Greer, or the police, Darwin wasn't sure. All he knew was that he needed to find Dr. Greer as soon as he could.

He sprinted his way across the walking bridge that connected the research and development department and the aerospace engineering department. But just as he got to the end of the bridge, he noticed that Dr. Greer was across the way on the ground floor below the bridge, talking to one of his colleagues. Darwin stopped suddenly, cupping his two hands over his mouth.

"Dr. Greer!" he shouted at the top of his lungs.

The whole area on the ground floor went silent and looked up at Darwin, including Dr. Greer. Darwin motioned with his hand for him to come over. Dr. Greer paused and motioned to his colleague that he would need to step away for a second.

"I'll meet you at your office!" Darwin shouted again. Dr. Greer looked a little embarrassed, as now everyone on the floor was looking at him. He nodded to colleagues, acknowledging that everything was okay and to continue work as usual.

When Dr. Greer got to his office, Darwin was already in there, pacing back and forth.

"What was that about? You can't just come barging in here, screaming as loud as you want, people will get wor—"

"I had another dream," Darwin interrupted.

Dr. Greer stopped and looked at Darwin, waiting for him to continue, but Darwin turned around and kept pacing.

"And? You've had dreams before," Dr. Greer said anxiously.

"Not like this one, this was different."

"How so?"

"I understood them," Darwin said. "They spoke to me. Well, it wasn't English, and it wasn't their usual language, but somehow I was able to understand what they were saying. It was as if I had suddenly learned a new language fluently in my dream, and the second I woke up, it was gone."

Dr. Greer slowly sat down in his chair behind the large mahogany desk that stood in the corner of the room. "Well, what did they say? What happened?"

"I was on the beach, all alone, miles of soft sand and crashing waves," Darwin started, still pacing back and forth. "I was walking along the beach, the warm sand sliding through my toes. I remember stopping to look up at the sun and to admire the view. I took a seat on the sand and closed my eyes. Why? I don't know. The warmth of the sun on my face just felt so good, and the sound of the waves was so relaxing." Darwin continued, "I thought about what the world would be like, if there was peace and tranquility between all people on Earth. What if they could feel a moment like this one in unison, one sun shining on us all on one planet? What if we stopped and recognized what the sun has given us, this beautiful world that we call home? Then maybe, just maybe, people would try to make their home a better place for themselves and for the rest of society. The sun provides the means necessary for the earth to exist, but without a unified people who love and care for one another, what is the point of it even existing? These were all the thoughts that were going through my head as I sat there with my eyes closed."

Darwin paused for a moment, and Dr. Greer patiently waited for him to continue.

"When I opened my eyes, I noticed out of the corner of my right eye that something was beside me. I turned and saw a Floranian sitting next to me with its eyes closed, facing in the same direction, toward the sun. I didn't flinch or shake at all. Normally, I would've, if all of a sudden I opened my eyes and another person was sitting right beside me. Instead, there was a sense of calmness that came over me."

Darwin stopped pacing, pulled up one of the chairs, and sat it down across from Dr. Greer.

"I looked at him for a bit and thought maybe I should say something or tap him on the shoulder, but he looked so at peace with himself that I didn't do anything. It was as if he were in a completely meditative state."

"Was this one of the same Floranians you had encountered in your dreams previously?" Dr. Greer asked quickly, one eyebrow raised.

"No, I didn't recognize him," Darwin said. "I knew he was a Floranian, though, based on his appearance. I don't know how long I waited there, but when he finally opened his eyes, he just looked out at the ocean, it was like he didn't even know I was there. I coughed initially to see if that would get his attention, but he just kept looking straight ahead. Then, he spoke. Like I said, it wasn't English, but I could understand everything he was saying perfectly. Initially he started saying what a beautiful day it was and how amazing the view was. He mentioned that he had never been here before. Since I didn't know where I was either, I asked him. 'This beautiful planet you call Earth,' he said. Surprised by the fact that I was able to understand him and vice versa, I asked how we were able to understand each other. He told me that I was given the power of understanding when I was created, that it was with me all this time, but I had to open my heart to receive it when I needed it most."

Dr. Greer listened to Darwin intently. The fact that Darwin was able to communicate directly with Floranians through a verbal language was a massive breakthrough. The implications that it would have on intergalactic diplomacy in the future were huge. It was never indicated in the instructions from Florana in creating Darwin that he would ever gain the capacity to understand and speak their language. It was now apparent that he could within the right state of mind, with an open heart.

"So, then what?" Dr. Greer said, eagerly waiting for the story to continue.

"It was a long conversation, and I'm afraid I can't remember some of the specific details. The whole thing seemed to be happening so fast."

"Well, was there at least anything new that we perhaps didn't know before?"

"I'll give you all of the details that I can remember, but the reason I came here so quickly was because of what happened at the end."

Dr. Greer nodded his head quickly for Darwin to continue.

"They want to visit Earth," Darwin said, his voice filled with both wonder and the gravity of the situation.

Dr. Greer's eyes grew wide, his mouth dropped open slightly, and he couldn't seem to find his words. "Or I guess I should say they *are* going to be visiting," Darwin added.

"How do you know for sure?" Dr. Greer asked cautiously.

"He told me. He said it was their dream to finally come into contact with life outside their planet. They have been doing research and explorations, looking for life on other planets for over a thousand years."

"A thousand years?" Dr. Greer asked sharply. "Their technology must be even more advanced than I thought. If they have historical documents, recordings, evidence of these explorations from that long ago, I can only imagine what their technological capabilities are now."

"Well, that's the other thing. Their life expectancy seems to be much higher than ours, or perhaps their definition of time is different than ours. The man told me had been living for a hundred and thirty-five years and that he was the average age for most Floranians."

"Incredible!" Dr. Greer rushed to his desk to start writing down some notes, but was quickly interrupted by Darwin.

"But, there was something that happened that was the most concerning to me."

Dr. Greer put down his pen and looked back up at Darwin.

"At the end of the conversation, when he was explaining to me the details of how they were planning to visit Earth, a loud bang blasted through my ears, and when I opened my eyes after the loud noise, the Floranian man slowly collapsed to the ground, holding his chest, blood flowing out of a wound. I looked around to the other side and could see an Earthling holding a pistol, standing a few feet away. He stared me down for a second and then turned around and walked off, out of sight. I didn't get a great look at him, but I'm almost certain it was an Earthling, based on the fact that he didn't have the typical spotted skin of Floranians. But it's weird because in all of my dreams that I've had regarding Florana, an Earthling has never appeared in them, even in the dreams that take place on Earth."

Darwin finished and Dr. Greer looked back at him with concern.

"What do you think that means?" Darwin asked.

Dr. Greer sat back in his chair. "And nothing like this has ever happened before in your dreams or visions, you've never seen Earthlings before?" Dr. Greer asked again to be certain.

"No," Darwin said, shaking his head.

"Well, we've always assumed that your dreams were accurate thoughts and images of Floranians, but of course we can't be a hundred percent certain."

"If it is, though, what could it mean?" Darwin asked anxiously. "Could it mean that if Floranians come to visit, that Earthlings would kill them? Is it a sign of war?"

"I don't know, Darwin," Dr. Greer said, shaking his head. "You know dreams can also be visions of the subconscious mind. It could simply be that in your subconscious you fear for the safety of Floranians, should they come to Earth."

Darwin sat there and thought for a moment. It was a possibility that the episode could have simply been a product of his subconscious mind, but this dream seemed different. He couldn't quite explain it, but it just felt more real than any previous dream or vision he'd had before. Perhaps because it was the first time he had truly communicated with his fellow Floranians.

After Darwin had finished telling Dr. Greer the concerning portion of his dream, he shared with him the rest of what he could remember from the conversation. Darwin had asked a lot of questions in the dream, as he felt he might never again have the opportunity to communicate with Floranians through a common language.

Among finding out that the life expectancy of Floranians was more than double that of Earthlings, he also discovered that Floranians ate very little, living off a diet that was entirely plant-based. Animals and other creatures existed in Florana, but the man didn't go into any details on what these particular animals were or looked like. He learned that Floranians lived a rather simple life. They worked hard but did so for the common good, not for their own interests. In fact, everyone worked together to build a strong and unified community, one in which they could all count on. When Darwin asked why Floranians did this for each other and how it was possible that they could get everyone to agree on this common practice, the man said, "We are all working together to prepare ourselves for the next world." When Darwin asked the man what he meant by "the next world," he responded that Darwin and the rest of Earthlings would find out in time.

Floranians had built their communities from the ground up to ensure the future of their society would always be keeping the betterment of the world in mind. Starting at the grassroots level enabled their people to have a sense of purpose in contributing to the common good of the world. This concept fascinated Darwin. Of course Floranians, despite their concept of working for the common good, had considerable investments and resources in their space technology. For them, discovering life on other planets was a part of their overall purpose.

Florana's concept of time was also much different than that of the earth. The planet orbited their sun in full every 446 days, and each day was thirty-two hours. Of course, the man had explained that these would be considered the equivalent of how time is measured on planet earth. On Florana, they did not call these days, hours, or years. However, despite the fact that it took Florana longer to make a complete orbit around their sun than it did for the earth, Florana was rotating at a faster rate. While the earth rotated around the sun at a speed of about eighteen miles per second, Florana rotated around its sun at nearly forty-four miles per second.

Because of the speed at which Florana rotated around its sun, time on the planet itself moved much more quickly than what one would experience on the earth. They'd estimated that if a Floranian were to visit planet earth, for every hour that passed, two-and-a-half hours would pass on Florana.

Of course, the most important piece of information of all was the intention of Floranians to visit Earth. The man had indicated they were building a massive spacecraft, which would penetrate the black hole just as their ship carrying Darwin's DNA had done previously. They hand-selected thirty individuals to travel on this voyage. Their aim was to learn more about the culture on Earth and see if there were resources that could be shared and exchanged between the two planets. Floranians would also help Earthlings voyage to Florana, should they desire to.

Unfortunately, the man was then shot in Darwin's dream before he could share any more details of their journey to Earth. Darwin hadn't even gotten his name. He didn't want to simply keep referring to him as the Floranian man, so until he met him again, he decided to call him Benedict—which meant blessed—as Darwin considered the appearance in his dream to truly be a blessing of the highest order.

Dr. Greer called an immediate meeting with the head advisors on the Floranian research team. He wanted to get them up to speed on everything Darwin had just divulged to him, but to keep it private even among other NASA employees until further action could be determined. Could they reveal this information to the world? If Darwin's dream was in fact accurate, then Floranians had every intention to visit Earth, and not just one or two people, but thirty of them. The fact that the world had become so divisive and violent purely from the fact that Darwin had been a Floranian living among them was enough cause for concern to announce that they were intending on sending thirty more of their people. On the other hand, if they didn't reveal Florana's intention to the public, they would one day arrive without any notice, which could have an even greater adverse reaction.

Either way, Dr. Greer knew the news wasn't going to be received well, at least not for the anti-Neila. He didn't want to be the only one to make the decision on how to proceed. It had to be discussed with his team to decide on the best course of action that would result in the least amount of backlash or violence.

The team spent a whole two days coming up with an action plan, and there was a great deal of back and forth on how the plan was to be orchestrated. Some people felt the information needed to be announced to the world right away. After all, what if the Floranians were to land on Earth tomorrow and the world was not prepared for it? This was their main argument, that an alien race landing without warning could have serious repercussions on society. On the other hand, some felt that they couldn't take a risk of announcing something like this simply based on a dream that Darwin had. It was not a certainty that Darwin's dreams of Florana were accurate or in fact real.

Although Darwin wanted to be a part of the planning process, Dr. Greer felt it would be best if he let the team put the strategy together themselves so that emotional bias would not play into Darwin's decision making. This frustrated Darwin, as their decision would have a great impact on his life and well-being on the earth.

Darwin waited patiently for two days in anticipation, waiting to hear from Dr. Greer and the other eight team members. He didn't leave his apartment for the whole two days—too nervous and anxious to interact with anyone. He barely slept and although he knew that his bodyguard, Sid, was worried about him, he left Darwin alone as he had requested.

Darwin spent those two days meditating and praying, trying to get back to the same dream state he had with Benedict the Floranian. He wanted to ask more questions this time: How their government system was run on Florana, if they had one? Did people believe in a higher power or the God that Earthlings referred to? Did Florana experience sects or factions in religions or belief groups in general, as Earth did? He realized that all he wanted to ask before were measurable scientific questions, but when he thought about it more, he wondered what the people of the world would really want to know when communicating for the first time with an alien species. Did the Floranians believe in something greater, something more powerful than their material existence?

Darwin had always been a scientific person, and not one for spirituality, but after that dream with Benedict, something changed in him, and he soon realized that there had to be something more to life than what science could explain. He realized that science and spirituality had to go hand in hand, that they must complement each other in order for one to fully understand the truth of the universe itself.

After a long forty-eight hours confined in his apartment, drifting in and out of a meditative state, only stopping to eat and drink occasionally, Darwin finally received the call he was waiting for from Dr. Greer, asking him to come to HQ so they could go over the strategy and timeline for next steps. Darwin said he would, but also wanted to know what their ultimate decision was before coming in. He was too impatient to wait. Standing there, waiting for Dr. Greer to answer, Darwin realized he was holding his breath.

"It's complicated, Darwin," was all Dr. Greer would say. "It would be better to discuss it in person."

"Are you making it public, or are we keeping this information confidential?" Darwin blurted out in frustration.

There was a long silence on the phone, and after clearing his throat, Dr. Greer answered, "We've decided that for now, we're not going to announce anything until we have more proof."

Darwin stood there, phone in hand, his face a mask of confusion. "What kind of proof?" Darwin asked. "I gave you all the proof you need."

"Darwin," Dr. Greer said patiently, "we can't be sure that this dream you had indicates that Floranians intend to visit the earth. The dangers something like this can pose to the world if we were to announce it could be catastrophic. Imagine how the anti-Neila would react if they knew an alien life form was coming to inhabit our earth, you've seen what they've done now, we just can't take that risk."

"You're the one that told me my dreams were real," Darwin replied urgently.

"Yes, but I never said it with an absolute certainty."

Darwin hesitated for a moment. He wanted to choose his words wisely before proceeding. How could Dr. Greer contradict himself so greatly? He was the one pushing for Darwin to believe that his dreams were an indication of reality while he had remained skeptical all this time. Now he was saying he didn't believe him?

"So, you expect me to just carry on like nothing has happened? To maybe have this happen one day and run that risk when we get there?"

"Look, Darwin," Dr. Greer responded, his voice calm and soothing despite Darwin's agitation. "I know this isn't easy, but it's the best thing we can do for the people of the world at this point. We will continue to do research, continue to investigate and see if what you dreamt—"

"No!" Darwin interrupted. "I'm telling you this was a different feeling, it was real, it was genuine. I can't quite explain it, but it was like they were calling to me, wanting to give this message to the world. We have to prepare the earth for this, otherwise it's only going to end in bloodshed. Why else do you think an Earthling shot Benedict at the end of the dream?"

"Darwin . . ."

"He shot him because he was ignorant, he didn't know who the man was, he just saw him as something different from him, wanting to invade his land!" Darwin's voice started quavering, "We have to show people that we can't keep doing this to each other. We can't keep fighting and killing those who differ from us in their appearance, culture, and beliefs. Otherwise, we'll never learn!" He slammed his fist down on the counter so hard that the cupboards shook a little. Darwin continued, "So far, all that Floranians have done is provide us with information on their world and how to create one of them, they haven't given any indication that they are a hostile species. Why should we be afraid of them?"

"Look, Darwin. I know this is . . . emotional for you," Dr. Greer said, trying to find the right word. "But, this is what's been decided. Like I said, we'll continue to look into it so as to better understand the validity of these dreams you have."

Darwin exhaled loudly in frustration, sitting down in a kitchen chair and feeling like all the air had just been drained out of him.

"In the meantime, you let us know if you continue to have any other dreams. We need to start documenting everything. I may even have you spend a few nights here in the lab, so we can monitor your brain activity while you're dreaming, see if we can find anything there."

Darwin didn't respond, he was too angry to say anything to Dr. Greer right now. He knew that once a decision had been made, it was final and there was nothing he could do about it. He had run into this type of situation far too many times before.

"You still there?" Dr. Greer asked.

"Yeah, sounds good," Darwin replied, rolling his eyes. He wanted to slam his phone down in frustration, shatter it to bits.

"Anyway, I still want you to come down to headquarters. We can talk about this more tomorrow afternoon, what do you say?"

"Sure," Darwin responded quickly. He was about to hang up the phone, but then wanted to ask one more thing. "Is Tyler a part of this committee?"

Dr. Greer paused and answered, "Yes, he is. If it makes you feel any better, he wanted to announce it to the public immediately."

Dr. Greer and Darwin said their goodbyes and hung up the phone. Darwin sat there thinking, unable to keep the disappointment he felt from rushing through his body. He needed to think, and he needed to talk to someone who would understand what he was going through. He picked up the phone again and started dialing. Darwin listened as it rang four times with no response. He was about to hang up when he heard someone say, "Hello?" in a quiet voice.

"Hey Mindy, it's . . . it's me, Darwin."

"Oh, hey, Darwin! How are you?" Mindy replied, clearly happy to hear from him.

"I'm good, I'm good. Hey, um, are you free at all for breakfast tomorrow?"

CHAPTER 30

The next morning at nine sharp, Darwin arrived at a coffee shop called Strand, a few blocks from his apartment complex. He grabbed a table for two by the window, as he was the first to arrive. Darwin couldn't stop fidgeting with his hands, and he kept tapping his feet so much so that the person sitting at the table in front of him looked around to see where the noise was coming from. Darwin stopped once he realized how annoying it probably was for others. He placed his hands in his lap and tried to keep them as still as possible. He was nervous, but not because he was meeting Mindy again, a girl he'd been attracted to for a long time; it was more about what he planned on telling her.

Just then, Mindy walked in the door. She looked as pretty as always. Darwin stood up and waved; she smiled when she saw him across the way and made her way over to the table. Darwin stayed standing and gave her hug.

"Hey! How's it going?" she said enthusiastically.

Darwin loved the fact that Mindy was always so joyful—after all, it was nine in the morning on a Tuesday, and most people were irritated or frustrated with having to go to work, but this didn't seem to faze Mindy. She was as happy and cheerful as ever.

"I'm good," Darwin replied. "Thanks for meeting me."

"Of course! So, do you come here often?" she asked with a smile.

"Um, every now and then, since it's close to where I live," Darwin stammered almost apologetically.

"Yeah, it's a great neighborhood. I've got to come here more often," Mindy said, looking around briefly before focusing her attention on him. "So, how is everything?"

Normally, Darwin was fine starting off with some small talk, but really he had asked her to come here for a reason and he wanted to get it out as soon as he could. "Um, things are . . . okay. Not too bad."

"Oh, just okay, huh?" Mindy said, looking at Darwin with a half-smile.

Darwin didn't want to keep beating around the bush. He was nervous and stalling.

"Actually, Mindy, there was something I wanted to talk to you about."

Mindy's face went from a wide smile to quickly furrowing her brow. "I just didn't know who else to talk to, and I knew you'd be a good person to ask for advice."

"Of course, what is it?" Mindy asked, looking curious.

Darwin looked at Mindy and hesitated before speaking. Right before he opened his mouth, the waitress came by to take their order.

"Can I get you guys anything?" she asked.

"Oh, um, I'll take a bagel with cream cheese," Mindy said with a smile.

"And for you?" she asked Darwin.

"I'll just have a decaf coffee with some buttered toast, please."

The waitress wrote down the order and made her way over to the kitchen. When she was out of sight, Mindy motioned for Darwin to continue.

"You remember how I said I couldn't tell you certain things that were confidential to NASA?"

Mindy moved her head back and then nodded slowly, confused as to what Darwin was going to say next.

"I need to tell someone." Darwin sighed. "Some of the confidential information I'm just . . . worried."

Darwin proceeded to tell Mindy everything he knew about Florana and the future plans between the two planets. He told her about the dream and everything Benedict had told him. In addition, he also told her the most important part, what Mindy had wanted to know for years now: Floranians might be visiting the earth again.

He went into detail about the most recent dream and the plans Floranians were making to visit Earth, and of course, the most concerning part for him, where Benedict was shot by an Earthling. Mindy was absolutely fascinated by the whole thing. Her green eyes were fixated on Darwin's and her mouth hung open without her even realizing it. She asked question after question and wanted to know more and more, even things Darwin didn't know himself.

"So, do you think it's really going to happen, Floranians are going to come to the earth?" Mindy asked breathlessly, her eyes opened wide in curiosity.

Just then, the server arrived with their breakfast. They were quiet for a long moment until she put the plates down in front of them and walked away.

"I don't know," Darwin said, picking up a piece of toast and biting into it, chewing rapidly. "All I know is, we can't have them come when this world isn't ready to receive them," he said once he'd swallowed. "There's already enough violence and hatred internally, I can only imagine what they'll do when thirty aliens from another planet set foot on their land."

"And NASA isn't going to say anything?" Mindy asked, wrinkling her smooth forehead while picking up her bagel.

"At least not for now, no," Darwin answered, wiping his lips on a napkin.

"But why?" she asked.

"They have their reasons, security for the people, lack of proof that my dreams mean anything."

"I mean, sure," she said, still chewing, one hand covering her mouth. "But this is pretty significant, the fact that your dream was so detailed should say something, and you've been having dreams like this all your life?"

Darwin shrugged; he had already fought this battle with Dr. Greer, and it wasn't worth explaining to Mindy. Although, meeting with Mindy this morning wasn't just about telling her all of NASA's confidential information on Florana; he had a plan of his own and he wanted to tell someone about it. He needed validation that maybe, just maybe, it wasn't crazy.

"I'm going to announce it myself," Darwin said suddenly.

"Announce what?" she asked, putting the bagel down.

"I'm going to tell the public about my dream. They need to know, they deserve to know."

Mindy looked back at Darwin, struggling to find the right words to say.

"Do you think that's a good idea?" Mindy asked tentatively.

"I have an interview with CNN next week, I can do it then," Darwin said, his voice firm.

"Whoa, whoa, slow down a second," Mindy cautioned him, holding up one hand. "Do you understand the severity of what you're planning to do? You'd be committing a felony by leaking confidential government information, it's a serious offense."

"That's fine. They can put me in jail for it then," Darwin replied calmly, much more calmly than he actually felt inside.

"Darwin, this could end up being really bad. I mean, are you really willing to throw away everything you stand for and go against the people who created you?"

"I know, I know," Darwin said wearily. "But the way I look at it, the whole situation is going to be bad either way. The best thing we can do is prepare people for what may potentially be coming. We have to change people's mindsets on life visiting from other planets, we have to help them see that we're all living creatures, living in this universe, and that we should accept everyone who has pure intentions and a heart to do good in this world. That's on us, we as a people have the capacity to do this."

The waitress came by with the check, placing it gently on the table, and Mindy sat there expressionless.

"Can I get you guys anything else?" the waitress asked brightly, shoving a pencil into her jet-black beehive hairdo.

"No, thank you. This is perfect," Darwin said and the waitress walked away with a smile.

"What if you didn't have to outright say that you knew Floranians were coming to visit the earth?" Mindy asked.

"What do you mean?"

"I mean, what if you could inform people, start educating, and preparing the world of a visit from Floranians just as a precautionary measure, and without having to overtly go against NASA's orders. In other words, you claim that you don't know anything, but you subtly prepare people for this."

"Sure, but they may start speculating that I know something. Besides, I highly doubt Dr. Greer would be okay with something like this, knowing that most people will then start to fear that Floranians are coming."

"But they are coming, Darwin. The best you can do is start the process without having to explicitly say that it's going to happen." Mindy continued, "Tell them what you just told me now, how the world needs to be freed from ignorance and prejudice and not be afraid of those we are unfamiliar with or different from us."

It wasn't a terrible idea, but Darwin had already made up his mind. He wanted to tell the world what he knew, and he didn't care if that meant he would go to jail for leaking classified information.

"Please just consider it," Mindy pleaded with him after seeing the displeased look on his face.

Darwin looked down at the table, unable to meet her level.

When Darwin got back to his apartment later that morning, Sid was waiting for him dressed in his usual formal attire, sunglasses shading his eyes. Normally, Sid would have gone with Darwin to breakfast, but Darwin intentionally told Sid not to wake him in the morning, as he would be sleeping in.

"Where have you been? You told me you were sleeping in this morning!" Sid said as he saw Darwin coming up the stairs, the worry on his face quickly replaced by anger. "You know my job depends on making sure you're safe at all times."

"I know, Sid," Darwin said, feeling sorry that he had worried Sid, who'd always protected him without fail, who'd always made sure he was unharmed. "And I'm sorry, I just needed some time to myself this morning to get out and get some air, clear my head, you know?"

"That's fine," Sid said, removing his sunglasses so that Darwin could see the deep creases that lined his eyes, "but you do understand that I could get fired for not knowing your whereabouts. If you need your space, I'll give you space, but I've got to keep a watch on you and at least know where you are."

"I'm sorry, Sid. I'll let you know, moving forward. I am fine on my own, you know, it's not like it was years ago when the announcement first came out," Darwin said, trying to move past Sid to get to his front door. But Sid moved slightly, blocking Darwin's way; he wasn't going to be able to enter until Sid had his say. Darwin knew from experience that when he wanted to be, Sid was like a brick wall. Immovable.

"But people are still protesting, and it seems now more than ever. I'm just doing my job," Sid said. They looked at one another for a long moment, and Darwin saw fear in Sid's eyes for the first time.

"I know, Sid," Darwin said, as Sid moved away from the door. "I appreciate that."

Darwin walked into his apartment and went straight for the couch. He plopped himself down in one of the seats and feeling a little tired, he kicked off his shoes and laid down lengthways. He thought more and more about what Mindy had said and whether he should take her advice. Dr. Greer's voice kept ringing in his head over and over, "The decision has been made."

More than anything, Darwin wanted to know the details of the Floranians' supposed visit to Earth. This was what had been keeping him up at night, especially given the fact that Dr. Greer and his team had chosen not to make the information public. He wanted to know when they were coming, and what their objective was in visiting in the first place. More importantly, he wanted to warn Benedict that the people of the earth weren't quite ready, and that it would be best to wait until humans could become more open to the idea.

Darwin slowly started drifting off, his eyelids getting heavier and harder to keep open. He could feel himself slowly starting to fall into a dream state, the sounds of the city outside his window fading away. The car honks and train horns faded into crashing waves, crashing yet peaceful.

He looked around and realized he was on the same beach where he'd spoken to Benedict. The day was bright and sunny again, the waves lapping against the shore.

Excitement quickly rushed through Darwin, as he had been waiting to talk to Benedict once again—he still had so many ques-

tions for him. He looked around but saw nothing other than the sand and the endless expanse of the sparkling blue ocean.

Slowly, Darwin started walking down the beach in hopes that Benedict would appear somewhere, just as he had in his last dream. Then Darwin remembered Benedict had shown up after he'd sat on the beach, closed his eyes, and began meditating. Darwin stopped dead in his tracks, sat down on the warm sand, and did just that.

Sure enough, just as he'd drifted off into a serene state, he felt a thump next to him on his right, as if someone or something had just fallen down next to him. When he opened his eyes, the same Floranian man he'd encountered before was seated next to him: the man he called Benedict.

Benedict didn't have his eyes closed this time, but was instead looking out at the ocean view, with a peaceful look on his face. Darwin wasn't sure if he should say something or wait to be spoken to.

They sat there for what seemed to be a good two minutes before finally Benedict spoke, "You came back?"

"Um, yeah, well, I'm not sure how I got back, but here I am."

"You chose to come back. If you didn't want to come, you wouldn't have," Benedict said. "You wanted to see this place again, and you opened your heart and saw beyond the material things of our worlds."

Darwin nodded his head; he did in fact want to return to see him again, but he didn't know what Benedict meant by opening his heart. "Sorry, what do you mean by opening my heart? You mentioned this last time as well."

"Well, you were always given the ability to understand our language in your own way, just as everybody has the capacity to know and understand their purpose in life, but only the pure at heart can truly comprehend what this means—especially when they need it most."

Darwin still didn't quite fully understand, but he let Benedict keep going.

"You see, Darwin, a lot of people in the world you live in have forgotten what it truly means to be alive. They have let the material things in life get in the way of what really matters. Pride, ego, and tradition have all gotten in the way of spirituality."

"I'm sorry, but I still don't understand," Darwin asked, narrowing his eyes

"As Floranians, we all believe that there is a greater purpose which we do not yet fully understand, but it's been said that only those with a pure and open heart can gain a better understanding of what that purpose is. Darwin, you've been living in a world that has been consumed by materialism, and naturally you have assimilated to this cultural belief. But when you come here, you've been able to put all of those material aspects aside and have opened your heart to discover your true self."

"So, this is Florana?" Darwin asked. He had never confirmed that earlier in his previous dream. The man nodded his head and looked out at the ocean, his expression serene.

"This is one of our biggest oceans on the planet, we call it Hergovna. Our planets are very similar, you know, same type of atmosphere, like Earth, our planet is covered mostly in water, nearly eighty percent of it, and we have vast mountain ranges across of all our continental land."

"How do you travel across your bodies of water?" Darwin asked. Benedict smiled and looked at Darwin, his face beatific.

"Darwin, many of these questions that you ask me I'm sure you're very curious about, but why don't you ask me what you really wanted to know before entering this dream?"

"Sir, the last time we spoke in my dream, you were killed while you were telling me of your intention to visit Earth. Why did this happen?" Darwin asked.

"I'm not quite sure," the man answered calmly. "Perhaps you have the answer to that?"

Darwin was a bit confused. How would he know why he was killed in a dream by another Earthling?

"Dreams are often our subconscious trying to tell us something. We were in your dream, not mine," Benedict added, as if this were completely obvious.

"So, you're saying it happened because this is subconsciously how I feel?"

"Perhaps." Benedict shrugged, still looking out at the water as he smiled softly. "Or possibly that you fear something terrible will *happen, if we visit Earth."*

Darwin sighed with relief. It was almost as if Benedict had read his mind.

"Yes, I do fear for your people's safety on Earth. I've seen how things have transpired over the last few years, ever since the discovery of Florana was made public, and many of the reactions have been less than welcoming. The people have become violent, divided, and filled with hate. I would honestly strongly advise that you don't visit Earth, at least not now."

Benedict continued to smile, and Darwin couldn't understand what could possibly arouse such an expression in a conversation like this.

"Darwin," Benedict said, "when we sent your DNA to Earth a long time ago, we didn't just do it to see how one of our own would fare on another planet and how he would be treated by its recipients, we also did it so that this individual would help others understand and accept an alien population such as ourselves, in case they feared us or were adamantly opposed to our very presence."

"But how could I, just one person, influence an entire world? One with so many opponents to the idea of Floranians?"

"You're a smart guy, Darwin. I'm sure you'll figure it out," Benedict said, looking at him.

It was impossible, Darwin thought, given the current state of the world. Everyone was on edge, including those who supported Florana.

"And then what?" Darwin asked.

"Once you feel that the earth is ready, we'll come. Until then, we'll take your advice and stay put on our planet," Benedict said, reaching out and picking up a handful of sand, then letting the grains slip slowly through his fingers. The smile faded from his lips.

Darwin nodded in agreement. He was glad that the Floranians were willing to patiently wait while everything on Earth was sorted out in preparation of their arrival.

"Thank you, sir. I'll do my best," Darwin said. "By the way, I never got your name the last time we spoke. I've been calling you Benedict to Earthlings who are a part of the research team."

The man smiled again and said, "You may call me Benedict, if that's the name that called to you after our first interaction." And with that, Benedict stood up and Darwin found himself doing the same, not quite sure what he was doing or why. Was this the end of their conversation? But before Darwin could inquire aloud, Benedict turned around and started walking away.

"Wait, is that it?" he shouted. He then suddenly heard some soft booms off in the distance, which became louder and louder with every boom. The booms were then suddenly accompanied with his name being shouted. Benedict continued to walk off, and didn't respond to Darwin's calls.

Darwin woke up to a loud pounding on his front door, the sound reverberating in his head.

"Darwin! Darwin! Open up!" Tyler's worried voice shouted outside the front door. "Come on, man. I know you're in there. Sid said you were inside."

Darwin slowly walked over to the door, still hazy from the dream, his thoughts thick and foggy. When he opened the door, he could see the relief on Tyler's face.

"Geez, man, where were you? I've been knocking for like five minutes straight," Tyler said, resting one hand on the doorframe.

"Sorry, I just . . . I feel asleep on my couch. I guess I didn't hear you."

"I was worried. I wasn't sure what happened."

"Yeah, yeah, I'm fine. Come on in. What's up?"

Tyler entered the room and made himself comfortable on the couch, where Darwin had just been sleeping.

"Well, I wanted to talk to you about the decision that was made earlier today about not going public with your dream. Dr. Greer said you sounded pretty upset, so I thought I'd come over here to check on you."

"Yeah, I'm fine, buddy. I'm fine," Darwin said before Tyler could really get into it. He walked over and sat on the couch beside him. "Listen, before we talk about that further, I have to tell you something, something important—I had another dream."

CHAPTER 31

Darwin and Tyler arrived at NASA HQ, making their way quickly to Dr. Greer's office. Darwin had just described everything that had happened in his dream to Tyler in detail, as it was still fresh in his memory, and Tyler wanted to tell Dr. Greer right away, in order to get his thoughts on the matter. Unlike most of the team, Tyler had been one of the few who voted to have the information from Darwin's first dream be made public. After hearing this second one, he told Darwin that there was no doubt in his mind that something needed to be said to the world.

"No, absolutely not!" Dr. Greer said, looking up from a stack of papers on his desk. His expression was pale, drawn, and more than a little alarmed. Darwin and Tyler had just finished telling him Darwin's dream, requesting that a public announcement be made immediately. "We cannot announce something that we have no concrete proof of. It's out of the question," Dr. Greer said, his face flushing a deep crimson at the very suggestion.

"Dr. Greer," Darwin said. "I know, as a scientist, this is something that is hard for you to believe, that events in a dream could actually be real and accurate, but I'm telling you, these last two dreams were nothing like I've ever had before. I was connected in some way to this man—it was like he was trying to use me as an instrument to connect the people of Earth and Florana. I know I can't provide any empirical evidence of this, but I know this is true, and it would be a mistake to not say anything to the world about this."

Dr. Greer scratched his head, and Darwin could see by the uneasiness in his expression that he was conflicted. "Do you realize how it's going to come off, if we brief the president on this? I highly doubt he is going to be okay with making this type of information public to the world," Dr. Greer said.

"He trusts you," Tyler said evenly. "You've been serving this country for over three decades, and he trusts your judgment."

After a good two hours of further discussion, Dr. Greer finally agreed to reveal Darwin's dreams to the world, as long as he made it clear that they weren't a guarantee of what was to come. Although people needed to be prepared, he argued, they also needed to be eased into the idea. Dr. Greer also agreed to allow Darwin to make the announcement in his CNN interview, pending the president's approval, of course. As he heard Dr. Greer give his approval on the matter, Darwin realized he was shaking. In fact, it felt as if he were vibrating from head to toe. He smiled broadly, unable to stop the waves of joy coursing through him.

Three days later, NASA had received the necessary approval from the president, despite some initial pushback. However, the president warned them that they could not indicate that Darwin's dream was in any way a fact or a reality, similar to what Dr. Greer had cautioned. Simply put, the dreams were theories that might or might not prove to be true.

That week, Darwin prepared day and night for his interview with CNN, spending a good five hours writing down his speaking notes, constantly making revisions. Every day leading up to the interview, he rehearsed what he wanted to say at least eight times, sometimes even more if he felt he didn't nail it perfectly. He wanted to be sure that he covered every aspect of the dream, so nothing was left out. Some parts had already started to get fuzzy, so he wrote everything down to ensure he wouldn't forget a single detail.

Mindy was the first person Darwin told about the interview. Darwin could tell she was relieved to know that he was no longer going against NASA's wishes, and wouldn't be committing a crime for leaking classified information. She was, however, nervous. The ramifications of revealing such information could be disastrous, she told him, her voice shaking slightly, since Darwin might be targeted as the main enemy or culprit by anyone who was anti-Neila.

The CNN interview was pretty standard, as these things went. Darwin had been asked to discuss his cause and his life in general. Networks often asked Darwin to do such interviews, given the level of his fame around the world. However, CNN had no clue what Darwin had planned to reveal in the course of the interview, and as such, they would be finding out at the same time as the rest of their viewers. The fact that this wasn't being publicized as a ground-breaking interview, though, would mean that the news of Darwin's announcement wouldn't be seen live by the majority of the world, and would rather be revealed over the course of a few hours as the news caught on.

When Darwin awoke the morning of the interview, he was disappointed that he hadn't had a single dream about Florana since the one he'd had previously, right before Tyler's pounding on the door had woken him up. He'd been hoping to have one last dream with Benedict for some additional words of inspiration or advice, but perhaps it just wasn't meant to be.

For some reason, everything seemed to be moving in slow motion that morning for Darwin. Showering, eating his bowl of cereal, putting on his suit, walking out to the car with Sid; it all seemed so gloomy. Darwin didn't know why; this was an interview he should've been excited about—it was what he had wanted all along, despite Dr. Greer's decision not to make the information from his dreams public. So why did he feel so down?

Every step he took required more energy than usual. It was almost like the feeling Darwin would get in the mornings when his mother had dropped him off at school. Every step leading up to the building would fill Darwin with trepidation. He had always liked school and loved learning, but the way he was treated there made him dread entering that building back in Crimson every day. If this was how he felt about going to school every day, then why on earth should he do this interview with CNN? It had to be the jitters, Darwin thought. It was only natural to be nervous, and his body and mind were telling him to not go through with it in order to soothe his anxiety.

Knowing that he had to do the interview, though, Darwin tried calming himself down as much as he could. "It'll be all right, just relax, breathe," he kept telling himself on the car ride over. He tried distracting himself with music and blaring it loudly as he passed through the group of protesters outside his house, but that didn't work as well as he'd thought it would; the shouting and chanting could still be heard over the loud music through his headphones, and even though Darwin tried to look away, he could still see the protesters with their signs, which seemed to be getting more offensive by the day, in his peripheral vision.

Since repeating coping statements to himself over and over wasn't really working, Darwin decided that perhaps it would be best to meditate for the remainder of the ride to the interview. Darwin had been mediating on a daily basis ever since his last dream with Benedict. It helped him to relax and connect with his soul.

Darwin sat and meditated, hoping he would perhaps fall asleep and see Benedict again in his dream before doing the interview, but he never fell asleep. As hard as he tried to meditate, he couldn't quite get into a relaxed-enough mood, not with everything on his mind and all of the noise from the street. Every time he closed his eyes, the livid faces of the protestors rose up behind his eyelids, their faces full of rage.

When Darwin arrived at CNN, he and Sid were greeted by one of their staff members, a young blond man with long hair and a goatee, who took Darwin to his changing room. Darwin didn't need to change, as he was already dressed for the interview in a navy suit with thin, white pinstripes, and a clean white shirt underneath, but he was asked to wait there while they were waiting for his segment. A spread of food was on a table in the waiting room, fresh fruit, vegetables, and fine cheeses with crisp, seeded crackers. Sid helped himself, piling a paper plate high with food, but Darwin wasn't in the mood to eat, still too nervous for the upcoming interview. His nerves felt like they were jangling as loudly as bells.

"We'll be on in about fifteen minutes, okay?" the staffer said.

Darwin nodded his head and Sid, his mouth full of crackers, nodded as well.

It felt like the longest fifteen minutes of Darwin's life. The only thing he could do was stare at the ground while Sid continued to dig into the food, until he'd cleaned his plate and refilled it twice. Darwin didn't want to meditate or go over his talking points; he wanted to clear his head as much as he could and not overthink anything. He thought about how the world would react to the news that thirty Floranians wanted to visit the earth. How would the anti-Neila react? How would even those who supported Florana react? They might like the idea of life on other planets, but how would they feel if these life forms entered their world, not knowing much about them or what they wanted? That line that Tyler had said to Darwin back in high school still rang in his ears, "People will always fear what's different from them." *Am I making the right decision?* Darwin wondered. *Is making this announcement foolish?* He didn't want to be responsible for a catastrophic war between the two planets or more terrorism at home. The thoughts of increased violence on Earth made him extremely uneasy, and his heart began beating rapidly, a sour feeling filling his stomach.

"Darwin, they're ready for you," the same blond staffer said as he opened the door to the changing room. Darwin took a deep breath and proceeded out of the room with the staffer.

"And now, let's welcome Darwin Sanders back to the CNN newsroom. As many of you know, Darwin is an advocate for Floranian and interplanetary research and an ambassador to the world. Darwin, it's great to have you here again," the news anchor, Josh Sloven, said. Sloven was a handsome young man with sharp, chiseled features, his dark hair perfectly groomed and parted to the side.

"Thank you, Josh. Good to see you again," Darwin replied, trying to mask his nervousness with a smile.

"You know, Darwin, I think the last time we had you on the show, you were promoting one of your causes around education and the importance education has in particular on the younger generation. I think it was about a year or so ago?"

"Yeah, it was, and I'm still focused on that goal today, among others."

"And how has it been going? I know you've given many speeches and presentations at schools throughout the DC area in hopes that kids will be inspired to focus on their education."

"Yes, that's true," Darwin said slowly, noticing that his hands were shaking uncontrollably under the table; he silently willed them to be still. "I just feel that deep down," Darwin continued, "education can potentially solve many of the problems in this world. You look at everything that plagues the world today, violence, terrorism, racism, sexism, prejudice, social inequality—all of these things can be avoided with proper education."

"Uh-huh, I see," Josh said, looking back down at his notes. "And what do you propose should be done regarding this need for education?"

"Well, first and foremost, I think we all need to start encouraging kids today to do whatever they can to serve their fellow people and make education their top priority to do so. And to help make this a reality, we need this to be encouraged at the top levels of our government. More funding for education and less for things like defense must be a priority. In the long run, the more we spend on education, the less we'll need to spend on things such as war. It's a long-term investment that will promote the betterment of the world."

"Interesting," Josh said brightly, looking down at the notes in front of him. "So, Darwin," Josh said, changing the subject, "tell me, what's the latest on Florana? Do we know where the planet is located in Andromeda yet, or are we still working on making contact with the Floranians in the near future?"

Darwin hesitated a moment before answering, wondering if he should come out and say what he knew about Florana or at least what he had been seeing in his dreams. He gave a little nervous laugh and took a sip of water to stall a bit longer.

"Ahem, um. Well, you know, there are things I can't really share with you," Darwin said as he put his glass of water back down, biting his lower lip. This was his last chance to say anything about his dreams. Did he want to risk the potential violence that would come as a result of his announcement? Or was it worth it for the world to know the truth? "But what I can tell you is this: there is a new development that I can speak to, for which NASA and the president have granted their approval."

Josh's face lit up at the possibility of intrigue, a juicy story. He looked at Darwin expectantly, waiting for him to continue.

"We believe, or I guess I should say we are fairly certain, that

Floranians intend to visit Earth."

"What . . . what do you mean they intend to visit Earth," Josh said slowly, in astonishment.

"Just like I said, they plan on visiting Earth sometime in the near future." There was a long pause, and Darwin saw the fear creep over the news anchor's face, his skin turning white.

"And Darwin, you indicated that you and NASA are 'fairly certain.' What evidence do you have? What has transpired recently that we weren't aware of before?"

Darwin took a deep breath, his spine tingling. This was it. This was the moment he'd been waiting for.

"My whole life I've had these dreams," Darwin said, "visions, premonitions, whatever you want to call them. As a kid, I wasn't really sure what they meant, but they were very vivid, very real to me. I would always be in another world, a beautiful place, but one I was unfamiliar with. Of course, when I was kid I didn't know where I came from, or who I really was, so I just assumed they were dreams that seemed very lifelike. Just weird dreams like everyone has."

Darwin took another drink of water, as his mouth started feeling dry.

"And it wasn't just that I was having dreams at night while I was asleep—sometimes I would go into these dream states during the day, when I was completely awake. After finding out I was from Florana eight years ago, the dreams became more vivid, as if I were actually experiencing everything I was seeing in real time. I soon realized the dreams were taking place on Florana, and that the people in my dreams were actual Floranians."

"You saw other Floranians in your dream? What did they look like?" Josh asked quickly, clearly excited by the prospect.

"Like me, actually. Same spotted skin, same build, and stature."

"So what does this have to do with your belief that Floranians are potentially coming to Earth?" Josh asked curiously.

Darwin decided he would skip over all of the other details and get to the point, as he could tell that's what Josh was looking for. "Well, in the last couple of dreams I've had, I was finally able to make contact with a Floranian and communicate with him in a form I could understand."

"What do you mean?" Josh asked, leaning slightly forward in his chair.

"The language wasn't English. I don't know what it was, but I could understand this man completely, and he could understand me. Whereas in my previous dreams, we couldn't communicate verbally with each other at all."

"Hmm, I see." Josh sat back in his chair again, seeming a bit more skeptical. "And what did you talk about?"

"Well, we talked about a lot of things. I asked a lot about their planet, their people, their culture. I had so many questions, like anyone would when meeting someone from another planet."

"And so, it was in this conversation that he told you they intend to visit Earth?"

"Well, sort of." Darwin shrugged. "He started talking about it, but we were cut off abruptly when I woke suddenly. It wasn't until the next dream that he confirmed their intention to visit."

Josh stopped and looked at some of his notes before proceeding, clearly thrown off by this sudden revelation. "Well, I've got to tell you, Darwin, this whole thing sounds a little," he looked up in the air to find the right words, "far-fetched," Josh concluded. "You're telling me that based on some dreams you've had, Floranians have communicated to you their planned invasion of Earth?"

"It's not an invasion," Darwin said defensively. "They want to know more about us, who we are, what our planet is like, and how we can help each other, share resources . . ."

"And how do you know that?" Josh said tersely, cutting Darwin off.

"Because that's what they told me." Darwin started getting a little heated. Josh noticed that Darwin was starting to get angry, and changed his tone quickly.

"Okay, okay." Josh chuckled, holding up his hands. "So, in this dream, a Floranian man told you that they were coming to visit. Did he give a time, though?"

"I told him that the world isn't ready yet."

"Not ready?" Josh asked, narrowing his eyes.

"Yes, we are not ready to receive them. We need to figure out our own differences and issues first, before we welcome another alien race to Earth."

"So, I have to ask, when *will* we be ready?"

Darwin picked up his glass and took another drink, swallowing hard before answering. "I don't know the answer to that question," he said soberly, aware that it wasn't the answer that Josh, or anyone else watching, wanted to hear. But Darwin knew he had nothing else to offer; not yet.

All around the world, as the interview unfolded, people were slowly starting to react. What started out as concern from those watching at a restaurant just outside of the DC area, slowly turned into a commotion, when people began walking out of the restaurant abruptly, some even angrily.

In Boston, people took to the streets to begin shouting their displeasure toward the idea of Floranians visiting Earth. "Dar-win, don't let them in! Dar-win, don't let them in!" a small crowd starting chanting downtown. Some of the other shouts were crueler, chants such as "Blow them up" and "Death to Florana" could soon be heard across the town as people began to emerge from their houses in the middle of the interview.

Even in Chicago, a city with a majority population of Florana supporters, fighting began to erupt between the supporters and the anti-Neila. The anti-Neila began rounding up their weapons, and what had started out as a small fight between two people slowly turned into a riot. Cars were tipped over and streetlights crashed down to the pavement, not just from the anti-Neila side; supporters were vandalizing property, as well.

When the interview ended, Darwin walked out of the CNN newsroom with Sid by his side, still feeling wired and somewhat elated from all he had said on camera. Upon opening the front door, he was greeted by a handful of reporters from different networks, as well as a small crowd of people shouting derogatory statements. It was clear that in their minds, this was all Darwin's fault. They believed that he had influenced the Floranians in coming to Earth, and his constant spread of propaganda in support of Florana had brainwashed those who were on his side.

"Get off this planet! Nobody wants you here!" one man shouted.

Sid stood in front of Darwin and guided him to the car. People began hurling trash at him. One threw a water bottle, which nearly hit Sid directly in the head, had he not ducked away quickly. As others nearby started noticing the commotion around the newsroom, they made their way over and joined the protest as well.

"Get in the car, Darwin! Get in!" Sid shouted to Darwin as they reached the car door. Items continued to be hurled at the car after they entered the vehicle, and what was once ten or so people quickly became a crowd of thirty angry protestors, shouting and launching trash at the car.

The news on television quickly turned to the sudden protests and riots that were breaking out all over the nation. They had never seen such a reaction happen so quickly—it was as if the Rodney King or OJ Simpson verdict had just been read.

Mindy was watching the news at home, watching the people who'd taken to the streets, anger contorting their faces as they yelled at the top of their lungs. Watching them, she felt horrified that her fears had come true. People would be divided even more than they had been, and the fear of aliens invading the planet would only create more anxiety and chaos. Besides this, though, Mindy also feared for Darwin's safety.

Just then, Mindy's cell phone rang. "Hi Mom," Mindy said distractedly as she picked up the phone.

"Oh, thank God you're okay!" Mindy's mom said, on the other end. "You know I've been trying to call you for the past half-hour!"

"Oh, sorry, Mom. I kept hearing my phone go off, but I didn't want to miss any of Darwin's interview."

"Darwin? That boy who is creating this whole mess?" her mother said with obvious disdain.

"It's not his fault, Mom," Mindy replied, much more patiently than she really felt. "If people weren't filled with so much hate, maybe they would understand and not act so violently."

Mindy heard her mom scoff.

"Listen to me, Mindy. You come home right away. I know you thought moving to DC would be a fun and new experience, but, like I told you before, it's much too dangerous."

"What?" Mindy shouted. "Mom, I'm twenty-six years old, and I make my own decisions. I'm not leaving!"

"Mindy, that city is about to implode," her mother said breathlessly. "There will be riots, shootings, stabbings, you name it. I can't in good conscience have you stay there."

"Mom, I'm not going anywhere," Mindy said sternly.

"Don't take that tone with me, young lady," Mindy's mom replied, her tone a warning that Mindy had heard many times before. The difference was that this was the first time she didn't care. "This boy has brainwashed you. What if these aliens wipe us all out in one swoop!"

Mindy had had more than enough. Her mom's ignorance had finally put her at her wits' end.

"I'm not going anywhere, Mom," Mindy said again. "All my life, you've been feeding me all of this prejudiced garbage, when it came to Darwin, and I believed it. I thought there was something bad about him, something awful. I thought he was dangerous, all because of what you and Dad said about him—and his kind. I didn't talk to him for eight years because of you! I cut off all contact with someone who was so kind to me and everyone he met, because of *you*." Mindy paused to see if her mother had anything to say, but there was nothing but silence. "And I'm not letting you do that to me again."

She slammed down her phone. Her hands were shaking with anger and her heart was beating rapidly. She sat back down on her couch and took a few deep breaths, waiting for her mom to call her back, either to apologize or yell at her more. But she never did.

Darwin arrived back at his apartment, and as they pulled into the complex, the car was now covered with eggs and the remnants of overripe tomatoes. The protesters standing outside his home added to the collage of food flung against the car.

Sid escorted Darwin up the stairs to ensure he was safe, and when Darwin entered his apartment alone, he slowly moved to the couch, every step feeling like he had just run a marathon. He flung himself on the couch and started to cry. Darwin had suspected the reaction from the public would be bad, but he didn't expect it to be this awful, with riots breaking out within a matter of minutes, and half of the world was still sleeping! Only time would tell how bad things would get once the interview went viral.

It was clear to Darwin that an overwhelming amount of work needed to be done in order to free people from their own prejudices and ignorance. Reversing this would be no easy task, and if the people of Earth refused to come together and understand their greater purpose in life, Floranians would never come to Earth. It would simply be too dangerous of a prospect. The question for Darwin now, as he lay there motionless on the couch, the last rays of daylight fading to dusk, was a difficult one. Was he willing to sacrifice everything he held dear, for the betterment of the world? As Darwin's eyes slowly closed and he slid into sleep, he wondered if he was even up to the task anymore.

CHAPTER 32

Tyler made his way down the corridors of NASA HQ to Dr. Greer's office, in order to discuss the conversation that he'd had with Darwin over the phone that morning. He knew that the conversation likely wouldn't be taken well by Dr. Greer, and having difficult conversations with his boss gave Tyler no pleasure at all.

He knocked on the door to Dr. Greer's office softly, almost hoping he wasn't there.

"Come in," he heard Dr. Greer shout. Tyler took a deep breath and opened the door slowly, peeking his head in. "Oh, Tyler," Dr. Greer said, sitting at his desk, his head bent over his laptop. "What can I do for you?"

"Do you have a second to chat?" Tyler asked, opening the door a bit wider.

"Of course, come on in," Dr. Greer said, closing his laptop with a sharp click as Tyler sat himself down in one of the chairs across from Dr. Greer's desk. "What's up?" Dr. Greer asked, leaning back in his chair a bit, his eyes fixed on Tyler.

"Well, sir, I just got off the phone with Darwin."

"And?"

"He's not doing the best."

"What seems to be the problem?"

"Well, he really wants to get back out there again. Do what he was doing before, giving talks, meeting with students. He wants to finish what he set out to do—to help prepare this world for a potential visit from the Floranians."

"I don't think we're quite there yet, Tyler," Dr. Greer said, losing eye contact with Tyler as he opened his laptop again. His fingers started tapping the keys.

"Sir, with all due respect, it's been a month since he's been able to leave his home. I understand why you're doing it, but this is borderline house arrest."

"He needs to stay there, for his protection. We'll know once it's safe, we just need all of this to settle down a bit," Dr. Greer said sharply.

"I've visited him a few times, he just seems miserable. You know him, he wants to be out and doing things, giving back to the community. By keeping him at home all day, we're depriving him of that. He's a prisoner in his own home."

"And what? Would you prefer for him to be killed?" Dr. Greer said, sternly now, looking up from the computer screen and staring right at Tyler.

"Absolutely not, sir, but we also can't keep him locked up just because something might happen to him one day. He has to be able to live his life."

Dr. Greer leaned back in his chair and took a deep breath. "I'm not sure if I've ever shared this with you, Tyler, but a long time ago, I had a son. His name was Casey."

Tyler nodded wordlessly, waiting for Dr. Greer to continue.

"And one summer afternoon when he was five years old, Casey drowned in a pool in our backyard when I was looking the other way. I was distracted by some food I had just burned in the kitchen. Just like that, he was gone. I won't look the other way again, Tyler. Not now. Not ever."

Tyler watched as Dr. Greer's dark eyes turned glassy, his expression far away. There was a long moment of silence in which Tyler desperately wanted to speak, to offer Dr. Greer some words of condolence, but he knew that as much as he wanted to reach out to his boss and mentor, it was best to stay quiet. Tyler knew that above all else, Dr. Greer was a private man, so private that Tyler had never guessed he'd once had children of his own.

"Since the CNN interview over a month ago," Dr. Greer said, choosing his words slowly and carefully when he began speaking again, "there have been four terror attacks, twelve shootings in the United States alone, fifteen stabbings, and over twenty riots all over the world. Things are just starting to calm down," Dr. Greer said, taking a deep breath. "Let's give it another week, Tyler. All right?"

Tyler nodded again, looking down at the floor and away from the pained look in Dr. Greer's eyes. Darwin wouldn't be happy about the news, and Tyler had done all he could. But the decision, as always, was ultimately up to Dr. Greer, and there was no real way for Tyler to challenge him. Not without losing his job, his future, his stability—his life.

Back at Darwin's apartment, Sid was stationed outside his front door, and two other bodyguards were stationed down at the bottom, near the gate of the complex. Dr. Greer had even had to request the presence of patrolmen outside Darwin's home, as he'd been receiving death threats in recent weeks.

Inside the apartment sat Darwin at his kitchen table, eating a bowl of cereal, the look on his face blank. He was anxious, not to mention a bit stir-crazy—he hadn't been able to leave his apartment since the interview, and the limited interaction he'd had with people had made him feel he was losing his ability to socialize. He noticed that he had started talking to himself a lot, humming, singing, and even having full-on conversations, as if there was another person in the room. He'd read virtually every book in his house, and had requested for Sid to bring him more.

Every now and then, Tyler would come visit. They'd play chess together, and Darwin would often ask when he was going to get his life back again. For her own protection, Mindy's visits had been rejected, and even though she and Darwin talked on the phone every so often, it just wasn't the same. The only person who Darwin consistently saw every day was Sid, and he wasn't exactly the most social person in the world—their conversations were generally more formal in nature, limited to things like politics and the weather.

What bothered Darwin the most, though, was that his isolation didn't allow him to work on what was most important to him—doing whatever he could to help people look past their differences for the sake of future generations. It was clear to Darwin that in moving forward in the future, life on planets besides Florana would likely be discovered, and that future generations would need to live in a world where interplanetary life and communication both existed and was accepted. How could one possibly expect them to do this and tolerate other alien life, if their parents and earlier generations continued to pass down the hatred from generation to generation?

That evening, Darwin had another dream. This one didn't feature Benedict, but as the dream began, Darwin knew he was certainly on Florana. There was the seemingly endless jungle, with its tangle of trees, and through that jungle there was a large mountain range with a long canyon that stretched into the cavernous distance. Darwin didn't see any Floranians this time, but unlike the dreams he'd had in the past, instead of running toward the shriek of the sirens that would always blare off in the distance, he decided he would lie down and stare up at the sky, take in the bright stars that shined down upon him.

The view of the sky on Florana was absolutely spectacular. Because the planet was much closer to the center of the Andromeda galaxy compared to Earth in the Milky Way, Darwin could see nearly twice as many stars as he could on Earth. Not to mention the fact that Andromeda was also a much larger galaxy than the Milky Way, at over one trillion stars, which was ten times the amount in the Milky Way.

As Darwin lay there looking up the stars, he wondered how much more life there could possibly be in the vast universe. The fact that Andromeda possessed so many stars, and was only a fraction of the size of the entire universe, was absolutely mind-boggling to him. There had to be life all over the universe. Perhaps it wouldn't be life as both Earthlings and Floranians knew it, but some kind of life had to be out there, and he knew we were all connected in some way or another, and the longer he lay there staring up at the sky, the more emotional Darwin started to become, thinking about the endless possibilities of life on other planets, or even what life might be like after death. He thought perhaps the images taken by the Hubble telescope of these far-off, massive nebulas and supernovas millions of light years away could be avenues leading to other dimensions. Were there portals or channels somewhere that led to other dimensions of space and time? There were so many questions, so many things about the universe still unknown.

When he stopped to realize the complexity and magnitude of it all, he began to laugh a little at how consumed we were as individuals with our own selfish desires, fighting with one another over mundane issues, shunning people because of their race or ethnicity, and for what? To glorify one person over another, just to prove superiority and dominance? All Darwin could do was shake his head. We were sitting in an infinite universe with over a hundred billion galaxies around us, and yet some people on Earth just seemed to care about themselves, always thinking inwardly and never contemplating the larger plan of existence.

Darwin woke up from his dream, blinked a few times before rubbing his eyes to fully wake up. It was 5:00 a.m., and the sun still hadn't risen. The streets outside were quiet, and all that could be heard was the sound of crickets chirping peacefully outside his window.

After trying to fall back to sleep, Darwin finally gave up at 6:30 and decided to get up and start his day. He thought about potentially going outside, against NASA's orders—he knew Sid was likely still sleeping. But then he remembered that the two guards at the gate of the complex rotated on twenty-four-hour shifts, and he knew he would be stopped there if he tried going any further.

When Darwin turned on the morning news, the first story was about another terrorist attack, this one in Germany. Someone had bombed the home of a family who had started a foundation to support Florana. The goal of the foundation was to raise money and resources to support space exploration. They were well-known throughout their town for starting this foundation, and had actually received considerable support from German citizens. Unfortunately, a group of anti-Neila had placed a homemade pressure-cooker bomb outside their front door late at night. The bomb had killed five of the family members, leaving one survivor, who was critically injured— a child, just eight years of age.

It was a horrific story and despite the fact that only a few were killed compared to other terror attacks that had been occurring throughout the globe, this one was more unsettling to Darwin. He quickly turned off the TV and stared for a while out the kitchen window. How much longer was this going to be? Darwin asked himself. How much longer would he have to be kept in his apartment? Another terrorist attack would only be more of a setback for Darwin on the road to Dr. Greer granting him his freedom again. Dr. Greer was waiting for things to settle down, before putting Darwin back in the public eye. The problem was that things only seemed to be getting worse.

Darwin knew that he could no longer sit back and watch the horror and violence occurring right before his eyes, without doing anything about it. He was tired of seeing the countless number of children being killed as a result of this violence. Darwin knew he had to talk to Dr. Greer and convince him that, despite the danger society posed to him, it was time to stand up and start doing something about the ills plaguing the world.

Darwin immediately ran to his room and grabbed his notebook; the ideas for what to say in his next speech were flowing rapidly through his brain. He wanted to convey everything he had pondered over the last month in his isolation, as well as touch on points he'd made in the past. He was writing so quickly, the words streaming from his mind to his pen. Normally it took days for Darwin to write and prepare his speeches, but this one only took him a matter of hours. It was as if some magical force was working through his body to deliver the words in the precise way they needed to.

After finishing up the speech, Darwin immediately called Dr. Greer to convince him it was time—time for him to get back out into the public and do whatever he could to promote the betterment of society and the world as a whole. This time, Darwin wasn't going to take no for an answer, no matter what.

CHAPTER 33

Three days later, Darwin paced back and forth in his kitchen, rehearsing his speech. Sid had taken his suit to the dry cleaners, after it had been stuck in the closet for over a month. Darwin was nervous, but not for his safety; more about the fact that he would be out in public after over a month of isolation. Darwin hadn't seen anybody but Sid and Tyler during that time, and he wasn't sure if he still possessed the executive presence needed for a speech like this. He felt anxious and wasn't sleeping well at night, tossing and turning in his narrow bed until he often just gave up and watched the sun rise outside his bedroom window in a tangerine ball of light.

When he started stumbling over his words, he decided to sit down and take a few deep breaths to relax himself. Darwin wasn't sure who was more nervous for today, him or Dr. Greer. Three days prior, after talking to Dr. Greer for a nearly an hour, Darwin was finally given the approval to appear in public again, to continue delivering his speeches and attend volunteer events. The president also came around to approving this idea, after a long talk with Dr. Greer. The president's biggest concern was the security of the people. As he pointed out, not only would Darwin be at risk out in the public, but other lives would be in danger as well.

Sid knocked on the door and brought in Darwin's suit, and asked if he needed help putting it on, but Darwin just shook his head *no*.

"I'll wait for you outside, then," Sid said.

Darwin put on his suit like on any other day, starting with his pants and a button-down shirt, cliffing the cuff links, and putting on his tie. He threw over his jacket and leaned over to put on his shoes. He took one last deep breath, and made his way outside, where Sid was waiting for him.

The speech was being held at the Capitol Building, where presidential inaugurations occurred. Darwin looked forward to attending the charity fundraiser for cancer research, his first public appearance since the CNN interview. Although he'd initially struggled to draw a comparison between cancer and his cause of promoting Florana, he was certain his analogy would resonate with the audience. Darwin had always had a great deal of support in DC, given its majority liberal population, and people were looking forward to seeing and hearing from him again.

The car in which Darwin was traveling on his way to Capitol Hill was escorted by three police motorists, and to Darwin's surprise, there were hardly any protesters or people shouting and hurling foul things at his vehicle. Perhaps the increased security had scared off the few anti-Neila in the town.

When Darwin arrived, he was greeted by Tyler, who was planning on being up on the stage during the speech. Darwin approached Tyler, each of them with a large grin on their face. Tyler opened his arms to embrace Darwin, as he laughed.

"Good to see you, buddy! Glad you could make it out." Tyler was dressed formally in a black suit, with shiny black shoes to match. His dark hair, streaked with gray, was fashionably messy, as usual.

"Thanks, Tyler, I have to thank you, as well. I know you likely had a part in convincing Greer to spring me from house arrest," Darwin said gratefully.

"It was all you, my man. You're the one who convinced him otherwise," Tyler said, patting Darwin on the back. "Tell you what, after this, let's go get a drink and catch up. What do you say?"

"Works for me!" Darwin said, smiling. He then went on to clasp his hands and tap his thumbs together rapidly, waiting for it to be time to head up to the podium.

"You nervous?" Tyler asked, looking down at Darwin's hands, which were shaking.

"Um, a little. I just haven't been out in a while. It's going to be weird, seeing people again. I just don't want to screw up on my first appearance."

"Ah, you'll be fine," Tyler said optimistically. "You always start out a little nervous, and then your nerves calm right down once you're up there and talking."

Tyler did have a point, and this was usually the case with Darwin when it came to giving speeches. The anticipation and anxiety leading up to the speech was horrible for him, but once he stepped onto that podium and began talking, all his nerves would melt away and he would suddenly possess all the confidence in the world.

"Like I always told you, even if you're not feeling that way, just act like you're confident on the outside, and no one will be able to tell the difference."

"You're right," Darwin said, now putting his hands down by his sides. "You know, Tyler, I never really thanked you for being there for me, for being my friend in those days back in high school. And then you still were there for me, even after you moved to a different role at NASA. I was upset when I first found out that you'd lied to me, but at the end of the day I was happy to have a friend beside me . . . even if you did get paid for it."

They both laughed, and Tyler said, "It may not seem like it, but you've actually taught me a lot about myself during these past few years. At first, I thought I was just going on an assignment for a few months, I would do my job, and then come back—it was that simple. But I ended up making a friend out of it. And I know your goal is to motivate others to serve and care about and respect one another. But before I met you, I didn't really care much about anyone but myself—I was only looking out for my own interests. You've changed that for me, and I think that says more about you than it does me."

Darwin smiled softly, but before he could thank Tyler for his kind words, a staff member approached, clipboard in hand. "Okay, Darwin, they're ready for you," he said. "Follow me, and I'll take you to the podium."

Darwin took a sharp breath and made his way toward the staffer.

"Good luck out there," Tyler said. "I'll be on the stage behind you."

"Thanks, Tyler. Don't forget, drinks after this!" Darwin said.

"I'll be there!" Tyler said enthusiastically, with a wide grin.

Darwin slowly walked up the stairs to the stage, and waited for the emcee to introduce him.

"Ladies and gentlemen, we'd like to thank you for attending the president's charity event to fight cancer, your donations have been greatly appreciated. Now it is my pleasure to welcome our first speaker of the night, Darwin Sanders."

The crowd cheered and clapped as Darwin made his way on stage. He shook the hand of the emcee and made his way over to the podium for the first time in weeks. Darwin could feel his heart beating through his shirt, and he tried breathing slowly to calm himself.

He cleared his throat in the microphone and looked out at the audience. There were a lot of people in attendance—it had to have been over a thousand, he thought. He looked around at all the people, most of them with happy expressions on their faces. Then, just before he was about to open his mouth to begin, he looked down in the front and saw Mindy cheering him on. They made eye contact and smiled at each other. And as he took in her open, expectant, and beautiful face, the red hair that tumbled to her shoulders and the way her green eyes lit up at the sight of him, his nervousness evaporated.

"Good afternoon, everybody," Darwin began. "It's great to see all of your faces again, I know that I've been out of the public eye for quite some time, but I want you to know I was always thinking about you, the people of this world, looking forward to the day when we would meet again. Over the past month, I had a lot to reflect on. We've come here today to support the fight against cancer and to find a cure for this deadly disease. We've done our best in terms of research to find a cure and investing in the proper technology that will allow those with this terrible disease to prolong their lives. It's interesting how the human body has so many organisms, properties, functions that all work together for the body to live and prosper. We have hundreds of bones, muscles, lungs for air, a heart, and a brain, and yet they all have to work together like a well-oiled machine so that the body can function." Darwin stopped, and took a drink of water.

"But then there are things that happen to the body that impede its ability to function properly. Take cancer, for example, uncontrolled abnormal cells, growing at a fast rate, which results in the form of a tumor, eat away at certain parts of the body. If the tumor isn't removed, it can continue to grow, and the cancer can spread." Darwin looked around at the audience and found Mindy again, who was listening closely, and she smiled when she realized Darwin was looking at her.

"Now, I know that most of you would like for me to talk about what I discussed on CNN. I'm sure you have a lot of questions. Are we in danger? What do Floranians want from us? How do we know they won't be hostile? Unfortunately, I'm not going to be answering these questions here today. Instead, I want to talk about how we as a people must come together for the common good and the betterment of the world, just like the human body needs all of its bones, muscles, and organs to work together to have a functioning body, so that we can succeed and prosper.

"Many of you know now that I have these dreams where I feel connected to the people of Florana, and you might choose not to believe in them, and that's completely fine. But I firmly believe that we are all, the whole universe, connected in some way. That we all share a similar bond, similar properties, which make this universe function. There is a reason we have been put on this earth, and we will never quite know why or what our purpose is. There are higher factors at play that we will likely never understand. But what we have to ask ourselves—if we are, in fact, a part of some larger and higher plan—is: are we doing our part on this planet to ensure that we all work together, that we care for one another and love one another, so that the earth can function properly with all of its inhabitants, and function properly with the rest of the universe?

"How can we possibly expect life from other planets to come visit Earth in such a hostile environment? An environment where its own people don't care for one another, fight with one another, and even kill one another, all because of their differences in race, beliefs, religion, wealth, gender, and sexual orientation? We all must be unified, if we are ever to see the people of this earth function together and live in harmony. Only then will we have succeeded as a human race.

"We live in a great day, where we know we are no longer alone in this universe, that life on other planets does exist. But just as we need people to come together on this earth, we also need to come together with those living outside this world."

Darwin stopped to take another drink of water, but before the cup reached his lips he could hear a slight commotion coming from the front row, on the right side. A woman shouted, and a couple of people were knocked over by a man who was wearing a dirty brown trench coat and making his way toward the front of the stage. The man looked furious, and had no regard for the people he was shoving out of his way. Security started to make their way toward the man, and Darwin put down his cup and moved away from the podium to see what was going on.

As the security guards drew closer to the man, who was still shoving people out of his way, the man reached into his coat pocket and pulled out what looked like a gun, the metal flashing in the sunlight. People around him started screaming and running away frantically. Darwin quickly turned to Mindy and motioned for her to run. The man holding the gun screamed at the top of his lungs and fired off two rounds of bullets, which echoed through Capitol Hill like loud fireworks being let off on stage. All of a sudden, Darwin felt a sharp pain go through his chest, then a stinging and burning sensation flooded him. But the feeling was so quick and fleeting that Darwin felt completely fine after the initial pain.

Then, Darwin felt his chest, and when he removed his hand, it was covered in blood, the viscous liquid dripping from his fingers. People in the crowd were screaming, and Tyler ran over to Darwin's aid as soon as he saw the blood.

"NO!" Tyler shouted as he sprinted across the stage toward Darwin.

Darwin also heard Mindy, who hadn't moved, despite Darwin's urging, shouting in a frantic panic.

When Tyler reached him, Darwin began feeling incredibly weak, and the room started spinning, the faces of the audience blurring together. He felt as if he was about to collapse. Blood was flowing onto the ground like a spigot sprinkling water, and the drops of blood quickly turned into a crimson pool.

"Somebody, call an ambulance!" Tyler shouted frantically, bending over Darwin's body.

Mindy rushed onto the stage and crouched down at Darwin's side, tears falling down her cheeks.

"It's okay, Darwin. Everything is going to be all right," she managed to get out through the tears. "Don't worry, we're going to get you out of here."

Darwin tried to speak back, but nothing came out; he was losing blood at an incredibly fast rate, and was slowly starting to lose consciousness. His breathing sounded more like gargling, as blood oozed from his mouth. The world went from spinning to fading into blackness.

"Where is that ambulance?" Tyler shouted, his face full of anger and terror, his eyes wide.

"It's on its way!" a man off in the distance shouted over the chaotic screams from the crowd.

Mindy grabbed Darwin's head and propped it up on her lap, while the rest of his body lay there, absolutely limp. Blood was falling onto her jeans, and her tears started to mix with the thick red liquid. Mindy looked down at Darwin, with his head in her lap; his eyes were now completely closed, and he lay there motionless.

"Darwin, you're going to make it through this. Come on, I know you can. You're going to go on and do great things in this world, I know it," Mindy said, choking back her tears that flowed ceaselessly from her green eyes. But Darwin didn't move; his face was turning as pale as milk, and when the ambulance finally arrived, cutting through what remained of the crowd, Darwin Sanders was pronounced dead at the scene.

The news of Darwin's passing quickly spread throughout the world. Some of the anti-Neila cheered and celebrated, and the supporters watched the news in horror. There was a sense of darkness that spread across the globe that day. Never in history had there ever been a known alien living on planet earth—and he didn't even survive to see his thirtieth birthday.

Dr. Greer, who watched the live broadcast from his office, was in a state of shock. It was his worst fear coming true. He had wanted to keep Darwin in hiding for a longer period of time, knowing that appearances in public would be a danger to him. NASA employees walked by his office in tears, and couldn't bring themselves to enter. They could see him through the window, staring blankly at his desk. He must have sat there for a good hour, not moving at all, until he finally broke down in tears.

Tyler went with the paramedics to the hospital, his hands and clothes covered in Darwin's blood. The whole time he sat there in disbelief, watching the blood dry, turning from red to a dark brown. He sat in the hospital for two hours, not knowing what to do next, tears slowly streaming down his face. He replayed their time in Crimson over and over in his mind, rewinding the tape, and all he could think about was how much he was going to miss his friend.

Mindy went home after the ambulance took Darwin away, and spent the rest of the day in her bed, eventually crying herself to sleep. The whole thing was more than she could bear, and her tears soaked through the pillow that night as she thought of him, and on many nights after that. Who knew what they might've been, if only they'd had more time for a real chance at happiness?

Later that evening, the president made a video address to the people of the world from the Oval Office, while sitting soberly behind his desk.

"My fellow Americans, and people of the world," the president stated. "I'm saddened to say that I come to you this evening with this address from the Oval Office after a terrible tragedy has been committed on American soil. Earlier today, Darwin Sanders was shot and killed at a charity event supporting the fight against cancer. And although this loss may seem like just one person to some, it is in fact much, much more than that. We learned eight years ago that an alien nation had come into contact with the earth, and with that they had given us a gift, a gift that turned into the incredible person, who we knew as Darwin Sanders. Darwin was a Floranian living in our world. He fought every day to promote Floranian research, and did his part in making this world a better place, a world in which he hoped that alien life would find hospitable.

"Sadly, we have seen more terrorist attacks, murders, and riots in the past year than we have ever seen in years past. Although we sometimes try our best to get along, something always seems to set us apart from one another, differences between us that allow violence and hatred to exist. I ask you, how can we possibly expect life on other planets to even want to set foot on Earth, if we can't even treat one another with respect and dignity? How could they ever come here, knowing that we killed the only extraterrestrial life form to have walked on Earth? I urge you all to reflect on the words Darwin Sanders delivered today, before he was shot: 'We must fix ourselves first, if we are to ever to be met by life from other planets. We all must be unified, if we are ever to see the people of this earth function together and live in harmony. Only then, will we have succeeded as a human race.'"

With that, the screen went dark.

The world was never quite the same after Darwin's passing. His death only created more division and outrage between Floranian supporters and the anti-Neila. Violence and crime increased throughout most of the United States, and in other parts of the world, as hatred and dissension grew, infecting the world like a cancer.

A few years later, Dr. Greer resigned from his position at NASA and ended his career with retirement. Those who knew him well remarked that he was never the same after Darwin's death. As the years passed, he grew quieter and quieter, until the day he peacefully died in his sleep. Mindy never married, and Tyler quit NASA and traveled to Japan, living out in the countryside. After Darwin's untimely death, the Floranians never appeared on Earth, nor were they ever heard from again. Eventually, the idea of making contact simply slid away like sand through one's fingers. The Floranians disappeared completely, as if the whole thing had been merely a dream or a vision. As if they'd never graced the world with their gentle presence at all.

ABOUT THE AUTHOR

Jamaal Aflatooni is a local author to the Bay Area living in Walnut Creek, California with his wife and daughter Eliana. Growing up in his hometown of Pendleton, Oregon, Jamaal always had a passion for astronomy, writing, and science fiction novels, Carl Sagan's *Contact*, in particular. Jamaal studied sociology at the University of Oregon where he grew an interest in the study of society, cultures, and lifestyles. Witnessing the divisiveness, bigotry, and violence plaguing our nation inspired him to write Space Between Us, a story about a boy, but more so, a story about us as a society.

We want to encourage you to support independent bookstore by visiting your local store and ordering this book from them.
Also, if you enjoyed this book we invite you to take a moment to rate it or write a review on *Amazon*, *Goodreads* and *Google Books*.

You can follow Jamaal on:
Facebook at: https://www.facebook.com/jamaal.aflatooni
Instagram: @jaflatooni
Twitter: @jaflatooni
Space Between Us page:
https://www.facebook.com/Space-Between-Us-103642621010939/

Thank You!

Made in the USA
Monee, IL
12 October 2020